Praise for

AWARDS

GOLD: Nautilus Book Award for Best Fiction, Large Publisher (2016)

GOLD: Sarton Women's Book Award for Contemporary Fiction (2015–2016)

GOLD: Independent Publisher Book Award (IPPY) for Best Regional Fiction, Australia and New Zealand (2016)

SILVER: Reader's Favorite Book Award for Women's Fiction (2016)

CALL MY NAME

"An **emotionally piercing and absorbing** account of turbulent female friendship over time, *Call My Name* is also a keen meditation on the powerful pull of connection and belonging—the places and people that shape and change us, forever calling us home."

—**Paula McLain**, New York Times bestselling author of *The Paris Wife* and *When the Stars Go Dark*

"*Call My Name* reminds us that love calls us to be generous rather than possessive and that we can go on, even when terrible things happen, because we're profoundly connected. Layered, sometimes shocking, yet shining with goodness and hope, **it's exactly the kind of story we need right now.**"

—**Barbara Linn Probst,** Award-winning author of *The Sound Between the Notes* and *The Color of Ice*

"Filled with **authenticity, compassion and grace**, *Call My Name* will find its way deep into your heart and soul, and stay with you long after the last page has been turned."

—**Sally Cole-Misch**, Award-winning author of *The Best Part of Us*

"Vivid setting, dynamic plot, and likable characters come together beautifully to deliver an **emotionally compelling** tale of friendship, love, loss, and forgiveness. A fantastic read."

—**Jodi Wright**, Award-winning author of *How to Grow an Addict* and *Eat and Get Gas*.

"**This is a love story**...of couples, of friends, of families. It doesn't shy away from the messiness of love, the inevitable complications of long-lasting love…Most contemporary in its inclusion of topics such as adoption, abortion, and surrogacy, it also looks back on the atrocities of war. A page turning saga that is fresh in its story, yet provides the warmth of an old-fashioned classic.

—**Romalyn Tilghman**, Award-winning author of *To the Stars with Difficulties*, 2018 Kansas Notable Book of the Year.

"*Call My Name* felt so intense and raw that I choked up a few times while reading it…brings out the true essence of friendship. **Powerful and inspirational.**"

—**Readers Favorite, 5 Star Review**

"…realistic, pulled at my heartstrings… unforgettable characters… **A masterpiece.**"

—**Readers Favorite, 5 Star Review**

A DROP IN THE OCEAN

"In *A Drop in the Ocean*, protagonist Anna Fergusson learns that love is about letting go. Jenni Ogden takes us on a sweeping journey, rich with unique characters and places, moving backward and forward in time, to reach this poignant and heartfelt lesson."

—**Ann Hood,** New York Times best-Selling author of *The Knitting Circle* & *The Book That Matters Most*

"Reading *A Drop in the Ocean* was everything a reading experience should be, endearing and enduring, time spent with characters who seem to be people I already knew."

—**Jacquelyn Mitchard,** #1 New York Times best-selling author of *The Deep End Of The Ocean*

"Readers will enjoy this novel of second chances, not only at love but at life, reminiscent of Terry McMillan's *How Stella Got Her Groove Back*"

—**Booklist**

"A novel about turtles, the fragility of life, and the complexity of love . . . a story to savor, discuss, and share."

—**Barbara Claypole White,** best-selling author of *The Perfect Son* & *The Promise Between Us*

"A quietly majestic book, taking on quests for identity, for connection, for love, for self . . . a book to lose oneself in— and then share, enthusiastically, right away."

— **Robin Black,** bestselling author of *Life Drawing*

"A complicated, deep and passionate love affair that transcends stereotypes. . . . Ogden brought the island to life with her words. . . But the book's real treasure is how island life changes Anna. . . ."

—**Story Circle Book Reviews**

"...Life, love, and loss are strong themes that will lure readers back to this beautifully woven journey of second chances...a powerful read that I highly recommend."

—**Readers' Favorite,** 5-star review

"Evocative and thought-provoking, *A Drop In The Ocean* is a story about belonging—and the ripples that can flow from the family we choose to the family that chooses us."

—**Anita Heiss,** Best-selling author of *Tiddas* & *Barbed Wire and Cherry Blossoms*

"Jenni Ogden is a natural storyteller who writes characters to care about."

—**Nicky Pellegrino,** author of *One Summer In Venice*

THE MOON IS MISSING

"Jenni Ogden is a beautiful writer. In this tale of domestic suspense, she tells the story of a neurosurgeon bedeviled by her own sophisticated brain and the memories of a long-ago tragedy that still has the power to destroy her and her family. Pick up *The Moon is Missing*. You won't put it down."

— **Jacquelyn Mitchard,** #1 New York Times best-selling author of *The Deep End of the Ocean* and *The Good Son*

"With gripping scenes set during Hurricane Katrina and on a remote New Zealand island, this tightly-woven family drama —fueled by long-buried secrets and a daughter's desperate need to answer the question, 'Who am I?' —is ripe for book club discussion."

—**Barbara Claypole White,** bestselling author of *A Perfect Son* & *The Promise Between Us*

"Jenni Ogden's powerful novel, *The Moon is Missing*, is a mother-daughter coming of age story exploring a woman physician's passion-driven work, the terrible mistakes and long-held family secrets that haunt her life, and the power of loving connections to heal. The evocative settings on three continents are an added bonus!"

—**Barbara Stark-Nemon,** author of *Even in Darkness* & *Hard Cider*

"...Beautifully written ... characters were immensely believable...Ogden did not shy away from the harsh realities of what can happen when someone in a family is experiencing panic attacks and trauma from the past. Katrina was a tragedy... the novel really paid homage to the medical staff who worked tirelessly to make sure people were evacuated...."

—**Readers' Favorite**, 5 star review

Also by Jenni Ogden

FICTION

A Drop in the Ocean: A Novel

The Moon is Missing: A Novel

NONFICTION

Fractured Minds: A Case Study Approach to Clinical Neuropsychology

Trouble In Mind: Stories from a Neuropsychologist's Casebook

Call My Name

Call My Name

A NOVEL

JENNI OGDEN

This is a work of fiction. Names, characters and incidents throughout the novel are the product of the author's imagination. Any resemblance to actual persons, living or dead, is entirely coincidental. Actual locales and events are used fictitiously.

Quotes from *Winnie the Pooh* by A.A. Milne, *Anne of Green Gables* by L. M. Montgomery, *The Velveteen Rabbit* by Margery Williams, and lyrics and music of "Ain't We Got Fun" by Raymond B. Egan and Gus Kahn are all in the Public Domain.

A catalogue record for this book is available from the National Library of New Zealand.

First Edition: September, 2022

ISBN 978-0-473-62961-8 (Softcover)

ISBN 978-0-473-62962-5 (Hardcover)

ISBN 978-0-473-62963-2 (E-Book)

ISBN 978-0-473-62964-9 (Audiobook)

Cover by Sea Dragon Press

Cover photograph of two women: Getty Image by Catherine Delahaye. Sky background from Canva.

Published by Sea Dragon Press

www.jenniogden.com

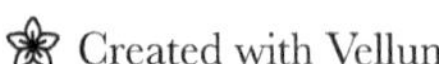

—For my friends from the past who are still my friends today—
From schooldays and with whom I shared the highs and lows of growing up, and music, music, music! - Jan, Jennifer, and Karen (Go, Fivefolk!)
For our friends from 1970s Australia, with whom John and I shared long hair, free-range kids, and crazy parties where we danced like no-one was watching: especially Ann, Peter, Jill and Jim, Robin and Mike, Neal, Annette and Jim (and Jeremy who is out there somewhere!)
And for my loyal same-generation family who are also always friends: Margaret and Edward, Lynn and Simon.

"Pooh!" he whispered.

"Yes, Piglet?"

"Nothing," said Piglet, taking Pooh's paw. "I just wanted to be sure of you."

— *Winnie the Pooh* by A.A. Milne —

Contents

Part One

KILLARA – ALWAYS THERE

1960 - 1975

"Kindred spirits are not so scarce as I used to think. It's splendid to find out there are so many of them in the world."

— *Anne of Green Gables* by L. M. Montgomery —

Chapter One

Cambridge, England, August, 1969

I LISTENED WITH HALF-CLOSED EYES TO BEN'S EASY VOICE, HIS banjo cavorting in and out of his words. I'd heard him singing this folksy, bluesy, almost ballad before, but this time, tonight, it felt different, as if he and I were alone in the smoky room, the others sent packing to their own flats and bedsits, to their ticky-tacky student halls scattered around Cambridge University's ancient walls. I opened my eyes and squinted through the dimmed space that separated me from him, filling in the details I couldn't really see, partly because I wasn't an owl, partly because of the students sprawled on the floor in front of me, partly because my contact lenses needed a good clean. He was the sort of man I never thought I'd meet, let alone attract. Gorgeously lanky with olive skin and a head of tight black curls just long enough to be sexy, and twinkling brown eyes behind black-framed glasses. Charming Scottish accent and ultra-smart as well as a musician of multiple talents—banjo, guitar and piano that I knew of—and the main singer in this student folk/blues band, the Cambridge CrapOuts. He was far from a crap-out, having handed in his PhD thesis in Ornithology yesterday. Birds. His first love. Gannets, falcons… Not me, not yet. But there it was, as crystal clear as the sea on the bluest day on the Great Barrier Reef. I had fallen in love.

A hint of a cramp low in my belly with its signature dull ache jerked me out of my daze, and for a second my breath stopped dead as relief churned, cheering wildly, through my body. I sucked in a stream of beer-stained air and let it out again. Sliding off the stool I was perched on at the back of the room, I grabbed my bulky fringed batik shoulder-bag and snuck out into the hall and into the bathroom. Thank the Lord. I'd been praying that two weeks late didn't mean the worst…although I'd counted back the days to the one only night we'd not used a condom; exactly halfway, as it turned out, between my regular-as-clockwork periods. Whoever really ended up pregnant after one measly slip-up? I pulled my slightly grubby makeup purse from my bag and retrieved a tampon, always ready for those times when, mostly in the middle of a meeting, the period pain decided to appear. Usually annoying, but not tonight. Not even if it meant I would be shy about making love later, if Ben suggested I stay over.

I undid my trousers and wriggled them down along with my knickers, looking confidently for the red stain that would vanquish the haze of anxiety that had dogged me for the past week or so. Nothing. White as the sands on Killara beach. They were pristine knickers purchased in a pack of three from Marks and Sparks in honor of my new hobby of weekend—and sometimes bonus Wednesday night—shack-ups with Ben. Just in case he decided to check my knickers when he ripped them off. I shoved the tampon in hard and waited thirty seconds before pulling it out again. Zip. Shit. *Give it time. The cramps have just started.* I pushed the tampon back in and wriggled into my sexy knickers and denim bell bottoms—another new purchase. As I washed my hands I felt it. Or didn't feel it. The cramps, the dull period ache, had disappeared.

~

I WALKED TO THE FAMILY PLANNING CLINIC FROM THE university, hoping the exercise and almost hot summer air would calm me down. My appointment was for 1pm, so I would be ridiculously early. I was already sick with nerves. Or perhaps morning sickness. Why the hell hadn't I been on the pill? After all my campaigning for the right for it to be prescribed for unmarried women? And here's me, idiot, relying on condoms. I'd thought about starting the pill, of course I had, but how could I have told Ben? He'd have assumed I slept around. I could hardly say I was on it because of our relationship. I don't think it has even entered his mind that we're a couple.

What if I were pregnant and I couldn't get a termination? I knew the abortion laws as well as anyone; I'd been at the front of a protest march through central London on the day the Abortion Act came into being, campaigning against the restrictions on who could have one. I never thought I'd be one of the women who had to suffer in real life. Would I have to lie to two doctors; convince them a baby would destroy my life, my mental health? Truth is, one day I would love a baby. Three perhaps. Preferably with Ben. Who knew nothing about this. One day, but not now.

Gilly thought I should have told him. "It will bring you closer," she said. "Isn't that what you want?"

"Don't you dare tell him, not even a hint," I hissed, petrified suddenly that she would, that I should never have told her. I only did because she'd had an abortion, and now considered herself an old hand.

"Of course I won't," Gilly said. "Promise. But wouldn't Ben support you if he knew? It's his bloody fault for not wearing a condom. Why should we women have to take the blame? It pisses me off."

"I don't want him to know. We've only been dating for three months, and I don't want to scare him off."

"Well, good luck with that if you are preggers and the good doctors can't find a single sign that you might spiral into deep depression if you had the baby. You have to give them some reason to allow them to bend the rules," she said. "You'd better polish up your acting skills."

I saw a nurse first, who was very gentle with me, to the point where I was almost in tears. She didn't ask me much; just why I thought I was pregnant and what options I had considered. If I were pregnant, she told me, the doctor would talk to me about my wish to have a termination. Then I was left alone to complete a questionnaire on depression, whether I had suicidal thoughts, if I relied on alcohol or drugs to get me through life. I considered answering a few of the questions with blatant untruths, but couldn't in the end. I knew about these sorts of tests from the courses I'd taken in psychology to balance my English major; they had tricky lie detector questions embedded in them. I'd have to rely on this carefully chosen Family Planning Clinic's reputation for interpreting the abortion restrictions liberally.

My arguments that to go ahead with this pregnancy would clearly result in more harm to my mental health than terminating it at this very early stage, when it was only a ball of undifferentiated cells, would be thoughtful, emotional, intelligent. I was only 22, just graduated from Cambridge Uni with an Honors degree, and only a month into my first job as an assistant to one of the editors at a small publishing company. On the path to a career in publishing, and writing novels on the side. Must the future I'd been working so hard to achieve be upended by one carelessly stupid but surely understandable mistake? One still starlit night in a field of silking corn, when my boyfriend and I were picnicking after a strenuous evening standing like statues and watching the flights of falcons, and desire took us by surprise? That neither of us had thought to include a condom in our daypacks?

In private defence of myself, I hadn't wanted to miss that moonlit moment of magic; I had the hots for Ben and at that moment he had the hots for me. But nothing about this new relationship was certain yet, even though I'd already known I wanted it to be. And I still wanted it, but the words 'love' and 'commitment' hadn't been voiced by either of us. I had thought it, wished for it said, but not this way. Not because Ben felt duty-bound because I was pregnant. He was a decent person, and I knew he would feel exactly that, duty-bound, if I told him we'd been unlucky, and then I would be in the position of having to decide whether I wanted to have a baby now. Ben would never put pressure on me to have an abortion, of that I was confident. And if I went ahead with the pregnancy, what sort of long-term partnership could Ben and I expect under those forced circumstances? No, this had to be my decision.

But to one day have a child, to have children, to be a family, to make a family, was so much part of my very essence, my ultimate goal in life, that it was a terrible decision to have to make. I had to remind myself that this wasn't the end of the story; I could have my children later, when the time was right. A child born to a solo mother, or to two parents who were only together because the father felt duty-bound was not part of my dream for a real family. The sort of family I had lived with and aspired to, but had never had for myself.

I DIDN'T NEED ALL MY COMPLICATED ARGUMENTS, OR TO HINT at desperate psychological consequences if I had this baby. Dr. Jackson was calm, down-to-earth, and acted as if she did this all the time. Which, of course, she did. It was only me who was the novice. My first ever internal exam was hardly pleasant but not as embarrassing as I had imagined it would be, and once I had pulled my jeans back on she gave me the news. Yes, my late period and tender boobs were telling me the truth; my cervix had changed color and was softer. But she would need me to pee into a bottle as she required confirmation from a pregnancy test before proceeding with a termination. If I was up to it she had thirty minutes for our first interview, and if we needed more time, that could be scheduled for a day later in the week. I had to return anyway for my second interview with another of the doctors in the Family Planning Clinic. They both needed to be convinced that a termination was the best option for my mental health, especially as I was a healthy young woman and there was no physical reason why I couldn't carry a baby to full term.

Dr. Jackson looked at me with her calm brown eyes. "At six weeks the embryo is the length of a grain of rice, but it is already beginning to look like a baby," she said. "It has a heartbeat, its head and body are defined, and its arms and legs are tiny buds." She poured a glass of water and handed it to me. I gulped it down.

"There's no rush to make a final decision. If necessary you can leave it for another four weeks, even a little longer, as long as it is in the first trimester."

I heard her soft voice but the rice-sized embryo stayed put in my head. A heart. Beating. Not an undifferentiated ball of cells.

"You might find it helpful to talk to a friend, if you are sure you don't want to involve the father. We have a psychologist here in the clinic you can talk it all through with, as well as Doctor Webster and myself. Then if you are certain you want to go ahead, and we agree that that would be the best option, I'll use manual vacuum aspiration to remove the contents of the uterus. It's a very safe procedure. The actual aspiration only takes about 15 minutes and can be carried out with a local anesthetic here in the clinic. We can even schedule it on a Friday so you'll have the weekend to rest before returning to work."

Eight days later, it was done. Ben, thank goodness, was away on a field trip; he had left the previous weekend and wouldn't return until Monday. I would be back to normal by then. Back to normal and on the pill. Gilly had been my strength, and had come in with me to the clinic and driven me home in her beloved yellow VW Beetle. I felt empty and soaked in guilt. More because I hadn't told Ben than because of the abortion. The hours of counseling I'd had with the two doctors and the psychologist had confirmed for me that this was the right decision. One day, I told myself, if we became a long-term couple, I would tell him.

Chapter Two

I SQUASHED THE GUILT INTO SOME FAR CORNER OF MY MIND, but at times the emotions insisted on welling up in spite of my life being mostly happy. I loved my job as trainee assistant editor, reading the submissions of would-be novelists who sometimes sent in stuff so bad I thought my own work would some day stand a chance, and sometimes words and sentences that shimmered on the page and made me both jealous and exhilarated.

Life with Ben was good; the words 'love' and 'commitment' still hadn't passed his lips, and I wasn't going to be the first to utter them, but it was early days. Ben's easy manner attracted friendship, and the vast house he shared with three other guys seemed always overflowing with students. They cooked up cheap meals in the kitchen, played guitars and banjos and the ancient piano that sat in one corner of the large main room with its tattered armchairs and posters of Che Guevara, Bob Dylan and Joan Baez, smoked endless cigarettes and sometimes pot—although drugs of any kind were still fairly scarce—and on weekends got pissed. During the week the alcohol was kept to a minimum; these friends of Ben's were serious students with research on their minds and the intelligence to know when and how long to party.

At the end of a Saturday night jam session, for Ben and me it was a toss-up whether we should walk for 45 long minutes through the silent Cambridge streets and bed down in my clean and tidy room in the clean and tidy flat I shared with Gilly, or in Ben's rumpled sheets and tumble of blankets on a mattress on the floor of a bedroom he shared with a bearded giant called Don. Don was not intrusive and snored on happily on the few occasions Ben and I slept together there, furtively making love under the unwashed sheets. But I yearned for a place of our own that had the warmth of his pad but gave us a measure of privacy, and as a bonus, clean bedlinen.

My own work sometimes took rather a back seat, and I would often find myself at 2am on Monday morning, reading the submissions I had brought home to read in the weekend. Ben never suffered from this problem; he could switch effortlessly from guitar-playing sexy lover to serious, dedicated post-doctoral research student at will.

One October day I came home to find mail. Not a common finding, real mail. When I did get mail it was usually an aerogramme, its thin blue paper folded over on itself, the stamp printed on the outside. The aerogrammes I did get were always from Aunt Cathie and Uncle William, my unofficial foster parents. They would each write a paragraph or two in their familiar dear writing, Aunt Cathie's in blue ink and Uncle William's in black. So I knew the cream-colored envelope made of heavy paper, must be from Cassandra. Unlike her parents, she didn't suffer from redundant post-war thriftiness. I could feel the silly grin on my face as my eyes feasted on her loopy violet writing. It was ages since she'd written. Ages since I'd written to her. I dropped my backpack and went into our tiny kitchenette. I'd make a nice cup of tea and plate up a cracker and cheese to savor with her news.

The six months Cassandra and I had spent hitchhiking around Europe in between my starting my Honors degree at Cambridge, and Cassandra returning to Australia, seemed a lifetime ago. Four years in fact. Our adventures in Europe had been spectacularly successful, bar a few mishaps like Cassandra leaving her wallet in the Parthenon, and me getting food poisoning in Turkey. I lost my virginity, and Cassandra, who had lost hers already, became more experienced. We'd both survived our intense but brief romances, and apart from a few minor spats when tiredness and hunger got the better of us, we stayed friends and between us made many more. After she flew back to Australia, leaving me in Cambridge, we were soon taken over by our new lives and our promises to write monthly didn't last.

Cassandra, as always, had stayed well ahead of me, life-wise, having moved to Brisbane and gained her qualification as a kindergarten teacher before landing a job in a posh private kindie. The last letter she'd sent, months ago, had been full of a fellow from Sussex, a law student. Sebastian. A name hard to forget and typical of a lover of Cassandra. I searched my memory. Brooks. Sebastian Brooks. I remembered grinning at her description of his family, toffy-nosed British aristocrats who sent Sebastian to boarding school when he was a toddler. Sebastian had fled to Australia to escape them, and would cut off his right arm before taking their blackmailing money. Whether Cassandra had been playing the drama card or telling the truth, who knew? She'd probably moved on to some chap called Julian by now.

My tea made, I collapsed into a beanbag and turned the envelope over, my finger poised to rip it open.

~

When Gilly walked into our flat, I was a mess. Tears, red nose, snot.

"Hey, what's the matter?" she said, dropping into the beanbag beside me.

I flapped the letter at her. "I got a letter from Cassandra… it made me homesick."

"She's your half-sister isn't she? The one you backpacked around Europe with?"

"My foster sister, not my half-sister." I grabbed more tissues out of the box and blew my sore nose again.

"Do her letters always do this to you? Seems a bit extreme."

I shook my head. "No. I think it's just… just her news. And she wants me to go home next month for her wedding so I can be her bridesmaid…"—my voice petered out— "but I can't, can I?"

"Given your state, perhaps you should. Did you know she was getting married?"

I shook my head. "No. She's pregnant."

"Ah. It's that, isn't it. She's pregnant and you're not. It's brought it all back. You think you're cool with it and then out of the blue, something triggers it and the emotions go crazy. It happened to me too, months after I thought I was over my abortion."

I buried my face in my hands and we sat there, not talking. I heard Gilly get up and the kettle boiling. She handed me a cup of hot tea and I sipped it. On the coffee table sat my last cup of tea, a white glaze over it's cold surface, Cassandra's letter in its fancy envelope shoved beneath the plate with its uneaten cracker and cheese.

"I can't afford the flights to Australia and back," I said, a while later. I'd had a shower and washed my hair and felt vaguely human again. "My salary barely pays my rent. I'll take forever to save up enough."

"At least you don't have to pay back a student loan, like me," Gilly said.

I knew I should be grateful for that, but it wasn't helping me yet. While I was at Uni, my scholarship plus my weekend waitressing job had covered most of my expenses, including my rent, but now I had graduated, the scholarship money had stopped. I blew my nose again.

"Perhaps Cassandra could help out? After all, she wants you to be her bridesmaid." Gilly pretended to gag; the only color she wore was black. "Could she or her parents loan you the cost of the flights?"

"They would but they wouldn't let me pay it back. I don't want that. They did so much for me when I lived with them. When I left, I was determined I'd be one hundred percent independent of them, and that's that."

I leaned over and pulled the envelope free of the plate. I turned it over, my blurred eyes moving over Cassandra's violet writing on the back. She'd sent it from Killara, not from Brisbane where she lived now. *Sender,* she'd written. A bolt of homesickness churned up from the depths of my gut. *Cassandra Tulloch, Killara, Oak Beach, Port Douglas, Far North Queensland.*

Chapter Three

Auckland, New Zealand, May, 1960

Two months after my thirteenth birthday, I became an orphan.

I found my mother when I took in her tea before I left for school, hoping it would wake her up enough to say goodbye. My nose twitching with the smell of vomit and gin, I carefully placed the mug of tea on the apple box by her bed, then picked up the bottle lying on the worn blanket and placed it upright beside the mug and the empty pill container. Mum was on her side, dried vomit coating her chin and the sheet beneath her head. She looked different from the other two times I'd not been able to wake her, and although I'd never seen a dead body before, not in real life anyway, I knew that's what I was looking at. Already not my mum, but a corpse, vacant and cold. Just in case I was wrong I held my hand over her mouth and felt no breath, gagging as my fingers grazed the bits of carrot and horrible mince we'd had for dinner last night. Stumbling down the hall and into the bathroom, I turned the tap on full and washed my hands and then my clammy face. Wringing out the flannel I took it and a towel back to Mum's bedroom and did my best to wipe her face and the sheet clean before wriggling the towel under her head so the disgusting dried mess I couldn't get off was covered. Then I did what I'd seen in the movies and pulled the bedspread up to cover her face.

After four weeks in a foster home, and when the nicer kids at school had stopped tiptoeing around me as if they thought I might break or bawl or something, the school psychologist who had been giving me grief counseling drove me into central Auckland for a meeting with Miss McGregor, the head of Child and Family Services. I'd met her before, the day after Mum died. She looked slightly less frazzled this time than she had on our first meeting after I told her my father didn't exist as I was the result of a one-night stand with a nameless sailor, my mother was an only child, and both her parents were dead. After she'd sat me and my psychologist down with cups of tea and chocolate biscuits, she pretended to look at the papers inside the file she was holding and said "Do you know Mrs. Tulloch?"

I shook my head. "I don't think so."

"Cathie Tulloch. We found an old Christmas card from her amongst your mother's things. It had her address on it and so we contacted her in Australia."

"Australia?"

"Yes. She and her family…" — she smiled at me and my heart sped up while my stomach did a somersault —"they live in Queensland, way up north, where it's always lovely and warm." She had a thick sweater on, but her hands were practically purple. Her office was colder than our apartment used to be when the gas bottle for the heater ran out. Even I was freezing and I had my school coat on as well as a sweater.

"William Tulloch—Dr Tulloch—is a professor at the university, and the son and daughter..." —she looked down at her notes—"Pete and Cassandra. They're thirteen just like you. Twins."

I swallowed the taste that churned up from my stomach to my mouth. "Why didn't you give me the card? Shouldn't I have been given all my mother's things?"

"The card is the only item we kept and you can have it, of course. We didn't want to raise your hopes until we'd contacted Mrs. Tulloch. We wanted to make sure she still lived at the same address."

"I've never heard of her. I didn't know Mum knew anyone in Australia."

"Mrs. Tulloch said they'd lost touch. She'd written to your mother since that card but her letter was returned and stamped as unknown at that address. She was very upset when I told her that your mother had passed away. She and your mother were close friends in Singapore during the war."

"But Mum was in a prison camp for practically the entire time."

"Yes, I know. They were both prisoners in the same camp in Sumatra."

The psychologist put her warm hand on mine. A memory flickered in my head. "Cathie. I think I remember Mum talking about her. She came to stay with us when I was little but I can't remember that and I didn't know her name was Tulloch. She gave me a kangaroo. Not a real one. Obviously. A stuffed toy." I blinked hard. "I still have it."

Miss McGregor pulled a card from beneath her notes and looked at it as if she hadn't seen it before. "She and her husband want you to go and live with them. The Social Services in Queensland interviewed them and are sure they will be a wonderful family for you."

The card she handed me was homemade and yellowing, with a photo stuck on the outside. I'd never laid eyes on it before; they must have found it in Mum's old desk amongst all the overdue electricity bills and rental demands. It didn't look very Christmassy; more like a holiday photo, palm trees and a blue sea. Lovely and warm. I opened it and there was another photo stuck on one side of the card with a message written in neat letters in real blue ink on the other. I peered at the black and white photo. A family all in shorts. A tall thin man with glasses and dark hair, a tall woman with shoulder-length curly blonde hair, and in front of them, two skinny kids; a boy with fair hair holding a bow and arrow and a girl with dark plaits and a hugh grin. The ink on the inside of the card was faded but I could still read it.

December 15th, 1956.

Dearest Jess,

Happy Christmas! I think of you and Olivia often and so wish you could come to Killara for a long stay. I probably wouldn't recognise Olivia now. She was only two when we were last together and she'll be nine now. The twins are nine as well of course. Cassandra is quite her own person already and I know she and Olivia would be great friends, just like we were.

Please write or even phone me if you can (reverse the charges) so we can find a time for you to fly over, perhaps during Olivia's next school holidays if you can take time off your work (are you still working in the same Old People's home?). I can pick you up from Cairns airport. William and the twins can't wait to meet you. The airfares are our treat.

Love, Cathie

Below was a phone number and address. *Killara,* it said. No street name or number. *Oak Beach, Port Douglas, Far North Queensland.*

Chapter Four

Far North Queensland, July, 1960

Aunt Cathie—which is what she asked me to call her—was waiting for me at Cairns Airport. She hugged me so tightly the second she saw me that I knew I was going to like her. Especially when she let me go but kept hold of my arms and looked at my face as if she was saying goodbye to someone she loved, not someone she'd just met. She had tears in her eyes and I had to look down. "Sorry," she said. "It's been so long and I can see Jess in you. Your eyes are exactly like hers, rainy-day gray."

It was a mighty relief. I'd been having nightmares about child slavery even though we'd talked on the phone a couple of times before I'd left New Zealand.

July in Auckland was full-on winter; rainy and cold. I was rugged up like an eskimo when I got on the plane. Here it was like opening the door of a hot oven when we pushed through the airport doors and walked outside. Crazy that it was mid-winter here too. We had nearly an hour's drive to get to Killara. Aunt Cathie drove the massive green 4WD Landrover like a fighter pilot. I grabbed the door handle as she raced around hairpin bends with the blue sea and white beaches a gob-smacking drop below, just missing other even bigger 4WDs and trucks whizzing past us the other way. My experience of driving anywhere was fairly limited and mainly in slow buses that stopped every five minutes.

It was hard to imagine Mum and Aunt Cathie could ever have been such close friends, they were so different. But they must have been for her to take me on. Mum looked like me, nothing to write home about. In real life color Aunt Cathie was even more beautiful than in the black and white photo in the Christmas card; tall and tanned and her eyes were so blue they were practically violet. She had messy curly hair cut quite short at the back so that it stood out like a ballerina's tutu. It shone gold in the hot sun and made her look like a 1930s model who rode horses along windswept beaches, which in fact, she did. She talked a bit about their horses while we were driving, and told me about Queensland and how all the stuff about everything killing you up here, from crocodiles to spiders and snakes and stinging jellyfish and even plants, was a load of poppycock. "They are around," she said, "but they have not a jot of interest in humans." Apparently Cassandra, Pete, and Uncle William, which is what she said I should call him, couldn't wait to meet me. She'd refused to let them come with her to the airport so I wouldn't be overwhelmed. She glanced at me and grinned when she said that. "Cassandra can be a bit over-the-top when she gets excited," she said.

I FELL IN LOVE WITH KILLARA BEFORE I EVEN SAW THE HOUSE. The 4WD turned across the highway that stretched for thousands more miles up the East coast of this massive country, and drove through a wide driveway that divided a vast green flat area of short grass with lines of tall coconut palms sauntering across it. KILLARA, it said on the wooden sign at the beginning of the drive. Not a big flashy sign to go with the wide expanse of well-tended coconut palms, but a rough sign, a sign that looked as if it had been there long before these sky-high palms had even been planted. That's when I felt the surge of heat deep in my belly.

The coconut plantation ended abruptly and the drive continued through a jumbled mass of trees of all sizes and forms, some with big white flowers. Up a rise we drove and there was the house. It was entirely not what I was expecting. I'd imagined that the house on an estate with a name like Killara would be a sort of Australian version of Tara in *Gone With The Wind* with stone pillars and servants—a cook and a cleaner at least—and beautiful antiques everywhere.

The dark blue wooden building that spread before us as Aunt Cathie and I got out and let our legs fill with blood again, was long and wide and beautiful. It had a white corrugated iron roof curved over at the edge and a verandah with a white balustrade across the front and around the sides. "It's called a Kneeling Queenslander," Aunt Cathie said, a laugh in her voice as I followed her around the side to the wide steps that led up to the verandah. "The true Queenslander is perched up on a high basement to keep it safe from floods, but this one is low to the ground."

The big french doors all along the front of the house were open wide. Aunt Cathie started up the steps but my sneakers were bolted firm in the broad-leaved tropical grass as I stared at the view. The house was on a sort of plateau on the top of a rise and in front of me was a wide area of grass. Around its edges were trees and palms and jungly stuff, but only small bushes in front, some of them covered in flowers. The trees had been cleared away except for lower down the slope, and from the grass you could see clear across the bluest sea. Through the lower trees peeked a golden sand beach. I didn't care about Tara any more. Who needed antiques and chandeliers?

I turned around and looked up at the tall man from the photo. He was standing on the verandah with a girl who looked nothing like her photo. Tall and tanned like her mother but with the darkest eyes, masses of thick dark wavy hair halfway down her back, and a face that made Aunt Cathie's seem sweet rather than beautiful. "Olivia Newman, you're finally here," she said, her voice a bit like her mother's, which I'd decided must be a result of a private school education or being upper class.

"Hullo," I said, trying to disguise my common New Zealand accent and furious with the flush that I could feel shooting up my pallid neck. "It's lovely to meet you."

"Oh my God," she cried—I soon discovered that Cassandra never screamed—in her posh voice. "I LOVE your accent. Speak, speak, so I can hear some more!"

And there it was, my future set out before me in that single two second interaction. The drama, the dominance, the manipulation, the generosity, the smothering, the wealth and education and land and privilege—the startling wonder of this almost woman from a world I'd never even dreamed I'd ever enter.

THE HOUSE WAS PERFECT AS IT TURNED OUT. NOT AT ALL posh. Inside it had dark wooden floors and white walls and dark beams in the big main rooms with high ceilings, almost like a church. There were faded rugs everywhere and a mish-mash of wooden furniture and saggy couches. Through french doors I could see the green forest and blue sea, although the flyscreens over the doors with lots of bird and insect splatter on them got in the way a bit. Wooden fans spun from the high ceilings in a romantic fashion.

Cassandra led me into a bedroom with twin beds, and said I could have the one under the window if I liked. It was clearly hers going by the bedside drawers which had on the top a framed photo of a horse, a horsey magazine, and an apple core.

"No, that's yours. This one is fine," I said, dumping my day pack on the other bed.

"I can shift in a jiffy. No prob. It's nice sleeping under the window if you're not used to the heat."

"No really, I'm good here." I was blushing again and shoved my damp hair back from my hot face, trying to ignore my reflection in the mirror on the chest-of-drawers opposite the two beds. Straight lank hair that Mum had called marmalade, but more like a horrible chewed gingernut, pale boring face with freckles, and at least half-a-head shorter than Cassandra.

"I insist," Cassandra said, pushing her bedside drawers across the space between the beds. "Shove those other drawers over here. They're empty so you can put your stuff in them."

"Thank you," I said. "That's awfully generous. Perhaps we can swap beds every week or something."

"God no, that would be a drag." She righted the horse photo that had fallen over in the shift. "Do you like horses?"

"I don't really know any," I said.

She grinned. "You're funny. I was worried we wouldn't hit it off and be stuck with each other in endless misery. But you're exactly the sister I would have chosen if I'd been given any say in the matter. It's dire having only a brother. I'll teach you to ride in a jiffy."

She ordered me to get my swimming togs out of my case and led the way back to the kitchen. A boy with dirty-blonde spiky hair was leaning on the bench eating an apple. "Gid-day," he said. "I'm Pete, the black sheep." His accent was a sort of cross between upper-class and Australian drawl.

"Hi," I said, going red as usual. "I'm Olivia."

"Thought you might be. Do you want an apple?"

"OK. Thanks."

Cassandra rolled her eyes and Aunt Cathie frowned at her. "You can all have drinks first before you go to the beach."

I took the icy-cold glass from her and laid it against my cheek, then skulled it down. "Yum."

"Have another. It's mango juice," said Aunt Cathie, but Cassandra was already shoving me out the door as if the beach would vanish if we didn't get to it immediately.

The track wound through the bush for quite a long way with divine seats every time there was a glimpse of the sea. Not that we stopped to sit on any of them. At the bottom just before the sand there was a shed and a loo, and Pete disappeared into the loo while Cassandra and I got changed into our swimming togs in the shed. I thought Cassandra would strip off her clothes without any hint of modesty and I'd have to as well, but she turned her back which was a relief.

The sea was heaven, absolute heaven. Warm and soft and barely a ripple. I discovered soon enough that it wasn't always like that, but it was most of the time. We swam inside a giant net that was attached to poles on the sand like an enormous drowned hammock. I thought it was to keep the crocs and sharks away but it was to keep stinging jellyfish out. It had a few holes here and there—bigger than the tiny netting holes, I mean, obviously—but none of us got stung so either the jellyfish were giants or just couldn't be bothered to sting humans. Pete said that they didn't even need the net in winter because the water was only 79 degrees, too cold for stingers, but it was too much of a hassle to take it in every damn May.

I SOON GOT USED TO EVERYTHING, EVEN THEIR ACCENTS AND Cassandra and Pete's bickering. Aunt Cathie and Cassandra talked all the time, which was tiring at first but it meant I didn't have to come up with stuff to say. I especially liked the Professor (that's what I secretly called him even though I was meant to call him Uncle William). He wasn't much of a talker unless it was worth it, but he always treated we three teens like adults with valuable opinions. I really looked forward to dinner time, not just because of the yummy food but because everyone argued and carried on about all sorts of things. Sometimes I thought of home and our lonely meal times, mostly because Mum was usually too tired to talk much and it was sausages or fatty mince if we were lucky. It was best not to think about it and concentrate on getting used to this bizarre new world.

Off the main living room where the kitchen and the old scrubbed wooden table where we ate was, there was a big room with a giant desk and a saggy couch and saggy chairs that didn't match and heaps of bookshelves with books piled up everywhere. I thought it was the Prof's study but he said he didn't have a study, it was a room for reading or sleeping or eating cake or anything else pleasant and was for everyone. He showed me lots of fascinating old books and there was even a copy of *Gone With The Wind* just like mine. He said it was one of his favorite novels, and so was *Wuthering Heights*, although he thought Catherine Earnshaw was a silly girl thinking she could love one man while marrying another for his money.

It turned out that Uncle William was an important author in Australia and had written two novels that had won prizes. He didn't tell me this of course, but Cassandra did one day to stop me 'banging on' about how interesting he was. I felt too embarrassed after that to ask her what the books were, and I skulked around the bookshelves, pretending to look for other books but really looking for his name on the spines. No luck. One day near the end of the holidays, Uncle William asked me what I was currently writing and I didn't know what to say. Then he said that when he is writing something new, he always thinks it's terrible and has a hard time showing it to anyone, even a proper editor whose job it is to read drafts and help the author shape them up. So I told him I was sort of mucking around with a story set in Yorkshire (where I'd never been but where Mum had grown up and her parents lived before they died so I knew something about it other than from Emily and Charlotte) and he said he'd be delighted to read it whenever I thought it could do with another author's eye.

Chapter Five

In spite of our polar opposite personalities, Cassandra and I became friends. Best friends. Actually it probably worked because we were so different; she always had to be the center of attention, and I detested the limelight. At school we didn't spend much time together, but at home we were rarely apart. She was fun and I'd never had a friend even remotely like her before. In New Zealand, the girls who let me hang out with them were either the other kids from the wrong side of the tracks and had nothing much to laugh about, or were outsiders for other reasons. Even when I occasionally got pissed off by Cassandra's bossiness, she never minded, and sometimes even apologized. I never forgot that I'd been hoisted on her out of the blue, and how generous she'd been right from the start. But I never forgot, either, that I wasn't really a Tulloch, especially as my Kiwi accent persisted in spite of my efforts to change my vowels.

When we made those silly secret wishes on New Year's Day every year, my wish was always the same; that one day I'd have my own family. Sometimes I added a second wish; that I'd become a writer of novels that would make me entirely independent and with luck would also win an award or two.

Cassandra didn't have any burning ambitions other than to have five kids and ride every day. She was horse mad like Aunt Cathie and that was another reason I didn't entirely fit; I seemed incapable of relaxing around horses, and I soon gave up pretending. Uncle William said he was on my side although in fact he was a perfectly good rider himself. Pete could ride but didn't; he preferred the farm bike.

It turned out that the Tullochs weren't as wealthy as I'd thought. I discovered this at Sandalwood Private School for Girls (motto: *Sandalwood Brings the Sweet Smell of Success*) where lots of the girls were really wealthy. According to Cassandra, the Tullochs were classed as 'comfortably off'. She found this very amusing. University professors weren't paid big salaries and Aunt Cathie didn't have a job, although she did lots of volunteer work. Cassandra went to Sandalwood because the local state schools had a poor record of educational achievement, and the Tullochs believed education was much more important than a fancy house and overseas holidays. Pete had refused to go to the private boys' school that was the twin of Sandalwood, and instead got the bus to the state school in Port Douglas. Perhaps that's why he fancied himself as the black sheep. His real name was Gideon, but he'd decided he wanted to be called Pete when he was about six.

I discovered that Killara — which was an aboriginal word meaning 'always there' or 'permanent' — hadn't been in the family for generations but had been an abandoned, overgrown coconut plantation that Aunt Cathie and Uncle William bought for a song after the war. They'd lived in the worker's cabin—now called the Shack—while they gradually saved enough money so they could rebuild the old homestead which had been partly destroyed by a fire. It had been called Killara when it was built in the nineteen thirties. The Shack was full of junk now and swallows flew in and out of a broken window and made their nests in the rafters.

Neither Cassandra nor I managed to find out much about

Mum and Aunt Cathie's friendship, except that they knew each other casually when they were both working in Singapore as young women before the war. Uncle William told us a bit, and said we weren't to talk to Aunt Cathie about it as it upset her too much. I knew Mum had been a nurse in Singapore, and Aunt Cathie was a waitress. They were both part of a group of Australians and New Zealanders who met up at Raffles to dance and drink cocktails. Then when Singapore fell in 1942, they ended up on the same evacuation boat sunk by the Japanese and were stuck in the same Japanese prison camps in Sumatra until the war ended in 1945.

Cassandra and I talked about it quite a lot at first and decided that nothing could be deeper than a friendship between two women fighting to survive in a prison camp. We pledged to strive to make our friendship as deep in their honor.

At Sandalwood, Cassandra and I were in different academic streams; I was in the A stream and she in the B stream. But when it came to everything else, Cassandra was the star. She was in the top tennis team, the top swimming team, the dressage team, and the horse jumping team (it was that sort of school). She was elected head of the student council, organized the dances with the private boy's school nearby, and for a while went out with their Head Boy. In our final year she was the Deputy Head Girl. It was only because of her that I was even a prefect.

I was hopeless at all sports and detested organizing things. But in truth I didn't care because my passion was reading and creative writing. After my first year and coming top in English, Latin and French, and second in Science, Geography and Math, I was taken on as a special project by the head of the English Department, Miss Brontë. I called her Emily inside my head as I figured Emily was more darkly dramatic than Charlotte, but her first name was sadly Sue. Sue Brontë. I ask you, what was her mother thinking? She didn't seem much older than us, but I suppose she must have been twenty-five at least as she had all sorts of degrees. According to Cassandra, Uncle William had taught her when she was at uni. He thought she was A++. If it hadn't been for Miss Brontë with lots of backup from the Professor, I would never in a million years have won the scholarship to Cambridge. It included all my fees, board, text books and spending money for four years of an English and Creative Writing degree. It even included my airfare from Australia to England.

We finished at Sandalwood in early December, 1964. As soon as Pete's school broke up he disappeared to Melbourne where he got an apprenticeship as a motor mechanic. Cassandra and I worked our butts off as cleaners in Cairns Hospital for twelve weeks to make some money so that we could embark on our big Overseas Experience. We were both 18, me only two days past my birthday, when we boarded our plane for London. How free I felt as I showed my ticket to the air hostess, paid for by my scholarship. I knew Aunt Cathie and Uncle William loved me, almost like a daughter, and I loved them back. But never again would I have to rely on their generosity.

When Cassandra flew back to Australia, six months later, she was fizzing over starting her new life, far away from Killara. "I'm not going back home," she'd been telling our new friends in England. "Brisbane is days and days drive from Killara." It was true, Cairns was over 1000 miles north of Brisbane, and they were still in the same State. Those sorts of distances were hard for Brits to get their heads around. But at least it was drivable. Not like the 9000 miles that now separated me from the place I'd called home for the last five years.

As I waved my dearest friend goodbye at Heathrow, my feelings were all over the place. But the tiny trickle of homesickness soon turned to intoxication as I gazed out the train window on the return trip to Cambridge. I tried to imagine what this landscape must have been like in 1209, when the University of Cambridge was founded. Nearly 600 years before Europeans settled in Australia. Yes, it was time for me to discover at last my own life.

Chapter Six

Cambridge, England, October, 1969

Ben saved me from my distress over missing Cassandra's November wedding, then staying on in Australia for a tropical Christmas. He didn't know why I was really so down; I stuck by my decision not to tell him about the abortion. But he understood homesickness, and how upset I was about missing Cassandra's wedding.

"Come with me to Scotland for Christmas and New Year," he said. Then with a wink, he broadened his accent. "First footing 'n' a' that. Lassie, ye hae nae experienced New Year if ye hae nae lived in bonnie Scootlund." He grinned. "An' Mum will be ecstatic."

"What about you?" I asked. "Will you be ecstatic?"

"Goes wi'oot saying, hen," he said, pulling me into a hug.

Our Scotland holiday was wonderful. Ben's parents reminded me a little of Aunt Cathie and Uncle William; not to look at but in their natural welcoming ways. The walks—mostly uphill—Ben took me on into the nearby Cairngorms immersed me in memories of wild New Zealand. When I was about ten, Mum and I had spent a whole week driving around the foothills of the Southern Alps, camping in rough campsites, cooking over a camp fire. Looking back, I have no idea how she managed to afford it, but as a child that didn't even enter my head. One of my few happy memories of us. It seems to me now that it was her final attempt to pull herself out of her depression. She'd lost her job before we went on our trip and when we returned she couldn't, or didn't, get another one. Then came the longer drinking spells, the pills, the inability to lift herself out of bed and out of darkness.

PERHAPS BEN AND I WERE BOTH LOOSENED BY TOO MUCH whisky on New Year's Eve, but one of us said the magic words first and the other said them back. We didn't share our new commitment with Ben's parents, but our relationship felt different after that; deeper, truer.

Back in Cambridge, on the surface we continued as before —living separately, spending Wednesday nights and weekends together. But in a new bonding venture we joined the Cambridge anti-Vietnam war movement. Britain hadn't added to the US madness and sent troops, mainly because of the opposition from the British public, but Australia had, and Pete, Cassandra's twin, was one of the unlucky ones. The new friends we made through the movement—some of them were Australians and New Zealanders—assumed we were a couple, and I finally felt confident that we were. It gave me the excuse I needed to tell Ben I had decided to go on the pill. He was all for it, and said he'd spend his condom money on my favorite chocolates from now on. I didn't mention that he could have discarded the condoms months ago.

In February, Ben began looking for academic positions, as his postdoctoral research funding would come to an end in August. We talked about it, endlessly, and I got upset, and he suggested I might come with him wherever he ended up. He applied for lots of lecturing jobs in the UK, USA, and Australia, and got offered one in Durham, one in Iowa, and one in Brisbane. I had a miserable few days and nights while he decided which one to take, but the hot sex I withheld from him while he mulled it over worked, and he made the right decision. His boyhood obsession with the Great Barrier Reef and its birds may also have had something to do with it.

Brisbane, September, 1970

In my letters to my Tulloch foster-parents and Cassandra—no longer a Tulloch but a Brooks—I'd said we were arriving in Brisbane in October, but when the university suggested Ben arrive earlier so he could participate in an ornithological conference being held at his new university, I decided not to reveal our earlier September arrival date. Cassandra loved surprises.

We arrived at 6am, jet-lagged after a 30-hour journey, and for most of the day wandered like zombies around the motel the university had paid for, trying to stay awake. We found out some more about tomorrow's big anti-Vietnam war march being held as part of the Vietnam Moratorium Campaign. It was advertised everywhere. Its mission was to force a withdrawal of Australian and other foreign troops from Vietnam and the repeal of the 1964 National Service Act. Pete's birthdate had been drawn in the conscription ballot in January, 1967, and he'd been drafted after only a few months into the Second Battalion of the Royal Australian Regiment, surviving thirteen months in Vietnam. His regiment returned to Australia in June 1968, and on completion of his two years full-time service he was discharged from the army but put on the active reserve list. That was one of the issues Australians were protesting about. Not only were these guys forced into the army for two full-time years just because their twentieth birthday happened to fall on a date drawn out of a hat, after that they had to serve another three years on the active reserve list. So poor Pete was drafted back into the same regiment for a second stint in Vietnam in May this year. I had a personal reason for going to this march.

I didn't phone Cassandra until the evening. No answer so I phoned Killara and got Uncle William. When I heard his beautiful voice my throat closed up. It had been over five years. His voice changed when I managed to croak out my name and that I was back in Australia. "Olivia, my love," he said. "It's been too long."

Aunt Cathie was out at some charity thing, and he thought Cassandra and Sebastian were in Melbourne for a few days. I was gutted. But we chatted on and I told him Ben and I were planning on going on the anti-Vietnam war march tomorrow.

"That's good," said Uncle William. "I'm surprised Cassandra and Sebastian aren't back for it. They've been pretty involved in the moratorium. Perhaps they're going to the Melbourne one; that will be the biggest. There are marches in all the cities. Australia is finally catching up to the world on this."

"What about Pete?" I asked, heat pulsing in my face as my callousness hit me. Perhaps he was already home?

"He's on his second tour of duty, as they euphemistically refer to it," said Uncle William.

"Still? How's he coping?"

"His rare letters don't let on, but he seemed keen to do a second stint so I suppose he must either get something positive out of it, or he believes in the cause."

"God, surely not? I thought he hated it when he was called up?"

"Pete was never easy to read. We can only hope the Australian troops are brought home soon."

"Aunt Cathie?"

"She finds it hard having him over there. It brings back all her worst nightmares."

"I'm glad we're here for the march. Pete will be OK. He's tough."

"Our beloved black sheep," said Uncle William. "But even black sheep can pine for their home paddock."

~

THE END OF THE MARCH AND THOUSANDS WERE MILLING around, hugging and laughing, finding old friends, eating hamburgers and kebabs at the food stalls—the atmosphere was more like the finish of a fun run than a march against war and forcing our boys to be part of the killing. And to be killed. Ben hadn't wanted to linger, and I followed him as we wove through the crowds, reluctant to leave the color of it all so soon but wanting less to lose sight of him and be stranded without a ride back to the motel.

The jolt that stopped my heart when her face flashed past —or more accurately as I passed her face—turned me around even as I yelled out Ben's name, pulled for the first of a lifetime of times in both directions. Cassandra won of course. She was talking animatedly to a group of people, every one of whom had their eyes glued to her beautiful glowing alive face. I broke through them, my arms outstretched, grabbing the sleeves of her jacket, probably grinning, perhaps even weeping, who knows? Pure happiness. We had found each other again.

Cassandra's hands jerked outwards as she tried to shake me off, and then recognition dawned and we were hugging, pushing out to arms length, laughing, crying. God knows what happened to the admiring group; they melted away, likely ran away as fast as they could. She looked incredible. Still taller than me by half a head, long dark hair flowing and waving and glinting with hints of auburn down her back, braided headband, feather earrings, enormous round dark glasses balanced on her perfect nose, palest pink lipstick as fresh as if she'd just applied it to her curvy lips with a brush dipped in dew. A short brocade fitted jacket with large lapels over a dress covered in a collage of small flowers ended mid-calf, permitting just a glimpse of her long brown legs before they disappeared into short, laced-up, thick-soled boots. I felt like a leftover from the dark ages with my babyish face with its freckled upward tilted nose and round black-lined eyes, my mousy ginger middle-parted hair falling demurely and smoothly down my back, the Mexican peasant blouse, the white shiny fake-leather miniskirt and the knee-high white boots.

"Olivia Newman, what in Jehovah's name are you doing here?" Cassandra said, hugging me again. "You haven't changed one teensy bit."

"Well, you have. I almost walked right past you." *Liar.*

"Bullshit." She grinned. "But here we are again, just the two of us."

Then Ben was there beside me, cross about searching for me in the crowds. He'd seen photos of Cassandra and me in our demure school uniforms, and in scruffy jeans with backpacks, but Cassandra as Queen of the Flower People was something else entirely. Perhaps I should have felt at least a twinge of apprehension as she took in my adoration of Ben in one glance and folded his right hand in both of hers. She turned towards me, looking over the top of her sunglasses—which had magically slipped down her shapely nose just the right amount—her gold-flecked brown eyes sparkling. "My God, Olivia, now I know why you never sent me a photo. Where did you find him? Is he permanent?"

Ben seemed perfectly content to leave his hand in both of hers; she was stroking the fleshy base of his thumb now, so why would he not?

But I didn't feel jealous, not the slightest. I could almost feel my chest puffing out like a proud hen. Proud of Ben and that he found favor with Cassandra, and proud of Cassandra, that she was my bosom buddy. Happy that the two people I loved most in the world liked each other.

"Ben, this is Cassandra," I said, my voice squeaking with excitement. Their hands parted company. Ben was not a man to gush or pronounce niceties, and he didn't then. "Great to meet you, Cassandra," he said. "I know how close you and Olivia were at school. You've got a house in Brisbane?"

"We have, yes. Oh, Olivia, you'll love our place," she said, all her attention back on me. "It's a massive old falling-down farmhouse on an acre of land just out of town, right on the river. A sort of alternative Killara. You must come back with us now. You can stay the weekend so we can catch up properly. Jumping Jehovah, I've missed you so fucking much." She grabbed me and swirled me around and then we were both giggling like schoolgirls.

"Where the hell is Sebastian?" She swung first one way and then another, scanning the crowds. "He was here a minute ago. Never where he should be."

My eyes watered behind my sunglasses. Now I was jealous. To have found her again only to have her undivided attention whipped away. That I had Ben, only minutes ago the center of my life, didn't even occur to me.

"There he is," she said, her hand shielding her eyes as she peered into the sun. "Sebastian," she yelled. "Guess who I've found?"

A tall silhouette emerged from the glare, a frosted glass in each hand. A young God. Long and lean with smooth brown skin and a face like Tutankhamun. Chiseled fine features, burnished hair in a mop of silky unbrushed waves cascading over his forehead and almost tangling with the dark lashes framing his smoky-gray eyes, his full lips so perfect that I barely registered the stubble on his upper lip and square jaw. The few photos I'd seen of him were a pale copy of the man.

"Hullo Olivia," he was saying, as I forced my mouth shut, having realised I was gawping at him. Cassandra was introducing Ben now and Sebastian thrust the glasses into Cassandra's hands and shook Ben's. He turned his eyes back on me. "Beer, Olivia?"

"Oh no, it's yours; no, it's fine thanks."

"I shall get two more. These are for you and Cassandra."

His voice was nice, not Eton, just refined enough. Yes, they were exactly right together, Cassandra and Sebastian, a beautiful, beautiful couple.

Sebastian and Ben wandered off to get more beers. Cassandra winked at me. She had removed her dark glasses. "Olivia, my friend, we have both struck gold, I see."

AMBER WAS FIVE MONTHS OLD, TODAY BEING LOOKED AFTER BY a friend but usually cared for full-time by Cassandra. She had, Sebastian informed us, been born in the bath, extracted by her father while the midwife watched. The bath was a massive old tub balanced over a fire pit on the rough grass outside their house. To one side of it was a freestanding brick fireplace with a high chimney, and the grass sloped down to a wide river about a hundred meters from the house.

The baby was sweet, and Cassandra lay back in the swing chair on the deck, her expression dreamy as the baby suckled, seemingly for hours, from her full creamy breast. Every so often the tiny hand clasping her breast would relax and Amber's rosebud mouth would slip off the erect nipple, exposing a dark areola that was surely two voluptuous inches in diameter. Cassandra was completely relaxed about this, leaving her breast exposed, and indeed sometimes both breasts. She'd never been prudish when we were teens, but she hadn't pranced about naked either. Childbirth had changed her. She was a natural, an earth mother, a woman fulfilled.

My breasts swelled and my body throbbed as Cassandra tilted her head upwards so her lips could meet Sebastian's as he leaned over her. I looked at Ben, wanting him, but he was engrossed in a book he'd found on the coffee table.

Feeding over, breasts put away, and baby burped, changed, and kissed goodnight, we became ordinary people again. Sebastian cooked steaks on a barbecue plate over the fire, potatoes were shoved deep in the coals, and Ben and I were pointed at the extravagant vegetable garden and told to gather the makings of a salad, and then make it. After more beers and two bottles of cheap red wine, we happily agreed to their command to stay the night. The giant water bed in one of the four large bedrooms was a new experience for us, and we rocked ourselves to sleep with the stars shining benevolently through the expansive, bird-shit-splattered, curtainless window.

Sunday dawned lazy and late and we ate and walked and talked, Cassandra and I often separate from the men. It felt like home. During our dinner of salad and barbecued herb-heavy mince patties—Cassandra hadn't gone so far as becoming vegetarian, thank god—Cassandra made an announcement. "We've decided you need to come and live here with us. This house is way too big for three and it is seriously ridiculous for you two to pay for some scummy apartment. We bought this house for almost nothing, so all we have to pay are the rates and electricity." She surveyed us all, queen of her domain. "And best of all it would be so cool to have this much fun all the time."

Ben and I looked at each other and then at Sebastian. He smiled his sweet smile and nodded. "This home from now on shall be our home. Cassandra has spoken, and you must obey." He raised his hand in a mock salute. "And I'm in total agreement with my wife. I too would love you to share our pad if you think you could stand us and a yowling baby."

"I haven't heard her crying once," I said, every cell in me jittering.

"That's very generous," said my sensible Ben, "but perhaps we should give it a few weeks. Olivia and I haven't even decided yet if we want to live together on a long-term basis. We need to settle in a bit first."

A knot in my chest squeezed and I held my breath.

"Come on, Ben, you adore Olivia and she adores you. Move in here," said Cassandra.

Ben's hand squeezed mine as he gave Cassandra one of his nicest smiles. "We'll think it over very carefully, I promise."

I started to pull my hand from his, but his grip tightened.

"What is there to think about?" Cassandra appeared oblivious to Sebastian's stern look and the hovering tension.

"Give it up, Cassandra," Sebastian said, his voice quiet. "It's Ben and Olivia's call, not yours." He turned away from her and towards us. "We're here for the long term, and we'd love you to share the old pile with us. Whether it's next week or next year, or in another life, no matter. Now, anyone for tea?" His eyebrows went up and his face relaxed back into its usual grin. "A homemade mint and lemon concoction?"

"I'd love some," I said, my heart still thumping the adrenaline through me.

"Sure," said Ben, "And then we've gotta go. I've got a conference to attend tomorrow, not to mention meeting my new colleagues."

Under cover of the firelight I glanced at Cassandra. I knew Ben. If she kept trying to organize him I'd never change his mind. She looked at me and I narrowed my eyes.

A perfectly calm and lovely smile lit up her face. "Sorry Ben, sorry Olivia, sorry sweetie," she cooed, blowing a kiss to Sebastian with her last sorry. "I got carried away. It's so exciting to have found Olivia again, that's all. No more from me on the house sharing, I promise. All that matters is that we're all here in the same city."

~

WE HAD OUR FIRST ARGUMENT ON THE DRIVE HOME. I couldn't stop myself bringing it up. "Haven't we had an amazing weekend? Isn't it a fantastic place? How cool of them to ask us to share it with them."

"Yes, yes and yes, but it's too soon. It's one thing having casual house-mates and quite another to live with close friends. And you and Cassandra are clearly that."

"Yes, we are, and you and Sebastian could be too. He's lovely."

"And in time we'll find out whether we might all make a go of living together. Even if we do decide it would have a good chance of working, we would have to sort out the financial situation properly."

"Cassandra has heaps of money and she told me that Sebastian's parents are practically aristocracy in England. You heard them, they own the house, and we can pay enough rent to cover all the rates and electricity so it would be good for them too."

"But not necessarily for me. I like to make my own way."

"You're making excuses. The money thing can be sorted easily. It's because you don't want to live with me. That's what this is all about, isn't it?" I could hear my voice rising and made an effort to pull it back.

"Don't you think we should try living together for a while first? Just us? What say it doesn't work out?"

"Of course it will. I love you and I thought you loved me. Is that a lie?"

Ben kept his eyes to the front, and I forced my gaze away from his set expression and watched the tall trees on the side of the road light up in our headlights before being plunged back into gloom.

"Well, is it a lie? Do you love me or not?"

"You know I do. That's not the point. Living with another

couple could stress our relationship and I would prefer we learn about each other's habits without that."

I counted the dead kangaroos on the side of the road: one, two three. Expendable, beautiful animals. Shit, I hated being like this, the child who didn't get her way. I snaked my hand across the gap to Ben's knee. His warm hand covered mine and a blast of hot crazy happiness filled me up again. Ha. Cassandra was always going to come second in my needy little heart.

Chapter Seven

Brisbane, January, 1971

"Finally, you're home," Cassandra crowed, grabbing my hands and pulling me around in a madcap whirl.

Four months it had taken. We'd come to an agreement about money; Sebastian and Cassandra reluctantly. But Ben was adamant; we would not be sharing their house unless we paid one hundred percent of their rates and electricity. This was still well below what it had cost us to rent one place jointly in Brisbane—our short-term experiment that seemed to have convinced Ben that he liked sharing a bed every night with me. We each paid into a kitty to cover groceries, but that didn't come to much as they had a highly productive garden, mainly due to Sebastian's efforts. He was passionate about all things green and loved nothing better than to be mucking around in the dirt, or building a new hen house.

It was mid-January, hot and humid. Freeing myself from Cassandra's dance I plopped down in a beanbag and looked around the big room, part horrified, part thrilled. How had we collected so much junk? Books, magazines, piles of clothes—

most not worn since I'd arrived in hot Australia—odd bits of crockery and cutlery, pots and pans, photo albums, papers of indeterminate content, Ben's guitar, bathroom contents from makeup to odd bits of soap, pillows, cushions, sheets, towels, sandals, sand-shoes, boots, beads, headbands, earrings, belts, two more beanbags, two desks. Oh yes, and framed photos: one of me with Mum on a rare happy day and another with the Tullochs on my eighteenth birthday; Ben's family, Killara in the 1960s, my favorite photo of Ben — why would I need this beside my bed here?— and his favorite photo of me.

Amber, nappy half-off, was crawling around in the mess pulling bits of paper from files, sucking on scissors from the bathroom box, and generally having a jolly fine time. Sebastian and Ben were slumped in the old cane chairs on the deck, beers rapidly disappearing down their thirsty throats, Oscar, the latest member of the Brooks family, a soulful black Labrador who had failed his final test as a dog for the blind, was asleep across Sebastian's feet.

Cassandra—well Cassandra, unlike the rest of us, looked clean and cool and was sorting through box after box, arranging china on shelves in the kitchen, lugging books into our new bedroom and stashing them in some sort of order known only to her on the brick and board bookshelf that she had, the day before, put together in preparation for our arrival. I was looking forward to the feast she would no doubt have pre-prepped earlier for later. I took a long slurp of my ice-cold mango juice. I was happy; very, very happy.

Cassandra and Sebastian had cut short their summer at Killara—oh how I'd yearned to be there with them—and returned to help us shift in. Ben and I had until the end of January off; Ben from the university and me from my new job as junior editor at Stoddard and Jones, a small local publishing company. It felt quite different from the stuffy publishing company I'd worked for in Cambridge, and even though I had to begin at the bottom again, filing, posting rejected manuscripts to dejected writers, and making coffee for the staff of seven, I devoured every moment. Over my holiday break I'd been given two manuscripts to read and comment on. They'd been read by and considered 'possibles' by Louise Jones, part owner and senior editor who had taken me under her wide and flowing culottes.

On my own writing, not much was happening. I was halfway through chapter twenty of my first attempt at a full novel, and getting that far had taken me two years. Becoming a novelist was an elusive goal. I knew the rare few who made a living from it were forced to do other things as well. My fantasy of sitting at my typewriter for forty hours a week and tapping out my imaginary worlds and page-turning stories was likely going to stay a fantasy.

Even Cassandra had taken time off from her role as chairwoman of the local kindergarten committee (and Amber wasn't even old enough yet to go to kindergarten); from her position as secretary/treasurer of the Feminist Action group; from her night school pottery classes. One activity she hadn't sacrificed for us was her riding. She didn't have her horse here, their acre being too small, so she drove to a stable not far distant to ride, three times a week. And she never took time off from her earth mother role. I could feel myself slipping back into my place in her life as if the years apart had never happened. Amber, Sebastian, and me; we all let her organize our lives and sometimes even our feelings. But never Ben. I think even Cassandra had worked out that he was a lost cause.

At least Sebastian was on the right path; he was half way through his one-year internship in a prestigious family law firm. If he got through it, he'd be promoted to junior lawyer, on the path to partner, Cassandra's dream job for him. Only once did Ben comment to me that Sebastian didn't want to be a partner, or even a lawyer, particularly.

"Why doesn't he do something else then?" I asked, as I cuddled into Ben's bare chest one Sunday morning.

"If Cassandra had her way, he'd be in criminal law. Much more prestigious than family law. But even she can see that he has no aptitude for that. This is a second best for her, partner in a good family law firm. At least she approves of him helping families and kids in need." Ben yawned and stretched his hands above his head, dislodging me from my cozy roost. "Poor Sebastian will do whatever it takes to make her happy, so I suppose when he gets to partner level he'll make the best of it."

"That's crazy thinking," I said. "Cassandra wouldn't want him to do something he doesn't enjoy."

"Well, my sweet, how about you seed the idea in Cassandra's head that being a market gardener or a cabinet maker is much more prestigious than being a lawyer?"

I pushed myself up on one elbow and looked at Ben, his sleepy brown eyes kissable without their glasses. "Are you happy being a university lecturer? Truly, deeply happy?"

"Dunno about truly, deeply, but as a way to spend my week days I like it more than anything else I could do. Right now lassie, I'd sooner be truly, deeply inside you." And he slipped the straps of my nightdress off my shoulders.

Perhaps it was because they'd both grown up in the UK, or perhaps because they were both gentle, generous types. But for whatever reason, Ben and Sebastian soon became close mates. I even had to quash the occasional niggle that their friendship was the key to our move rather than Ben's desire to discard his independence for a life harnessed to me. Cassandra irritated him sometimes, but she also made him laugh, and being Ben he respected the deep bond Cassandra and I shared.

We were all involved with the local branch of the Vietnam Moratorium Campaign, and Ben and Cassandra were quickly recruited onto the organization committee. Sebastian became their legal advisor although he was still not fully qualified, and together he and I drafted submissions and information pamphlets. Away from these duties we often split ourselves differently; Sebastian and Ben in intense discussion about politics or conservation or on a long day's hike, and Cassandra and I at the Feminist Action group, or taking off on a sunny Saturday with Amber and a picnic basket, basking in a lazy day lolling about on one of the gorgeous beaches north of Brisbane. Sorely bloody needed after a particularly heavy feminist meeting. Feminists—at least the women in our group—were not big on humor or good ole fun. They lightened up at the end-of-year party when they brought along their partners, mostly males, although there were three intriguing and rather scary butch partners. Two young Aboriginal men played the didgeridoo and bongo drums all night and into the dawn as we danced randomly around, the sweet smell of cannabis filling the air. Babies were bound with long flowing scarves to backs or fronts, toddlers wandered amongst us, bawling when they were stood on, older kids played ghosts outside and climbed sky-high eucalyptus trees in the dark.

We somehow got home—Ben driving at his usual steady pace in spite of having smoked his share of joints—and after a sleeping Amber was deposited in her cot we carried on for another few hours, but with our own choice of music. I was floating on the few puffs I'd allowed myself; it didn't take much. I was wary of alcohol and usually kept to one glass of wine on special occasions, vivid images of Mum slumped senseless and dribbling on the couch or dead in her bed usually intervening when I was tempted by a second. But at least Mum hadn't smoked, likely because she'd spent any spare money on gin. Thankfully cannabis was unheard of back then.

Cassandra kept the vinyls spinning—her fine motor coordination was still sufficiently reliable to manage the tricky business of placing the needle on the edge of the record without it screeching across to the center. She was one of those people who could appear to be drinking as much as everybody else but in fact didn't. For every three drinks others had she was still on her first, surreptitiously drinking very slowly while acting as crazily as the drinkers. She looked as if she'd come straight from Woodstock — and she was genuine, in her way. A simple life, healthy, home-grown food, love for her family and friends, free-spirited children, earth-mother values, peace not war.

Cassandra's influence was subtle but we weren't unaware of it. None of us wanted to be out of control, out of our minds. We wanted to make Australia a better place, change the world. And that fine resolution we agreed on that mellow night near the end of 1971, required the use of our minds as well as our hearts. So we sang along with James Taylor's best-selling, Grammy-winning version of Carole King's 'You've Got a Friend,' dubbed as 'our song' by Cassandra, and shared —with Cassandra as well—our last ever joint.

"Pete's back home." Cassandra glanced up from the letter she was reading, her face tense. Her lips quivered and I stumbled towards her, nearly tripping over Oscar, asleep in a patch of winter sun at her feet.

"It's all right. He's home now. He'll be OK," I said. I was at the back of her chair, my arms on her shoulders. The letter she was holding was covered in small neat writing. It was from Aunt Cathie, not from Pete. My mouth suddenly dry, I croaked out some words. "Is he OK?"

Cassandra nodded, her body relaxing a fraction as she dropped the letter and bent over, her head in her hands. I waited, my hands rubbing her back. After a minute or two she sat up and leant her head against me.

"Sorry. Don't know where that came from. I must have

been more worried than I realized." She stooped and picked up the letter. "Mum says Pete… Hang on, I'll read it."

Her finger moved down the page and stopped at a line near the middle. "'Pete looks tired and he's so thin, but we're fortunate he hasn't been injured. He doesn't talk much about Vietnam, apart from saying it was pretty tedious most of the time. It wasn't like their first tour. Even Pete admitted that was terrible.' "

Cassandra shuffled the page behind the next one and kept reading, silently now. I tried not to read along with her, but my eyes caught my own name near the bottom of the page. I quickly scanned the last lines.

'It would be so nice if you and Sebastian and little Amber could come home for a few days to see Pete. He's planning on leaving soon for Melbourne. He thinks he'll have more chance of finding work there. Please bring Olivia, we miss her so much and Pete loves her. It's long past time that we welcomed Ben into our family. Love and hugs, Mum.'

Chapter Eight

We were met at Cairns Airport by Aunt Cathie and Uncle William, but no Pete. Aunt Cathie ignored Ben's outstretched hand and hugged him, and my stomach calmed. Twenty-four years old and this was the first time I'd ever introduced them to a real boyfriend.

After Amber was cooed over, Sebastian vanished to collect poor Oscar who had been in a dog cage in the hold of the plane, and all seven of us plus dog piled into the 4WD, Amber perched on Sebastian's knee. On the drive north along the mind-bogglingly gorgeous coastline, we didn't talk much. At last the familiar sign swung into view, the black letters of *Killara* shimmering through the heat and my tears. How had I stayed away so long?

Ben and I were given the guest room with the double bed.

"Aha," Ben said. "I see why you love these guys so much. I was expecting separation and creeping along corridors at night."

"Nope. Aunt Cathie is not the prudish type. She did ask me if we were engaged though when we talked last week. As if I wouldn't have told her."

"And?"

"And what?"

"Did you tell her any more about us?"

"What's to tell? She knows we live together. I told her I was on the pill, though. If I hadn't told her she would be constantly worrying that I'd get pregnant. Like Cassandra. You don't mind, do you?"

"No, of course I don't mind," Ben said. "She's your mother, pretty much."

"I wish."

"Come on, Olivia. Lighten up."

"And if I got preggers, you'd have to marry me," I said.

Ben raised his eyebrows and looked over his glasses. "Touchy." He pulled me to him and kissed me. I tightened my lips but he laughed through his kiss, making my lips tingle. I succumbed like a woman in love.

We sat on the rear deck with its cover of wisteria for a very late lunch—so heavenly to be back in the tropics where it was hot even in mid-winter— and while the three men stuffed themselves with cold lamb and salad, we three women just picked at it. Although I did manage to chomp through two cheese scones. Still no sign of Pete.

"He disappeared this morning," Uncle William said. "Told us he needed to check on a mate of his who was in Vietnam too. He knew you'd be here by lunchtime. I'm sorry, it's very rude of him." Uncle William's gentle face looked worried more than annoyed, and Aunt Cathie's brave attempts to fill us in on the local gossip didn't fool me one bit.

"He'll show up when he's ready," said Sebastian. "It must

be a hell of a thing getting used to civilian life after Vietnam. Perhaps he needs to spend time with guys who have been there too and understand what it's like."

Aunt Cathie lent across the table and put her hand on Sebastian's. He smiled at her and my heart squeezed as I saw the love in her eyes.

WE'D GIVEN UP WAITING AND HAD DECIDED TO WANDER DOWN to the beach when Pete showed up. I must have been expecting him to look tanned and rough and fit after so long in Vietnam. God knows why. I suppose because he'd looked tan and rough and fit ever since I first knew him. A soldier who could come through two tours in Vietnam without a scratch. Denial I suppose. I'd read up on some of the operations his battalion had been involved in during their first tour; the exploits of the second tour were not public yet. It was difficult to believe anyone could get through such horrors without their minds closing down or shattering into millions of pieces. And here he was, pale and thin with his hair so closely shorn he may as well have been bald. It almost looked as if he had no legs inside his jeans, his T-shirt was two sizes too big and he looked shorter than I remembered. He'd never been more than an inch taller than Cassandra — a great triumph for her as a teen—but with her masses of hair she looked taller than he was now.

I hung back as he hugged Cassandra and then Sebastian; Amber was missing, down for an afternoon nap. "Hi Pete," I said, feeling ridiculously shy.

"Olivia. Long time." He stuck his hand out as I lurched forward for a hug, but caught himself and opened his arms as I stumbled into them. I felt his quick squeeze and he stood back. I blew my nose as Cassandra, her eyes still teary, introduced him to Ben.

We were saved by Aunt Cathie pushing him down before a plate of food - it was four o'clock by then but she probably thought he could do with as many lunches as he could fit in, given his scrawniness. The rest of us stood there, even Cassandra, not knowing whether to watch him eat, or escape to the beach. Then Uncle William put one arm around Cassandra and the other around me and said he had a few beers and some nice red wine with our names on it. "We'll keep Pete company while he eats something to make his mother happy."

Pete did manage to scoff a huge plate of food and drink his way through a lot more beers than any of us, but at least that relaxed him a bit. After a couple of hours the lunch was replaced by dinner; a roasted chicken and all the trimmings. I escaped to help Aunt Cathie in the kitchen and she chatted on as if everything was entirely normal. We filled the space in the air until we had to go back outside where the men were now discussing, of all things, the antagonism over the war and the marches and submissions to force the Australian Government to withdraw all troops from Vietnam. At first I thought Pete was agreeing with them, more by his silence than anything he said, until he slammed his beer bottle down on the table, making every one of us jump.

"Fuck you. You're as fucking bad as the rest of Australia. You don't know a fucking thing about it. Sitting about in your nice little universities and law firms and having fun with your piddling marches and fucking rotten egg throwing." He picked up his beer bottle and swilled whatever was left then fired it over the balustrade onto the lawn. "I've a fucking good mind to join up for the regular army. At least they get off their bums and do something about the bloody Vietcong. You yellow-bellied lot just sit back and watch the Commies murder little kids and women and every fucking thing that moves in South Vietnam." He rose out of his chair and I shrunk into mine. "Well bully for you. Hope it makes you sleep well at night."

Pete disappeared on his old motor bike and didn't come back the next day, or the one after that. Then Aunt Cathie got a call from a woman called Maggie who said she was Jake's girlfriend. Jake turned out to be the guy that Pete knew from Vietnam; he'd been back longer then Pete. Maggie said he was safe at their house and she'd phone Cathie every day to tell her how he was doing. The kindness of strangers. On her next call she said a bit more; Pete and Jake spent most of their time getting drunk, but she'd heard Pete tell Jake that he wasn't going back home until we'd left. After Aunt Cathie hung up, her face drawn and old—she was only 55 but nothing like having a son in Vietnam to pile on the years—Sebastian phoned Maggie back and got her to reveal what Pete had actually said.

"Something like 'I'm not going home 'til Cassandra and the lot of them have pissed back off to their holier-than-thou marching team,'" Maggie said. "You probably didn't want to hear that. But they're all like that when they first come home. He'll get over it."

"Thank goodness he has Jake to talk to. Thanks for looking after him."

"No problem. Anyway, what on earth is a marching team? I thought only girls joined marching teams?"

That night Sebastian and Ben sat out on the verandah, leaving the rest of us in the big room, reminiscing, laughing, crying a little and catching up on everything that had happened in the years since Cassandra and I had left home for our European adventure. They were still out there when we gave up and went to bed. In the morning Cassandra called a family meeting. I thought Ben would balk at the very idea, but he didn't. Later he admitted to me that it was a relief to have it out in the open. He and Sebastian had been going over and over their motivations for being so antagonistic towards the Vietnam War, and how that had expanded to include antagonism towards the soldiers who had been sent to fight it. I'd been having similar thoughts. Over the past year the newspapers had been filled with 'incidents' of aggression towards returning servicemen, almost as if they were responsible for the Government's policies. Almost as if the soldiers believed in what they were doing.

"Well, Pete seemed to believe in what he was doing," Cassandra said.

"That's probably the only way our boys can live with themselves," Aunt Cathie said softly. "Otherwise they couldn't survive."

"I don't think he has survived. He's nothing like he used to be. He needs to get help, but I don't suppose the bloody army is going to provide any of that." Cassandra's face was white with anger.

Ben took my hand and held it tight. I knew he could feel my insides shaking. I had never seen Cassandra angry before, not like this.

"That's why we must keep the pressure on the Government," Ben said, his own usually calm tone not quite as calm as usual. "They have to withdraw now. We'll bring it up for discussion at our next Moratorium meeting. Make everyone see that we have to welcome the soldiers home, stop blaming them, really listen to their side. That isn't incompatible with hating the war and hating our involvement in it. We need to keep at the government to put their money into rehab for those guys, not just leave them to rot. That's as bad as forcing them to do their dirty work in the first place."

"And Pete? How will we get through to him? How will I get through to him? He's my twin. If I can't talk to him, who can?" Cassandra said.

"Sweetheart," Sebastian said, "it'll take time, a long time probably. Leave it for a while. Poor guy, he's only been back a few weeks."

"But what if he does join the regular army? Just to get back at us because he sees us as against him, not against the senseless killing?"

"He won't," said Uncle William. "Or if he does, he won't be going back to Vietnam. I think the organization and discipline the army provides suits Pete. He'll have made some lifetime mates in Vietnam and many of the men in his battalion are career servicemen. Who are we to decide what's best for him?"

Chapter Nine

Brisbane, 1972

The hours I spent dreaming about the novelist career I was determined to have almost equaled the hours I spent in my head rearranging the words and sentences in my own novel. Turns out the bum-on-seat hours weren't quite so easy to stack up. Mostly I kept to my regime of writing before breakfast, but evenings were difficult. A small child did not encourage a writing career, even when she belonged to someone else. When Amber was in bed, I could rarely fight the temptation to sit around with the others, drinking another glass of wine, talking about everything and nothing, quite often listening as Ben played his guitar or banjo, trying out new riffs and breaks and singing in his folksy, easy baritone the folksy easy songs of love and freedom that were so much part of our privileged hippy lives.

Cassandra often joined him. She had a beautiful voice, untrained and pure and true. Sebastian would haul his bongo drums from under the bed, or when Ben's mood changed and became more bluegrass Sebastian would grab the largest brown stoneware jug from Cassandra's collection of stoneware jugs and bottles arranged with casual design in the corner of the kitchen. Holding it in both hands, he would produce farting noises by buzzing his lips across its mouth, invariably startling Oscar out of his dreams or whatever mischief he was about, causing him to stretch his neck up and emit a series of wails and moans even more mournful than Sebastian's. Cassandra would add percussion by shaking her rattles or scraping her washboard with a wooden spoon, and changing her voice from pure to country.

I had no instrument and no ability until Ben and Sebastian constructed a tea-chest double bass for me. I practiced it gleefully, never quite sure if the gruff sounds I was producing were the right ones or not, but when Ben's banjo was doing a jig, Sebastian's jug and my tea-chest sounded exactly the thing. Then we'd all sing. Sebastian—in between farts—and I were strictly chorus and backers, given our less than perfect abilities to stay on note when Ben and Cassandra took off on one of their harmonious couplings.

We got into the habit of inviting one of Cassandra's musical friends around every other weekend. Meredith played the fiddle and turned us into a band so fine that it cried out for a name. The Krazy Killara Jug Band became so famous that we played twice at birthday parties in other crazy people's houses.

My novel did grow, word by word, sentence by sentence, month by month. It also shrunk quite often as I ripped pages out of my typewriter and screwed them into furious balls to pelt at the wall.

"What's the problem?" Sebastian asked, when I appeared late one evening after forcing myself to write as they relaxed.

"It's too bloody hard. I should stick to publishing other people's novels."

"What's hard about it? You've got all the words. All you have to do is arrange them."

"I'll arrange you," I said, picking up a cushion and firing it at him. But I was smiling again.

By late February it was done. Secretly I hoped it was far removed from an early draft, but out loud I claimed it as the beginning of a long revision process. Only I had read it. When I was asked what it was about I fumbled with a description but usually admitted it was a historical novel set on a New Zealand high-country sheep station in the 1860s. A childhood dream, although I'd only set foot on one once, during my camping trip with Mum.

Cassandra was busting to read it. "Someone has to read it first. Who better than your best friend?"

"Family and best friends are the worst critics. They always say nice things whatever they really think."

"Promise I'll be honest. Go on, be brave."

I succumbed as I always did, and could barely sit in the same room when she was reading it. I tried to decipher her expressions and judge her involvement or boredom by the speed with which she flipped through the manuscript pages. When she occasionally scribbled something in the margin—I'd agreed she should make comments and corrections as she went through—my pulse sped up.

Ben was tuned in to my tenterhook behavior and suggested I find somewhere else to be when Cassandra was 'working on it' as she said. He'd also offered to read it but that would have been even worse, especially as I had a sneaking suspicion that it was really a women's book. Ben's idea of a good novel was the latest Man Booker prizewinner, well named as the winning books were usually authored by a man.

"Finished," Cassandra declared, one late Sunday afternoon.

I sat motionless, my shining career balanced on her next words.

"Want a cuppa? Then I'd better get Amber her dinner."

"Cassandra, you cow. What did you think?"

The cushion I hurled at her bounced off her newly pregnant belly, but at least my body parts had come alive again.

"Loved it, silly. It will be a best seller, I'll bet my marriage on it."

"Really? You're just saying that."

"I know what I like and I love this. Why don't you send it to Dad next? You'll have to believe him."

"No way. It was bad enough waiting for you to finish it."

"Well, once it's published, millions of people will read it and some of them won't like it, so you'd better toughen up."

I SENT IT OFF TO UNCLE WILLIAM AND GAVE A COPY TO Louise, my boss at Stoddard and Jones. Then I stopped taking the pill. A sort of reward perhaps. Ben was not deeply enthusiastic and argued that we had years yet before we needed to start a family. But he gave in on the condition that I didn't orchestrate our lovemaking around my fertile times. I buried my guilty thoughts about not having told Ben yet that we'd been pregnant before. It was too late now to raise it. Instead I congratulated myself on my courage back then; it would have been way too soon for Ben. Now was perfect and I daydreamed that my debut novel and our very own baby would share a birthday. Of course I knew that was a fantasy given the time it took for a book to be published. But I was willing to settle for our baby being born around the time of the printing of advance review copies of *A River Through Time*.

I don't know which was more agonizing; waiting to see if my period would appear or waiting for feedback on my manuscript. The Professor's comments came back first. Then Ben's and finally Louise's. I was prepared for her opinion by then as I had already been close to suicide and back.

Cassandra read all the comments and told me I was being ridiculous. "They are simply telling you how to revise it, not to burn it," she said. "Put the whole thing away for a month and then read the comments again. They all said the story was good, most of the characters were engaging, and the writing was excellent."

"And that it starts in the wrong place, nothing happens in the middle, the parts I thought were my best are peripheral to the story and I should cut them, and the ending doesn't ring true," I said. "And Louise worries that it isn't commercial enough."

"So revise it. That's what writers do."

"How do you know what writers do?"

"I've read some of your books on writing, that's how."

I had almost digested the feedback on my literary masterpiece and was contemplating whether I should revise or put in bottom drawer when I knew, beyond all reasonable doubt, that I was pregnant. Again. I had, at some deep place, been afraid that I wouldn't get a second chance. That I didn't deserve it and was imagining my sore boobs. But by May, when my period didn't appear, their tenderness was unmistakable. I managed to delay seeing the doctor until my second period stayed away. I wanted him to give me a conclusive result. Ben came with me, although he was dispatched to the waiting room while the doctor probed my uterus.

That evening Sebastian and Cassandra concocted a magnificent celebratory dinner at which the men drank two bottles of wine while six months pregnant Cassandra and I drank unfermented grape juice.

"Now you two," said Cassandra, leaning over the table and fixing Ben and I with her most hypnotic gaze, "I want you both to be present at the birth of this little fella."

"Oh, I'd love to." My heart was knocking on my chest. "Are you sure? Won't it be too crowded?"

"Don't be silly. There's loads of room on the grass around the bath. I want all of us there, Amber too."

"Not me," Ben said.

I breathed out. I didn't really want him exposed to the whole thing. Or Cassandra exposed to him. Perhaps we weren't hippy enough for such intimacy with our closest friends. Silly really, given we sometimes swam naked in a secret river spot, all of us.

"Please," Cassandra said, her dark eyes and glossy hair and beautiful belly conspiring to beckon us into line.

"Don't leave me all alone," wailed Sebastian, fighting unsuccessfully to swallow his grin. "We'll all fit into the bath, as long as we're deliciously starkers and don't mind the odd foot in the crotch."

"Stop it, Sebastian," Cassandra said, her face scrunched into her sternest Women's Lib expression. "Ignore him. You can keep all your clothes on and stay dry. I want you there for Amber anyway. The midwife and Sebastian will be too busy helping me. Amber will need a few breaks for food and naps, but I definitely want you to make sure she's there for the actual birth."

"Olivia is your woman," Ben said. "I'll be backup, well outside the birthing coven. I can do the minding when Amber gets bored watching you grunting and groaning, and boil water or whatever you need."

"Ben, think of Olivia. It'll be great for you both to see a water birth so you know what to do when your baby arrives," Cassandra said.

"You know something that I don't know then," Ben said, looking at me, his brow a mass of furrows. "Olivia? I thought you'd decided it was best to have our baby in hospital? It is your first…"

"I haven't decided yet. Perhaps seeing Cassandra doing it in the bath will help us make our minds up. That's if you're OK about us being there, Sebastian?"

"Very OK. It's a wondrous experience. My woman is something to behold when she's in full cry."

Cassandra hauled herself out of the chair. "Well, I'm not

going to take no for an answer from you, Ben Appleby, not yet. You can decide on the day. Perhaps just come in for the crowning and birth if you can't cope with all my shouting and swearing."

When Cassandra went into labor on the first of October, the exact day the baby was due, Ben did come on board. Not for the whole thing, like me, but in and out with Amber. By the time the baby's head crowned nothing would have stopped him. He was almost as absorbed in the intimate family drama as I was. David was born eight hours after Cassandra's first contraction, slipping out into Sebastian's waiting hands and yowling lustily before his small body was completely born. It *was* wondrous and it did give me—Ben too, he admitted later—confidence. Cassandra made it look magnificent. Even her yells were invigorating, and at the end she had us all screaming along with her.

Chapter Ten

Killara, Christmas Day, 1972

God, those Tullochs! As crazy as a troop of Kookaburras at dawn. A picnic at high noon on a sweltering Christmas Day? Lugging crayfish and scallops and Christmas puddings down to the beach?

When I'd woken this morning my ankles had been so swollen I'd been tempted to stay back in the cool house with my feet up and an icepack on my aching head. But Cassandra was having none of it. "You can't miss all the fun. You'll be able to soak your poor feet in the sea. It's this heat that makes them swell. Mine feel as if I've got elephantiasis and I'm not even pregnant," she said, lifting one slim ankle and glaring at it.

Four weeks to go. It felt like a lifetime. I lumbered along the track to the beach behind Ben, who was loaded down with two deck chairs and a chilly bin full of beer. I stared down at myself. What a sight. Belly slick with sweat and ballooning out above my bikini bottoms. Why hadn't we stayed in Brisbane with Janice, my own midwife, ready and waiting with a nice sterile hospital close by? If anything went wrong Ben would never forgive me. He'd definitely never forgive Cassandra.

I closed my eyes against the glare, the memory of Ben's words from months ago echoing in my throbbing head. "If you want to be at the birth, Cassandra, great, but what's the problem with staying here in Brisbane and having the baby in the hospital?"

"Because, Ben, in the hospital, they will only allow you in, and even then they might chuck you out. You might get in the way or faint," Cassandra said. "That's why you need to have a home birth, Olivia. It will be heaven at Killara in that fancy spa bath Mum and Dad have got. Come on Ben, lighten up.You must admit it's a step up from our ancient bath on the grass."

So here we were. Of course. I patted our baby through my wet belly but he or she remained asleep. Two months ago a spa bath birth at Killara had seemed very romantic, but I wasn't so sure now. Thank heavens the midwife up here, what's her name again? Clara? Sarah? God, my memory's going too—Clara, that's it—at least she seemed very experienced and calm about it all.

Shit, it's hot. Why did I come again? Hey baby, let's grab the shade under that palm tree, bloody furnace, can't see for sweat, hey bubs, you having a nap? Yum, crayfish and scallops—you want some baby? Too hot? Tell me about it. Let's go lie in the sea.

Oh, bliss. Cool, cool water. Is that better bubs? Whoops, nearly lost my hat. Oh no. Funny taste, stomach churning, shit, shouldn't have eaten all that bloody crayfish, oh my god too late, gross… on no, here it comes again, yuk. Get out, crawl, mouth so dry, need water, SHIT pain, pain, no please no it's too early this isn't right I'm ripping open, so much blood, BEN, where's Ben? BEN, HELP ME.

An arm around my back, Cassandra's voice. Her words make no sense. "Breathe through it Olivia. Pant like we practiced. Your baby's coming, that's all. Ben and Sebastian can carry you up to Killara between contractions and we'll get you into the spa pool."

Ben's voice, rough and scared. "It's too early. Someone get up to the house and phone for an ambulance. Sweetheart, hang on, it's going to be fine, just do what Cassandra says and we'll soon have you home and the doctor will be there."

"Mum, can you go and phone the midwife?" Cassandra's voice yelling over the top of Ben. "She doesn't need an ambulance, she's having a baby for heaven's sake. Get the spa filled with warm water. It'll be hours yet."

The contraction let go and I could see again, shapes hanging over me blocking out the sun. Ben's hand on my forehead, unsticking my hair and pushing it back. "Sweetheart, are you alright?"

"Better now," I gasped as the next one bull-dosed in. "Shit, stop it, stop it, rub my stomach, shit no, my back..."

How did I get in here? My t-shirt was floating in the bubbles. Why is it so cold? Spa baths are meant to be hot.

Aunt Cathie and Cassandra were rubbing my back. "Cold, cold," I whispered.

"It's heating sweetheart, you'll feel warmer soon," said Aunt Cathie. "The midwife is on her way."

"Where's Ben? I want Ben."

"He's here, darling. He's just calling Cairns hospital. He wants you to go there to have your baby."

I looked at Cassandra's face looming over me, her mouth opening and shutting.

"Cairns? It's too far," I croaked. It was coming again, the pain slicing into me.

"Come on Olivia, pant like we practiced. Pant through it. Huh huh huh huh."

The water was red. "I'm bleeding. I shouldn't be bleeding. Where's Ben?"

"Here, sweetheart," and I saw his glasses all steamed up leaning over me. I reached up, grabbed him.

"The ambulance is coming from Cairns. They'll be here in an hour. Hang in there sweetheart, it's going to be OK, just do what Aunt Cathie says, come on, huh huh huh huh."

"Huh huh huh huh shit shit…"

"Turn on your hands and knees and see if that helps," Cassandra's voice said out of the red haze.

"Well now, this is a to-do," coming from somewhere.

"Thank goodness you're here." Aunt Cathie's voice. "Olivia, Clara is here now so we need to give her some space."

Hands turning me, prodding me. "Huh huh huh huh shit shit shit…"

"I'm going to examine you now Olivia, to see how dilated you are. Ben, you sit behind her and support her. Olivia, lean back on Ben. I'm going to put your feet up on the sides of the spa bath so I can get a better look."

Ben's in the bath with me, I feel his chest behind me, his arms holding me tight below my boobs, the pain receding, the midwife leaning in between my legs, pressure down there. "Shit shit…Ben…"

BRIGHT LIGHTS—TOO BRIGHT—HANDS TIED DOWN. MY HEART was racing. I licked my dry lips and forced some words out. "Let me go. Untie me."

"Ah, you're awake. That's good."

"Who are you? Where am I?"

"I'm Ginny, your nurse, and you're safe in Cairns Hospital. You've been asleep quite a while."

"Ben, where's Ben?" The nurse untied my wrist and I lifted my arm. The tube coming into it was red with blood. I tried to put my hand on my tummy, tell my baby we were all right. "What's this big hump in the bed?"

"You've got a bed cradle over your stomach to keep the weight of the blankets off it," she said, holding my wrist. "Careful with your arm, you need some more blood yet to make up for what you lost."

"Why? Oh, oh… My baby. Did I have my baby? Where is my baby?"

"Yes, you had your baby, and you're safe here. Your husband will be back in a minute. He just went to get a cup of tea and a bite to eat. He's been here, poor man, ever since you came back from theater."

"Please can I see my baby?"

"Soon, dear. The doctor will be here soon. Are you in pain? I can increase your pain medication if you are. Try not to cry. That'll only make you feel worse."

"Is it a boy or a girl?"

"Ah, here's your husband. He'll be very happy to see you're awake at last, so you'd better stop those tears."

"Ben, oh Ben." And my face was squashed into his neck, his lips were kissing my cheek, his tears were falling down into my mouth.

"Where's our baby? Is it a boy or girl?" I whispered.

His hands stroked my hair back from my face, his dark eyes floating in tears just above mine.

"A little boy," he said.

"Oh Ben, I was so scared. I thought he must have…"

"Shush, the important thing is that you're awake and you're going to be all right."

"What do you mean? Ben, I can't remember anything. I was in the spa bath. What happened? Why I am in hospital? How did I get here? Why can't I feel anything? Why aren't I sore?"

"You're on lots of drugs. You'll probably feel sore later. You passed out in the spa bath when the midwife was examining you and you were taken to Cairns by ambulance. Sweetheart, you had an emergency Caesarian. It had to be done quickly because you were hemorrhaging and the baby was stressed."

"Our baby. Is he all right? Can I hold him?"

"Olivia, sweetheart, I'm sorry. Our little boy, he's perfect, I've seen him. Olivia, darling, he wasn't able to cope with it. The doctors tried but they couldn't get him to breathe."

"What do you mean, what are you saying, are you saying he's dead?"

THE NURSE WHEELED IN A COT AND BEN AND I LOOKED INTO IT at the perfect little face swaddled in a white shawl. On his tiny head was a blue knitted hat with a bobble on top. The nurse lifted him out gently and put him in my arms.

"Oh, you're warm, little boy. Ben, he's warm, he's alive." The joy was bursting out of me as I opened the shawl and touched his sleepy little body in its blue all-in-one.

"Dear, I'm sorry. He's warm because I put a hot-water bottle under the cot sheet. I wanted him to feel warm when you held him. It helps some mums. I'm sorry, Pet."

I shut out her voice as my tears plopped onto my baby's sleeping face. Ben's trembling shook me as he reached between me and our son and took off his blue hat. He already had a fuzz of black hair. It would be like Ben's. I could see him so cute toddling about with wild black curls.

We named him Archie for Ben's grandfather who died in WWI. Archie Appleby. He'd got so cold by the time they took him away from us.

I couldn't go to his funeral. How can such a little baby who hasn't had any life yet have a funeral? I hated funerals. I'd only ever been to one and that was the second worst day of my life. The third worst day now.

~

A Placental Abruption. That was the diagnosis. The doctor explained that it was likely that my headache and ankle swelling indicated pre-eclampsia and that might have been a factor. My placenta had probably partially detached from the wall of my uterus with that first strong contraction and loss of blood, and when the midwife massaged my stomach to try and turn the baby from a head-up to a head-down position the placenta became fully detached. If it hadn't have been for the ambulance's arrival right then I could have died. The only way they could stop me hemorrhaging was to perform a hysterectomy as soon as our baby had been ripped from me.

"If I'd stayed in Brisbane and got to hospital as soon as I had the first contraction, would he have been saved?" I managed to ask, two weeks later, just before I was discharged from the hospital.

"Both the baby and you would have had a better chance if we'd made the diagnosis of pre-eclampsia and placental abruption immediately. Then we'd have avoided manipulating the uterus and carried out the emergency Caesarian before the whole placenta detached. You've been very unlucky. One in a hundred women have a mild placental abruption and usually the baby and mother are both fine, but only one in 400 have a severe abruption. And that's the problem with home births and midwives; they aren't trained to deal with emergencies."

"So should the midwife have known and not tried to turn the baby? Shouldn't the bleeding have alerted her?" Ben asked.

"I don't think any blame can be laid there. She was in a difficult situation, a long way from a hospital, and she thought the best way to proceed was to get the baby born as quickly as possible. Indeed, it could have gone this way even if you had arrived at the hospital straight away."

I stared at him, my eyes dry and sore. I knew whose fault it was. The doctor's eyes became the brown eyes of the doctor in Cambridge. *At six weeks your baby has a heartbeat…*

"I'm sorry, Olivia. You've been through a terrible experience. But I'm pleased with your progress. A hysterectomy is an unpleasant procedure for a young woman to go through, especially as we had to sacrifice your ovaries as well. But the hormonal treatment will prevent you going into into premature menopause, so you won't have to deal with hot flushes and menopausal moods. On the positive side, at least you won't have any more periods."

Chapter Eleven

"Livie, Livie, do you want to see Mandy's new dress?"

I pushed my eyelids open and the blurry face of Amber slowly sharpened. She was standing by my bed, her head level with mine. I felt my lips curve upwards, a strange sensation. My hand reached out and touched her auburn curls. Her mouth opened and a burbling laugh flew out. She held up her favorite doll, its bright blue and red dress crinkling my eyes.

"Amber, sweetheart." My voice sounded croaky and unused and I cleared my throat and tried again. "It's a lovely dress. Did your Mummy make it for her?"

Amber shook her curls. "No, Grandma sent it in the post. She's got new pajamas too."

"Ah, Grandma is the best sewer. Do you think she might make me some new pajamas?"

She nodded. "When are you getting up? Is your tummy still sore?" Her chubby hand stroked my hand and my eyes filled. I blinked hard. She didn't need to see me sobbing. I'd barely stopped since we'd lost our baby; every thought set me off. My sense of time was shaky but I knew I'd been in hospital for two weeks and home a few days.

"Don't cry, Livie. It's all right. Me and Mandy can help

Mummy look after you." Tears filled Amber's huge eyes, the color of her name, and caught on her long black lashes.

I smiled at her earnest little face, my lips feeling easier. "Thank you sweetie. You've made me feel much better already."

"Amber, Amber, where are you hiding?" Cassandra's voice floated through the door.

"Oh, Mummy is looking for me. She said I couldn't come in and see you 'cos you needed to sleep all the time so your tummy could get better."

"Well, it's much better now so you'll be able to come and see me whenever you want."

Cassandra's long brown legs came into view. "There you are. I thought I told you to leave Olivia in peace? Sorry, Olivia."

"I've missed her. It's lovely to see her," I said, raising my eyes to Cassandra's frowning face.

"You're feeling better. Thank heaven. We've been worried sick," she said, sitting on the edge of the bed and pulling Amber between her legs. Their likeness struck me as if I'd never noticed it before.

"What day is it? How long have I been home?" I winced as my arm touched my breast.

"Just a week. The community nurse was here yesterday and has instructed us to get you up and walking around for a few hours every day. Don't you remember? She's been coming every day to massage your poor breasts."

"Oh heavens yes. I do remember. It's torture." Now that I'd woken up properly I had no problem remembering. I pulled myself into a sitting position as Cassandra grabbed a bright yellow pillow from the floor. Her fresh-air jasmine scent wafted up my sore nose as she leaned over and stuffed it behind me. Gingerly I pressed my right boob. Sore, but not as hard as it had been. The Oxytocin that had been pumped into me to try and stop the hemorrhaging had brought in my milk with a wallop. With no baby to suckle, my boobs had become engorged and my right breast had ending up with infected milk ducts. That led to my hot swollen breasts being massaged in an attempt to unplug the blocked ducts, and in turn the massage slowed the milk drying-up process. It also increased the strength of the stomach cramps that curled me into a tight ball so often I suspected I'd have a permanent hunch when I finally left my bed.

"It's so bloody unfair. You've had every possible complication." Cassandra pulled my hand away from my breast. "Don't press it. The nurse says you shouldn't massage it any more now the ducts are cleared. All that does is keep the milk coming. She recommends frozen cabbage leaves on the boobs to relieve the pain. I have a stack in the freezer; shall I get some?"

"No, it's OK. I'm sorry I've been such a nightmare. I can't seem to stop crying."

"How about I run you a cool bath and then you can get up for a bit? It's a gorgeous day. You can laze about on the deck, have a wander around the garden. Ben would be so relieved if you were up and dressed when he got home from the uni."

"I'll never forgive myself," Cassandra said. We were sitting on the old cane chairs on the deck watching Amber making castles in her sandpit.

"Forgive yourself? What for?" My stomach cramped and I held my back straight and tried not to wince.

"I should never have conned you into going to Killara and having your baby in the spa bath."

"Conned? Don't be crazy. I made my own mind up."

"Ben doesn't think so."

"Come on Cassandra, you're imagining stuff. Ben would never say that."

"No, he hasn't said it but that's what he thinks. He barely speaks to me. It's so tense whenever we're in a room together."

I reached over and took her hand. "You've been my life-saver. What would I have done without you looking after me while Ben's working? I know you only wanted me to have the same joy as you."

"Shit, now you've got me crying as well," Cassandra said, and we grinned at each other and simultaneously blew our noses. Amber started at the sudden honking and looked up from her sandpit, her eyelids jerking wide open. She chuckled. I blew my nose again, louder this time, and her bubbling laugh started both of us giggling. Oh, how good it felt.

I CAN DO THIS. NEXT WEEK. I'LL GO BACK TO WORK NEXT week.

I wriggled myself deeper into the beanbag and picked up the novel lying face down on the floor beside me. The words blurred as I tried to remember what the hell it was about and I threw it back on the floor. My fist crashed down after it, making it jump. Since when did I treat a book so badly?

I'll make dinner. At least that will get Ben off my case. I hauled myself onto my bare feet and unstuck my damp shorts from my butt. It was stifling even with all the doors and windows open wide. Opening the fridge door I let the cold air caress my skin, flapping my singlet to encourage it to wash over my hot, tight, boobs. I checked in the freezer compartment to see if there were any frozen cabbage leaves left. One. One? Why would Cassandra freeze one cabbage leaf? She knew I had two bursting boobs. Why wouldn't she freeze fucking cabbage leaves in pairs? Shoving the last one over my lucky left breast, I eased my singlet back over it. I'd discarded my support bra; it was way too hot for armor.

Dinner ideas? Shit, it was too hot to eat. Cold chicken.

We'll have that with salad and new potatoes; that'll have to do. Strawberries and ice-cream. At least Amber will love me.

Through the open door the sun flashed on the river at the bottom of the garden. I huffed out a hot breath. That's what we'd do. When Cassandra and Amber got back from their shopping trip and David woke from his afternoon nap we'd go for a swim. My first since… Why does every bloody thing have to remind me? When will it stop?

It was only a little whimper. I froze. This was the first time Cassandra had left me alone with David. "He won't wake until three and I'll be home by then," she'd said. I looked at the wall clock. Half past two. Little devil.

A louder whimper, then a full-blown cry. I covered my ears and walked out onto the deck. I wasn't ready to hold him. He was hiccupping now, crying that hungry, desperate cry. My hands went from my ears to my tingling, aching breasts. I pulled off my singlet and the warm wet cabbage leaf dropped on my foot. I cupped the heavy globes in my palms and massaged my breasts like a calf on an udder. I watched the beads of whitish liquid ooze out of each nipple and dribble through my fingers. Bringing them to my mouth I licked at the milk, then licked my other hand. I wanted to stretch my neck down and fasten my mouth around my tingling nipple and suck it, suck them both until they were empty like me.

I tiptoed into the dimmed nursery. "Hush, David, it's alright. Hush. Go back to sleep. Your mummy will be home soon to feed you." I shook his cot gently. He looked so small and angry, dressed only in a nappy, his sheet tangled at his flailing feet. Last time I'd been in his nursery he'd been in a cradle. He was only four months old. Why was he in this big cot?

"Hush, sweetie, please hush." My finger stroked his damp cheek and he grabbed it in his chubby fist and shoved it in his mouth. I closed my eyes as he sucked frantically, his mouth so moist and soft around it. The milk trickled down my naked front and I eased my finger out of the strong little mouth and lent over and lifted him out. Holding him close to my chest I rocked back and forth, back and forth, patting his bare back, but his hiccupping urgent cries kept on. I eased myself into Cassandra's nursing chair, the rocking chair made for her by Sebastian before Amber was born. I held his hot little body in my lap, his cries and mine all mixed up. And then he was straining towards my breast, its life-giving, unwanted milk dripping out faster and faster, falling onto his face and teasing his lips around his straining mouth and then he was attached, his face buried in my breast, the pain in my breast punching through me and curling my toes as he clamped his gums tight, his mouth sucking frantically, his body gradually relaxing as his little hand pinched me, his soft sharp fingernails biting into me and feeling so right. "Oh, my baby, my perfect little boy," I whispered, my tears slowing, my arteries pumping peace through my sad body. "I love you baby boy, I love you so much."

"Olivia, there you are."

My eyes opened and I felt the solid little body in my arms. I looked up at Cassandra, her face looming over me, her eyes wide, her mouth opening and shutting. I looked down at my bare breasts hanging over David's sleeping body, one little hand grasping my right nipple, a bubble of milk still dripping from it.

"What are you doing? Why are you naked?"

"Silly Mummy, Livie's been feeding David," Amber cooed, and I looked at her shining face, smiling up at me before she leaned over and kissed her baby brother on his cheek.

David's eyes sprung open as Cassandra took him away from me, holding him to her and murmuring into his ear.

"He woke up and wouldn't go back to sleep. I had to rock

him to settle him, that's all. I'd taken my singlet off in the kitchen to… to put cabbage leaves on my breasts, they were so painful. I just didn't have time to put it back on when he started to cry. We must have both fallen asleep, it's so hot in here."

Cassandra shook her head, her eyes seeing into me. "He'll be hungry then. Would you mind getting out of my chair so I can feed him?" Her voice was a spear of ice into my heart.

I grabbed the arm of the rocking chair with one hand and pushed myself up, my other arm across my guilty breasts. Cassandra already had her shirt undone and one enormous boob with its dark bullseye out before she sat down. Her hand pushed David's head towards it and I stood stuck to the floor, willing him to take it and suck her dry. Her strong brown fingers squeezed and her milk shot out, hitting David on the cheek. Her other hand pushed his head towards it and he shook his head and squawked but then his mouth latched on. Cassandra jerked back, and there was a popping sound as David was torn from her nipple. "Shit," she said. "Don't bite me, you little horror."

"He's a greedy boy," Amber giggled. "He'll burst his tummy if he drinks up all your milk too." She snuggled her head against Cassandra's arm. "David's already had Livie's milk. Let me drink out of you, Mummy. I won't bite you."

I backed out the door, my face burning. Why the hell hadn't I told Cassandra the truth? What was so terrible about feeding him when he was yelling and my poor breasts needed the release? It wasn't my fault that her baby's cries made my milk flow. It was just as good as her milk. Better probably. Mine was still full of colostrum.

~

"WHAT'S THE MATTER?" BEN WHISPERED, HIS NAKED WARM chest against my hot back. It was the middle of the night and neither of us had slept.

"I fed David this afternoon. He woke up frantic to be fed and Cassandra had left me to mind him. I couldn't help it. I tried not to pick him up. I tried to rock him back to sleep but my breasts were leaking everywhere and he latched on. I couldn't stop him. And Cassandra came home and found us."

"Bloody hell. Was she OK about it?"

"I lied to her, told her I'd just been rocking him and we fell asleep. But she didn't believe me for a second. She was furious."

"Oh, sweetheart, that's tough." His hands curved up and gently cupped my throbbing breasts. My tears fell faster and faster.

"I'll never ever feed a baby again, never."

"Well then, I'm glad you had that experience. Forget about Cassandra; she'll get over it."

"I won't though. It's not fair. What have I done to deserve this?"

"It isn't fair, you're right. But give it time. It's so difficult because it's too soon and you're full of hormones, and your body is still thinking it gave birth to a baby. You won't feel so sad once you've stopped producing milk."

"My body did give birth to a baby."

"I know, I know." Ben was rocking a little, back and forward, my back curled into him. "Try and relax, you're so tense. You need to get some sleep. Shall I make you a milky drink?"

I shook my head on the pillow. "No. Thank you. Just hold me."

"Always. And I'm going to find a way for you and I to have a break from here for a while. You can't begin to heal with a baby in the same house."

Chapter Twelve

"I've checked with the Heron Island Research Station and they've OK'd you coming with me on this trip," Ben said, carefully placing another dripping dinner plate in the dish rack.

I looked over at him from my horizontal position on the couch and took another long drink from my glass of icy chardonnay. "I don't think I'm well enough to go anywhere yet. Don't worry about me. I'll be fine. It's not as if I'm alone."

"You can rest just as easily on Heron. More easily in fact. You can sleep all day if you want under the trees on the beach. See some turtles, get in some snorkeling, watch the sunsets. Being away from this madhouse will be good for you."

"No. You go."

I winced at Ben's long sigh as he dried his hands on the tea towel and came over to me.

"Olivia, it's been eight weeks. You've barely left the house. You promised you'd think about us having a break from here a month ago. It's past time."

I saw the look in his eyes as I took another slurp of my wine. "Stop staring at me like that. This is only my second glass."

"At least your third, and that's after two G & Ts before dinner."

"So?"

"So you have gone from almost never touching alcohol to drinking multiple glasses every night. It's not helping."

"What's that got to do with dragging me on one of your field trips? As far as I can work out you all drink like bloody fish every night when you're in the field." I took another sip.

"Bullshit. A couple of beers at the end of the day is all I ever have. We have to take all our food and drink with us so it's a no-brainer not to bring wine and spirits. It will make it easy for you to give up."

"Give up? Are you implying that I'm an alcoholic?"

"Don't be smart. Of course I'm not. But any alcohol is only going to make you more depressed. You need to get out and do something."

"Thank you Dr bloody Freud. And for your information, I intend to return to work at the beginning of April."

"Then it's perfect timing. This Heron Island trip is for three weeks. You'll have a few days when we get back here to get ready for work."

"If I were you I'd take a sea-sickness pill," the woman at the wharf said as she handed me our boarding passes. I could see Ben through the door, stacking our boxes of food in the freezer container that would travel with us on the boat.

"It doesn't look too rough," I said.

"Once you're out of the harbor it'll be rough all right, and it will continue to be rough for the whole three hours. Unless you have a stomach of iron, you should take one." She pulled a square of silver from under the bench and ripped off two foil wrapped pills. "One for the trip over and another for the trip back. You're not preggers are you? You can't take them if you are. Or even if you might be."

I shook my head.

She winked. "With a guy like Ben Appleby in your bed, you might be on the return trip. He's a hunk."

I grabbed the pills from her hand, my face burning, and marched out the door to my hunk. Stupid woman. If only she knew. We hadn't made love for months. Not that making love would ever again make me pregnant. I could swallow poisonous pills and wash them down with alcohol as often as I bloody liked. I could do with a large G&T right now, and all we'd got were two dozen beers to last us three weeks.

"All set?" Ben said, smiling his hunky smile. He was buzzing with joy.

I nodded, smiling back, and held up the foil. "Sea-sickness pills. You didn't tell me it would be rough."

"Might roll about a bit. Funny how people imagine the sea out to the reef is like blue glass. But once we get there it will be. Day after day of sunshine and warm blissful sea and white sand and millions of beautiful fish and coral gardens for you to float over. You're going to love it."

"I know I will. I can't believe I haven't come with you before." My smile was stuck in position.

"Too busy working, that's why. But you're here now." He tipped my chin up and kissed me with his hunky lips and I kissed him back. Hopefully the ticket woman was watching and getting her little thrill. Imagining it was her.

It was rough. I silently sent my reluctant thanks to the ticket dame for giving me the pills. Sitting inside with the green-complexioned tourists who were going over to stay in the resort, I watched Ben through the window. He and his two PhD students, Larry and Joe, stood by the rail, getting washed by spray as the boat ploughed into the big swell.

But at last the sea calmed and Ben came into the cabin to drag me outside. "There it is," he said. "Heron Island."

I'd been to coral cays before, plenty of times, when Cassandra and I were teenagers. But not since I'd returned to Australia, and never on the Southern outer reef as Heron was. It was exactly like the posters, an enchanting white line with green in the middle and the bluest, clearest sea all around. The resort's marketing pitch was 'Just a drop in the ocean,' and it was. Perhaps it would help, being here. Away from the babies that were everywhere on the mainland, away from chuckling little David, away from Cassandra with her huge milky boobs. My hands touched my shrunken breasts, almost dried up now. Screwing my eyelids closed over my stupid tears, I took in some deep breaths of the salty warm air.

The noise hit me first as we walked down the gangplank; thousands of birds flying back and forth and shitting everywhere. The noise and the smell of tons of bird shit drying in the tropical sun. It was strangely pleasant.

Our house at the Research Station was a Queenslander, a bit like the house at Killara, except this one wasn't kneeling and was covered with bird shit and surrounded by broadleaved trees loaded down with scruffy nests, all with very cute white and black Noddy terns perched precariously on them. The noise increased around seven at night when the shearwaters crashed in from their long days at sea. Phenomenal flyers, they were clumsy on land and once they touched down they shuffled about looking for their burrow where their mate and chick were waiting to be fed. And all the while they howled, up and down the scale, all night. There were thousands of them on this tiny island, and when I woke sweating at 3am, they sounded like some ghostly orchestra. How would I survive three weeks of this?

The second night Ben took my hand and led me through the trees and onto the beach. Within minutes we saw a nest of baby turtles erupting out of the sand and scuttling, like clockwork toys, down to the sea. We flapped our arms at the seagulls and saved all but two hatchlings from their nasty sharp beaks. In the bright moonlight, the sea high over the reef, we walked around the island. Seventeen nesting turtles we counted, hauling themselves up the beach, spraying sand over us as they scrapped out their pit so they could deposit their eggs, dragging their great tired bodies back down the beach and sliding into the sea before the tide was too low to swim back over the reef.

Once these dedicated mothers had laid eighty or so eggs, returning on another two or three nights over the next weeks to lay more, their job was done. Never would they see their babies exploding out of the sand weeks later. Never would they cry salty tears as the gulls swooped and grabbed their babies, leaving some for the fish and sharks waiting for them if they made it to the water. Never would they see their babies die. Never would they be forced to watch other mother turtles with their babies. Somewhere out there in the depths of the ocean there must be a turtle god who truly cared about her congregation.

It took a week to stop wanting a drink, and I knew I was being shitty and bad-tempered. I drank oceans of mango juice with tonic water, determined not to beg Ben for one of his precious brown bottles. The first two nights he drank mango juice with me while Larry and Joe gulped down cold beers, but on the third night I somehow dredged up sufficient kindness to tell him it was OK, it wouldn't worry me if he drank, and I didn't like beer much anyway. Which was true; I preferred G&Ts and wine, but if he had poured me a beer I would have forced it down.

Then almost without my noticing, the yearning and the images of cold alcohol that dominated my mind around sundown faded, and I found myself enjoying delicious cold water again. I began to sleep, in spite of the howling birds, and no longer missed Ben when he was out bird watching with his students. Instead I wriggled my feet into my fins, spat in my face mask, clamped my mouth around my snorkel mouthpiece, and floated over the reef for an hour at a time, when the tide was high enough. When it wasn't, I lay on the sand and slept or read, or took myself on a reef walk. Sometimes I'd cry a little, but not often.

As our second week came to an end, two important things happened. I started writing again, and Ben made love to me.

We picked our way carefully over the beach rock—my almost healed skinned knees a warning not to rush—and sat on a slightly raised rock at the edge of the pink sea. It was almost low tide and we could see fish shapes swimming about the dark coral not a meter from where we sat. A group of eagle rays swam past, lazily looking for an evening snack. Ben took my hand.

"Will you miss this?" he said, his gaze on the horizon where the sun was fast dropping towards dark.

The tears were instantly in my eyes. I blinked and felt his fingers almost stroking my palm. The sun touched the water and I took a deep breath in. "Do we have to leave?" I said, knowing it was not really a question.

"We can come back. I was afraid you wouldn't feel as I do about being here. It's the first time you've been with me in the field."

"What about all those days trudging through the heat looking at your bird sites?" I said.

"Day trips are not the same. None of those places are like this." I squeezed his hand as the sun became a glowing igloo on the blue and pink glass.

"Watch for the green flash," Ben said, and we kept our eyes pinned to the sun. I had never managed to see the green flash that others said they saw in the split second the sun dropped below the horizon. I concentrated on holding my eyes open, refusing to allow a single blink. "Oh, I saw it, I did, I saw it, I'm sure I did."

Ben pulled me to him and I turned my face away from the sea and looked into his eyes.

"Olivia, let's get married," he said. "Is it too soon?"

"Too soon? Too soon? No, it's not too soon, silly. I didn't think you wanted to get married, ever."

"Perhaps I didn't, but I do now. I've grown up, I guess. Being married mightn't make any difference to how much I love you, but I want more than that. I want the old-fashioned commitment too."

I kissed his beautiful mouth and he kissed me back. "I'll love you forever, Ben Appleby," I whispered. "Birds and all."

Chapter Thirteen

Killara, July, 1973

Uncle William and I stood outside the same shed that Cassandra and I had used as our changing room on the day I first arrived at Killara. We were waiting for Mendelssohn's Wedding March to soar along the track from the ghetto blaster on the beach. The music began and Uncle William smiled down at me and pulled my hand through his bent arm. No majestic orchestra, but Elton John's familiar voice singing 'Your Song'. It shimmered in the sunlight and swooped through me, taking with it the scared flutterings that had been resident ever since I'd woken before dawn this morning. Ben must have chosen it for my entrance. So often when we danced to it he'd sung the words in my ear.

Uncle William stooped and kissed me on the cheek. "You look beautiful," he said, his dear voice sending shivers through me. "Thank you for asking me to give you away."

"Oh, don't. I'll start crying. Who else could give me away?"

"We love you, we Tullochs. You're part of us. Killara will always be your home."

I blinked hard. I didn't want to smudge my mascara before I even got to the altar. "I love you too. If I had a father I'd want him to be like you."

"Well, I feel like your father, and I know Cathie feels like your other mother." His hand stroked back my hair. "Jess would be so proud and happy to see you now."

I nodded, my throat tight.

"Are you ready? If we don't appear soon they'll have to start Elton all over again."

"I'm ready." And we walked elegantly down the few yards of track to the shell path that had appeared like magic on the beach, and followed it to Ben standing tall beneath a flower-entwined bower of drift wood. His long curly hair sparked in the sun and he had on a loose shirt, pale blue, and white flares. As he turned towards me I could see his eyes shining and his shirt pulsing as his heart pumped love for me, Olivia Newman. In a few minutes to become Mrs. Olivia Appleby.

AFTER THE NUPTIALS, PERFORMED BY A LONG-HAIRED YOUNG Presbyterian minister who seemed unconcerned by our request to have no mention of religion in his address or the vows—which we'd revised poetically from the traditional version—we wandered up the balloon festooned track to a feast set out on a long table on Killara's verandah. There were too many speeches probably, but no-one seemed to mind. Uncle William was eloquent and funny and Ben's father was warm and proud. He and Ben's mum seemed not in the least tired after their long flight from Scotland two days ago. We four each gave a speech; Cassandra first, then Ben, followed by Sebastian and finally me. We all said basically the same things. Then I tossed my posy of wild flowers up into the air and Pete, who had shown up the previous night having never replied to his invitation, caught it.

That was the sign for everyone to throw aside their solemn-occasion manners and let the party begin. The table was cleared and moved away and the dancing spilled from the verandah to the lawn. Sebastian was in charge of the music but I don't remember what any of the songs were, except the first, which was a medley that Ben had compiled for the traditional dance of the newly-weds. We were good together, dancing, Ben and I. (Although we had practiced a bit back in Brisbane, quite a bit really, with Cassandra and Sebastian and Amber joining in.) Everyone circled us and we began with a waltz, then the music morphed to a quickstep, then a tango, then the twist and back to a waltz again. At the very end it became "You've Got a Friend" and we pulled Cassandra and Sebastian onto the grass to dance with us. Soon everybody was dancing and singing along with James Taylor, even Pete.

But the best was still to come. At midnight, stars as only stars in the dark of a new moon night at Killara can be, Cassandra took our hands. "Bedtime for you two," she said.

"Ho, ho. We're not going to bed with all you lot still dancing. I suppose you think you'll stand outside the door and listen for the squeaking of the bedsprings. Make sure we have consummated our relationship." I grinned at her. She still looked ravishing, unlike the rest of us who looked as if we'd been dragged through a gorse bush backwards, as my mum used to say when she had the energy to notice me on a Saturday morning.

"We've got a surprise for you first. Get your sandals on and follow me." Cassandra was bubbling with something. Mischief?

"What are you up to, woman?" growled Ben, holding her hand high and twirling her around.

"You'll see," she said, leaning over, her hand on her side,

when they came to a stop. "Now do as you're told and get something on your feet. We're going for a walk."

She led us down the track towards the beach; Sebastian, Uncle William and Aunt Cathie, Ben's parents, Pete, and all our friends following.

"I think we're going for a midnight swim," said Ben. "Hope there ain't no crocs lurking, attracted by the music."

I shivered. "They wouldn't dare."

"If they get the scent of you they'll dare all right." He lowered his head and nuzzled my neck. "Yum."

"Stop it. Even Cassandra and Pete wouldn't make us swim."

Just ahead of us they'd stopped by the overgrown track that led to the Shack, long since fallen so far into disrepair that only broken lawn mowers and bits of horse tackle made it home. Sebastian was pulling at the bushes on the side of the track. They came away suspiciously easily. Cassandra shone her torch in the gap and we could see the old path, free of branches and covered with white beach sand, winding into the darkness.

"Come on," she squealed, grabbing my hand and pulling me after her.

"Aha, a secret tunnel," I heard Ben say. I realized he'd never seen the Shack.

We stumbled along, ducking a fair few low branches, and there in its clearing was the dear old Shack, shining and new, festooned with balloons and streamers and a banner across the deck that shouted "Welcome Home Olivia and Ben."

"It's for you. It's yours. So you can always come back and have your very own place." Cassandra and Sebastian's arms were around us, and then Aunt Cathie and Uncle William joined the party. Ben and I stood there, stunned, in the middle of them, totally unable to speak. They were all in on it, the Tullochs of Killara. They had planned it, had it rebuilt, and as we soon discovered had furnished it and stocked the kitchen with everything a newly-wed couple might need. Even our clothes and toiletries from the house had been smuggled down here while we were dancing.

Sebastian pushed us towards the steps. “Sweet dreams, guys. We’ll see you when we see you.”

Cassandra kissed my cheek and whispered, “Just shout out my name if you need anything. But I don’t think you will.”

Chapter Fourteen

In May, 1974, Sunny was born in the spa bath at Killara. As always, Cassandra flew through the birth but not with me nor Ben anywhere near. The morning she went into labor we drove to Port Douglas and had a very expensive lunch. By the time we got back to Killara, it was 8pm. We'd spent the afternoon swimming and walking the long Port Douglas beach in an effort to burn off the alcohol before the winding drive back.

Cassandra was wide awake, her new baby in bed with her, thankfully not attached to her breast. She looked up at me, a question hovering in her eyes. I kissed her cheek and then the silky head of her baby. "Can I hold her?" I asked.

"Oh, Olivia, yes, yes. I've been so afraid that you'd be too upset."

"Me too. But I'll be alright." Sunny was beautiful, with hair as bright as the star she was named after. My heart dissolved with love.

~

It wasn't until the end of the year that Ben and I returned to Killara. My first Christmas there since we lost our baby boy. The tiny tension lines between Ben's eyebrows disappeared when I asked him if we could afford the flights.

I was home again as soon as Aunt Cathie hugged me. Uncle William squashed me into his tall skinny body and kissed the top of my head as he always had, and, like magic, my stomach stopped churning.

Pete even showed up for a few days. He was quiet and often disappeared without saying where he was going, returning late at night or sometimes not until the next morning. Aunt Cathie couldn't hide her worry and hurt from any of us, although she tried. I wanted to hug her every time she walked past me but usually stopped myself. All that did was bring the shadows back to her eyes.

Sebastian had to return to his law firm in February. He didn't enjoy the daily grind of divorce settlements and custody battles; his passion was for the pro bono sideline he had taken on, working with groups of parents who wanted to adopt children from third world and war-torn countries. One evening, as he was telling Ben and me about one heart-warming case, Cassandra joined us. Within minutes she had taken over, first saying how wonderful his adoption work was and then adding a throw-away comment about a colleague of Sebastian's who'd been made a partner even though he was just 32.

"He's a born partner, poor bastard. Thank god I'm not," Sebastian said.

"You're only 28. You might feel differently in a few years time."

I avoided looking at Cassandra. Staring her down usually had no effect.

Sebastian shook his head, his grin plain joyful. "I'm betting I won't. Not about that anyway. Admin and worrying about balancing the books doesn't do it for me."

"Don't put yourself down like that," said Cassandra. "You'd be a wonderful boss. Much nicer than some of those ghastly suit types." She grabbed him around his neck and smacked a loud kiss on his cheek. "And I want to be married to a gorgeous Partner and don't you forget it."

Sebastian unwound her arms, his face as open and loving as always when he looked at her. Ben simmered beside me.

It was also time for Ben to return to work. Five weeks was already a week too long for him; he couldn't hide from me his boredom with women and kids. Even Uncle William escaped early every weekday morning to the university and didn't get back until dinnertime. I was tempted to go back with Ben, not because I wanted to leave Killara but because he was returning to Heron Island for another research trip. I could have joined him; I'd managed to get an extra two weeks holiday before I was due back at Stoddard and Jones. But I wasn't entirely sure he wanted me with him, spoiling the matey atmosphere that he thrived on, out in the field with his research colleagues and senior students, freed from the confines of the university. And Cassandra wanted me to stay; Aunt Cathie as well.

I enjoyed the kids. Amber was a bossy four-year-old, scarily like her mother in both looks and personality, David was an adorable toddler, and seven-month-old Sunny was perfectly named. Rather than reminding me to be sad, being with her gave me pure pleasure. I had moved on from the terrible day when David clamped his mouth on my breast and for a tiny moment sucked away the pain.

Cassandra and I spent hours together, often without the children; Aunt Cathie loved looking after them. It was almost like being in our early twenties again, carefree, and with our futures ahead of us. By the time we joined Ben and Sebastian in Brisbane, Cassandra and I had come up with two plans: a new house for her and Sebastian, and adoption for Ben and me.

~

"WHAT'S WRONG WITH THE HOUSE WE HAVE?" SEBASTIAN asked, when Cassandra explained her plan for a new one, the night after we arrived back.

"You know I absolutely love it, but we have three children now. It's not big enough. When you're made a Partner, we'll have to do some real entertaining. Our friends...your colleagues... they won't want to be driving all the way out here."

Sebastian's tanned face turned red. Cassandra had put her foot in it big time now. Not that she let that stop her.

"Amber will be starting school in May. I want her to go to one of the better schools in Brisbane. The local one is too countrified." Cassandra blustered on, oblivious to the tension steaming from Sebastian and my silent plea, *Stop now Cassandra, STOP NOW.*

Sebastian's eyes were slits. "Our local school here is perfectly fine, and all Amber's friends from kindergarten will be going there. She can go to one of your fancy city schools when she gets a bit older and can get herself there by bus."

Ben was twitching beside me. Feeling guilty probably. He knew damn well that this house being too small was not the reason for Cassandra's desire to build a new one. He touched my arm and jerked his head towards the door.

Cassandra was hammering more words at Sebastian. "I've interviewed some head teachers in three schools in the best suburbs in Brisbane and I want her to go to one of those. I'll drive her in and pick her up until our new house is built."

Stop it, you stupid stubborn woman.

"What about Ben and Olivia? Are you planning on chucking them out of their home too?" said Sebastian, his eyebrows raised.

"Don't be so mean. Of course I'm not. They can stay here. They might have a baby of their own soon and it's perfect for babies."

The silence was resounding. I could have banged her head

against the wall. How dare she bring up our adoption idea before I'd had a chance to talk to Ben. Sebastian's face had turned from red to white. My heart was pounding so viciously I had to sit down.

"I think you should apologize to Olivia and Ben." Sebastian's voice was deathly calm. "How could you forget?"

"It's OK. She didn't mean…" I began, but got no further.

"It's not OK," Ben said. "Olivia and I will find another place. You'll have plenty of room then and it's way overdue for us to get our own home."

"Ben, there's no need, man. We love you being here, we all do. Cassandra's lost her bloody marbles. We'll build an extension on the damn house. I don't want you to leave." Sebastian pushed past Cassandra and grabbed Ben's arm.

"Shit, I'm sorry Olivia. I didn't mean to let that slip out," Cassandra whispered. She was ghost white now.

I stood up, bugger my racing heart. "All of you shut up and listen to me." I was shouting. "Just bloody listen. Cassandra didn't mean it like it sounded."

They shut up, surprised looks on their faces.

"Cassandra and I were talking at Killara about our lives and had a few ideas, that's all. Just things to discuss with each of you." I glared at Cassandra. "Not bloody ultimatums."

"Sorry," she squeaked.

"One of the things was the possibility of us adopting a baby," I said. "That's what she meant about us having a baby. She just can't stop her blabber mouth sometimes." I looked at Ben, his eyes sparking through his glasses. "I was going to talk to you about it later, when we were alone."

Sebastian turned to Cassandra and she shrunk back. Never had I seen that before. Even when they were arguing furiously Cassandra never gave way.

"When will you learn to control your tongue?" he hissed.

Cassandra looked away, and I saw her back straighten as she turned to Ben.

"I'm sorry Ben," she said. "I'm really sorry. I've ruined it all now."

"Forget it. I'm going for a walk. Are you coming Olivia?"

"Um, yes. Yes, I'll come."

Ben was already out the door, Oscar padding silently after him. Oscar hated conflict.

I leaned over and touched Cassandra on the arm, giving Sebastian my best sympathetic look as I did so. "Perhaps you two can have a good talk and straighten things out. It really isn't such a big deal." I made for the door, turning back for one last platitude. "We'll see you in the morning, hopefully when we've all calmed down."

They didn't give any sign they'd heard me or that they would hear each other.

Ben mooched along, hands deep in his pockets, Oscar lolloping ahead. "Wait for me," I yelled. Was Ben walking even faster? I had to catch them up. Needed to explain. Come on, Olivia. Keep going. My breathing was jagged. I'd lost all my fitness since losing our baby.

Panting, I finally caught up. Ben glanced sideways at me. His jaw was set and my stomach clenched. God knows, he didn't deserve this. As my breathing slowed, the edge of his hand grazed mine and then our hands twisted and clasped. Oscar herded us closer like a couple of sheep. Ben stooped, picked up a stick and threw it. It was a feeble shot and Oscar was soon back, holding it in his soft mouth. Ben dropped my hand and chucked the stick again, this time with enough force to wrench his arm out of its socket. "Sometimes it seems that Cassandra means more to you than I do," he said, his voice low and his gaze still on Oscar.

My heart went out to him. How could he think that? "No,

don't say that. It's so not true." Was there a kernel of truth in what he'd said? Was there?

"How could you discuss us adopting a baby before we'd even mentioned it to each other? Are you scared of talking to me? Did you think I'd be against it?" He turned and looked at me, daring me to be honest, to admit that I cared more about Cassandra's opinions than his. But it was more complicated than that. So much more. I swallowed, trying to get the words right before I spoke.

Ben stared at me as if I were a stranger he didn't think he'd like. "This is our baby you and Cassandra were scheming about. My baby, if we ever do adopt." His words stabbed through the hot air.

Oh god. What had I done? "I'm sorry," I whispered.

Ben walked ahead and I stumbled after him. "I know I've hurt you, but I didn't mean to, surely you know that. We won't talk about adoption again until you want to, and I'll never talk to Cassandra or anyone else until we've made our decision."

"Decision? That implies there is something to decide, not something we haven't even begun to talk about."

"Oh bollocks. This is getting ridiculous. You're determined to have a fight." I didn't know if I was furious or miserable; whatever, I was crying.

Ben was ahead of me again, Oscar by his side, no more sticks to chase. I snuffled along, my mind a mess of things I wanted to say but didn't know how to without making things worse.

"Sorry," Ben said, stopping suddenly. "I'm being a prick."

We turned to each other and I looked into his eyes, soft again behind his glasses. Both his thumbs came up and wiped away my tears and I cried harder; then he was holding me close and Oscar was circling our legs, taking care of his unpredictable human charges.

Chapter Fifteen

Two weeks later when we'd all calmed down, Ben and I began the search for a house to rent and Sebastian and Cassandra started looking for the perfect section in the best suburb to build their 'forever' family home. They were keen for us to stay where we were, but Ben remained adamant; it was time to begin our own lives. The hippy years were over. He came home one evening with his hair—not the Afro of his student days, but still quite long—cut close to his head, a cap of tight springy curls. For a few days I felt as if I were married to a stranger, but once I got used to his new look, I loved it. He had a beautifully shaped head; who would have known? His glasses went next, the heavy black frames changed for oval wire ones. My lovely Ben.

Sebastian, inspired by our glowing admiration of Ben's new look, had his longish hair cut as well, and shaved off the stubble he usually wore. Cassandra approved his new smart look; I knew that she thought that his young, too casual style had been a factor in his failure to be made a partner in the law practice. At least she kept her thoughts to herself this time.

Cassandra's long hair was next, with a neat straight trim of its long luscious ends, and an elegant upswept hairstyle on the days she wore one of her new business suits. ("What business?" muttered Ben.) The loose locks went with her new summer dresses pitched just above her knees and showing off her stiletto heels. My wardrobe was modernized as well; I even splurged on one business suit for future power meetings in my fantasy role as a fully-fledged editor with my own list. The beads, headbands and miniskirts were added to Amber's dressing-up box and the floaty long skirts were relegated to the back of our wardrobes to be brought out for the occasional retro weekend when the hot weather insisted on an old-fashioned barbeque on the back deck.

One Saturday I was marched off by Cassandra to a hairdresser/beauty therapist establishment in town where I survived a total image update. Lunch and the purchase of a summery and flattering dress followed, a late Christmas present from Cassandra.

"I can't accept all this. You've already given me a Christmas present."

"You can and you will. You are my best friend and if you make a fuss I'll strangle you."

That evening she presented me, with much drama, to the men, and to my boss Louise and her husband, Jonathan, who had been invited for dinner. After recovering from the shock, they said all the right things. I was stunned, myself. It took a while to recognize the sleek and gorgeous woman-of-the-world in my mirror. Chin length, side swept, pale coppery hair, glowing complexion with subtle smoky eye makeup—the replication of which took me weeks to master—, perfectly defined lips. It was startling how it changed my attitude towards myself. I felt like an editor of note, and better still an author to watch. On Monday Louise took my fantasy another step nearer to possible; she confirmed my new position as a full editor with a list of my own.

Cassandra had taken a week or two to persuade Sebastian that it was time to build the house of her dreams. He'd always loved carpentry; his beautiful wooden toys were snapped up in the first half hour at school fetes, and the intricate rocking horse he'd made for Amber had earned the status of family heirloom, its carved saddle and mane maturing like red wine as each new Brooks child loved it. So once he got his head around the idea of moving, Sebastian began designing their new home. Cassandra, thank heavens, left him to it. Sebastian's trust fund, an advantage he'd always struggled with, came into its own. Their enthusiasm was catching, and although we couldn't afford the mortgage on a new house, we could now afford to rent somewhere pretty nice.

It was fun, and brought us all together in new ways. Adult ways. In our spare time we began packing up the old house, refreshing the paint here and there, making repairs to the deck (the men, not we women), and getting it ready to sell. We needn't have bothered as it sold for a handsome profit the weekend it went on the market. We wailed and sang all the old songs that night and wore our oldest clothes and cooked sticky pork ribs on the barbecue while the kids played in the bath that Amber and David had been born in. How could we have thought we'd be happier away from here? How could we live as two families instead of one?

BEN AND I RENTED A MODERN THREE-BED APARTMENT ON THE second floor of a small, attractive apartment block overlooking the river and with ferry access five minutes walk away. From there the ferry took us across the river to the city center where we both worked. Our new home was full of sun, had a large private balcony, and required new minimalist furniture.

Sebastian and Cassandra bought a large section in a leafy suburb close to the best schools. It had perfect contours and views over the city one way and across the river the other, a gift for the up-and-coming young architect who took Sebastian's plans and turned them into a five bedroom, three bathroom, concrete, wood and glass work of art. Meantime the Brooks family rented a large house nearby to live in during the build.

As all this house hunting was going on we began the long process towards an overseas adoption. Sebastian's stories had torn our hearts and it had been an easy decision to hope for this, rather than an Australian adoption. In any case it was pretty much impossible to adopt from within Australia. Single mothers were thankfully no longer routinely coerced into giving up their babies.

Our application to the Adoption Services Department went through quickly, thanks to Sebastian, and we moved into our new apartment just in time. Around came two pleasant assessment officers to interview us on why we thought we'd make good parents. Sebastian had given us the lowdown, but it was still nerve wracking. After they left we looked at each other, our almost desperate desire to be potential parents exposed.

We passed with flying colors and attacked the next steps with passion. We knew from Sebastian how long overseas adoptions could take. He had advised us to stick with government-to-government adoptions and steer clear of private orphanages in third-world countries. Black market baby trafficking was rife and adoptions from private orphanages made it more likely that the baby you thought was a genuine orphan or had been voluntarily given up by the parents had in fact been stolen or bought. Sebastian had even had cases where the Australian parents thought they had adopted their child officially, only to be challenged a year or more later by the biological parents coming forward saying they had been the victims of baby kidnappers, or with sad stories of being coerced into selling their babies so they could support their other children.

We wrote letters of inquiry to embassies and government-run orphanages in Thailand, Philippines and Sri Lanka. We wrote to Mother Theresa in India and got a hand-written reply telling us gently she could not help. We joined the local support group for overseas adoptions. We filled out overseas application forms and by mid-March had our names put on the list for a child of either sex, aged from birth to two years old in Sri Lanka, one country that appeared to have less trafficking than some of the others.

Now it was a waiting game. Sebastian put us in touch with a social worker in Colombo, who kept the pressure on the Sri Lankan social services that arranged adoptions. I packed our bags in readiness for the telegram that would tell us there was a child waiting for us across the seas. Medications, nappies, soybean milk—many of the children were allergic to cow's milk—small bribes for officials (ball-point pens) and orphanage staff (bras and makeup), and baby clothes in a range of sizes. Long skirts and long-sleeved tops for me, as trousers and short skirts were not approved of.

We got permission from the owner to re-paint the perfectly pristine second bedroom in our apartment. Ben turned it into a room that was so full of exuberance and joy that I asked him to shift my desk in there, just until our new baby arrived. I knew he thought I'd get little writing done after that, but he was wrong. I discovered it energized me and my second novel began to take shape. I had failed to find an Australian literary agent to take my first novel or me on—agents were thin on the ground and not much interested in a novel set in 1860s New Zealand—and *A River Through Time* was now languishing with the editor of a small publisher in New Zealand. Even that small step forward was courtesy of Louise. The editor was a close friend of hers. I tried not to beat myself up about the who-you-know-not-how-good-your-book-is thing. Louise's friend or not, she would surely only accept it if she thought it worthy in its own right. I refreshed my old dream of my debut novel being published at the same time as our baby found a home here with us.

~

On April 4th, Sebastian arrived at our door. It was Friday night and we were listening to a Sonny Terry and Brownie McGee record Ben had discovered on one of his regular forays through the second-hand record bins at his favorite record store. Our first thought was that something terrible must have happened. Sebastian walked straight over to the TV and turned it on. It was 10:05pm and the late evening newsreader was reporting some grim news about a four-car pile-up outside Sydney.

"What's happened?" Ben had switched off the record player and was standing next to Sebastian, his eyes on the TV. "What's our beleaguered Prime Minister being accused of now?"

"Saigon. Babylift. Wait, they must have it on soon."

Vietnam had been back in the news lately. Da Nang had been taken over by the North Vietnamese and Saigon was under attack and expected to fall. The longest war in modern history was finally nearing its chaotic and horrifying end. A few days ago President Gerald Ford's announcement that the U.S. government would begin evacuating orphans from Saigon had raised a smidgeon of hope that a tiny few of the innocent victims might be saved. The rescue plan was dubbed Operation Babylift, and American families were flocking to take the orphans into their homes. Many of the children had been fathered by American servicemen, and when we heard the news we'd wondered about the responsibility of Australia in this; our servicemen had fathered children there as well. Our interest and concern were likely more intense than that of most Australians, given our current obsession with our own overseas adoption plans, our long association with the anti-Vietnam war lobbyists, and Pete. So we'd been relieved when, on April 2nd, Prime Minister Gough Whitlam announced the Australian government's plan to evacuate about two hundred orphans to our country.

"Is it the orphan rescue? Have they arrived?" I said, too impatient to wait for a solemn-faced newsreader to enlighten us about whatever had got Sebastian hotfooting it over here late on a Friday night. Before he had a chance to reply the item was on. We listened in silence; horrified silence. A few hours ago the first US Babylift plane had departed from Tan Son Nhut Air Base in South Vietnam, bound for the Philippines; from there the orphans were to be flown on charter flights to their new homes in the United States. But the C-5A Galaxy, a massive troop and cargo carrier with 330 defense staff and children from Saigon orphanages packed into the troop and cargo compartments, crashed near Saigon. Early reports were of an explosion on the plane shortly after takeoff. The plane had swerved back, crash landing in a rice paddy, skidding for half a mile or more before breaking up and bursting into flames when it hit a dike. The area was difficult to access but some survivors had already managed to get themselves away from the wreck. The death toll was expected to be high.

Ben got the whisky out and we sat there, stunned.

"Those poor children," I whispered. "How can any of them survive that?"

"Is it sabotage? This will probably stop the whole baby evacuation. None of the kids left waiting for their planes will stand a chance now." Ben's glasses were off and he was rubbing his eyes, a sure sign of distress.

Sebastian looked gray. "That's what I've come to talk to you about. A Qantas plane is scheduled to land in Sydney tomorrow with possibly two hundred orphans on board. They were evacuated to Bangkok by the Australian Air Force before this crash." He stopped, and I held my breath. The silence seemed endless.

"I wondered..." —he looked at me, at Ben— "perhaps

you might be willing to take one of the children? I've talked to the officials and they say that with my recommendation and given you've passed all the adoption requirements you would almost certainly be approved. You'd have to give up on the Sri Lankan adoption though."

"Heavens," was all I could say.

Ben, his glasses back on, had his hand on mine. "Olivia, we have to do this."

"Yes, yes, of course we do. Oh, Ben, I can't believe it. Tomorrow…"

"Hang on a bit. You need to think this through," Sebastian cautioned. "I'm not sure you'll have much choice; the kids are all ages and you might not get a baby. And they've likely spent their whole lives in hell and then been uprooted and herded onto a plane. They won't understand English, and a lot of them will have health problems. We can put in a request for a young child or baby based on your request to Sri Lanka, but I'm not sure how much say you'll have. Many of them will have disabilities, severe malnourishment, war injuries, not to mention psychological problems."

"When do we need to make a decision?" Ben said, his voice shaking.

"When they arrive they'll have to spend two weeks at the Quarantine Station at North Head in Manly. Or in hospital if they're really sick. So you have some time, but not a lot if you really want to go ahead," Sebastian said. "I wouldn't be surprised if lots of parents want to adopt one of these waifs, and some of them won't have thought too much about it. It's not something I believe anyone should go into without a lot of preparation. And you've got that. So my feeling is that we should get all the Adoption Services and legal formalities ticked and signed off as soon as possible. That might also give you a better chance of being allocated a baby. I know that's what you really want." He looked at me, his expression so full of kindness.

I felt Ben's arms around me and then Sebastian was holding us both.

"Yes," I said. "We're ready. So ready. Let's not waste a second."

"Ben?" said Sebastian.

"Not a second. We have enough love for the whole two hundred." He kissed the tip of my nose. "But we'll begin with one."

Part Two

MOTHERS AND DAUGHTERS

1975 - 1983

~

“Sometimes” said Pooh, “the smallest things take up the most room in your heart.”

— *Winnie the Pooh* by A.A. Milne —

Chapter Sixteen

April, 1975

We flew to Sydney two days later so we could be there as soon as the children were released from the Quarantine Station or the hospital. Sebastian was also acting for two other prospective adoptive families who wanted to adopt Babylift babies instead of waiting for other overseas adoption possibilities to become reality. So we all took the same flight, excitement and nerves bonding us together. Ben, Sebastian and I were going to stay with Uncle William and Aunt Cathie who had insisted on flying to Sydney where they'd rented a big house for ten days. Cassandra remained reluctantly in Brisbane, minding the fort and the three children. Sebastian told us she'd begged him to let them adopt a Babylift child as well, but he was against it. He strongly believed that parents already in the adoption process should be prioritized. "And we," he said, smiling gently at me, "have the good luck to be able to have our own children."

The day after we arrived Sebastian had all the formalities

completed and we were approved. Then he managed to get permission for us to accompany him when he visited the Royal Alexandra Hospital for Children, and the Quarantine Station. Many of the one hundred children in the hospital were too sick for us to see, but others were in the big ward, suffering from 'minor' illnesses such as pneumonia, severe diarrhoea, infected stumps where once they had a leg or arm, severe malnutrition, or poorly treated burns. Most of them lay silent and wide-eyed in their beds, shocked and still. We were too shaken to visit the Quarantine Station that same day, and needed the love that Aunt Cathie and Uncle William wrapped us in that evening.

The next day we were more emotionally prepared, we hoped, for the Quarantine Station. To accommodate another one hundred children, two former hospital wards had been converted into a combined nursery, eating area, and medical examination room. It was bustling with activity—nurses and volunteers, many of them Vietnamese students who could talk to the children in their own language, doctors, and staff from the station. Representatives from various adoption agencies, church as well as government, were sifting through forms and trying to match up approved parents with children. Sebastian was clearly well-known and respected by everyone; until then we hadn't realized how passionately involved he had been in the overseas adoption minefield. Neither had it really sunk in before that he did all this work free of charge.

There were many frightened, shocked and screaming children of course, but also some who were taking it all in with big eyes and big smiles. Milk, food, bandages for lesser injuries, new clothes and toys, and most of all hugs; they were in heaven.

"Can we help?" I asked one of the senior nurses. "Are we allowed to touch them?" I thought perhaps we would be stopped for some quarantine reason.

"As long as you are healthy, no colds or anything, and you are aware that most of the children have scabies and nits; yes, you can help. Try to keep your hair away from their heads. We're treating them all but it takes time."

We didn't get back until 7pm that evening. Sebastian had dragged us away.

"We must go back tomorrow," I said, tired and buzzing with the emotion of it all.

"Why not," Sebastian grinned. "You should have been a nurse, or a nanny, not an author. Now go have a shower and wash your hair with this." He produced a bottle of foul-smelling nit shampoo. "No dinner until you are clean as a whistle; outer and underwear changed as well."

WE MET LILY THE NEXT DAY. I FOUND HER LYING, QUIET AS A little mouse, in one of the cots near the very end of the long dormitory. The small card stuck on the end of the cot said "Reference number: SAF87. Name: Lily. Birthdate: Unknown. Estimated age: 11-15 months. History: Abandoned at orphanage, January 10th, 1975; no papers."

Lily was clutching a pre-loved koala, one of the thousands of toys that had flooded in from Sydney wellwishers. I fell in love with her on sight. I murmured softly to her in a language that she didn't know, sung a lullaby in a voice that was strange to her, held her in my lap and gazed at her delicate face as she emptied a bottle of milk faster than I could have downed a glass of water.

I took my eyes off her only when Sebastian and Ben appeared at my side. Sebastian was reading Lily's identity card. He smiled at me. "I thought you might want to introduce Lily to Ben. When you're ready, come and see me. I'll be over at the adoption desk."

~

WE TOOK HER HOME EIGHT DAYS LATER. SHE'D PASSED ALL HER medical tests and was 'free to go.' Sebastian had continued his magic and passed us papers to sign that handed her over to us. The official adoption would come later but for now we were her foster parents. After she was discharged from the Quarantine Station we stayed for another three nights with the Tullochs. They too fell in love with her. Cassandra phoned constantly for updates, as did Louise, and of course Ben's parents from far away Scotland. They were, I think, a little stunned by the rapidity of their new grandparent status.

Lily had bonded to me to such an extent that I couldn't put her down without her protesting with a high repetitive mewling noise. Even Ben could hold her only if I was right there as well. So I walked around with her on my hip; she had apparently been toddling at the orphanage and when she first got to the Quarantine Station, but now refused to put any weight on her tiny feet. She weighed only 12 pounds, the size of a healthy three-month Australian baby. We put her in our bed in the rental house so I could sleep with her cuddled into me. If I wasn't there she would begin her mewling again. If she fell asleep and I tried to creep away, her big eyes would snap open and fill with tears and her cries would begin afresh.

Within two weeks of getting her home and in her own colorful bedroom, she looked like a different child. She was beautiful, her dark hair, raggedly short-cropped at the Vietnamese orphanage to dishearten the nits, soft and clean now and giving her a fashionable and very huggable urchin look. Her bronchitis was rapidly getting better, and the scabies scars on her wrists and ankles were fading. Her milky-tea skin, dull before, now had a soft glow. Her main health problem was a persistent diarrhea and we had to limit her food intake as she would eat every last rice grain on the plate, picking each one up with delicate fingers and stuffing it in her mouth.

~

Lily was our miracle child in another way. Three weeks after our return to Brisbane, I got a phone call from Pete.

"I'll be in Brisbane tomorrow," he said. "Is it OK if I come and stay for a few days?"

I almost dropped the phone. I don't think we'd ever had a call from Pete before.

Ben was looking at me, his eyebrows arched above his glasses.

"Does Cassandra know you'll be here?" I asked.

"Dunno. I'll phone her and let her know," Pete muttered. "Thought it was time I met this new baby Mum and Dad are so excited about."

"Oh, Oh, um, that's lovely. Where are you now?"

"Stuck in Melbourne, same tedious job. I could do with a break."

"Lily's still settling in; she's quite anxious around anyone but Ben and me still," I burbled.

"If you don't want me there, just say. I don't want to get in your way."

"No, no, you must come. We'd love to see you. I'm just surprised, that's all."

"Right. I'll see you about two. I'll grab a cab."

"No, don't be silly. Give me your flight details and Ben will pick you up."

"She'll be right, See ya tomorrow eh? Gotta go." The phone went dead.

It was a Saturday, thank goodness, and Ben wasn't due at work. I'd taken six months maternity leave. Our apprehension infected Lily and she clung to me more than usual. We cleaned the apartment and tidied away the baby paraphernalia and made up the bed in the third bedroom. As if Pete would care.

Half-past three and no sign of him. We'd almost got past our nervousness; now we were pissed off. He'd changed his mind and hadn't bothered to call. We talked to Cassandra who was as surprised as we'd been; Pete hadn't phoned her to tell her he was coming.

I'd just lifted Lily out of her warm cot—we'd managed to get her down for an afternoon nap—when the door bell rang. Our apartment had outside stairs to our door; it wasn't one of those apartment blocks where visitors had to buzz to be let into the building. Ben opened the door.

"Sorry I'm late. The plane was delayed," Pete said.

Ben shook his hand and I caught the embarrassed look that flashed between them before they collided clumsily in a man-hug.

"We'd almost given up on you," Ben said. "Come on in. Is this all your luggage?"

"Yep." Pete dumped his small backpack on the floor and looked at me standing by the table, holding Lily. "Hi, Olivia." He moved towards us and I stroked Lily's back, murmuring to her. We'd been home only three weeks and she still refused to go to anyone but me and Ben. Even Sebastian and Cassandra hadn't yet managed to gain her trust.

"Hullo Lily," Pete said softly.

I turned her around so he could see her face. "She's too shy yet to go to anyone," I said.

Pete said something in Vietnamese. It hadn't occurred to me he might speak the language.

I felt Lily's little body relaxing. Her eyes were wide.

Pete kept talking to her.

She strained forward and her arms reached out. Pete looked at me, a question in his eyes. I nodded and he took her from me. Lily sat there in his arms looking into his face, and her little hand came up and touched his lips, still talking to her in her own language. Pete's eyes were tearing up; he was shaking.

Ben was beside me, his arm around me. We watched, no

words possible, as Pete walked out the open french doors onto our balcony, crooning to our baby, singing almost, walking with her back and forwards. We could hear her babbling back to him, then her little chuckle; the chuckle that was still rare for us to hear.

Chapter Seventeen

Pete stayed for a week and he spent so much time with Lily that I almost felt jealous. But then I'd watch them together. She was thriving and Pete's relationship with Ben was deepening every day. Apart from one afternoon when he went over to Cassandra's for lunch, he stayed close to Lily.

When Ben returned to work, Pete and I were thrown together. I'd seen him only twice since Cassandra and I had left for our European experience when we were eighteen. I had almost no real idea of who he was. Or who he had become, as Ben had once commented in one of our discussions with Sebastian and Cassandra about the aftermath of the Vietnam war. When Lily was having her afternoon nap I would usually have a sleep too, but sometimes Pete and I would sit on the balcony and talk. Pete wasn't one for talking much about his Melbourne life; he worked for an insurance company and had a 'casual' girlfriend. "She's smart and likes a good laugh but I don't think it will last. She's too good for me."

I soon got the message that it was pointless trying to put a more positive spin on it. One afternoon I asked him if he missed the army. It was hard to imagine what it must have been like going from a war zone to an insurance office.

"Yep, sometimes," Pete said. "I miss the guys more than the army. It could be pretty damn tedious for weeks on end; not much different from the insurance business really. Just less comfortable."

"Do you keep in touch with anyone over there? I guess you made some Vietnamese friends in all that time."

He didn't say anything for a few minutes and I knew I'd stuck my giant foot in it. God knows what might have happened to anyone he'd known there.

"Not really," he said. "We weren't so popular with the locals. It's still a mess there anyway, and no-one is where they were any more."

By the end of Pete's stay, Lily was pulling herself up on the furniture, and walking with help. According to Pete, some of her babbling, especially when he conversed with her in Vietnamese, sounded almost like words—Vietnamese words. Every night he taught Ben and I how to say a few more words and simple sentences, and we decided that we would find someone to teach us properly; perhaps a Vietnamese student. Pete never missed an opportunity to encourage Lily to say 'Mum' and 'Dad,' pointing to us as he did so, and repeating it. The first time she said "Mum-mum" and lifted her arms up to me, we were all there, and our clapping and "Good girl, clever girl" soon had her repeating it again and again.

On Pete's last night I prepared a special dinner. Pete had shown me how to make a few Vietnamese dishes and I'd found a Vietnamese cookbook in a local bookshop and wanted to surprise them with some new recipes. The Brooks family, including Oscar, arrived late afternoon, and Lily became the center of attention for Amber and David. Sunny, who was about the same age as Lily, was petite, but still made Lily look like a delicate doll. Lily had been happy in the children's company from the first days after we brought her home, and loved gentle Oscar. Adults were the problem. She still tensed and clung to me if anyone other than Ben, Pete, or I wanted to hold her, much to Cassandra's disappointment.

That evening, after the Brooks family had departed and Lily had been bathed and put in her yellow all-in-one, Pete asked me if he could give her a bottle. He was holding back tears as he fed her and Ben and I had to disappear into the kitchen, busying ourselves washing up. We all went into her bedroom to tuck her up and kiss her goodnight. I pulled the string that set her music box playing a very short version of Mozart's "Elvira Madigan" and we tiptoed out. The music died away and quietness reigned for perhaps ten minutes and then she began to cry. We left her for five minutes, hoping she'd fall back to sleep. But not tonight; perhaps she was overtired, over-stimulated by the big day she'd had. Perhaps she sensed her Uncle Pete was leaving, taking her language with him. Ben went to her first and tried to calm her, then I tried, but to no avail. It was a long ten minutes before Pete appeared at the door. "Shall I have a go?" he said.

Ben and I went back into the main room, tense and exhausted. We'd decided that we shouldn't bring her out of the bedroom when she wouldn't settle; we didn't want her getting the idea that she could stay up longer if she made enough fuss.

Within minutes her crying had stopped and we looked at each other, partly relieved and partly not—how unfair that Pete could calm her when we, her parents, couldn't. We tiptoed to the bedroom door. She was lying in her cot, her eyelids fluttering closed as Pete, his hand on her little hand, sang to her.

When we were back in our easy chairs, stiff whiskies poured and blissful silence from the bedroom, I asked Pete what he'd been singing. "Was it a Vietnamese lullaby?"

His pale skin flushed and he took another sip of his drink.

"Not really; I just make the words up as I go along. It's a common tune in Vietnam, but I don't know the words."

"What were your words?" Ben asked. "What did they mean?"

Pete shrugged. "Just words, nothing in particular."

"They sounded beautiful," I said. "I'd love to know them. Perhaps we could learn them and that would help us calm her. You could write them down and when we find someone to teach us the language we'll ask her to teach us how to say them properly." I reached over to the coffee table and picked up my notebook; the one I recorded every tiny milestone in Lily's life. "Please? Could you write it in here?"

He nodded and took the notebook and wrote a sentence. "That's basically all it was. I just repeated it."

Ben and I looked at it - Đi ngủ đi con gái của tôi—and tried to say it. Hopeless.

Pete grinned and repeated it and we tried again.

"Better," he said. "Keep practicing."

"What does it mean?" I thought I recognized one word, *ngủ* - sleep—from the words we had learned this week.

Pete was blushing again. "Go to sleep my baby daughter."

"Oh, that's perfect, thank you," I said, my heart weeping for him.

Ben had got up and was over at Pete's chair. He took the whisky glass from his hand and pulled him up and hugged him. I blinked hard and stayed where I was.

"It's OK," I heard him say. "She's yours too, Pete."

He told us about Nhu then. He had met her in a Saigon nightclub on his first tour in Vietnam. His Unit spent a few weeks of intensive orientation in Saigon before embarking on active duty. Nhu worked as a barmaid, and lived with her grandparents, parents and seven younger siblings in a shack in one of the poorest areas of the city. She was nineteen, beautiful, and smart, and it was love—for Pete and he believed for her—at first sight. After that they met whenever he got a leave pass and could get into Saigon. Their only way of being together was to pay for a room in one of the dives that catered to servicemen, renting out basic rooms by the hour.

When Nhu discovered she was pregnant he stopped her having a backstreet abortion, determined to find a way to marry her and bring her and their baby back to Australia. When their battalion returned to Australia in the June of 1968 he had seen their one-month old daughter—they'd named her Linh, gentle spirit—only twice.

He managed to keep in touch with Nhu through letters and photos he sent to his army mates in Vietnam. They took them to Nhu and sent her letters and reels of film taken with a camera Pete had given her, back to Pete. By the time his battalion was ordered to return to Vietnam in May 1970, he had made contact with a chaplain in Saigon who was willing to marry them. But just before they arrived in Saigon, on the sixth of May, Viet Cong terrorists killed hundreds of civilians in raids throughout the city. Nhu and Linh, now two years old, were killed along with most of Nhu's family and an estimated 450 other civilians. Pete finally tracked down two of Nhu's younger brothers who had escaped slaughter by hiding in a storm water drain for three days. Only then did he stop hoping.

Neither Ben nor I spoke during Pete's almost emotionless telling of his story. When he'd told it, he sat stooped, with his elbows on his knees, his hands and head dropped low. My throat was still tight and aching when Ben managed to get out some words.

"Would you show us some photos?" he said. Not "I'm sorry, that's terrible, shit man, I understand now," or anything else trite, but simply "Would you show us some photos?"

Pete stood up and went into his room. After a minute or two he came back and handed Ben a scruffy, bulging envelope. "There are a few there." Then he disappeared back into his room.

We looked through them: Nhu sparkling and lively; Pete buzz-haired and so young; a tiny dark-haired baby; a family outside a shack, Nhu in the middle; and then photo after photo of a little girl growing up, sometimes alone and sometimes with other children or older people who must be her grandparents and great-grandparents, and sometimes with Nhu. Every black and white image spoke of love.

Around midnight Ben disappeared from our bed and I heard the murmur of their voices as I dozed and woke and dozed again. Ben crept back to bed as the dark window was beginning to lighten, and we slept locked together until Lily woke us at seven. When Ben stumbled into the kitchen to get her bottle and make us a cup of tea, Pete had gone. The note he'd left for us said simply, "Thanks, I thought I'd get on my way before Lily woke. Kiss her for me. Love, Pete." And below the note was a photo of Linh with a wide smile, aged about two. On the back was written "For Lily, your cousin Linh in Saigon, April, 1970. Now a gentle spirit, Love, Uncle Pete."

After Pete left, Lily was puzzled for a while, babbling a name that we decided was her name for Pete. A few days later Aunt Cathie phoned. Pete had appeared on their doorstep the day he left us in Brisbane. He'd come to tell them about Nhu and Linh. She and Uncle William were heart broken, but relieved too, as they felt it was a turning point for Pete. Before he had flown back to Melbourne he had seemed already more like the Pete they remembered from before he went to war.

We began our Vietnamese lessons, taught by a patient student who came to our apartment every Sunday morning and stayed for a Vietnamese lunch. Lily listened in, delighted as we practiced her beautiful but oh so difficult language. She continued to thrive and was soon toddling confidently, even without Ben or me in sight.

Cassandra and Sebastian finally became part of Lily's trusted circle and I began taking her to a mother-and-baby morning twice a week, organized by the overseas adoption support group. We became friends with the two families—Sebastian's clients—who had also adopted Babylift babies. One family had adopted a little boy of two, and he thrived along with Lily. The other family had a terrible time with their baby girl, who became very sick and spent two months in hospital before she died. Sebastian was shattered and made it his mission to find them another baby who had been medically assessed and was considered healthy before he even told them about her. Ten months later they had a beautiful Sri Lankan daughter.

We were one of the lucky Babylift parents. Because Lily had been abandoned, we were able to go through the formal adoption procedures in July, just three months after we met her. We were asked to decide on a birthdate. A date in 1974 of course, the year before her flight from Vietnam. We chose the eighth of April, the day we met her, the day we fell in love.

Chapter Eighteen

Brisbane, April, 1976

A River Through Time, published a year after Lily's arrival, flopped so badly it couldn't even be found in those remainder troughs outside cigarette-selling newsagents. This was in spite of the New Zealand publisher making a nice job of it and it receiving two generous reviews in the main New Zealand newspapers, and another in a popular women's magazine. Distribution attempts in both New Zealand and Australia had been modest but not modest enough, and I'm guessing that ninety percent of my total sales were courtesy of the book launch generously hosted by my favorite small independent bookstore in Brisbane, with Cassandra throwing herself into spreading the word and organizing fingerfood and wine. We'd had quite a crowd as a consequence and I sold out of books; all thirty of them. Three months after the launch my bestselling debut was dead in the river. I told myself I didn't care, and that my passion was editing the novels of real writers. In truth it was mothering that filled me up and sent me into a dreamless sleep within minutes of climbing into bed each night.

I'd semi-reluctantly returned part-time to Stoddard and Jones six months after Lily's arrival, but by the time her second birthday came around I'd begun to itch for something more. Upping my hours at the publishing house? Pottery, painting, a night-class on the dark history of Australia? Nothing appealed. So I began again to write. It was a struggle. By the time I'd picked Lily up from crèche, made dinner, and we'd gone through the bath and story routine before sleep time, I was too tired to focus, and on the days I stayed home, she was home. I fancied I'd found a story I could make sing, but I couldn't get into it. When I grumbled to Louise about my procrastination—for heaven's bloody sake, I had two authors with babies and they seemed able to write while breast feeding—she asked me what my story was about. "Three very different families who meet at an overseas adoption support group, and their interactions and ups and downs as they go through the adoption process. That's the frame at least," I said. "It should be easy."

Louise shook her head. "Far too soon. Perhaps by the time Lily is a teenager you'll be distanced enough to use your own experiences as a stepping-stone for fiction. Even if you decide to write a memoir, you'll need distance first."

My shoulders lifted as my guilt flew away. Until Lily was a lot older, I'd put all my creative efforts into editing the manuscripts of other authors, especially incredible mothers who could do with as much support as I could give them.

When I told Ben, he high-fived me. "Thank god for Louise," he said. "How about we drop Lily off with Cassandra and go to the movies tonight?"

Brisbane, April, 1978

We celebrated Lily's fourth birthday in style. Birthdays for four-year-olds are really an excuse for an adult party. Obviously no parents are going to dump their toddlers and leave. Cassandra offered their home with the garden and pool as the venue, rapidly following her offer with "Sebastian and I'll be assistants, that's all. It will be your party. I promise absolutely, truly, deeply, that I won't take over."

When I repeated her lavish promise to Ben, he was delighted. "Sebastian must have beaten her over the head with a dead mouse to get her to agree to that."

We were tempted by her offer. Our pool-free, garden-free apartment was already causing us to count our pennies, looking for ways we could acquire our own house. A place to call home. The problem was our standards. My standards primarily. I wanted a house with a garden; a home that would last us forever.

But it didn't take us long to decide we'd have Lily's party in our apartment, however humble. Cassandra didn't invent ever more reasons why this would be a bad plan, and Sebastian came up with a doozy of an idea. "Live music, that's what you want," he said. He had his best mischievous grin on, so I assumed he was joking.

"These are four-year-olds, not teenagers," Cassandra said.

"Amber loved dancing to our music when she was four."

"Oh me, oh my, the man is referring to the one and only Krazy Killara Jug Band." Ben struck a pose and began playing an imaginary banjo, making vaguely tuneful plucking noises with his lips. Sebastian grabbed a milk jug from the table and held it to his mouth, farting merrily in time with Ben's plucking. Before you could say Mr. Bojangles I was boom boom booming in my deepest voice and hauling back those strings on ye old double bass, and Cassandra—six months pregnant—was in full voice, her bluegrass, hoe-down country finest.

Our kids appeared at the door; they'd been playing perfectly happily in Lily's bedroom. Sunny and Lily instantly got the fever and joined in, each dancing to their own tune.

Amber and David looked briefly aghast but soon capitulated. It was some minutes before we came to an extended, loud, and energetic finale and fell on the floor, the kids immediately taking advantage and jumping on top of us.

"You can't be serious?" I said, when I'd stopped giggling. "What would our guests think? The adult ones, I mean."

"They'd be into it. Let's do it, I say," said Sebastian. "Then we'll *all* have fun."

"Every morning, every evening, Ain't we got fun?" sang Cassandra, twirling around with Amber.

"Not much money, Oh, but honey, Ain't we got fun?" we all hollered.

And so we did. Sebastian, bless his hoarder's heart, had carefully stored my tea-chest double bass, his bongos and Cassandra's washboard and shakers in the shed on their new property. Cassandra's core still hid a seam of golden flower child—I was pretty sure that would glow when she was six feet under—and her treasured collection of jugs now graced an elegant corner of their elegant floor in their elegant hallway. Ben would never give up his instruments; he even played them occasionally, sometimes to amuse Lily. I hadn't realized how much I'd missed our music making. For Ben it must have been so much more of a void.

The final party count was fourteen adults and seven kids aged from one to seven. The Brooks family, the other two Babylift families and a young couple with a little girl who Lily had befriended at crèche—well more accurately, whose mother I had befriended. Louise and Jonathan of course. And Meredith, our fiddler from the olden days; an invitation to her was essential once we'd decided to stage a comeback tour of the Krazy Killara Jug Band. Pete didn't need an invitation. He'd become a regular house guest, arriving for a long weekend about every six weeks, always overloaded with treats for Lily and the Brooks children, and cheese, chocolate and wine for we adults.

It was, we reflected, in the midst of the chaos after the guests had departed, a success. No-one left early, no kids were sick, the adults got on and no-one got completely blotto. The Jug Band went off like a didgeridoo on moonshine. Our unsuspecting new friends were probably a tad bemused and bewildered, but they soon revealed their hippie hearts and our intimacies sprang to new heights. We gained a comb-and-tissue diva, a spoons maestro, and in Pete, a bongo drum-plus-saucepan banger with a rhythmic ability far superior to Sebastian's.

Lily did have a screaming fit when everyone had left and I tried to put her to bed. "Overtired, overstimulated," we said wisely, and had another glass of wine, chilled out—us, not the red wine—to the max as our favorite James Taylor rendition of "You've Got a Friend" set us smooching. How very satisfying it was to be so normal; a real family with a gorgeous four-year-old, and friends who loved to dance.

CASSANDRA'S BABY WAS DUE ON JULY 2ND, AND SHE ASKED ME to come to Killara for the birth. I was thinking up excuses when she reminded me that I'd missed Aunt Cathie's previous two birthdays. They were going to celebrate her sixty-second on July 5th. So I negotiated some leave in return for working four days a week when I returned to Brisbane. Ben stayed behind with a full-on research schedule, and Lily and I flew with Sebastian, Amber and David to Cairns; for me it would be a ten-day break. The airlines didn't permit heavily pregnant women on their planes, so Cassandra had driven up with Sunny a week earlier. Even with a stomach so huge she could barely reach the steering wheel, she seemed to have no problem with the three-day marathon. Timing wasn't an issue as we all knew Cassandra's baby's arrival would be exactly as planned. As she had so far produced girl, boy, girl in that order, she said this latest would be a boy, and that he'd be born three days before Aunt Cathie's birthday.

And so he was. Fred. Not Frederick, but plain Fred. Sebastian chose the boy's names: David and Fred. Cassandra chose the girl's names: Amber and Sunny.

"Let's go into Port Douglas for lunch," Aunt Cathie said, two days after the birth. "Just you and me. I want to hear all about your editing and your writing. Sebastian can mind Lily along with his rowdy lot. I've got to pick up some supplies for my birthday dinner, anyway."

By the time our pears in red wine sauce were set in front of us I had spilled out all my angst about my failed ability to write. "Sorry," I said. "I thought I was over this writing fantasy. It's not as if I don't love my work as an editor. And every minute I'm away from Lily I want to be back with her." I felt Aunt Cathie's hand on mine, and I smiled at her, blinking away the ridiculous tears that came out of nowhere.

"Olivia, there is no rule that says a woman can't follow many passions. In fact I believe that the more passions you have the better person you'll be and the better mum and wife as well. The very first thing William said to me after you arrived at Killara, such a sad and self-contained child, was that you were a writer."

"I'm sure I never admitted that. I was in awe of him, especially when Cassandra told me he wrote books that won prizes."

"I asked William what gave him that idea, and he said it was because your eyes shone when he showed you the library and when you talked about books. He recalled that he'd offered to read anything you wrote if you wanted another writer's opinion, and you literally glowed."

"God, how embarrassing. I do remember him saying that though." Dear Aunt Cathie, her face so soft. I leaned over and kissed her cheek. "How can I ever thank you both. I'm not sure I ever have. You gave me such a wonderful life, so much love and caring."

"We loved you from the first moment. We have as much to thank you for."

"Heavens, this was meant to be a happy pre-celebration of your birthday, not a crying jag," I said, grinning as I pulled a pack of tissues from my bag and passed one to her.

"It's time I told you more about your mother, and what she meant to me," Aunt Cathie said, when we'd stuffed our screwed-up tissues in our bags. "Would you let me? I think I'm ready at last, after all these years. And now that you have your own little daughter, your mother's story will mean so much more."

I yanked another tissue from the pack and dabbed at my eyes.

"Why don't we take a walk along Port Douglas beach?" said Aunt Cathie. "That seems like a good place to talk. It's a long story so it will need a long beach. Who knows, perhaps some of what I tell you will find its way into one of your novels. Jess would love that; she'd be so proud."

We walked in silence for ten minutes. "Perhaps it's a story you could write?" I said. "Lots of people find writing therapeutic. Uncle William could give you some guidance if you needed it, and I'd love to as well if that would be helpful."

"No, I could never write any of it down. Talking about it will be hard enough, but I owe it to you and Jess."

"It's OK, Aunt Cathie. I don't need to know. Why should you bring it all back now? Let it be."

Aunt Cathie stopped walking and turned towards the blue sea, so peacefully empty of people and only one yacht in sight. "I've thought about it a lot since you lost your baby and almost lost yourself," she said, her voice quivering a little. "I wanted to tell you your mum's story then, to help you understand. Jess was inspirational for so many of us in the prison camps. She showed us what it is possible to endure if you hang on to hope."

An acrid smell invaded my nostrils and I gagged, slamming my hands over my mouth. Mum was there, staring at me behind my closed eyelids. If I reached out I could touch her, lying on her side, vomit coating the pillow beneath her white face. Heart thumping, I swallowed and swallowed, willing myself not to vomit.

"Olivia, are you OK?" Aunt Cathie rubbed my back.

I nodded and lowered myself onto the sand. Aunt Cathie sat down beside me.

"Sorry, sorry," I said. "Mum… how she looked when I found her… it all came back to me."

"Oh love. I should never have brought it up."

"That hasn't happened for a long time. I'd forgotten how awful it was every time I allowed myself to think about it." I looked down at our hands, Aunt Cathie's stroking the back of mine. I breathed in slowly and out again, in and out, and my heart gradually calmed. "I'm OK now. Let's walk again."

We continued along the beach in silence as I struggled to get my thoughts straight. Should I try and explain? Poor Aunt Cathie, after all this time getting up the courage to tell me things she'd found too painful to talk about, even to Uncle William or her own children, and I reject her.

"When you said how inspirational Mum was, it brought back the worst times for me," I finally said. "I know there were good times too, and I know she loved me, but mostly all I can remember are all the days she was too depressed or drunk to even get out of bed." I stopped and turned to Aunt Cathie. "How could she kill herself, knowing I would be the one who would find her? I was only thirteen."

"I can't answer that, and I can't understand it any more than you can. I have to believe that she didn't mean to die. The Jess I knew would never have left her child. Never."

"I've told myself that too, over and over. What else can I

think when I look at Lily? How can any mother leave her child, hurt her child?"

"Only when she is so depressed and so very very traumatized that she can no longer think straight or manage herself."

"But you went through the same hell as she did, and you're the best mother in the world."

"The luckiest mother, perhaps, and I have William. When we were in the prison camp it was Jess who was the strong one, and she saved me. Me and my child."

"Your child? You had a child?"

"Yes, for a while. He died in the camp but he would have died much sooner if it hadn't been for Jess."

"Does Cassandra know?"

Aunt Cathie shook her head. "I've never been brave enough to tell her or Pete. William knows. He met my little boy before Singapore fell. When we were all so young and naive."

"You knew Uncle William back then? I thought you met in Australia after the war. That's what Cassandra told me."

"In Singapore we were part of the same young crowd, mostly Australians and Kiwis, drinking and dancing at Raffles. I was in denial about what was happening in the real world. All I did back then was look after my baby while Charles—he was my husband—was away at sea. I'd met him within a month of arriving in Singapore. The first time I'd ever been away from Australia. Waitressing on a working holiday."

I looked over at her, but she was somewhere else, her gaze towards the horizon. After a while she continued. "William knew what was going on outside our cocoon; he'd been turned down as a serviceman because of flat feet, so he signed up as a war correspondent with the Australian Broadcasting Service. They were lucky to get him, he'd just completed his PhD in English literature. And Jess knew more than the rest of us as well. She was working as a nurse in Singapore. You must know that?"

"I did know that, and that when Singapore fell the ship she was on with hundreds of evacuees was sunk by the Japanese, and that she spent years in prison camps. I tried to find out more from her but she'd get angry. She said that talking about the war and all the terrible things it did to people gave it respect it didn't deserve."

"You were only a child. How could any mother tell her child about such atrocities? I still can't tell my children."

"I understand that now, but back then I felt shut out. If she could have talked to me, perhaps I could have helped her. At least I would have understood why she was so messed up." I'd stopped trying to hide my tears.

Aunt Cathie didn't say anything. I'd made her feel bad now. Why couldn't I keep my selfish thoughts to myself?

"You and Mum were on the same ship?" I asked, after we'd walked a while.

She nodded. "Me and Andrew. He was only three."

Chapter Nineteen

We turned back then, stopping for a cup of coffee in a café almost empty of happy beach goers. We needed to ground ourselves in this modern world before driving home to Killara, and the chaos of kids and birthday preparations. I tried to find a happier topic.

"Were you and Mum close friends when you lived in Singapore?" I asked.

"Social acquaintances, that's all. We were pretty different. Me with my baby and social life. Even servants. It's not that we had much money; all we white people had servants. Jess lived in the nurses' home attached to the hospital she worked in. She was a pioneer really. After training in New Zealand she was in the first small group of NZ nurses who joined the Australian nurses in Singapore. For Jess, sun-downers at Raffles gave her a chance to forget the maimed young soldiers she nursed in the hospital."

"And your husband…?"

"He was a navy lieutenant and on leave when Singapore fell. It was his ship we were all crammed on to."

"Was he in a camp too?"

Aunt Cathie's hands came to her mouth and her eyes screwed shut.

Why couldn't I shut up? Find something pleasant to talk about? "Let's not talk about this any more," I said, pouring another glass of water and pushing it towards her. "You're exhausted. You can have a nap while I drive home."

"Charles and many of the other servicemen who made it to the beach in Sumatra after we were sunk were massacred by the Japanese. Marched just out of our sight and shot."

I took her hand. I didn't know what else to do.

"When we were finally discovered in the camps and shipped back to Darwin, William somehow tracked us down in the hospital we ended up in. We were all pretty weak. I wasn't too bad. Not like some of the others." Aunt Cathie's voice was so soft I had to strain to hear her. "If it hadn't been for William, encouraging me to start living again, I'm not sure what would have happened to me. My father had died while I'd been away, and my mum had aged terribly. She'd lost my brother as well. He was killed in Greece in 1941." She picked up the glass and took a sip then put it down again. The sun slanting through the café window emphasized the fine lines around her violet eyes, and I could see she was far away. The waitress came past and collected our coffee cups and said something. I shook my head and she moved off.

Aunt Cathie blinked hard. "Why William fell in love with me I'll never understand. I looked like a walking skeleton. But he did..."

"He'd loved you ever since he met you in Singapore?"

"I didn't even know he'd fancied me back then. Hadn't a clue." She laughed and I started. I too had forgotten where we were. Out the café window I'd been seeing war ships on the ocean off Port Douglas beach, and barbed wire along the sea front.

"What happened to Mum when she left the hospital?" I asked.

Aunt Cathie's eyes overflowed as she took both my hands in hers. "She went back to New Zealand. I'll never forgive myself. I knew that she was in a dark, dark place. I should never have let her go back. I abandoned her when she needed me most. In my very darkest times in camp she never abandoned me."

THANK GOODNESS FOR CHAOS. ONCE BACK AT KILLARA IT took over and gave us both a way to bury our sadness. Aunt Cathie's birthday was wonderful, although as it neared midnight it seemed to me the shadow behind her eyes deepened. Two days later, when we were all back to our normal routine, she appeared on the deck of the Shack where Lily and I were staying.

"I have a plan," she said, her eyes soft as she scooped up Lily and held her close. "Why don't we turn this into a research project? Lots of novelists do research for their books."

"You mean about you and Mum?"

She nodded. "I wouldn't want the true story told without Jess's agreement, and that can never happen now—but I know it will inspire you. Perhaps it can become a novel. Even if it isn't the true story, it would still honor your mother and all those women who have been forgotten."

"Your story as well," I said.

"Yes, mine as well. I can't talk about it with Cassandra and Pete, not yet. Pete is still grappling with his own war traumas, and baby Fred needs a calm, happy mother."

"Are you sure? They're your children. I think they'd want to know."

Aunt Cathie sighed. "It's me I suppose. I'm not ready to tell them. Our research project might help me to work through it and find the words to share it with them one day."

"What will we tell Cassandra?"

"The truth, I suppose. I'll talk to Cassandra. It's my problem, not yours. I'll explain that I'm telling you because it's your mother's story, and I owe Jess that." She sighed again. "Even William only knows bits of it."

My stomach lurched. How did I get into this? I didn't want to know any more. I'd closed all the bad memories of Mum off long ago. Nothing Aunt Cathie could tell me could change the truth; that she neglected me.

"Olivia, if my memories inspired you to write a wonderful novel, think how right that would be. Imagine how happy it would make Jess if she could know that all these years later she'd helped you with your writing in such an intimate way."

Aunt Cathie planned to talk to Cassandra that afternoon. I gathered up all the children, except of course for baby Fred, and drove off to another beach, leaving Cassandra with Sebastian and her parents. When we got back around five that evening, Cassandra, Sebastian and little Fred were missing. "They've taken over the Shack for the night," Uncle William told me. "Cassandra needs some time to process this. Do you mind staying here with us?"

Next morning, after a sleepless night, I took off again, this time taking only Lily with me. How ever did we think this would work? Poor Cassandra.

I crept back into the house mid-afternoon and found Cassandra and her parents out on the verandah, empty tea cups and a plate with four scones on the table between them.

I felt like a stranger walking in on them.

Aunt Cathie smiled at me and held out her arms to Lily. "Olivia, I'm so glad you're home. We kept some scones for you both. Sebastian and the kids have gone down to the beach for a swim."

"I'll make another pot of tea," Uncle William said, his

kind eyes creasing up as he looked at me. "You look as if you could do with it."

I nodded, no words to say, or no words to say that I could possibly squeeze out of my tight throat.

"Chill out, Olivia," Cassandra said as soon as I'd sat down. "I've got over my tantrum. I've talked it through with Mum and Dad, and I understand. I'm sad, but I'm not going to let it get to me." She held my gaze as she covered her mother's hand with hers. "I'm so proud of Mum that she's brave enough to talk about it. I wish she would let me listen in, or for you to tell me what you two talk about, but I understand why that would make it too hard for her."

Aunt Cathie stroked Cassandra's long thick hair. Physically, I'd never thought of them as similar, but now I saw that I'd been wrong.

"Sweetheart," Aunt Cathie murmured, "I'm hoping Olivia will write a wonderful novel about another woman, other women, heroic nurses like Jess and ordinary women like me. That will be easier for you and Pete to read."

Cassandra caught her mother's hand and brought it to her lips. "I know, Mum," she said. "I'm sorry I made it harder for you."

"Never. You've never made anything harder for me. Now, my love, I want to hear your laugh again before the children come back and wonder what your father and I have been doing to you." She looked at me, her smile the same one I'd known since I was thirteen. "You too, Olivia. No more worried looks."

I sniffed and grinned at her, and then at Cassandra.

"Come here, you," she said, and our hug was still happening when Uncle William plonked down the teapot.

Chapter Twenty

Sebastian and school-kids Amber and David had to return to Brisbane the next day, but the rest of us had another week. We set up a schedule. Every morning Aunt Cathie and I would sit on a shady part of the verandah at the side of the house, a cord from a power point snaking through the open window to my tape recorder on the low table between our old easy chairs. We began after breakfast and at mid-morning Cassandra or Uncle William would ring the bell that had always been used to alert missing children to lunch or dinner. That was the sign for us to move to the front verandah or lawn where our morning tea would be set out—iced tea, scones or dainty cucumber sandwiches, sometimes a scrumptious chocolate or carrot cake. All prepared by Cassandra. Uncle William had no lectures that week so was able to stay home and work on his own writing. He always appeared when the cake did, and the kids ran in and out, grabbing food and drinks and vanishing again.

Around eleven, Aunt Cathie and I would reluctantly return to our work stations and continue until half-past twelve when the bell would ring again for lunch. After lunch, we'd all doze or read. But before I dozed I would make brief notes about what that morning's tape included. Aunt Cathie had decided to tell me her story in chronological order as much as possible, and that helped, and a trip to the Cairns library to read what I could find about the fall of Singapore and the horrific Sumatra prison camps filled in some of the background. I was shocked at how little there was. Aunt Cathie was right; these women prisoners, many of them civilians, had been forgotten.

Afternoons and evenings were for relaxing, swimming, hiking, making huts in the tangled rain forest. Once I'd made my notes I tried not to think about any of it; when we began again next morning was soon enough. Unfortunately my off-duty mind had other ideas. Sometimes I couldn't get to sleep and sometimes I woke in the early hours, horror freezing me to my hot sheets as whatever nightmare I had been immersed in faded.

One morning, Aunt Cathie asked me how I was coping. "You look worn out, dear. I think this is all too much. Why don't we have a break for a few days?"

Too much for me to hear? I could feel my insides curling in shame. It was unimaginable, the things that had happened to Aunt Cathie, and we were only as far as her evacuation by ship with thousands of other civilians and servicemen. A ship that my mother was also on. We were still only in March, 1942, and I knew that the internment camps in Sumatra hadn't been freed until late in 1945.

And it *was* almost too much for me to cope with, sitting on a peaceful verandah in the Australian tropics listening to Aunt Cathie's still vivid memories of herself as a young woman working as a waitress in a hotel in Singapore, falling in love with a young naval officer stationed there, becoming a mother for the first time, drinking and dancing at Raffles. The disbelief as she and Andrew were taken by her husband to the docks and pushed up the gangplank of an already overloaded ship. The relief that Charles was on the same ship, and found her the second night and lay with his long arms around her and Andrew on the hard deck, sandwiched between hundreds of others until his turn on watch. The fear and chaos when the very next day the Japanese attacked them. Scrabbling for life jackets and the relief when Charles appeared with one small enough for Andrew. His strong hands tying Andrew to her chest with Cathie's long blue scarf. Jumping over the side, her eyes closed, thinking Charles would follow. The noise of the ship breaking in two and her desperation to get away from the flames roaring and spitting debris on the giant swell that sucked and pulsed across the ocean as the ship sank, pulling her down with it. Kicking, kicking, Andrew's face jammed hard into her chest, coming up spluttering, Andrew coughing up water, the sea on fire and no ship. The masked faces of the Japanese bomber pilots staring down at her as she tried to cover Andrew with her body without drowning him, the screaming of the planes, the staccato of the guns as their bullets ripped across the water setting bodies leaping into the air before floating or disappearing below the crimson ocean.

The man who reached down from a crowded lifeboat and grabbed Andrew, Cathie's desperation as she tried to reach other hands stretching down as the lifeboat lurched away, the relief when it turned and came back and she was hauled up the side, landing on top of Andrew, his screams the sweetest sound she'd ever heard. Five days of tropical sun beating down, the boat getting less crowded as the dead were hoisted over the sides with a quick prayer to take them to the bottom of the sea. The thirst, the unbearable thirst, the urge to gulp down the few sips she allowed herself from her own ration after Andrew had sucked his and most of hers from the tin cup. The kindness of the teenager who gave her own ration to Andrew as her gunshot-smashed stinking mess of leg sucked the life out of her. The swim when finally, finally, land appeared. A swim through breakers that crashed her and her precious boy down on sharp coral, stinging and adding to the festering cuts and scrapes already covering them. Forced to sit on the mosquito-infested beach, her three-year-old tight to her chest, his crying silenced by exhaustion and starvation. No-one crying, no-one speaking, only coughing, spluttering, moaning as slit-eyed Japanese surrounded them, bayonetted rifles ready to kill. More people washing onto the beach, crawling through the gentle waves lapping the sand. A boat full of men, navy men, one of them taller than the others. Staggering up the beach, uniforms barely recognizable, faces swollen and burnt.

"Charles, Charles." Her voice a croak. Standing up, waving both her arms. "Charles, I'm here, I'm here." Her head cracking, pain searing through her, her face hitting the sand, Andrew whimpering, a gun above her threatening to hit her again. Watching through the soldier's legs for the tallest man as the men are hit and herded and marched along the beach and around the point. Jumping, jumping as gunshots ricochet through the air, through her screaming head, on and on. Forced along the beach with the other women and children, around the point and past the pile of bodies. Hit by a rifle butt, the Japanese soldier with the face of a child dragging her away from the edge of the pile and a body so gangly she knew it was Charles, the man she loved, the father of her son.

"No, no, I don't need a break. But you do, Aunt Cathie. I feel terrible that I'm putting you through this. We don't have to do this. It's too much."

The look on her face was almost funny. Surprise? Determination?

"I want to tell you. I want you to hear it. It's a relief to realize how clearly I can remember it all. So often back then I feared I was losing my mind. But for you to hear it for the first time—that's why I couldn't tell Cassandra and Pete." She leaned over and touched my cheek. "I was no hero, but so many of the women were. Your mother especially. I know it's hard now, but one day you'll write a story that will help you understand, and Cassandra and Pete too."

~

I WAS COMMITTED TO WRITING A NOVEL NOW, AND ASKED Louise for another week's leave. We waved Cassandra goodbye as she set off with Sunny and Fred on the long drive back to Brisbane, and Aunt Cathie and I resumed our daily interviews.

They were precious, those days with Aunt Cathie, although without Lily's cute chatter and wide smile greeting me when I emerged from the filth and disease and hunger of the Japanese prison camps, I would have crumbled. Sketching an outline for the novel also helped me draw an emotional line between fact and fiction. When Aunt Cathie and I were locked in the past, Lily played happily in the library while Uncle William read and wrote, my girl proudly ringing the bell for morning tea and lunch. She and her Poppa—the Brooks children's name for their grandfather—even made scones on occasions. I'd never had grandparents and often wished Ben's parents didn't live so far away. I wanted Lily to have all the family love I never had. So the bonding going on between her and Poppa and Grandma—Aunt Cathie—filled me with joy.

I could find only one book that gave any insights into the lives of the women imprisoned in the Japanese camps; *White Coolies* was a nurse's memoir published in 1954. Had most of those women survivors, like Aunt Cathie, keep their memories from their families as well as away from public scrutiny? Was this to protect their families from distress, or was it the only strategy they had available to deal with the trauma? My long felt anger over the Australian and US Governments' treatment of the victims—soldiers included—of the Vietnam War was swallowed by a new fury. Why had so many governments stayed silent about these women and men who were left to their 'fates' for four interminable years after the fall of Singapore?

I began to think of my mother as Jess, rather than Mum. The two were hard to reconcile in my tired head and aching heart. Cathie remembered Jess as a natural leader in the camps. "She was an experienced nurse; nothing seemed to phase her. When we were sick, in our hut the only face we wanted to see was hers. Once when she had been staying in another hut for two nights because they had so many cases of typhoid fever, three of our women marched over there and dragged her back. We had fewer cases because of Jess's regime of trying to keep things clean, but one of our children was burning up. Jess could be tough—behind her back some of the women called her 'Mother Crocodile'—but she had our respect. She knew how to raise us up when we lost hope." Aunt Cathie smiled. "Like you, she had a way with words."

It took a long time for Aunt Cathie to find the courage to tell me what happened between her and Jess that elevated my mother from leader to savior. The Japanese guards were cruel but disciplined; physical and emotional abuse of their women prisoners under the guise of punishment was a daily occurrence, but sexual abuse was rare. Early in their imprisonment a soldier discovered raping one of the women was shot, and his victim was tied to a pole in the middle of the yard in the searing heat without water or food for three days and nights. Almost unconscious, she was then thrown into the isolation cell. They saw her body being dragged away next day.

I knew, the morning Aunt Cathie told me this, that something terrible was coming, and I found it impossible to eat the biscuit and cheese Lily offered me so sweetly. "Sorry, darling, I ate too much breakfast," I said, my stomach churning.

"Perhaps we should leave it for today," Aunt Cathie said, when we were back in our interview chairs.

I shook my head. "No, tell me please. It won't get any easier if you leave it."

"I'd taken Andrew to the latrines. It was dark but he had diarrhea. We all had the runs most of the time. There was a moon, I remember, and that made it a bit easier. The rats were everywhere, day and night, but fearless at night. Andrew was terrified of them. We were coming back when I was jumped by one of the guards, the most vicious of them all. He shoved me down in the stinking mud and I shouted to Andrew to run back to the hut. The guard kicked him and he fell over and sat there screaming. Then I was hit across the face so hard I nearly passed out. No one came. No one. The hut was only a few yards away."

She was shaking, and I put my hand on her arm.

"I heard her before I saw her," Aunt Cathie said. "Jess. The guard already had his pants down and was trying to untangle my dress from the mud. Jess was standing right there, pushing him off me. 'That woman has venereal disease,' she yelled. 'THE POX.'"

Aunt Cathie screwed her eyes tight, her face white under her tan. "God knows how he understood, but somehow Jess got through to him. She'd been learning Japanese—she'd had to treat sick guards as well so she probably knew the words for sickness and disease at least, probably the Japanese word for Pox; nothing about Jess would surprise me. Venereal disease was common enough in the soldiers she nursed in Singapore. The guard spat at her and butted her with his head. I thought he was going to let me go. But he was disgustingly aroused,"—she shuddered—"and he grabbed my legs and forced them open. Andrew was screaming and Jess was shouting, and then she pulled her shorts down, then her pants, and pushed herself, jutted her… her hips… in his face. 'I want it, do it with me,' she said, almost sexually, almost as if she wanted him. 'I'm clean, I haven't got the pox. Take me.' And she sat down on me so I was under her, her legs open wider than mine and I felt her whole body jump. He was ramming into her and pumping up and down, I could feel every thrust through my body—he must have been ripping Jess in pieces. Andrew was crying so hard he was hiccupping and I tried to call to him to go to the hut. Jess's back was squashing my face so I couldn't breathe and then she rolled off me into the filth and the brute was gone."

The vomit burned up into my throat and clamping my hand over my mouth I lurched to the balustrade. Leaning over it I emptied my breakfast into the bushes below.

Chapter Twenty-One

Uncle William found us there on the verandah. My retching had brought him running.

He looked after us both as if we were sick, running us baths, putting scented oil in them, making us soft boiled eggs and toast, tucking us up on the couches in the library and playing soft beautiful music on the stereo. Lily stayed with us, 'reading' stories to her doll and perhaps to us, and after her afternoon nap returned dressed in a child-sized nurse's outfit Aunt Cathie had in her big trunk of dress-ups for the grandchildren. I opened my mouth so she could pop the thermometer in, frowning and shaking her head when she took it out and looked at it. The irony was not lost on me; that my daughter's way of making her mother and grandma smile again was to nurse them. I had memories of Mum in a nurse's uniform. For a while, off and on, she'd worked in old peoples' homes, although I don't think she ever went back to hospital nursing after the war.

It seemed like days before we had the courage to resume our 'research' interviews. Uncle William wanted us to stop completely. "I thought that talking about it all would be healing. Cathie love, you were right. Some things need to be buried forever. I'm sorry." He had tears in his eyes as Cathie went into his arms, and I backed out of the room. Ten minutes later he found me and apologized.

"It's not your fault," I said. "I needed to know. She was my mother."

"She saved Cathie and Andrew. That's what you must keep clear in your head."

I nodded. He seemed to need my forgiveness.

Aunt Cathie understood better. "Tell me when you're ready to begin again," she said next morning.

"Begin again?"

"With our story. You can't leave Jess there. I can't leave her there."

"What more is there to tell?" My stomach churned. "More horror, more depravity? You could never tell me the truth after this. I'm too cowardly to hear it without breaking down."

"You'll find the strength to hear the truth for my sake as well as yours. For your mother's sake. I need to get it all out now. Do you want to get the tape recorder?"

"WHEN WE CRAWLED BACK INTO THE HUT THE WOMEN WERE all in their bunks, pretending to be asleep. Not one of them asked us if we were OK. Not one. Usually we women supported each other, shared what we had, tried to raise up those of us who were too depressed to live. But that night fear took over. Jess had nursed and helped so many of them, saved the lives of at least three of their children, and this is what they gave her in return."

The heat boiling through me was in Aunt Cathie too. Her eyes were glittering, turning her gentle face into the face of a stranger. She was back there, her hate, her anger, her fear—all of it—raw again. "A few nights later the guard returned to our hut and marched Jess out. She came back with her hair a mess

—she was always telling us we should keep our hair combed because of lice, so for her to have messy hair—and her legs were covered in mud. She crawled into her bunk without saying a word. After the rape, the woman who shared Jess's bunk moved in with another woman whose daughter's death had left a gap. No-one wanted to share with Jess, so Andrew and I shifted to the bunk underneath hers. I tried to talk to her but she shrugged me away. I should have tried harder. No-one else went near her."

I couldn't move, couldn't think, tried not to feel.

"Every few nights after that the brute would be back and Jess would go off meekly with him as if she wanted to. I knew, we all knew, that they were having sex. I finally got her to tell me what he had over her."

"How could she?" The words catapulted out of my mouth. "Perhaps she did want it. That's how I was conceived; a one-night stand." Where did those words come from?

"Listen to me, Olivia. The guard told her that if she didn't have sex with him every time he wanted it, he'd force himself on me and on my Andrew too. Jess knew the guard would be punished, probably shot, if she told the commandant, but she'd be shot as well. That's how the Japanese dealt with sexual misconduct."

Stop. Please stop. I'd somehow got myself into a corner of the verandah, hunched on the boards, my arms around my bent legs, my head buried in my knees.

"Most of the women lost respect for her after that, although they still needed her when they were sick. I tried to tell them why she was doing it, but they wouldn't listen. She was an outcast."

I raised my head and peered up. Aunt Cathie was standing at the verandah railing, looking over the bush. What was she seeing? The steaming jungles of Sumatra?

"But Jess found a way to get the bastard in the end."

Never had I heard her use such a label. She turned around

but her face was in shadow and I couldn't see what was marked on it.

"She offered to work for the camp commandant as his secretary and made herself so valuable to him that she was able to get extra rations and medications for the women and children in our hut, even the ones who were so nasty to her. Of course they could be all sweetness if they saw food coming."

"How did she get him? How did she get the bastard?" I said, standing up and spitting the last word out.

"Once she had the commandant's trust, she told him about the guard. He disappeared the next day. Shot, I hope. With his cruel eyes wide open."

"Oh, my god. What did she have to do to get the commandant's trust? What Aunt Cathie, what did she have to do?" I was shaking her shoulders.

Aunt Cathie grabbed my arms and held them still. "He didn't rape her. I'm sure he respected her. Jess even grew to like him. Not all the Japanese were brutes."

"How can you know that for sure? Jess wouldn't have been able to tell you."

"She told me enough. Her relationship with the commandant was a good one. She came to see him as a friend. She even cared about him. I know it's impossible to believe, but I did believe it."

"How could she? How could she care about the man who was in control of her; who followed such a brutal regime? Was food more important than self-respect? Was it?"

"Until you're starving it's impossible to know what you'd do. Jess somehow found a way to see some good in that one man, and it was that that helped her to survive, not scraps of food. She shared those with all the women. When Andrew was four, he got malaria and would have died if Jess hadn't been able to get quinine from the commandant. I can't think of him as despicable, Olivia. I can only think of him with gratitude."

"But Andrew didn't survive. Jess couldn't save him. Her wonderful Japanese boss's medicines couldn't save him. Why don't you hate him?"

"Andrew died from dysentery and cholera a few months before we were finally found. Jess helped me bury him. So many crosses. I wonder if they're still there, buried in the jungle? Many of the women died of starvation and dysentery, and most of the small children. Even the guards and the commandant were starving by the end."

Lily and I left Killara a few days later, and saying goodbye at Cairns airport was gut wrenching. Lily caught our mood and began to cry, clinging with her brown dimpled arms to her grandma. Her Poppa kissed her and then me, and we stumbled to the end of the boarding queue.

I did tell Ben that story, the true story. I had to tell someone, and it couldn't be Cassandra. For her and Pete I would write a novel, a novel where I could leave out what I couldn't bear to remember, leave out the more-terrible-than-fiction parts I didn't want her and Pete to know.

Before I'd left Killara, Aunt Cathie had decided that William could listen to our tapes. He'd heard the worst, anyway, after my breakdown. So he was the obvious choice for my first editor. I thought about what he'd said to me in his kindly way the day I arrived on Killara's doorstep, orphaned and damaged. If only he'd known back then what his author's eye might one day have to read.

"Be honest with me," I said, when twelve months later I phoned to warn him to expect what I hoped was a reasonable draft of *Daisy's War*.

"Expect nothing else. Not a single dangling participle will escape my red pen."

"Good. But you know that's not all I need. I want to know

whether I've captured the essence of Cathie and Jess's story, but managed to turn it into fiction. I don't want Cathie to have to re-live the worst horrors again and again. She doesn't want thousands of readers she doesn't even know intruding into her and Jess's past."

"No, she's clear about that. And she wants Cassandra and Pete to be let in gradually."

"Will she tell them everything one day?" I asked.

"I don't know. I suspect she would want that to be a joint decision between you and her. She sees you as the guardian of your mother's story."

"My mother's terrible secrets, you mean."

"Is that how you see this? Terrible secrets your mother had a say in?"

"We all have choices."

There was silence on the end of the phone.

"I know what you're thinking," I said. "I know I can't possibly understand how it was for her. I know that. I'm trying to forgive her, but I'm not there yet. How could she be so casual about sex after the war? Tell me that?"

My mouth was desert dry as I handed the packaged manuscript to the postmistress. I'd written it too fast, I'd skirted around the bad bits. Perhaps there was nothing left worth reading?

I'd put everything, everything, into this story. I'd burned through it, draft after draft. Even on the three days each week I worked at Stoddard and Jones I rose at dawn and wrote for three hours, and after Lily was in bed locked myself to my typewriter late into the nights. I agonized over every word, every sentence, hoping they were giving life to gentle Daisy, my protagonist, and her stroppy friend Gillian. On a good day I thought I'd succeeded in capturing their personalities in a way that was *not* Cathie or Jess, but somehow honored them anyway. Their complementary essences— at least as I imagined them as young women— I'd scattered across many of the women in the camp; a bit of Cathie here, a bit of Jess there. Some of the horrors they'd suffered were shared around as well. Not the worst horrors. I was still a long way from confronting the rape and my mother's forced prostitution even in a fictional, watered down version. And my mother's relationship with the commandant would never appear in this or any novel. I couldn't even look at it in my own head.

Chapter Twenty-Two

Brisbane, April, 1979

So many of the milestones in our lives seemed to fall around Lily's birthdays. So in April on the week Lily turned five, Ben and I moved into a home of our own, ten minutes walk from the Brooks house. The mortgage was manageable with Ben's senior lectureship salary and the jaw-dropping advance *Daisy's War* had won. Our garden was perfect; a large, sloping, private bush section with a view of the river—not the panoramic view Cassandra had but a very pretty one never-the-less. It wasn't the rural setting we'd once thought we'd want, but it didn't feel at all like a suburban location.

Yes, we'd finally joined the mainstream; probably the last of our hippy friends to do so. It was all about education, and right-of-entry for Lily to one of the top state schools, the same one Sunny attended. The two girls were inseparable, holding hands as five-year-olds do, going on adventures with their dolls and teddies and wombats and koala bears. One day Cassandra and I were in the kitchen cooling ourselves with iced tea when they appeared in the door frame, hands joined, faces aglow, and announced "We're twins."

"Goodness," said Cassandra. "So you are. How will we ever tell you apart?"

"You can," said Sunny earnestly. "Lily has a green sunhat and I've got a red one." And off they went, satisfied that they'd explained the one difference that would help their mothers tell their daughters apart, one with violet eyes and bouncing golden curls and the other with eyes of chocolate and shining midnight hair swinging past her small shoulders.

Brisbane, April, 1981

We delayed celebrating the publication of *Daisy's War* until after Lily's seventh birthday. We didn't want her to feel second best. I still had flashes of guilt when I thought about the writing schedule I'd stuck to so selfishly when I was writing that book. Never again I told myself.

Now I wrote nine to three on the days I wasn't at Stoddard and Jones, and a couple of hours after Lily had gone to bed. In May I took a few short breaks without pay from my day job, as Ben called it, for book tours around Australia and New Zealand, followed by a two-week tour in the UK. By July I was exhausted and hanging out for a holiday at Killara. Ben's university position was a bonus as his breaks usually coincided with Lily's, and we, with Cassandra and her kids, spent the mid-year break there, determined that no work commitments would distract us. Not a smudge of regret did I feel abandoning the final —hopefully — revision of my third novel. After *Daisy* it had been easy to write, partly because it was a major re-working of the manuscript I had shelved when *Daisy's War* took precedence. I'd decided that the 'fictional' overseas adoption story I'd begun so long ago was too autobiographical, and it had morphed into a novel about a rural

English family who took in two children evacuated from London in WWII and adopted them when their parents were killed.

Cassandra had read *Daisy's War* of course, but she didn't try to get out of me which parts were most closely entwined with her mother's experiences. "I'm not sure I'm ready to go there anyway," she told me. "One day perhaps, when the kids have all left home. David is in tears if he finds a baby bird out of its nest. He can tell if I'm upset however hard I try and hide it."

So our mothers' war was consigned to the shadows, and I began to believe my own fiction; Daisy and her fellow prisoners somehow became the truth, their gruesome but heroic exploits replacing the horrific realities that Jess and Cathie had almost not survived when they were younger than Cassandra and I were now.

By September the English evacuees novel was with my publisher, and to my ongoing disbelief, the hype around *Daisy's War* hadn't abated. I seemed to have broken out at last; the volume of books sold in Australia and UK had elevated me to a best-selling author in those countries. US still to crack.

The pressure was now on to complete a novel every twelve to eighteen months—preferably twelve; the eighteen was insisted on by me at the risk of falling out with my publisher—and I reluctantly resigned from Stoddard and Jones. Some days I yearned for the busy office and nursing my authors up and down and up the mountain track I'd so recently traversed, but on the positive side, writing from my study at home meant I could spend more time with Lily. I wrote from nine to three and never a second longer. A friendly and chatty student came in once a week and vacuumed and cleaned the bathrooms and toilets. I found it hard at first; it seemed a big and somehow rather unethical leap to go from being the child of a mother who cleaned houses when she had the energy, to paying someone to do mine.

"You're living in the dark ages," Cassandra said. "Your student needs the money and your house is a doddle to clean anyway. If you had to do it you'd never meet your deadlines."

My student cleaner chatted nonstop while she cleaned so I got no writing done anyway. Instead of cleaning I got back into cooking and baking and making my own bread, and enjoying Lily's hi-jinx when Sunny or one of her other friends came around to play, and often to stay the night. I resumed my old regime of rising at 5am and writing for three hours.

In October that same year *Daisy's War* was shortlisted for a major literary award. It was a really big thing, with the winner to be announced at a glittering affair in London in late November. It was so ridiculous that in my head it became almost something to be ashamed of. It was a scam. One of the judges must have had a mother who'd been a prisoner of war. They'd been told they had to have at least one woman on the shortlist, and my novel was the only one written by a female that the majority of the three-male-one-female judging panel didn't hate.

My British publishing company was excited—it was their first book ever to make the shortlist—and insisted I go to the awards ceremony. They opened their wallets and coughed up the money for the airfares and accommodation in London for five nights for Ben as well as me. I'd do a short book tour immediately after, whether or not I won—which obviously I wouldn't. Both Pete and his new bubbly Kiwi girlfriend, Julie, were in their second year of a teaching qualification at Melbourne University, and by November their course would have finished for the year, so they offered to stay in our house and look after Lily. Sunny booked herself in for the duration. "Pete's my uncle so it's only fair," she said.

"Ha. This is going to be worth watching," Cassandra

crowed. "If they can survive our terrible twins, teaching classes of 30 will be a doddle."

"And they'll discover whether they can stay together for the long haul," I added.

I WAS INTERVIEWED ON NATIONAL RADIO, ON TV CHAT SHOWS, and on the TV bookclub for literary snobs, a show that had previously ignored me. I told them all that awards and all that jazz didn't matter to me. Nice to be recognized and hopefully good for sales but really? I knew dozens of novels that were better written than mine, were more engaging, more literary, reaped more glowing reviews from eminent reviewers. "It is interesting," agreed the TV bookclub interviewer, failing in her effort not to look down her nose. "*Daisy's War* is such a *commercial* success—I suppose because it's women's fiction." The other three shortlisted novels were all by well-known literary novelists. All men. Mine was the outlier.

Ben had no time for my protests. "Enjoy it. Say after me: 'It's OK to feel good about this. I have bloody well earned it.'"

I didn't go quite that far, but I stopped expressing my doubts. On the day of the award ceremony I was sick with nerves. I had secretly written out a few sentences of thanks, just in case, although I knew it was stupid to even think it possible. Enjoy the moment, I begged myself. Concentrate on all those famous writers you'll meet.

I was nervous about that as well. We'd received the seating plan for the silver service dinner that was to be held in the evening at Claridge's Hotel. My heart practically pounded out of my chest when I read the names of our dining companions. And I was seated next to an author whose books put him easily in my top five.

The award ceremony was at 3pm, and in spite of the afternoon hour, dress was black tie. For Ben that is. For me a long, slinky, dusky-blue gown. I think the idea was that we could go straight from the award ceremony to the bar and get satisfyingly pissed before dinner.

We were ready by 2pm. Ben looked divine and I scrubbed up quite well myself. Then the phone in our bedroom rang.

"Leave it," Ben said. "It's probably the bellboy to tell us our taxi is here."

But I picked it up anyway. Perhaps I had a premonition.

"It's Dad," said Cassandra. "He's had a stroke and…" Her voice filled with tears and my world stopped. I closed my eyes and took a breath. "I'm coming. We'll be there as soon as we can."

Sebastian's voice. "No, no. It's not too bad."

Cassandra's muffled sobs swam across the endless miles of phone line.

Sebastian again. "His doctor doesn't think he's in any danger of another stroke so don't cut your trip short. William will likely be in a better state to see you anyway in a few days."

"Aunt Cathie? Is she OK? Cassandra sounds a mess."

"I'll look after them," Sebastian said. "Cathie is keeping calm. Pete and Julie are flying up from Brisbane today. They're bringing Lily."

"Sorry, sorry, Olivia. I should have waited and phoned you tomorrow. Your awards are today aren't they?" Cassandra's voice wobbled and I felt my face crumpling.

"Go and enjoy your moment, 'Livie," said Sebastian. "Do it for William. Cassandra will be fine. It's just the shock. Her Dad is her rock."

Chapter Twenty-Three

We left instructions with the hotel to book flights for tonight if possible and get the message to us at Claridge's. Any flights, however expensive. If two weren't available, book one.

I wanted to wait while they phoned the airline but Ben made me get in the taxi. In the glittering ballroom I sat in the front row with the other shortlisted authors and took in a word here and there. When the contents of the envelope were read out I sat like a ninny until the man next to me nudged my arm and said, "You need to go up on stage. Congratulations!"

Somehow I got there and took the silver trophy and made some sort of thank-you speech. Then Ben was beside me with his hand on my back, guiding me through the clusters of people with their mouths hanging open and words coming out.

"Are you sure you want to go home?" he asked, when we'd found a quiet corner in the lobby. "We're booked on a flight to Brisbane leaving in three hours, then a connecting flight to Cairns. But we could see if there was a flight tomorrow. It seems a pity to miss the dinner. William and Cathie wouldn't want you to miss it. Cassandra wouldn't either, not really."

"No, now. We must go now. They need me."

~

Twenty-four hours of flying—first class seats and food didn't ameliorate my distress—then another four hours from Brisbane to Cairns. After a late-night arrival we grabbed a taxi and made straight for the hospital. Aunt Cathie and Pete were in the small waiting room at the end of the ward, not talking.

Why aren't they talking? Where's Cassandra? And then Pete was hugging me, and at last I was in Aunt Cathie's arms.

"Olivia, darling, thank you for coming. You didn't need to hurry back." She reached out and took Ben's hand. "But I love you both for doing it."

"Uncle William? Is he…"

"He's tired and still rather confused. It was a significant stroke but not a massive one, but it's near the speech area. So he's having trouble with his speech. His right side is a little weak too."

A shudder whipped through me. "That sounds bad."

"He's alive, and that's all that matters. He'll get his speech back, I'm sure of it." She pulled a handkerchief from somewhere and mopped at my face. "Why don't you go in and see him? They've dosed him up and he's in and out of sleep, but he'll know you're there. Cassandra's with him. Tell her it's time we all got some shut-eye."

"We can't go back to Killara. What if…?"

"We've got three large motel units with a spare room for you and Ben five minutes from here. Sebastian and Julie are there now with the kids," Aunt Cathie said, touching my cheek. "You look as though you could sleep a week."

"Lily? Is she really here too?"

"Of course. That's her Poppa in there." Aunt Cathie

reached for a chair and collapsed into it, tears at last spilling from her eyes.

"Come on Olivia," said Pete, when we'd got ourselves back in line. "I'll show you Dad's room. You can drag that sister of ours away from him. She needs some shuteye too."

Ours? Our sister? Pete thinks of me as their sister?

I held my hand out to Ben but he shook his head. "No, sweetheart. I'll see William tomorrow. It's you he needs to see now."

I tiptoed into the room. It was lit only by two night lights and Cassandra was a shape hunched over the bed.

"I'm here," I whispered, and she jumped and turned around.

"Olivia?"

I tried to smile, but the tears started again. "How is he?" I was still whispering.

Cassandra leaned back and I saw Uncle William's face, his eyes closed, his mouth open and his breath coming in little snores. His hair seemed grayer and his chin and cheeks sprouted stubble. I'd rarely seen him unshaven and never, I suddenly realized, had I seen him asleep. Perhaps he always looked like this when he was asleep? Older. Old. I touched his hand, stroked it, but he didn't stir.

"He looks peaceful," I said.

"He's drugged up, that's why." Cassandra's voice was so full of tears she could barely get her words out.

"Oh, love, come here," I pulled her up and into my arms. "It's OK, he'll be OK, I promise." Her body was heaving and I rocked and rocked her, but she couldn't stop, couldn't calm herself. "Hush, hush, don't cry so."

"I'm not crying. I'm tired, that's all. "

"It's alright to cry. He's your Dad."

She pulled back, her eyes still crying but a tiny smile on her face. She nodded. "How did you get here so quickly? You didn't need to come so fast. Dad's not going anywhere, and I'm fine really."

"You're not fine. You're not fine at all."

"I am. I told you, I'm just bloody tired."

"Oh, Cassandra, it's sort of a relief that you're letting yourself cry. You are always so… so in control, so able to be sensible and together and the one everyone looks up to to make everything right."

She sniffed and hauled a wad of tissues from the pocket of her jeans. She blew her nose and I hauled some tissues from my jeans pocket and blew mine. She grinned at me and I grinned back.

"Wha..aa, wha…"

Cassandra was leaning over the bed before I even realized where the sound was coming from. "Dad, Dad, it's OK. I'm here."

I gazed down at his dear face, his left eye open and looking at us, his right eye fluttering and not quite making it. "Hullo, Uncle William," I said.

"Dad, Olivia's home. She came back early from England especially to see you." She let his hand go and moved aside, pushing me down on the chair.

"Ol, Ol.. Damn," he said, his mouth lopsided and his words slurred. Cassandra leaned over in front of me and wiped the trace of saliva dribbling from the corner of his mouth. "It's OK Dad. Damn is right. You'll soon be able to say everything you want to say again. I'm going to help you. And now Olivia's here you haven't a chance of slacking off. She'll have the whip out if you don't get your participles perfect."

Uncle William's eyes closed and I think the left side of his mouth turned up a bit. We watched him in silence until his breathing became little snores again.

"We'll be back in the morning," Cassandra whispered, and bent and kissed his forehead. As I leaned over to kiss him his left eyelid fluttered open and he raised his left hand and touched my cheek. “Oli, Oli.. Prize?”

I swallowed and nodded. “I won the prize. Your prize too. Yours and Aunt Cathie’s.”

He nodded. “Our.. writ, writer.”

“Oh my god. You won? Shit, Olivia, that’s wonderful. Why didn’t you say?” Cassandra’s face had morphed from sad to happy in a second.

“I’d forgotten. It doesn’t seem very important.”

“It is to Dad, all of us. I’m so proud of you.”

“Thanks. It’ll sink in later I guess. Once your dad is back home.”

Out in the corridor, Cassandra hugged me. "It means everything to Mum and Dad, having you here. And I needed you."

I pulled out of our hug and tried to grin at her. "Who knew you had such a bloody loud voice? I could hear you calling out my name from 15,000 kilometers away."

Chapter Twenty-Four

Uncle William was transferred to a rehabilitation facility in Brisbane three weeks after his stroke, and Aunt Cathie shifted into the guest bedroom at Cassandra and Sebastian's house. We all took turns joining in his rehabilitation exercises; all the grandchildren, including Lily, as well as all we adults. Pete and Julie flew from Melbourne to Brisbane every third weekend, usually staying with us. Lily was in heaven; she loved Pete with a passion only equaled by his love for her.

In March, Lily's Poppa was deemed safe enough on his legs to be transferred from the inpatient program to the outpatient one, and we all celebrated his return to Cassandra's place, almost as home as Killara. According to his doctors his progress was remarkable. "Gold stars all round," said the psychologist in the rehabilitation center. "Recovering from a stroke is a family affair, and you guys sure stepped up."

By July Uncle William was pretty much back to his old self, the weakness of his right leg and arm so minor it was barely noticeable, and his occasional word-finding problems dragging him down to the level of most healthy 70-year-olds. But his near-death experience changed his work habits; no more going into the university four days a week as he'd been doing ever since his official retirement five years previously. Daily walks and writing from home was the plan, much to Aunt Cathie's delight and relief.

~

KILLARA, CHRISTMAS DAY, 1982

Christmas at Killara that year was precious. Uncle William was on form: his mind wry, his quotes apt, his love for his family total. And his family included us.

The heat was of course crazy as we lugged down to the beach chilly bins and cane baskets full of cold roasted chicken, glazed ham, seafood salads of scallops and crayfish and calamari and prawns and chunks of white fish, leak and potato pies, hard-boiled eggs, crisp green salads and Ben's exceptional potato salad, Aunt Cathie's homemade bread and Uncle William's bottles of home brew, Sebastian's banana cake, Cassandra's scones and millionaire's shortbread, Amber's afghans, my phenomenally impressive three-layer chocolate cake and fresh tropical fruit salad (with lashings of whipped cream in a separate container), actual fruit—mangos, pawpaws, and various strange tropical fruits Ben had found at the Port Douglas markets, the best Australian Shiraz and Chardonnay, and bottles of Pete's mango and lemon fruit cocktail. Sea-green picnic plates and cups and delicate glass wine glasses and the best cutlery and a plaid tablecloth with matching real cloth napkins had to come as well. "You want them, you carry them," Pete said to Cassandra. But I noted Julie taking pity on her and grabbing some of her load. She wasn't yet a fully anointed Killarian.

Sebastian herded the troops to the far end of the beach for the annual game of cricket, and Cassandra and I were left in peace to lay out the feast under the shade of a size 99 picnic umbrella. Uncle William had cried off too, with the excuse that it was too hot for his old bones. He was sitting nearby under a palm tree, reading to Fred. At four, he chose books over any other toy.

"Aha!"

Uncle William's exclamation drew my attention and I smiled at the enchanting tableau: he in his white straw hat, Fred in his sturdy brown body and red swimming togs. Poppa reading *The Wind in the Willows* to his youngest grandchild. The sounds of ball on bat and masculine yells and feminine hoots in the distance.

An intense sensation of… I wasn't sure; peace, contentment, luck—to be here and part of this family? No mere thoughts could capture it; all that mattered was to be filled up with it.

"The perfect quote for our picnic," said Uncle William, sharing his book with Fred, whose eyes were glued to the page. "Just look at Mole's round eyes. I wonder if they're bigger than his tummy, like yours?" Uncle William tickled Fred's tummy and he giggled. My gaze rested on Cassandra's face as she stopped being busy, her eyes hidden behind dark glasses as she looked at her father, his deep voice reading to her baby.

"'What's inside it?' Mole asks, eyeing a fat wicker luncheon basket. 'There's cold chicken inside it,' replies the Rat briefly; 'coldtonguecoldhamcoldbeefpickledgherkinssalad-frenchrollscresssandwichespottedmeatgingerbeerlemonadesodawater… '".

New Zealand, January, 1983

In January the whole family flew to New Zealand for Pete and Julie's wedding. Turns out Julie's parents were well-heeled and well-known in Auckland. Who would have guessed? Julie had a Kiwi accent almost as broad and state-school as mine. Bridesmaids Lily and Sunny ("We're way too old to be flower-girls," Sunny scoffed) were in heaven. Julie, bless her heart, consulted them on every little detail: the flowers, the table decorations, the menu, the dance music, the guest list and who should sit where…

It was beautiful. Romantic, perfect weather, glowing bride, dottily-in-love bridegroom. Lily and Sunny looked delicious, their hair twirled high on their elegant eight-year-old heads, and best men, Ben and Sebastian, strutted their stuff in matching hired suits and black ties.

"Perhaps I should buy one of these outfits," Ben muttered as we fell into bed in the early hours of next morning. "I seem to need one every few months these days. The economics of renting are getting are bit borderline."

A few hours later, the softer New Zealand sun high in the sky, we waved good-bye to the newly-weds as they were driven to the airport, thence to fly to Bali for their honeymoon. Then we said goodbye to Uncle William and Aunt Cathie who were driving to Wellington to stay with friends. All that done and dusted we were finally off for two long lazy crazy weeks at the beach. Julie's parents, who had turned out to be down-to-earth generous people with accents as broad as Julie's, had insisted on lending us their holiday house at Piha, the dramatic black iron-sands surf beach on the West Coast, not far from Auckland. "It's just a big old house. Nothing fancy," they said.

"I bet," said Cassandra, as we walked over to our rental vehicles, two required to accommodate all nine of us.

But in fact it was just that, an old wooden house with paint flaking off the walls, beds with sunken mattresses, battered tin pots and pans, no TV, and an outside cold shower and long-drop toilet. We fell in love with it on sight. It was Killara's poor Kiwi cousin.

And my-oh-my, the beach. Dramatic doesn't do it justice. It was early evening by the time we'd dumped our bags and groceries and walked across the dusty road and low sand dunes to the sea. The sand really was jet black, shot through with purple and blue light where the low rays of the setting sun hit it. The sea far out was the luminous blue of a summer evening with giant waves breaking and crashing down before flattening out and spreading across the fifty meters of wet sand left by the low tide. We flipped off our thongs and raced into the sea for our first paddle. Even though the waves were breaking way out, the wash from them swelled the shallow water near the edge from our ankles to our knees with each wave before the backwash sucked the sand from under our toes.

"It looks a bit wild," Cassandra said. "We'll have to watch the kids when they're swimming."

"It's got the reputation of being the worst beach for drownings in the country," Sebastian said cheerfully. "But ain't it grand!"

Chapter Twenty-Five

We agreed it was the best holiday we'd had in ages. Killara's sea was so different, usually calm, and the sand as white as this was black. We were used to surf beaches; in Brisbane we often took the kids to the beach so they could catch a few rides on their boogie boards. Apart from little Fred, they were all reasonably confident in surf. But this surf was a different beast, and when the tide was coming in and the surf was up we usually walked to the south end of Piha where the lifeguards were on watch and most of the swimmers obediently swam. Cassandra and I stayed between the flags with the kids, although this frustrated Cassandra. She'd rather be surfing with Ben and Sebastian. The three of them were all strong swimmers and sometimes swam, even at high tide, near our house at the far north of the beach where there were few people and no life guards. It gave me the shits.

At low tide we all stayed at the deserted north end near our house. It did look like fun as everyone but me waded out until the water was waist deep before jumping on the small waves that were the leftovers from the real waves that broke further out. Even those little waves packed a punch as they carried a mess of boogie boards like speeding bullets across the flats, sometimes tumbling the kids head over butt and dumping them giggling on the black sand. It took three days before Lily's glum face forced me to let her join the boogie-board frolics when Ben and Sebastian were surfing way out and thus useless as lifeguards.

"For heaven's sake, Olivia, it's only knee deep," Cassandra said, her irritation with my mother-hen behavior sending her eyes to the skies and back. Listening to Lily's joyous screams as she and Sunny jumped on a wave side-by-side and hurtled towards the beach finally got me hooked. By the second week I was almost as confident as my eight-year-old.

Our last day and it was another magical evening. Sebastian put his hand up as chef, with Fred as his assistant and Amber on patisserie. While they began their preparations for a special farewell dinner, Cassandra, Ben and I took the other three kids down to the beach for a last swim. We could see a few surfers and small groups of people still on the sand at the other end of the beach, but here we had the beach to ourselves. The tide was going out and fifty or so meters of shallow water lay invitingly on the flats. We spent half an hour wading out waist deep, turning and waiting for that perfect wave and jumping on our boogie boards at just the right moment so we were carried right onto the sand. We'd mastered it now, even I, the faint-hearted. Next year we would be in Hawaii competing in the surfing championships.

"Let's go for one last walk as far as Lion Rock," Ben said. "I want to take some pics. This is going to be one amazing sunset."

"Lovely. Come on you lot; get dried and let's march." I began to stuff hats and towels into my beach bag.

"No, I don't wanna," David said. "I want to get a few more rides."

"Me too," said Lily and Sunny, simultaneously as usual.

"One more, then we're having that walk," I told them.

"You two go by yourselves. Look at that sky; it's so romantic." Cassandra grinned at us and plunked herself back down on her towel on the sand. "I'll stay here with the kids."

"Sure?"

"Go. If we get too shivery we'll wander up to the house and see you there."

David was already halfway back to the sea, his boogie board clasped in front of him.

"Be careful, Lily," I couldn't help saying. "Don't go too far out. You know there are a few holes out there."

"We'll just play about on the small waves. See ya!" And she and Sunny ran after David.

"I'll watch them like a starving gannet," Cassandra said. "Now scram."

We strolled hand in hand along the iridescent wet sand; it was so black that it almost seemed like a mirror, reflecting a play of changing colors, as the sun sank nearer the sea. We could see Venus even though the sky was still quite light, and the pale three-quarter moon was already up, too impatient to wait for the sun to leave.

I walked a little ahead of Ben as he stopped to take a photo of some seagulls reflected in the iron sands. When he called my name I turned, and his camera clicked.

"Don't waste film on me, silly. You have so many already."

"You look so beautiful. The light's perfect." He walked towards me, snapping another shot, and I waited for him, my hair blowing forwards over my face, my bare feet in the still-warm sand, my whole being infused with perfect happiness.

We met with a kiss, which became a long kiss, and holding hands we continued to walk towards the main beach. We could see the lifeguards taking down the flags, another day of keeping everyone safe over for them.

"What a perfect day, a perfect evening. How lucky we are," I murmured, almost feeling teary.

Ben's arm went around me and I snuggled into him as we turned to go back towards Cassandra and the kids.

"Who's that?" Ben squinted at a figure racing down the beach towards us. "I think it's David. He's a bloody good little runner."

"Cassandra probably told him to come and hurry us up. The kids will be dying of starvation."

"What's he yelling for?"

Now I could hear him as well.

"I think something's wrong…" Ben's words hovered in the air between us as he ran towards David, leaving me stumbling to keep up, the fear pounding through me, my breath coming in gasps.

Ben's stopped, David's shouting, they're running again, away from me. I can't keep up. David's fallen and Ben's running ahead.

"David, David." I'm on the sand beside him, rasping so loudly I can't speak for a few seconds.

"It's Mummy, she's gone in to get Sunny and she's not moving and I think she's drowned." David's crying so hard I can barely understand him. I'm standing, pulling him up, shaking him.

"Speak more slowly. Is it Cassandra? Is your mummy…"

"NO. Sunny, Sunny. Mummy tried to save her but she's not breathing and Mummy couldn't make her breathe and now she's gone back into the sea, and she's going to drown too. I ran as fast as I could to get you to save them but you were too far away and it'll be too late now."

"What about Lily?" I scream.

"I told you, I think she's drowned too, I told you."

"David, run as fast as you can to the life guard and tell them to come as quickly as they can. Just go." I push him away and lurch after Ben so far ahead. Hurry Ben hurry, heart pumping, sand tripping dear god don't take Lily from me.

Ben crouching over our baby his head her head joining his head lifting his hand pressing down so hard on her little chest his mouth back on hers. Ben shouting "Come on Lily, breathe, breathe."

You'll break her chest it doesn't matter that's where her heart is make it beat please make it beat.

A terrible wailing. It's Cassandra, her neck stretched, her head back, her eyes staring, her arms holding Sunny.

Sunny.

Her golden curls black with sand and her small body shaking so violently. She's having a fit but I can't help her because Lily isn't breathing and why is Cassandra wailing and screaming? Her Sunny is still alive.

No, no, no. It's Cassandra shaking, not Sunny, because... because Sunny is dead.

Shove them away the bodies leaning over my baby her eyes closed her long hair wet her cheeks black with sand. NO DON'T COVER HER FACE SHE CAN'T BREATHE. "I'm here Lily. Mummy's here."

So many lifeguards. I can't see her, what's happening? Don't hold me so tight, Ben, let me go, I can't reach her. Please, please, save our baby. Make her breathe again. You're life guards, you know what to do, you're always saving people, you'll save her, you have to save her...

But they can't and she's blue and dead.

Sunny so limp in Cassandra's arms, her perfect little body, her hair wet and lifeless, her face in Cassandra's chest and Cassandra wailing and sobbing as if the whole world has ended. And it has but I don't believe it yet, not yet. I'm so so cold and Ben's wrapping me up in towels and almost carrying me to the house, following the lifeguards. They've got our daughters and I can't see them, and David is almost carrying Cassandra and he's only ten.

~

The police are in our house. They tell us our daughters have been taken away in the rescue helicopter to Auckland. We can see them later but not yet, they tell us.

I grab the policewoman's arm. "Have they taken them to the hospital?"

"I'm sorry. You can see them tomorrow."

"I want to go to the hospital now. Why couldn't we go in the helicopter with them?" My face is burning.

"I'm sorry. They need to be… need to be examined first, then you can see them."

Ben's behind me, holding my arms from pounding at the policewoman standing there in front of me, telling me I can't see my own daughter.

We're all sitting down with cups of tea we don't want, and the policewoman has taken Fred into another room, and the police are asking David and Cassandra what happened. As if it mattered now who is to blame. Whether it is us for leaving them or Cassandra for not watching them and not saving them.

I concentrate on David stuttering and stammering out the words that I can't, won't believe are true. "Lily was shouting, waving, and Mummy and me was on the beach and we ran down to the edge of the sea and we couldn't see Sunny properly and then we saw her and she was out way further than Lily, and then Lily was half walking, half swimming out too. She was trying to get to Sunny but Sunny kept disappearing every time a big wave crashed down, and somehow she'd got right out there where the big waves were."

Sebastian's arm is around David, poor little boy, shivering and shaking although only his white face is showing through the bundle of blankets wrapped around him.

"Mrs. Brooks? Can you tell us what happened," the cop asks.

"I could see Sunny's head between waves and then she'd be further out," Cassandra whispers. "I couldn't see her boogie board. I was getting to her as fast as I could and Lily was trying to get to her too. I think I told David to get help and to stay out of the water, I think I did do that."

"I did, Mummy, but I wanted to help you save Sunny first, and then I ran for Uncle Ben."

"You did the right thing, David," said the cop, and Sebastian moans and cradles his little boy, rocking to and fro, to and fro.

Cassandra starts again, her voice shaking and coming and going like the sound of waves. "I got past Lily because the water was too deep for her and I shouted for her to go back and I'd get Sunny, but then I was over my head and the waves were breaking on me and it took so long to get to her. She was floating face down and I got her turned over and held her face as high as I could out of the water and somehow I got her back. It was so hard and she wasn't breathing but I couldn't do anything until we were out of the water."

"But you didn't get Lily too. You went right past her," David sobs, his teeth banging with cold.

"Was Lily in trouble too at that point?" asks the cop.

"I think so, yes, she was, but I couldn't get to her because I couldn't let go Sunny's head and I needed to get her to the beach so I could get her breathing again."

The cop is looking at David again. "David, did you see what happened to Lily?"

"She was trying to get to Sunny and the water was up to her chest but then she went right under, and when she came up again Mummy was swimming past her and I screamed and screamed at Lily to come in and she was trying and she was waving her arms in the air and her boogie board washed right up on the beach and she had nothing to hang on to just like Sunny. Mummy had got Sunny and was coming back in but she went right past Lily and Lily was calling out her name. I could hear her shouting Cassandra, help me, and then she'd go under again and I didn't know what to do. Then Mummy got Sunny on the sand and all the water came pouring out of her mouth and Mummy started pushing on her chest and breathing in her mouth. And I thought I should go and help Lily because she still kept going under and then coming up and screaming and she was trying to catch a wave in but they were too big and just dumping on her. And I TOLD Mummy to go and get Lily and I'd keep trying to breath into Sunny because I knew Lily was going to drown too and I knew Sunny was already drowned."

"I'm sorry, Davie, I'm sorry baby." Cassandra is pulling David away from Sebastian. She holds him with her whole body, her sobbing so loud I have to jam my hands over my ears.

"You're doing well, David," said the cop. "Do you remember what happened next?"

"Can't we leave this until later?" Sebastian says. "He's only ten and he's in shock. I think you should talk to him and to Cassandra tomorrow."

"Of course, Mr. Brooks. Just another few minutes and we'll leave you in peace."

"I want to tell them." David pulls away from Cassandra, his face stained with salt and crying and snot mixed with black sand. "Mummy told me to run to the house and get Daddy and she went into the sea to save Lily, and I ran to get Ben and Olivia because I could see them coming back and I could get to them quicker than Daddy."

I squirmed as close to Ben as I could get, silent, numb, the words going into my ears and sitting in my head as if they weren't anything to do with us. I wanted to crawl inside Ben so we were the same person. That's all we were now and all we would ever be ever again, just us and no Lily.

Cassandra is on her knees in front of me, her hands grabbing my arms. "Olivia, I tried to reach her, I tried so hard, but she'd got caught in the same hole as Sunny, and the rip started taking me out as well. She was keeping her head above water some of the time and I finally managed to grab her and then Ben was in the water and got to us and took her and somehow I got back."

"Mr. Appleby?"

Ben's shaking so hard he's making my heart vibrate. "It was too late. I gave her mouth-to-mouth until the lifeguards arrived. But she didn't stand a chance, she'd been pushed under too often by the waves."

"Mrs. Brooks, are you saying Lily was still calling out when you went in to try and save her?"

"Yes, I don't know if she was calling out but she was still bobbing up and waving. I'm so sorry, if I could have grabbed her at the same time as Sunny. But I couldn't. And if I'd let go of Sunny she would have been swept away. I didn't know if she was still alive. I thought if I got her to the beach…"

There is no air in this room.

"I didn't think. I just needed to get her to safety. I couldn't think of anything else."

"Thank you, Mrs. Brooks. Thank you everyone. You've all been very helpful. I'm so sorry. We'll leave you in peace now, and come around tomorrow. You'll be able to see the little girls then; we can take you into Auckland. Is there anyone we can call for you?"

I lick my dry lips but no words come out. No one speaks.

"Well, we'll call the local doctor to come over; perhaps he can give you all something to help you sleep tonight."

"I didn't save them, I let them drown," Cassandra whispers. "Lily was trying to save my baby and I let her drown. I went right past her and I let her drown."

Part Three

BECOMING REAL

1983 - 1992

~

"It doesn't happen all at once," said the Skin Horse. "You become. It takes a long time. That's why it doesn't often happen to people who break easily, or have sharp edges, or who have to be carefully kept. Generally, by the time you are Real, most of your hair has been loved off, and your eyes drop out and you get loose in the joints and very shabby. But these things don't matter at all, because once you are Real you can't be ugly, except to people who don't understand."

— *The Velveteen Rabbit* by Margery Williams —

Chapter Twenty-Six

Brisbane, January, 1983

We flew home, all of us, our babies in boxes in the cold hold of the plane. There was a double funeral, a double burial, but I didn't go. I couldn't move from my bed. Julie stayed with me. I think Ben was scared I'd do something crazy. Julie should have still been in Bali on her honeymoon.

When Ben got home she left and Ben got into bed and curled himself around me shivering in the hot hot night. He was shaking with crying and I wanted to turn in his arms and kiss his wet cheeks and comfort him and love him but I couldn't move. He didn't talk about the funeral and I didn't want him to. He tried, later, the next day, but I put my hands over my ears and screamed at him to shut up. Later, a week perhaps, two weeks, three weeks, I don't know, he tried to convince me to come to the cemetery and see her grave. He said it was beautiful and peaceful and it would help me to say goodbye.

"I don't want to say goodbye. Why can't you understand that? Leave me alone."

I'll never go to that cemetery. I'll never look at all the cards and letters that came. I'll never read the cards Ben collected from all the flowers people sent to cover her coffin so they didn't have to see how small it was. I knew it was small because I saw it when they loaded it onto the plane in Auckland.

~

Brisbane, November, 1983

"You're a writer, Olivia. You need to write your feelings down."

I looked at her, the grief counselor I had been seeing for endless sessions, the desperate expression on her kind face almost forcing a jolt of something in my chest—guilt, I suppose—but then I was numb again. I shook my head.

"Please try, " she said. "I know you think it won't help, but it's been ten months now and you need to find your way out of this depression. For Ben's sake, even if you can't do it for yourself."

"Ten months since I last held Lily. Is it really that long? Why can't I see her face any more? If I didn't have photos I'd have lost all of her. "

"I know it feels so raw still, but time does heal. The first year is the hardest. It will get a little easier every day from now on." She leaned over and put her hand on my knee. I looked down at it, the hand of a woman who had lived longer than I.

"Have you ever lost someone?" I'd been coming here for months and I knew nothing about her. Perhaps she'd told me but I couldn't remember.

"My father four years ago and a dear friend when I was about your age," she said.

"How many children do you have?" I asked, trying my best to find something that would help me connect with her;

help me take in her advice on how to climb out of the darkness.

"I don't have children," she said. "I'm sorry."

"Don't be sorry. If you don't have children, you can't lose them."

"I do understand that I can't put myself in your shoes, but I've counseled many parents who've lost a child. Many—even mothers who have never even kept a diary—find that writing their thoughts and feelings down can help them. At first it might feel forced, false, but it will get easier."

"I'll try soon. I'm not ready yet. I can't write about losing Lily; I don't want to. I can't sleep if I let myself think about that. I can only get to sleep if I remember her before…I can see her still in my mind. I can feel her, smell her. I can't lose that, I can't. If I lose that I'll lose her forever." My tears were coming again as they did every day, every hour, every time I remembered. How could I have so many tears?

"Tell me. Tell me how you remember Lily."

"I've told you. You've seen photos. You know how pretty she is, her big brown eyes so twinkly when she's being silly, and like pools when I read her a sad story or she's watching a sad movie. Ben teased that she had a heart made of chocolate mousse it melted so easily. So different from Sunny. Her heart was like her hair, made of gold. It shone, but didn't melt like Lily's. Sunny liked adventure stories and scary Roald Dahl books."

"Do you think that's why they were such close friends? They complemented each other rather than competing?"

"They were only eight. I don't think they thought like that at all."

"Perhaps not consciously. But even young children can be competitive."

"No. No." I watched my hands shaking. They didn't seem to belong to me. I sat on them. "I don't know. My heart isn't soft like Lily's. Wasn't. I never used to cry all the bloody time."

"Perhaps you wouldn't give yourself permission before. Your heart was always soft, you'd just given it a protective coat."

I shook my head. "This isn't helping. I'm wasting your time coming here every week."

"Olivia, I know that you're frustrated with yourself, but this depth of grief is normal. You've lost a child. I promise you that with time the pain won't be so intense."

I blew my sore nose again. I bloody didn't have to go through this every week. At least when I was home I could watch some mindless thing on TV instead of thinking.

"Tell me how you remember Lily when you're trying to fall asleep."

"Her long shining hair, I'm brushing it and tying it back with a yellow ribbon. Her giggles when her Daddy tickles her, her little-girl sweaty smell before she has her shower and how delicious she smells from her favorite jasmine soap when I wrap her in her towel. Her cream nightie covered in violets, the one her Uncle Pete gave her, and how she feels when she hugs me goodnight and I nuzzle her soft neck and breathe her in. The way she holds her tongue between her teeth when she's coloring her elaborate pictures with glitter markers and felt pens and star stickers with puppies and fairies on them. Her long brown legs with bruises and scratches after we've been for a hike..." —I pulled more tissues from the box on the table and mopped up more tears and shoved the tissues with their tears in the plastic bag I carried with me—"and you can see I can't write any of it down because when I think about Lily I can't stop crying. All I can do is think about her, but sometimes I can't see her face any more. I can't dream about her. Why don't I dream about her?"

"Grief is different for everyone. Do you still need a sleeping pill to help you sleep? That might stop you remembering your dreams. Perhaps that's a good thing."

"Ben lets me have half a pill if I'm not asleep after two

hours or wake up too early before it's light and I can't stop shaking. I'm not trusted to keep them because I forget I've taken one and take another."

"That's another symptom of grief, not being able to keep track of everyday things."

"Poor Ben, how can he put up with me? He needs to grieve too, but he's so busy taking care of me, how can he? Please don't give up on me. I do want to stop crying but I can't, I can't."

"I won't give up on you, Olivia. You're not alone. Perhaps it would help to read about other parents who have lost a child? Winston Churchill, Dwight Eisenhower, Charles Darwin. Writers like you; Mark Twain, Charles Dickens, Sunny's favorite, Roald Dahl. Their grief, sometimes their guilt, was intense, but they survived and went on to do great things, write more wonderful books."

"Why are they all men? Where are the mothers?" I watched the red blotches creeping up her neck.

"I'm sorry. I didn't think." She covered her neck with her hand, her long pale-pink nails luminescent against her shamed skin. "I'll find some books for you where mothers who have lost a child share their thoughts, their grief; how they lived through it and came out the other side."

"They didn't lose Lily. How can they help me when they can't know how it feels to lose Lily? They didn't leave their little girl on a beach swimming in a dangerous sea."

"And nor did you. It was a terrible, tragic accident. It wasn't your fault. It wasn't Ben's fault."

"We trusted someone else to look after her and she didn't. She couldn't even save her own daughter." My eyes were aching, my throat was aching, my heart was breaking. I shoved more and more tissues into my plastic bag.

"Lily wouldn't want you to be so sad. She would want you to be happy, remember the wonderful years you had together, keep her memory alive but not stop living your own life."

"You can't know what Lily would want. She wouldn't want me to be without her. She would want me to miss her all the time, with every piece of me, and I do, I do. I ache to hold her, to smell her, to watch her bouncing on her bed, to feel as if I'll burst with pride when she sings and dances with Ben and Pete, and walks up on the school stage to get all the prizes for English, and Drama and Music, and Arithmetic and Art, and all the school kids clap and clap and cheer and stamp their feet because they love her so much."

"I know, I know. But you have those memories and they can never be taken away from you."

"But they've stopped being made. She'll never go to high school, university, find a soul-mate, have her own children, make me and Ben grandparents." My head fell down and I held it on my knees, so heavy with all the life our Lily would never have. "She wasn't just any little girl, she was our gift from Saigon. A gift her mother gave us out of all that horror and pain, and we let her down. We lost her, and we never deserved her."

"Olivia, look at me. I know you understand that this is grief talking. You need to use those strategies I taught you when you start thinking like that. Saying those affirmations that we came up with. Saying them out loud, under your breath, in your mind, whenever you start thinking like this. 'We loved Lily more than ourselves and she had a wonderful life. No-one was to blame for her loss; it was a tragic accident.'"

I tried to look into her face but it was a blurry nothingness.

"You can get through this, and you must, for Ben as well as for you."

I nodded. "I'll try. That's all. I'll try."

~

I STOPPED GOING TO COUNSELING AFTER THAT. I LIED TO BEN. I told him the counselor had decided I didn't need her any more; that the best thing I could do now was to get on with my life, our lives. That wasn't a lie; it *was* the best thing. My only lie was that it wasn't her decision, it was mine. I felt sick even so. Sick that I wasn't being truthful with Ben.

I forced myself to get up in the mornings to have breakfast with Ben before he left for work. I made myself a schedule and followed it. 9am: Do dishes, tidy up house. 10am: Walk to a café and order coffee and sit there for an hour with a book or read one of their magazines or newspapers. 11am: Decide what to have for dinner and defrost the meat and make sure I have all the ingredients. Midday: Make myself lunch and eat it and wash the dishes. 2pm: Have a rest on the bed. 4pm: Make a cup of coffee and drink it. 5pm: Start making dinner. Have a glass of wine or a G & T. 6pm: Ben gets home.

I had variations for different days of the week. On Mondays I did the grocery shopping which took all morning. On Wednesdays I vacuumed the whole house, which took all morning. On Fridays I cleaned the bathrooms and the kitchen sink and the fridge, which took all morning. On those days I walked to the café at midday and had lunch there instead of morning coffee.

Weekends were a relief because Ben planned what we'd do. He always made us go for a walk on Saturday and Sunday, whatever the weather. Sometimes we went to a movie or play on Friday or Saturday evening. Mostly we stayed home and watched TV or listened to music. Ben didn't play his banjo any more, and he didn't sing in the shower any more either.

Ben's parents wanted to fly over from the UK and stay with us but I couldn't deal with having anyone in the house, so they stayed in a motel. They'd even stayed in a motel when they'd flown all the way to Australia from Scotland for the funeral of their only grandchild. About three months after the funeral Pete and Julie came to stay. Ben invited them. I didn't try and stop him because I thought Pete would be good for Ben. I don't know if he was or not, but I suspect not as Pete was as devastated as we were. Poor Julie. If their marriage doesn't survive it will be our fault.

When Pete and Ben went out for a run the second day they were here, Julie tried to talk to me. She said she and her parents felt responsible because it was their house we were staying in when it happened. I told her that was ridiculous. That's the word I used, ridiculous. It is ridiculous to feel guilty about a house. A house can't be responsible for a little girl drowning. A little girl swimming outside the flags that the life-guards put up so that they can keep children safe.

"Two little girls," Julie said.

"Two little girls, yes, two little girls. Best friends forever," I said and we sat there beside each other, her hand holding mine. But I still felt alone.

Chapter Twenty-Seven

Brisbane, March, 1984

I FELT THE SOFT TOUCH OF HIS LIPS ON MY CHEEK BUT DIDN'T open my eyes. Too early, too early.

"Cup of tea," he said, as he did every morning.

"Wassa time? It feels as if I only went to sleep."

"It's a beautiful Saturday morning and we're going for a walk and a picnic. I've made it already, and all you have to do is get up, have a nice shower, scrub the sleep out of your eyes, wash your hair and make it shine, and we're outta here."

I squinted up at him, the light from the window above our bed too bright. "Why do I have to wash my hair? What's wrong with it?"

"You used to have such shiny swingy hair. Don't you remember? 'Clean hair is happiness.' That's what you used to say."

I pushed my hand through my gritty-feeling tangles. "Ugh, it's horrible. You go walkies, I'm too sleepy. It'll be good for me to have some more rest. I'll be much better when you get home. I'll even wash my hair."

"Come on sweetheart, do this for me. You'll feel better once you've had a good walk and breathed in all that lovely fresh air."

I pulled myself up in the bed and Ben tucked a second pillow behind my back. "Do I have to? I hardly slept last night."

"Well, you will tonight once you've had a day keeping up with me. If you don't get more exercise you'll lose the use of your legs."

"Don't be silly." I managed a grin. "Where are we going to walk?"

"I've found a track through some peaceful bush an hour's drive from here. There's the prettiest stream and birds galore. You'll love it."

"How did you find it? How do you know it's so nice?"

"I've been there a couple of times over the last few weeks. A friend told me about it."

"You've been going off on long walks without telling me? Who's this friend?"

"Olivia, you haven't been too interested in anything I've been doing, not for a long time. I know Lily's anniversary was tough on you, but you need to start making more effort again."

"Who's the friend?" I said.

"Does it matter?"

"I'm trying to be interested, that's all."

"Sebastian. We walked it a couple of weeks ago with Oscar." Ben had taken off his glasses and was looking into me.

"Oh, Oscar. How I miss him. I haven't seen him in so, so long. Is he OK?"

"For a fourteen-year-old, he's great. He misses you too. He was droopy when he caught on that you weren't coming with us."

"I didn't know you'd been seeing Sebastian. You should have told me."

"It was the first time for months. We've both been too tied up in our sadness to make the effort, but then Sebastian phoned me at work and, well he thought it was time we talked."

"How is he?"

"Do you really want to know?"

"How can you say that? Of course I want to know."

"He's a mess. He's struggling with it all, like us. But I think it's even worse for him."

"It couldn't be worse, nothing could be worse. He has other children to live for. That must help a little bit." My tears were coming again, plopping onto the sheet.

"That's not how grief works; you know that. And he's terrified that Cassandra won't make it back."

It was not until we were eating our sandwiches by the singing stream Ben had promised me, that he brought it up again. What he'd meant when he said that Sebastian was afraid she wouldn't make it back. I tried to close my ears but how is that even remotely possible? A design flaw. We can close our eyes or turn our heads away when we can't bear to see, but apart from clamping our hands over our ears, which looks plain rude, we're stuck with hearing every damn thing. I was a master at turning off my brain and letting the words wash through the mush between my ears when some boring suit at a party was droning on about the same thing those sorts of men always droned on about—money and how much they'd made, usually—but Ben never droned. He wanted me to hear what he had to say. That's what this walk, this picnic, was really about.

"Sebastian is worried about Cassandra. She's in a bad way."

I didn't speak. Couldn't speak. Of course she was in a bad way. We all were. Why did I have to hear this?

"She's been admitted to the psychiatric ward for the second time. Her psychiatrist thinks she might benefit from some ECT treatments."

Psychiatric ward? ECT? The words echoed around inside my head. "Second time? What do you mean, the second time?" The easiest of the three questions.

"She had a spell in there apparently about three months after Lily and Sunny's funeral. Sebastian said she wouldn't get out of bed and wouldn't eat. They got her through that and she's been on antidepressants and having therapy ever since, but after the anniversary of… of losing them, she had a relapse, and this time her depression is much worse."

"How didn't we know this when it happened the first time?"

Ben shook his head.

"You knew," I hissed. "You knew and didn't tell me. No-one told me, how could you?"

"Olivia, I didn't know. They kept it from both of us; everyone who knew kept it from us. I'm sure they thought we had enough of our own to deal with."

"But how could Sebastian not have needed to tell you? You're his closest friend."

"Sebastian felt that he couldn't talk to me because of you. You've forgotten how sick you were. You refused to even have Cassandra's name mentioned. You still can't say her name."

"I wasn't sick. I was grieving. And I love Sebastian. I'd never not want to be there for Sebastian."

"Sebastian and Cassandra are two halves of a whole. You can't be there for him and refuse to have anything to do with Cassandra."

"Telling Sebastian he couldn't see you even if she didn't want to see me? That's crazy. It sounds like her power trip to me."

"Sweetheart, Cassandra has wanted to see you, talk to you, ever since it happened. That's a huge part of why she's so depressed, why she had to be admitted to hospital. Sebastian says that she can't stop believing that it was her fault that Lily and Sunny drowned. The antidepressants aren't working. Apparently ECT is not the horror it used to be…"

"They can't give her ECT. That's barbaric. Stop them, Ben, please stop them." I was pulling at his clothes, grabbing his face to make him look at me, listen to me.

He held my arms down and I could hear my moaning as he pulled me into his chest and held me tight, stroking my back, my hair. After a while when I'd calmed down—on the outside at least— and we were gulping down the hot, whisky-spiced coffee from the flask, we tried to have an adult discussion.

"Sebastian is against the ECT, but he's scared," Ben told me. "She's not responding to medication as she should be. The hope is that the ECT will jolt her out of the depression enough so she can respond to drugs and more therapy."

"No. She'll lose herself. I know she will. I've read about what ECT does to some people. It makes them placid and bland. It destroys their memories…"

Ben looked at me, his face drained. If only we could wipe away *those* memories but not all the other good ones, that's what he was thinking.

"Would you see her, sweetheart; talk to her?"

"I can't," I whispered. "Please don't ask me." I couldn't look at him.

"Sebastian didn't want to ask, but he's desperate. He believes that the only thing that will save her from ECT or getting worse, is you. She needs to know you forgive her."

I closed my eyes and sat there, the sun hot on my head. Ben grabbed my arms and I flinched.

"Olivia, listen to me. She can't afford to get any worse. Think of Amber and David and little Fred and what they're going through. They've lost Sunny and Lily, and now they're losing their mother too. What about Cathie and William, after all they've done for you? They've been here for weeks, sitting with Cassandra hours every day, trying to get through to her."

"What about my feelings? What about me?" I shook off his hands but couldn't look at him. "Why is it my fault? How can everyone think that I blame her?" I felt Ben's fingers on my chin as he forced my head up. He was crying.

"Tell Sebastian that I don't blame her. He can tell her. You can go and see her and tell her. She'll believe you."

Ben dropped his fingers and put his hands over his face. His shoulders shook.

"I don't know if I'm ready," I whispered. "Perhaps I'll be able to see her in a few weeks. I'll try, I promise. Tell her I'll try."

Ben dropped his hands. "She doesn't have a few weeks." He took my hands, and his felt so cold around mine. Ben always had warm hands. "You love her. You will always love her, whatever she does. You have to see her and make her understand that. She needs you to tell her it was a terrible accident and it wasn't her fault. You should be supporting each other through this. We should all be doing that."

"Will you come with me?" I could hear my voice, high and needy like a child.

"Of course I will, if you want me there. I'll always be there with you, you know that." Ben stroked my hair back from my face.

"I'm sorry, I'm sorry, sorry. I know I've been useless, I'm being selfish. Ben, please don't cry. I know you've been so patient with me and she was your daughter too."

I felt his fingers on my cheeks and I took his hand and kissed it.

"I love you, Olivia. I'll do whatever it takes to help us get through this."

"I love you too."

Ben rested his forehead against mine. "Friends?"

I nodded, tried to smile, but my mouth was wobbling too much.

Ben's hands cupped my face.

"But I haven't listened. I haven't listened. I've left you all alone to miss Lily," I whispered.

"Sweetheart, Cassandra needs you," Ben said. "You and I, we can work through this later, but right now Cassandra needs you, needs you with every cell of her body."

Without Ben I would never have got through it. On the way there, I was imagining a dark, gloomy institution with figures in shapeless track pants shambling around corridors or sitting in a circle in front of a muted TV, mouths dropped open, eyes vacant, drugged and silent. Of course it wasn't like that at all. Money has its advantages. She was in a pleasant room of her own, sitting in a chair, dressed in nice pants and shirt, her hair much shorter, not shiny, but cleaner than mine usually is these days. But she was drugged and silent when the nurse opened her door and beckoned us to go in. Sebastian was sitting beside her, holding her limp hand. He almost leapt out of his chair and came to me, his gaunt face a punch in my gut. I reached for him and we clung together as Ben went over to Cassandra and bent and kissed her cheek.

That first visit almost made me give up. I knelt before her and took her brittle hands—her well-cut clothes couldn't hide her terrible thinness—and then I said her name. Her name. How strange it felt to hear it in my voice again. I was looking up at her drooping face, and she lifted her chin a little and gazed at me with her beautiful eyes and then tears fell out of them and she sat there without moving, without speaking.

"Cassandra, it's me. Don't cry, don't cry. You don't need to feel guilty. It was a terrible accident, I know that. I know you did everything you could to save them. It wasn't your fault. It wasn't anyone's fault."

Her tears fell faster but she didn't move or speak. She was like a statue crying. I was too late.

We went back three times after that, and each time she was less drugged, a little more alert, although the only word she said to me was "Olivia." On the fourth visit she touched my face. As I knelt down in front of her chair I heard the door close, and realized Ben and Sebastian had left us alone.

"I forgive you," I whispered. "Please forgive me for deserting you. I was a mess. I wasn't thinking straight."

"I'm sorry," she said, her voice swimming through an ocean of tears. "I'm sorry I didn't save Lily. I'm sorry."

WHEN I WALKED OUT OF CASSANDRA'S ROOM, THROUGH THE big windows in the corridor that ran along the front of the beautiful old house, I saw Ben and Sebastian walking in the park-like hospital gardens. I thought about joining them but decided I needed to hide for a while in the visitor's lounge.

Aunt Cathie and Uncle William were there. It was the first time I'd seen them since New Zealand. They'd aged so much I barely recognized them. My throat closed up as Aunt Cathie wrapped me in her arms and my hands found fragile ribs instead of the firm muscles they remembered so acutely. Over her shoulder my eyes met Uncle William's, his still as blue as I remembered but now shadowed by pure white eyebrows to match his pure white hair.

Cassandra was discharged from hospital ten days later and we visited her at their house every few days for weeks. Gradually her hair took back its shine and her children stopped hanging around her like worried mother sheep. I still thought of Lily every waking minute, but my never-ending tears seemed finally to have dried up. I put all my effort into being there for Ben, and when he organized a four-day trip to Heron Island, this time staying in the resort rather than the Research Station, we finally become lovers again.

Our visits to the Brooks home became less frequent; Cassandra invited us to small dinner parties on a couple of occasions and we had them over for barbeques. We went to all the children's birthdays, and we went to Oscar's funeral. Cassandra had fought to keep him alive; had tried to over-ride Sebastian's wish to have him put down by the vet after he told them that Oscar was so riddled with cancer that further surgery would only give him a few more uncomfortable months at best.

But Sebastian prevailed and alone took Oscar for his last ride to the vet, stayed with him, and carried his body home for the burial. Wrapped in his old blanket, he was laid in a grave under his favorite acacia tree with his collar, his chewed rubber bone, and a beautiful drawing done by six-year-old Fred: five almost recognizable figures in decreasing size, holding hands, a small figure with curly yellow hair lying on the ground with her eyes closed and her hands crossed on her chest, and a large black dog lying on his side, his legs stiff. Underneath was written, "Our family and Oscar. He was a good dog." Cassandra read a poem she had written, her tears as she read bringing tears to every one of us, and Sebastian threw on the first handful of soil.

Later, Sebastian told Ben that Cassandra's determination to keep Oscar alive at any cost was the first time he'd known for sure that she was fully herself again. "But for once I couldn't let her have her way," he said. "After all the devotion Oscar has given me… I wanted him to go peacefully, not be forced to live on when his time was up."

Louise took me back as an editor at Stoddard and Jones, and I threw myself into it. I had long since terminated my own contract with my UK agent. My writing was over, the novel I'd been playing with before we lost Lily abandoned in a box in the back of a cupboard. Ben had refused to let me burn it, or throw it out with the junk mail. How he thought it remotely likely that I would ever want to look at it again was mind numbing.

Ben and Sebastian's friendship grew ever stronger, and the light in Ben's eyes slowly returned. Yet as our lives returned to some semblance of normal, for Cassandra and me, it wasn't so easy. On the surface, our few meetings—Saturday coffee every few weeks with other women to keep the conversation going—were cordial and friendly. But beneath our fragile shells we understood that the extraordinary bond that had joined our polar-opposite spirits from the day we met was frayed beyond repair.

Chapter Twenty-Eight

Killara, May, 1985

Returning to Killara wasn't as hard as I'd feared. Perhaps because it was associated with so many memories, not only those of a dark-haired Lily giggling with her sunny friend on their very last Christmas. It was also me at thirteen, on the cusp of a new life; me at 26, being given away to Ben by Uncle William; me at 31, loving Aunt Cathie as she bravely told me about my mother.

The reason for our visit was Uncle William's seventy-third birthday.

"Seventy-third?" I said, when Aunt Cathie phoned me. "I thought you only celebrated the significant birthdays with a big bash."

"He's missed too many birthdays," she said. "There's been a lot going on."

So of course we went. How could we not?

Everyone was there, including Pete and Julie with their new baby son — William, for his Poppa, Billy for short. Sadness was banned. At the birthday feast Uncle William was back on full form, rolling out funny and eloquent toasts to everyone and everything; no stumbles over words tonight. Until the last time he raised his glass. "And finally, and most 'specially, a toast…" His eyes filled and I swallowed as he struggled to speak. The room was hushed with love for him. "A toast to our lost girls, Sunny and Lily," he said.

Ben and I made love that night in the Shack. How perfect to be here, alone, with the rest of them playing rowdy board games at Killara. We felt a little guilty to have it all to ourselves when the big house was so over-flowing, but Cassandra had insisted. "Later," she'd said, "the kids can spend a few nights sleeping in the spare room if you don't mind them."

"You know we don't mind them. It's a deal."

After Heron Island, we'd made love more than we ever had when we were exhausted parents. Once we found each other again it felt almost like desperation. A need to be as close to each other as we could, to inhabit each other so that for a few moments we could forget the void in our hearts. As the weeks piled one on top of the last, our lovemaking became less frenetic. More normal, I suppose, if normal for two people who had been together for sixteen years was this comfortable familiarity. For me, that is; Ben's passion was never in doubt. Whether this was a male-female thing, I didn't know. The only woman I might once have raised such an intimate topic with was Cassandra, but those days were gone forever. I had to make up my own mind.

Ben's deep breathing soothed me as I lay awake looking at the stars through the window, listening to the wind in the trees, the distant hum of the sea, breathing in the salty night air intensifying the scent of our naked bodies still tangled together in the hot sheets. He was beautiful, his smooth skin, his gentle mind. He didn't deserve a pedestrian love-life. Surely I could do better?

~

Next morning we ate breakfast alone on our deck, reluctant to join the others too soon.

"Sweetheart," Ben said, and I smiled at him, feeling at once twenty-one and thirty-eight, youth and experience rolled into a single sensuous body.

"Hmm?"

"There's something I need to talk to you about."

That sudden feeling of falling. "What? Is something wrong?"

"Nothing like that. I've been putting it off but I owe it to you…"

"You look so serious. Is it your work? What is it, tell me."

"It's Cassandra. She's…"

"She's what? Oh, please don't tell me she's sick. Not now just when everything is finally coming right again."

"She's fine. There's no easy way to tell you, so I'll just say it."

I looked at him, every muscle and tendon in my body tensed, waiting. For what I had no clue.

"Cassandra wants to… has offered to…"

"For heaven's sake Ben, just spit it out. It can't be that bad."

"She wants to have a baby for you, for us."

My mouth opened. Then shut. I looked down at my legs, bare and brown, my toenails painted dusky pink.

"I know it's a crazy idea, but she's so earnest. She really wants to do this and I couldn't talk her out of it. She begged me to ask you. She said she couldn't because you'd never let her if I didn't agree."

"How can she have a baby for me? What is she thinking?"

"She's looked into it all and Sebastian has agreed. She'll use intrauterine insemination to get pregnant and when the baby is born we can adopt it."

"Intrauterine insemination? Why? Why would she give up their baby? She'd never be able to do that."

"She'd use my sperm, not Sebastian's. So it would be our baby as much as theirs. And then we'd adopt it."

"You'd jerk off into a test-tube and a doctor would squirt your sperm into Cassandra and when she got pregnant we'd all be a happy foursome waiting for our baby to be born, except it would be yours and Cassandra's. Not mine. Not Sebastian's. We could all crowd around while she has it in the spa-bath. You could haul it out to make sure you bonded with it."

"Stop it. I knew this was a bad idea. I told Cassandra but she said if I didn't ask you, she would have to."

"And she didn't want to ask me if she could have my husband's baby? As if she didn't have enough of her own already." Hot tears stung my face as I crouched in front of Ben's chair.

"You need to calm down. Give it time to sink in; think about it rationally. Cassandra loves you. She believes this is something that would make you happy. It's an incredible thing she's offering us. You have to see that whether you want to accept it or not."

"You think this is a good idea?" The words choked out of me.

"I didn't at first; I felt just like you do now. But I've had time to think about it, and if it's what you want, then I do too."

"If we wanted a baby we could adopt. Why would we need to do this?"

"You told me, you told Cassandra and all of us, you'd never want to adopt again."

"Because we could never replace Lily." My tears started again.

"Sweetheart, we all understand no child could ever replace Lily. That's not what Cassandra thinks."

"You want this? You want us to adopt Cassandra's baby?"

"It would be half our biological child."

"Yours, not mine," I whispered.

"I hoped you'd want to be the mother of a baby that came from me," he said, and I laid my head on his knees and wept.

I KNEW I COULDN'T HIDE AWAY FOR THE REST OF THE DAY; I had to front up to Cassandra and somehow tell her I didn't want her child, her offer to go through all the waiting to see if she was pregnant and then nine months of pregnancy and labor and birth in her late thirties. And giving it away. To me. Her baby with Ben.

Ben had gone off somewhere to clear his head, whatever that meant.

"You have to come with me," I'd said.

"No. This is between you and Cassandra. We'll all need to talk later if that's what you two want."

"But I didn't ask for this," I whimpered, wincing at my tone. "Can't you tell her? You're the one she asked."

"Because it's my sperm she planned to use. I told her that if this is what you wanted, I'd oblige. It's your decision now."

He sounded so cold but I knew he wasn't. He was hurting. Was this what he wanted deep down? A child to carry on his genes? Had I missed how important that was to him?

I walked up the track to the big house, very slowly, desperate never to reach there. Unwanted thoughts chased through my mind. Cassandra and Ben. Ben and Cassandra. An image as vivid as the sea through the trees flashed behind my eyes: Ben's expression when he first met Cassandra when we were at that anti-Vietnam war march. Cassandra capturing his hand in both of hers and looking at him over the top of her dark glasses. I shivered in the warm air. I could hear her sultry, deep voice. I almost glanced around, she sounded so real. *"My God, Olivia, where did you find him? Is he permanent?"* Her thumbs fondling the soft base of Ben's thumb.

Stupid, stupid. Why was I remembering this now; how was I remembering it now? I'd never been jealous before, I'd never had a single reason not to trust them.

"Olivia. I was on my way to see you, and here you are."

I started, and turned from the view I wasn't seeing. This was a real voice. The sickness rose into my throat.

"Sorry," Sebastian said. "I didn't mean to startle you. Are you OK?"

I shook my head and Sebastian's gray eyes looked into mine.

"Hey, come here," he said and pulled me into him. We stood holding together, me with my eyes closed tight. The wild laugh of a kookaburra cackled out and as if by arrangement, we both pulled back and grinned.

"Let's sit," he said, plopping down in one easy movement, settling his butt on a ferny tangle under a tree. He grabbed my hand and I half fell, half collapsed, beside him. He wrapped his arms around his bent knees. "Tell me what you're thinking."

"You don't want to hear," I said.

"Try me. I'm a lawyer. Nothing surprises me."

I grinned again. Two grins since we met a few minutes ago. "I was imagining crazy stuff. Like whether Ben was... wanted to have Cassandra's baby."

"Yep. I know that crazy thinking. Me too. Cassandra has always loved Ben. Who wouldn't? I love the bastard myself. If they have a baby together they'll have something that will connect them in a way that I don't think Cassandra understands. Refuses to admit to herself."

I swallowed. The kookaburra laughed. I could see it now, sitting on a naked tree limb not ten meters from us. "Bloody bird. Shut up," I yelled, shaking my fist at it.

"So the question is, is it worth it?"

I looked at him, his burnished waves blowing in the wind, his square jaw unshaven, his perfect face as beautiful as it was when I first saw him. He raised his eyebrows and wiggled them.

I grinned. Three times now. "Stop it. This is serious."

"It is. Very serious. Having babies is a serious business. Especially when they aren't ours."

"If I wanted this baby and Cassandra was serious about doing this, would you be willing? How could you possibly agree knowing that it wasn't yours, and that you'd have to keep seeing it with us and watching Cassandra with it?"

"Good questions. Cassandra and I did go over all that, again and again. She thinks she can give you this baby absolutely and that she'll always think of it as yours, never hers. Perhaps she could. She has a determined streak."

I stopped myself rolling my eyes. "If she could, what about you?"

"If this is what you and Ben want, I want it too. Simple as that."

"What if she changes her mind when its born? I've heard of mothers who do that. Women who have babies for other women, I mean."

"Anything is possible. But I don't believe Cassandra would ever go back on her word."

"I'm sorry. I know she wouldn't… I don't even know why I said that. I've already decided this couldn't work. I feel terrible when Cassandra… you and Cassandra are offering this, and I don't want to hurt her. But I don't want another child. Ben suggested we look into adopting again and we decided no. I can't go through that again."

His warm hand covered mine and I closed my eyes and put my face to the sun, willing the warmth to take all this away.

~

Cassandra was waiting when we reached the house. She looked nervous.

"Thank you Cassandra. But I can't. It's too much, I'm sorry." I looked over her head, my lips pressed hard together and my nose stinging.

"Oh," she whispered. "It was just a silly idea. I thought you might think about it. I so much want you to be happy, and I can't bear you not to have your own baby."

"It wouldn't be my own baby though, would it."

"It would, it would. It would be Ben's and yours. Lily wasn't your own… wasn't genetically yours either, and that didn't matter at all. I need to do this for you. I want to. Please don't say no just yet. Think about it for a while."

"Giving me a baby won't change how I feel about losing Lily. You think you can make everything right, but you can't. Not this time." I jumped as Sebastian's hand gripped my arm.

"Steady on, Olivia. How about we leave this for now."

I nodded and turned away, blocking out Cassandra's white face.

Chapter Twenty-Nine

We left next morning. My feeble excuse, some crisis meeting at Stoddard and Jones that I had to be there for, was believed by no-one. I didn't care, I had to get away from them all. Their pity simmered in the air, stifling me, locking me out, blaming me for rejecting Cassandra's wonderful gift. Even Sebastian seemed to have swapped sides. Of course he had. Cassandra was his sun and moon and bloody stars. If she wanted to have his best friend's baby and then give it away to his best friend's wife, that was all right by him. Anything Cassandra wanted she should have. And I had the temerity to turn her down.

No-one said anything but I knew they'd been discussing it in one of their family meetings. "Oh, no dear, I'm so sorry you have to go so soon," from Aunt Cathie was the best they could do. Babbling on about me flying to Brisbane for the meeting and leaving Ben at Killara, and flying back to Killara right after it to finish our restful holiday. They knew they weren't fooling me into thinking they didn't know. It was all about keeping the peace, pretending everything was fine, we were all a big happy family.

Ben appeared at the last minute, looking as if he'd wiped

off his tan in the shower. "We have to get a move on. Our plane leaves at ten," he said, his tone the color of his face. "I've called a taxi."

That floored them.

"Don't be ridiculous," Pete said. "I'll take you. I was going into Cairns today anyway."

"It's fine. The taxi will be here in a few minutes. I called it a while ago. Silly to mess up your plans."

Cassandra sidled up to me and put her hand on my arm. I shrugged her off.

"I'm sorry, Olivia. We'll talk when I get back," she said, her voice quiet for once.

I turned and walked over to the table where the others were still sitting at breakfast, their bacon and eggs congealing on their plates. I leaned over and kissed Aunt Cathie on the cheek, then Uncle William, and tried to smile at Pete and Julia, who were looking a bit shell-shocked. Perhaps they weren't in on it. Ben nodded in the table's direction and kissed Aunt Cathie. By then Uncle William was up and Ben shook his hand. I wanted to cry. It seemed like he was saying goodbye. Goodbye forever, not just 'til next time.

We walked out onto the verandah and down the steps I'd first walked up when I was thirteen and homeless. On the grass looking over the trees to the sea, Amber was pushing Fred in the swing and David was hammering a nail into a red wooden truck I'd given him when he was five. At least they weren't in on the conspiracy. They came leaping over, and when Ben told them we had to leave, Fred jumped up and down chanting "No, don't go, stay here, it's the holidays for ages yet so why do you have to go?"

~

I WAKE SOMETIME IN THE EARLY HOURS OF THE MORNING, HOT and sweaty. Lily is hunched in my arms, her hair tickling my face. "Sweetheart," I whisper.

It's a dream. I know it's a dream. I push the pillow in my arms over the edge of the mattress, gently so it doesn't bruise when plops on the floor. I wipe my hair away from my face, then miss the tickle of it. I want to return to my dream although I always feel strange for hours after it, as if something has happened that I can't quite remember. But I know it's gone and I've got another day to get through. I know Lily mightn't come back again for weeks or months. One day she'll never come back.

Ben's lying with his back to me; we've barely spoken since leaving Killara. He seems to be sleeping, but it's hard to tell. I don't want to talk to him anyway. I creep out of bed and tiptoe into Lily's room. Closing the door I slide between her yellow sheets. They look gray in the dark but I know exactly their color. They feel damp and cold, and the thin summer bedcover sucks out the little bit of warmth left in my body. Winter in Brisbane isn't meant to be this cold.

THE DOOR OPENED AND BEN WAS THERE, LIGHT HURTING MY eyes.

"Here's some tea," he said. "You should get up and have a shower. I'll make some breakfast and then we'll talk this through." He dumped the tea on Lily's bedside table and looked down at me, no smile on his face, no kiss good morning, not even a pretense of caring.

I took my time but I knew Ben wouldn't soften until we'd had it out. I didn't even know why he was so angry. What had he expected? That I would do as I was told and thank Cassandra and let them get on with their cozy little plan to make us a baby? The memory of Ben and Cassandra ogling each other all those years ago was stuck in my head now, and then there were all those other times when they were alone together. Ben always pretending he found Cassandra a pain and Cassandra always carrying on as if Sebastian were the only man for her.

"It's time Lily's room was redecorated," Ben said. "We can turn it into a library. You've always wanted one. You can keep Lily's bookcase with all her books, and some of her pictures. The one of her and Sunny dressed as bunnies at their first ballet show perhaps. You love that one. Keep the others in photo albums. Not on the walls."

"I like it the way it is," I said, my eyes welling.

"It's two and a half years. It's not healthy. You need to let her go."

"I don't want to let her go. She's all I have."

"You'll always have your memories; we can remember her together. The happy times. I miss you."

I looked at him, seeing him at last, across the table, his eyes behind his glasses begging. I closed my eyes, fighting the ocean of tears pressing on my chest, the infinite ocean that grew inside me, pushing into the space where my uterus used to be, squeezing my broken heart smaller and smaller.

I was being pulled from the chair into his warmth, falling with him onto the floor, holding him and kissing the tears on his face and my tears on his face, his glasses discarded where they fell.

We built the library together. It was beautiful. Sebastian, maker of fine rocking horses, sourced the wood for the shelves, and he and Ben built them on the white walls while I followed along behind, stroking on the velvety varnish to bring out the grain. We moved my desk out of the guest bedroom that doubled as my study and placed it under the window in the new library, and above it I hung the picture of Lily and Sunny with their floppy yellow ears, painted pink noses and four black whiskers on each cheek, distorted by their huge grins.

When the shelves were filled with all our books in alphabetical author order (my 900 novels) and by subject matter (Ben's 900 biology and history books) we placed Lily's small bookcase with its tattered picture books and still new, big girl's novels, in pride of place against the end wall. Above it we hung three small pictures that seemed in this space to go together like family: our wedding picture; a rare happy picture of Mum and me aged seven; a picture of Killara with a young Cathie and William and gangly Cassandra and Pete on the deck. Then we invited the Brooks family for tea. Scones with raspberry jam and clotted cream.

Ben was right, and transforming Lily's memorial into a living, breathing library was a turning point. I even began doodling with a new story idea. I didn't think it would become a novel but at least it gave me some different people to think about if I couldn't get to sleep.

Two weeks, three weeks, four weeks went by and sleep became easier. My dreams began to have a scent; I'd wake happy, sniffing the air. I knew what it was immediately: Johnson's baby powder. It transported me back to the seventies and Cassandra's babies. Amber, David, Fred.

Sunny.

Not Lily. I had Jasmine talcum powder for Lily, right from her first bath the night we brought her back from the Quarantine Station to the house Aunt Cathie and Uncle William had rented in Sydney. In the rush and excitement of leaving Brisbane, I'd forgotten to put baby powder in my case of baby essentials. Aunt Cathie had given me hers. For our newborn son, who'd never had a chance to have any powder stroked over his soft skin, perhaps I'd had a tin of his own Johnson's baby powder waiting, or perhaps I'd planned to share the massive tin Cassandra had for baby David. I can't remember.

Another week passed and on the mornings I woke without the scent of the dream I yearned for, I was irritable, unsettled. Instead of joining my Stoddard and Jones colleagues for lunch in the small tearoom where they gathered to gossip and sometimes rave about a manuscript they were reading, day after day I found myself in cafés. Cafés swarming with young mothers, desperate for adult company, their Johnson's-baby-talced infants asleep in their prams.

"Ben," I finally managed to get out one night during dinner, "Ben, I think I've changed my mind. Is it too late?"

Chapter Thirty

Brisbane, September, 1985

Ben booked a table for four at one of the nicest restaurants in town, famous for its degustation menus, its quiet music, and its private tables. We'd never been there before and that, we'd decided, was important. Our initial instinct had been to meet Cassandra and Sebastian in the restaurant we'd been to so often as a foursome in those long-ago days when we all lived together as happy hippies. If this dinner turned out the way we hoped, it would be the beginning of a whole new relationship, almost a business deal, and we didn't want it infected by the past. When we invited Sebastian and Cassandra, we used the excuse that it was to celebrate Ben's 39th birthday; it seemed a good omen that it so conveniently fell in the week after I made my decision.

I was scared; we both were. What if my cold rejection of Cassandra's generous offer had turned her off the idea? What if instead they'd decided to have another baby of their own? Perhaps she was already pregnant? We would wait until well into the evening before deciding whether to raise the possibility of surrogacy. Ben told me it would be entirely my decision. He'd follow my lead.

~

"Wow, this is gorgeous," said Cassandra, as we were seated, each opposite our partners, at our romantic, secluded, candle-lit table. The lights of Brisbane spread out before us on the other side of the big window. "Is it only us?" Cassandra's eyebrows went up.

Ben nodded. "Yep, I wanted a quiet, gourmet night. I'm an old man now, not some young party-crazed punk."

"Punk," Sebastian snorted. "Never were you that. But this is nice. We're honored to be the ones to share such an Augustian occasion with you." He looked twenty-five in the soft light, his grin the same as ever.

Thank goodness for degustation. Small, beautiful bites of dishes that even with my stomach churning I could swallow. Lots of delicious wine. Ben was consuming more than usual. Luckily we'd been sensible and taken a taxi to the restaurant.

I tried to slant the conversation towards family. Theirs, and whether they were planning on any more kids. I didn't actually ask that, just watched for signs when they were talking about seven-year-old Fred's latest exploits at school.

"Well, only a few more years of those bloody primary school fairs, and Fred will be at secondary school. I bet you're hanging out for that," Ben said. "Grief, you've done your share of school runs." He stopped and counted on his fingers. "Already ten years of Parent-Teacher meetings and baking sponge cakes for school fund raisers."

Sneaky. I watched Cassandra's face.

"I'm with you there," said Sebastian.

"Spoilsports. It's not that bad. I'll quite miss it," said Cassandra. She sighed. "Fred's so grown up already."

"Come on, woman. You've had enough of little kids.

They're too damn exhausting for ancients like us," Sebastian said.

"Speak for yourself. They don't exhaust me. I can't wait until Amber has her first."

"She's only fifteen. I hope in heaven's name she waits at least another ten years." Sebastian put on a mock frown as he looked at Cassandra.

"I was twenty-three when I had Amber. But it was different then. Everything was so free."

The silence seemed to stretch into minutes, but was probably a few seconds. Were we all back there, flooded with those halcyon memories? Before I got pregnant with Alfie, before Lily, before everything changed?

Cassandra sighed again. "It's strange to think I'll never be pregnant again. I loved that, almost more than having little babies to look after."

Under the table, Ben's foot nudged mine. I swallowed a mouthful of red wine. "Why don't you? Have another baby, I mean. You always said you wanted lots of children."

"Ha. Even Cassandra isn't equipped to produce a baby without a man," Sebastian said, his grin flashing white. "Have you forgotten I had the cut years ago?"

"Are you kidding? You never told us," Ben said.

"Surely we did. When Fred was three. We finally decided enough was enough. Best decision we ever made. The world's got far too many damn people in it."

"It was when you were on all those book tours after *Daisy's War* was published," Cassandra said. "I think you were in the UK. I guess we just forgot to tell you. By the time you got home it was old news."

"We never even guessed. Are you sorry now?" My hands beneath the table were gripped together so tightly I could feel my nails biting into my palms.

Cassandra shook her head. "No. Not often, anyway. I'm getting too old for all that getting up in the middle of the night to feed a baby. I do miss the feel of being pregnant though. Bizarre, I guess."

"We wanted to talk to you about that," I croaked.

"What?" Cassandra turned her head and looked at me.

I forced myself to look into her eyes, their gold flecks accusing.

"Oh Olivia, I'm sorry. How bloody thoughtless of me; going on about babies and all that twaddle." She grabbed my arm. "I didn't think. I'm sorry."

"It's OK. It's not that. It's something else." I looked over at Ben. "It's… would you think about that idea of yours again? Having a baby for us?"

"A baby? You've changed your mind? Oh, my god, I can't believe it. Are you sure?" She turned to Ben on her other side. "Ben, is it true? Are you OK with it too?"

Ben nodded and I saw that he was tearing up. Cassandra still had my arm in an iron grip so I stretched my other hand across the table to Ben, and he took it. Somehow I found the strength to look again at Cassandra. "I wouldn't blame you if you turned us down after I was so horrible to you when you suggested it. I couldn't get my head around it. But I do want a baby, so much, and if you'll try and help us…" Tears fell down my cheeks and Cassandra was crying as well. Sebastian's arm was around me holding me tight and Ben was clinging to my hand. I felt encompassed by love.

Love alone wasn't able to still my fears as I learned more. Sebastian gave us the lowdown the next evening when we met at their house for an alcohol-free discussion. "For a while I've been part of an Australian-wide working group on the knotty issues around surrogacy," he said. "At the moment there is no legislature around it, and so it happens privately. So far there is pretty much agreement that commercial surrogacy should be illegal in Australia, but that altruistic surrogacy, where the surrogate mother does it because she truly wants to and not for money, should be permitted. But we need some guidelines and legislation. Of course there are some factions who think even altruistic surrogacy arrangements should be criminalized, but last year the Queensland Government produced a report that made a strong case for supporting it. It had numerous recommendations, and it'll probably take years before anything becomes law. As a lawyer I'd like to see some sensible and humane laws around it, but if I'm honest, it's a plus for us right now. If we decide to go with this, we can, and without all the red tape."

"So what happens when the baby is born?" Ben asked, his hand reaching for mine. "How do we become its parents? Surely that has to be a legal process?"

Sebastian nodded, and his usually benign expression changed. I suddenly saw him as a lawyer.

"That's the hardest bit; the adoption after the baby is born. The intended parents, both of them, even if the man is the sperm donor, need to legally adopt the baby because the parents on the baby's birth certificate are of right, that of the birth mother and her husband."

"Even if the husband doesn't agree?"

"Ah, that's where it's possible to get around it. If the birth mother and her husband sign a statement saying he isn't the father, then only the birth mother's name will be on the birth certificate. That leaves a possible chink in the adoption laws and the genetic father and his wife can apply for a Relative Adoption. There was a successful surrogacy and adoption case in Melbourne not long ago where the two women were sisters. Both couples have come to some of our surrogacy working group meetings. The birth mother was the sister of the adoptive mother, and the sperm donor was the adoptive mother's husband. They had counseling before the first round of artificial insemination to make sure they understood all the possible consequences, and still wanted to go ahead. Everything was carefully planned so later it would be easier to adopt. They made agreements about all sorts of issues to do with the pregnancy and birth as well as how much contact the birth mother and her husband and three kids would have with the baby once he was with the intended parents. Obviously, as they were sisters, the birth mother and her husband and kids were going to stay part of the child's life."

"Did the birth mother give away her baby as soon as it was born?" I heard the disbelief in my tone.

"In this case, yes. But that's up to the birth mother. Unofficially she can give it to the new parents immediately, or after a few weeks if she's uncertain, and they take over all the parenting roles. After four weeks they can apply for a Relative Adoption, if the birth mother, her husband and the biological father all sign statements that the child was conceived by sperm donation with the intention that the biological father and his wife would become the child's legal parents."

"Why are you talking about this as if it has nothing to do with us?" I could hear the quiver in Cassandra's voice.

"Sorry. The legal beaver in me raving on. I didn't want to assume anything yet. Not until we all know the facts."

"Well, I'm not a lawyer and I need to talk about it as something we're doing, not your clients."

"I think we can work it out," Ben said, the tension in his voice echoing his expression. "You're the birth mother, I'm the sperm donor. Sebastian's the guy who has to swear your baby isn't his and that he doesn't want to claim it, and Olivia waits in the wings and hopes the adoption goes through and she gets to be Mum."

"It seems too difficult," I said, the tears in my voice taking me by surprise. "I thought adopting Lily was hard enough, but this sounds much worse. What happens if we go through with it and then the adoption isn't approved?"

"That could happen," Sebastian said. "But if we do it

right — retain sympathetic lawyers and have in-depth counseling — I believe we'd have a very good chance."

"But we all know each other. Surely we don't need counseling. It will take too long," I said.

"We absolutely need counseling. All of us, separately first, then in pairs, and finally as a quartet. That's what I would request of my clients, and it makes sense. The judge will think so too, when it comes time for the adoption proceedings."

"I never found counseling much use." My pulse was thumping in my throat.

Ben's arm tightened around me. "Sebastian's talking about specialist adoption counselors, not therapists," he said. "Perhaps we should let the counselor decide how much we need. A child is a life-time commitment, and I'm betting there are issues that might arise that we haven't thought through in detail."

"That's right," Sebastian said. "Like the relationship of the baby to Cassandra. To me as well. Once you adopt the baby Cassandra will lose all legal rights, so we all have to agree that we, and our kids, continue to play some role in the child's life from then on. Obviously we couldn't go ahead if it meant we could no longer do stuff together as friends."

"It'll bring us together again, Olivia." Cassandra's brown and gold eyes glowed.

A shiver crept up my spine.

"We haven't really been together — not like we used to be — since Sunny and Lily died," she said, her voice soft.

I sighed. "I'll never be able to thank you enough if this works out. Never."

"I want to do this. You don't need to thank me. This means as much to me as to you."

"And to me and Sebastian," Ben said.

For a few seconds I'd forgotten they were there.

"Sebastian is the one who has to stand on the sidelines

while Cassandra has our baby." Ben looked at Sebastian. "Why would you do that? What do you get out of it?"

"Your happiness. Olivia's happiness. Cassandra's happiness." He grinned. "And I get to experience a bit of what my clients experience, and hopefully I gain a cute little niece or nephew. One that I can give back at the end of the day. What's not to love?"

Chapter Thirty-One

Over the next two weeks we had more discussions, Ben and I fluctuating between excitement and terror, Cassandra and Sebastian seemingly remaining committed. We battered Sebastian with questions; I needed to know every little detail. He contacted the two Melbourne couples and got their permission to share their story with us. Straight away they offered to meet with us; they were planning a trip to Brisbane soon anyway, as the sisters' parents lived here. Three weeks later, with the kids farmed out to friends' homes for the night, Cassandra put on one of her dinner parties. Eight adults — the two Melbourne couples and we four learners — and one gorgeous little boy, the one-year-old at the center of it all.

"It was wonderful," said Marnie, her eyes glowing in the candlelight. "When Toby was born right on our bed, we were all there. After I'd breast-fed him so he got the colostrum, I handed him to Brenda and Aaron. It was incredible, watching their faces. It felt right. From the moment of conception I'd thought of the baby as belonging to them. The adoption was just a legalization of that belonging."

"And we get a whole family of babysitters we know will

take care of our baby as if he were their own," Brenda said, her laugh so full of joy I found myself laughing with her.

After they left, the four of us had one more glass; whisky for the men and port for Cassandra and me. "Marnie is incredible," I said, snuggling into Ben. "Brenda too. They've finally made me believe it's possible. Marnie choosing to be a surrogate because she loved being pregnant and had already completed her own family. She simply wanted to give the joy of parenthood to a couple she cared about."

"What about the blokes?" asked Ben, tickling me.

"Huh, easy for them," I said. Across the glass-strewn coffee table I smiled at Sebastian, his long brown fingers massaging Cassandra's bare feet as she lolled on the couch. He was lit up from inside. Not just the whisky. I could see and feel his passion for this.

"This means a lot to you." My breath suddenly stuck in my chest.

"It's why it's so important to push for legalized surrogacy in Australia. Never for money. It must always be altruistic. Babies should never be purchased, however that is obfuscated."

'That will make it less stressful for everyone," Ben said. "Knowing it is all going to happen and not having to worry about the birth mother changing her mind."

"It won't prevent that entirely. Even in a legalized system, the birth mother will likely always be able to change her mind, right up until adoption."

"I'm not going to change my mind," Cassandra said, her voice drowsy.

We felt more confident after a meeting with our lawyer, a man who had, like Sebastian, been involved with complex overseas adoptions and was sympathetic to surrogacy. Cassandra and Sebastian had their own lawyer, likewise first checked out by Sebastian. Sebastian's adoption contacts also came in handy when it came to choosing our counselors. Pauline and Brian were a counseling couple, with biological and adopted kids of their own. Down-to-earth and overwhelmingly positive, they skillfully guided us through all manner of scenarios without reducing me to a quivering mess.

The hardest session was the one where we discussed where the baby was going to be born — in hospital, at Cassandra and Sebastian's home, or at Killara. In fact it was always Cassandra's call. The birth mother had complete autonomy over her pregnancy and birth. But we were all invited to share our feelings about it. Ben and I wanted it to be at Brisbane hospital; my disastrous spa birth experience still haunted us. But when Cassandra pointed out that the rigid hospital rules would never allow three support people in the birthing suite and she wanted us all there, we reluctantly agreed to a home birth here in Brisbane, close to the hospital, and not at Killara. Without asking me, Cassandra registered with Janice MacIntosh, the same midwife I had gone to when I was pregnant with our lost boy. She didn't deliver him because I was at Killara. Would the outcome have been so much better if she had? I hadn't seen her for over twelve years.

Luckily the GP who had been looking after the health of all four of us since our hippie days was sympathetic to our surrogacy plans; it helped that she'd known us for so long. She'd be the one who'd manage Cassandra's hormone treatments and act as a backup for the midwife should she need it. The whole thing was beginning to seem normal.

It was December before all the health checks were done and we and our counselors were satisfied that we understood what we were getting into, both short and long-term. They suggested we take a break over Christmas before the first treatment cycle began. Killara welcomed us, and I discovered, to my shame, that Aunt Cathie and Uncle William had not known back in July that Cassandra had offered to have a baby for us and I'd rejected her gift. It had all been in my suspicious mind. This time, together we told them, Pete and Julie as well, the night after we arrived. After a few moments of open-mouthed astonishment they seemed pleased, and by the time we had to leave, Uncle William and Pete were cautiously optimistic and Aunt Cathie and Julie plain excited.

As soon as we got back to Brisbane, Cassandra began a course of artificial hormone stimulation to encourage ovulation and stimulate the release of multiple eggs. This would increase the chances of conception, but also of course, of twins. We didn't dare voice the possibility of triplets. I would have quite liked twins, but I didn't mention that. At the peak of Cassandra's ovulation, Ben's semen, carefully washed by the sperm donation clinic to concentrate the motile sperm, would be inserted by the GP into Cassandra's uterine cavity using a small catheter.

"It doesn't always work straight away," Sebastian warned. "In fact it almost never works straight away. It usually takes months. Ten months is about average."

"Poof. I never had any problem conceiving the minute we stopped contraception," Cassandra said.

"True, and that might happen again. Let's hope so or poor old Ben will run out of porn magazines."

"Don't be so crude," Cassandra said.

"Me, crude? Wasn't that your thirty-ninth birthday we celebrated last week? I'm sorry to break this to you, but you're no longer the sweet thirty you were when Fred was conceived. And my sperm and your eggs were obviously madly attracted to each other. Ben's sperm might be shy."

"Too much information," I said, my face hot.

~

It was shockingly upsetting when the first cycle, then the second cycle failed. A rollercoaster of emotions. I dreaded this being our lives for countless months while we waited. My disappointment was tinted with something darker — a satisfaction that Ben's sperm hadn't been as keen to snuggle into Cassandra's eggs as Sebastian's obviously had been.

Ben dreaded his visits to the donor clinic to produce his sperm sample each month. "They have this cozy little room decked out with posters of Marilyn Monroe with her dress blowing up and some presumably erotic scene from *Gone With The Wind*; the scene where Rhett Butler looks as if he is about to strangle the scarlet woman. It's captioned: 'Frankly, my dear, I don't give a damn.' Very stimulating. Then there's the heap of turn-off, well-thumbed porn magazines."

So when he came home after producing the third sample and told me about the alternative method we could try, if that sample failed, I had to agree. "There's a special collector condom we can use. We have sex in the morning and then I rush the bursting condom to the clinic for processing. God knows why they didn't tell me this earlier. How could they think a poster of Marilyn Monroe would be better than you?"

I didn't enjoy it. I couldn't stop thinking about how those sperm squirted into me would then be squirted into Cassandra. After Ben came back from delivering his package to the clinic we talked for ages, and pretty much decided we'd stop the whole business if Cassandra hadn't conceived after the sixth sample. Of course that very first sample collected in our bed and my body did the trick.

I think Ben and I believed that once Cassandra was pregnant, our emotions would stabilize. We'd lived in the same house as Cassandra when she was incubating both David and Sunny, and we knew pregnancy and blossoming were synonymous for her. No nausea, no mood swings, no high blood pressure, no bloating. She was an Earth Mother. All we'd have to do was sit back and wait.

~

NOPE. EARTH MOTHER NO LONGER. CASSANDRA WOULD BE SIX weeks past her fortieth birthday when the baby was born in late February. Well into what the medical profession charmingly labeled a geriatric pregnancy. Eighteen months since she first suggested surrogacy. So her age was the explanation we all grabbed for as Cassandra wretched into the toilet bowl morning, noon, and night for the first four months, her moods fluctuating between irritable and depressed, her constant fatigue worrying Sebastian, who recalled how annoying he'd sometimes found her boundless energy during her previous pregnancies. I had another, clearly ridiculous, explanation; not that I dared voice it. Perhaps, in contrast to Sebastian's four offspring, Ben's baby didn't love floating around in Cassandra's amniotic fluid. But the anxiety and guilt I was carrying with me twenty-four hours a day lifted when, after four months, the nausea stopped and Cassandra reverted to her blossoming self.

The day of her twenty-week ultrasound was scheduled so we could all go, and somewhat to our surprise we were all allowed to watch. Such a cliché to weep, but that's what we all did. Boy, girl; we told the radiographer we didn't want to know. But I did look carefully. Not a clue. But that little face, the hands, the tiny mouth sucking a thumb, the heart beat. Another joy we didn't have with our baby son. Ultrasounds weren't routinely offered to pregnant mums back then.

As Cassandra's belly expanded, my feelings turned a touch green. Just a touch. More because of Ben's fascination with the whole process than because I wanted to be the one with the glossy hair and glowing skin. More because of Ben's gentleness with Cassandra, and his poorly disguised delight as he placed his hand on her growing stomach so he could feel the first kick, the second kick. He was sure it was a boy; such a feisty little chap. Was he remembering our baby? Before he was born he too kicked like a champion. I hated it when my thoughts went in that direction. I'd desperately try and block them out with memories of Cassandra's babies, all so wonderfully strong from the moment they emerged. If she gave us a healthy baby I would love her forever.

Chapter Thirty-Two

When Sebastian showed up at Stoddard and Jones in early December, my first thought, of course, was that something had gone wrong with the pregnancy. The plethora of possibilities that flooded my brain in the few seconds it took Sebastian to explain the reason for his first ever visit to my office was staggering. How can the mind and imagination work that fast?

"Sorry," he said, after he told me Cassandra was fine and he saw my relieved expression. "I should have phoned first."

I sat back down and waved to the chair on the other side of my desk. "So now my pulse is back in line, what's up? Have you written a memoir and now you're looking for a publisher? It would be a bestseller. All those men whose lot it is to be married to a surrogate. You could make it a self-help manual."

"Ha. Very amusing. No, I need a favor. I'm off to Melbourne for a week of meetings with our getting-surrogacy-legalized pressure group." He pressed his lips together, his forehead crinkling in a rare frown. "I don't like leaving Cassandra alone for all that time; she's struggling with dealing with our three hooligans, on top of the pregnancy, even though she tries to hide it. She's not sleeping well. Too bloody uncomfortable she says. Basically she's not the young thing she was with her last pregnancies. I wondered if you and Ben would come and stay in the guest room while I'm away; give her some support?"

"Oh, well yes, although I'm not sure I can take time off work," I gabbled, everything in me screaming *No*.

"No need for that. It's just in the mornings and evenings it would be good if she had some help. When chaos rules. I could ask Cathie and William to fly down, but I thought it might be nice for you to be involved a bit more with your baby's incubation. Do Cassandra's panting exercises with her." He grinned. "Ben can experience the delight of the foot massages for a few days."

"I'll need to check with Ben; when do you go?"

"Next week. Sorry about the short notice. Cassandra lost it with poor Fred last night; yelled at him to go to his room. That's not like her. And she and Amber are constantly at loggerheads. Teenage stuff, I know, but it's harder for her to handle when her back is aching and her ankles are swollen."

"God, I knew this was a bad idea. What on earth were we thinking?" The guilt seared through me.

"Don't be daft. It's a few weeks discomfort in a lifetime of one gorgeous kid."

"I'll come, whether or not Ben can. That's if Cassandra wants me to."

"Of course she does. She's sad she doesn't see you more often. She wants to share it all with you. The good things I mean, like her checks with the midwife; listening to the baby's heartbeat. Not the aching back."

Ben was enthusiastic. Too bloody enthusiastic. I was being ridiculous. Cassandra was big for 32 weeks. Bigger than she'd been for any of the others. She lumbered around, dark circles under her eyes, her hair the only part of her still glossy. If she needed her ankles massaged, I'd do it. Ben could entertain the kids. They loved him to bits.

It wasn't so bad. Apart from Amber, who seemed to have only three modes of behavior — picking arguments with her mother, yelling at her brothers, or sulking and disappearing into her room behind a slamming door—the atmosphere was reasonably benign. The house was always spotless as the cleaner came in four mornings a week. School mornings were chaotic of course and it was bliss to get to work and shut my office door. Evenings were less fraught, and Ben and I took turns making nourishing dinners that the kids wouldn't turn their noses up at. Spaghetti Bolognese, homemade pizzas, roast chicken, hamburgers. After dinner while the boys watched TV in the den—it was almost the end of the school year so no hassles over homework — we'd sit on the deck in the early tropical twilight, music wafting out the open French doors, the lights of the river and Brisbane spread out before us. Goodness knows what Amber did in her room. Hopefully not drugs.

"I'M SEEING MY MIDWIFE ON WEDNESDAY MORNING," Cassandra said on our first evening. "Nine-thirty. I thought you might like to come. Meet her again and hear your baby's heartbeat."

I glanced at Ben. Was she talking to him or me?

"Both of you, if you can," she said.

Mindreader.

'Wednesday? Can't do," said Ben. "My stage three lecture is at ten."

"Olivia? Could you come?"

"Are you sure?"

"Of course I am. I really want you to come. Sometimes I

feel like you don't want this baby." Her voice quivered.

"Oh, don't. Of course I want it. It's just awkward, knowing what to do without… without taking liberties."

Cassandra giggled.

I grinned. "That didn't come out right. But you know what I mean."

"So you'll come?"

I nodded. "I don't think I have any meetings. If I do I'll reschedule."

It was awkward, seeing Janice. Our last meeting had been in the weeks after I had my hysterectomy. She'd come around to the house to sympathize.

"You remember Olivia?" Cassandra said, when we first arrived at Janice's home where she saw her mothers. "She's come to listen to our baby's heartbeat."

Janice blushed and nodded, but didn't say anything. I stood in the corner while she examined Cassandra, wishing I hadn't come.

"Come on, Olivia," Cassandra said. "Your turn to listen in."

I pushed the stethoscope earpieces into my ears, and concentrated as the midwife pressed the diaphragm onto Cassandra's bulging stomach. Nothing. I closed my eyes. Hooves in the distance, galloping, coming closer. So rapid. "Oh, I hear it. I hear it."

"Lovely and strong," said Janice.

I opened my eyes, reluctant to lose the moment. I'd been so afraid it would take me back to hearing our son's heartbeat. But it was a relief, a breakthrough. Ben needed to hear it too.

"Our baby," Cassandra whispered. "Your baby. Yours and Ben's."

I blinked back my tears. Janice was over at her desk, the stethoscope gone. I touched Cassandra's smooth brown geriatric belly, the navel already protruding. "Thank you," I whispered.

~

It was the night before Sebastian was due back. I was exhausted. How Cassandra coped I had no clue; one baby was going to stretch us to our limit.

Please let him—or her—be healthy. Down Syndrome babies were born to one in a hundred mothers aged forty. Like every pregnant mother I worried. It felt wrong to even think that a baby who had a disability, any disability, would not be welcome. Of course he would, loved to bits. But there was no getting around it, I would turn forty in March, only two months later than Cassandra.

I quashed my selfish thoughts as I wiped down the kitchen bench. Blessed silence pervaded the house, all three hooligans doing whatever they wanted to in their bedrooms. Pouring three cups of lemon and ginger tea, I stuck them on a tray and walked towards the lounge. The door was ajar and the room seemed barely lit. Cassandra was probably asleep on the couch and Ben as usual crouched under the reading light engrossed in some bird journal.

I tiptoed in, glancing over at Ben's chair. Not there. Then my eyes adjusted and I saw that the shape on the couch was a prostrate Cassandra, and kneeling at her side with his head on her bare stomach was Ben. Ben with her hand on his head.

Somehow I caught the tray before it crashed to the carpet, but one cup hit another, the sound like a pistol shot in the still room. Ben's body jerked, his head swinging around. Cassandra turned on her side and in the low light I could see her glowing eyes, the look I thought she kept for Sebastian.

"What's going on?" I hissed, the tray banging down on the coffee table, slopping Cassandra's pretentious herbal tea over her pretentious pile of coffee table books.

Ben unfolded himself from the floor and stood up. "I was listening to our baby's heartbeat."

"He was so sad that he missed out on hearing it through the stethoscope on Wednesday," Cassandra cooed.

"Is that right. And did you hear it with your satellite ears? Did you get close enough?"

"Stop it, Olivia," Ben said. "Cassandra thought it might be loud enough, that's all."

"And?"

"It wasn't. All I could hear was her pulse."

"Surprise, surprise. Had you forgotten we learned from our own son that fetal heartbeats couldn't be heard just by sticking your ear on my stomach?"

"Calm down, Olivia," Cassandra said, hauling herself into a sitting position and pulling her top over her beachball. "Ben is this little person's Daddy. If he wants to get close to her, he can."

"Her, is it? Did the baby tell you that? I thought you'd decided it was a boy?"

"Not me. I've always known it was a girl. Girl, boy, girl, boy so far. So this one's a girl."

"Oh, for heaven's sake. Put the bullshit away. I'm going to bed. Your tea's all over your coffee table if the two of you want to lick it up."

I REFUSED TO GO TO CASSANDRA'S FOR WEEKS AFTER THAT. Ben wanted to invite the whole five of them over for dinner, but he wanted in vain. Bugger her.

Sebastian tried to smooth things over; goodness knows what twisted story Cassandra told him. He came to my office for a second time. "Come on Olivia, it's no biggie. I can understand why you're pissed off, but is it worth all this grief? Think of your baby. That's all that matters. If you continue with this you'll end up too angry to be at the birth."

"Aren't you worried? Your wife and my husband?"

"I was shitty with both of them when they confessed, but I do think they meant no harm. Sometimes, pretty bloody often actually, Cassandra is incapable of seeing things from any perspective but her own, and perhaps Ben did think he would be able to hear the heartbeat. Otherwise he wouldn't have had his ear to her stomach. Intimate, I give you that, but hardly foreplay."

He had a point. It was too late to change my mind over taking this baby. Ben's baby. He would never give it up. And I wanted it desperately. Desperately.

When I finally gave in and went with Ben to lunch at their house, Cassandra did her best to apologize. "Sorry, Olivia. We should have waited until you were in the room. It just never occurred to us that you would misread it. Sorry."

I felt as if we'd never got past being fifteen.

On the positive side, it was good to see the kids. I'd missed them. Amber especially. Poor thing. She had no way to escape Cassandra's grandstanding. After lunch she and I went for a long walk, leaving the others to entertain themselves. "I sometimes wish you'd been my mum," she said. "That baby doesn't know how lucky she is."

"Don't say that. About your mum I mean. You kids mean everything to her."

"I know. I don't suppose I really mean it, but sometimes…"

"Cheer up. You'll be off to university next year. Where are you thinking of applying?"

"Anywhere that is not in Brisbane. Uncle Pete and Julie said that if I go to Melbourne Uni I could stay with them until I found an apartment."

"Sounds perfect. Let me know if I can help you with applications. Are you still interested in psychology?"

"I don't know. Perhaps. But then I'd have to give therapy to control freaks like Mum." She grinned and took my hand as we turned and dawdled back to the house.

Chapter Thirty-Three

Brisbane, February, 1987

When the phone rang at four o'clock I was so engrossed in the editing of the manuscript of one of my best authors that I let it go to the answer machine.

"Olivia. Are you there? I've started."

I snatched up the phone. "Cassandra, I'm here. It's way too early, are you OK?"

"Two weeks early is nothing. This is my fifth, don't forget…"

As if I could.

"It's practically normal for experienced mothers to go into labor early. Anyway, this pregnancy has been different from my others right through."

"Have you phoned the midwife? How far apart are the contractions?" The words stumbled out of me as I shut down my computer and grabbed my briefcase.

"I'll phone her next. Then Sebastian. Can you call Ben?"

"Of course. We'll get over as soon as we can." I hesitated. "That's if you want us there."

"God, Olivia, sometimes you are as dumb as two thick planks. Of course I want you here. Both of you. It's your baby, for heaven's sake."

"Sorry. I'm leaving now. Shall I bring some food? We could grab some takeaways; the kids at least will be hungry."

"There's no rush. This new kid won't be here for hours yet. Get your toothbrushes and PJs and come when you're ready, after Ben gets home from the university. I've got salmon for the BBQ and salads all prepared for dinner, and a new baked loaf just out of the oven…" She giggled. "Very appropriate. Shit, here it comes again."

I heard her breathing as I pressed the phone hard to my ear.

"Bloody hell, that was a bit stronger."

"Have your waters broken?

"No. My contractions are.. just checking.. about ten minutes apart. So no panic. I might have a sit down. I'll see you a bit later."

"God, I can't believe it."

"Believe it, Mumsie. Your peaceful nights are almost history."

While Cassandra lolled in the spa bath on the back deck, water swaying up and down the sides with each contraction, we picked at our salmon and salad and then played Monopoly. David won. I had purchased just one property during the entire game.

Janice arrived about ten, Fred and David having been cajoled into their bedrooms with a promise to call them, wake them if they'd managed to fall asleep, when the baby was about to make an appearance.

While Janice examined Cassandra, Ben and I wandered out on the deck. It was one thing watching the baby emerge from between her thighs and quite another to be in the room during the preliminaries. Sebastian beckoned us back in time to catch the severe expression on Janice's face. "This baby has got itself into the posterior position," she said, frowning at Cassandra as if it were somehow her fault. "That's why you are having so much back pain. Your blood pressure is too high, so I think we'd better get you to hospital. You're not young and I'm not willing to risk any complications."

"No way," said Cassandra, before panting through what seemed like a pretty strong contraction. They were about five minutes apart now.

"I know you had your heart set on a home birth, but you'll be safer in hospital. I'll phone the maternity ward now and warn them you're coming."

"I said no. It's my body and my baby and I'm staying right here."

"Sweetheart, listen to Janice," said Sebastian. "It'll be fine. You can have the baby in hospital and you'll be home tomorrow."

Ben's tension zinged through the air between us.

"Come on Cassandra," I said. "Be sensible."

"They won't let you in with me in hospital Don't you want to see your baby born?" Cassandra said.

"Yes, of course, but not if there's the slightest chance it will go wrong."

"Phone the hospital, Janice," Ben said, and we all looked at him. "We'll get her in the car now."

"Who the hell do you think you are, ordering me around," Cassandra hissed, then grimaced as a contraction took over.

"The father," Ben said, ignoring her panting. He nodded toward Janice.

Janice sort of huffed, and tossed her head. She'd made little effort to disguise her disapproval of us being here at all, let alone as future parents of the baby.

"Janice, phone my doctor," Cassandra commanded. "If

you're not willing to help me with this then Diane will come over and deliver the baby."

"I'll call her," said Sebastian. "Let's at least see what she thinks. But if she wants you in hospital, that's what's happening. OK?"

"You're all a load of wimps. Call her."

Sebastian was back in a few minutes. "Well, that's made the decision for us. I got her daughter on the phone. Diane is away in Melbourne until Sunday. This baby won't wait until then."

LEAVING AMBER IN CHARGE OF THE TWO BOYS, WE SUPPORTED A panting Cassandra into the back seat of Sebastian's car and I got in beside her. *Please don't let me have to deliver our baby on the motorway.*

Janice's car shot off in front, and Ben followed us in our car. Quite a parade. At least Janice had agreed to be present at the delivery. Cassandra didn't know any of the obstetrics staff at the hospital.

During the twenty-minute drive she was so busy fuming she almost forgot to pant. My whole body was trembling as if I were lying in a too-thin sleeping bag in a tent in zero-degree temperatures, not in a car with the 28 degree hot night air of February Brisbane wafting through the open windows. Thank heavens the traffic was light and most of the traffic lights in our favor.

It was midnight when we arrived, and the hospital was dim and quiet and smelled of safety. My trembling felt more like a quivering excitement. I'd been dreading the home birth. Cassandra was met by a nurse and Janice, who must have broken the speed limit to get here so much sooner than we had. They stuffed Cassandra into a wheelchair and bustled off with the three of us following like obedient children.

"Who is the husband?" asked the nurse who stopped us following Cassandra through the swing doors.

Sebastian raised his finger.

"I'll get you to do some form filling and then you can gown up and go in to support her," said the nurse, her smile sweet.

"Can Olivia and Ben come too?" he asked. ""Cassandra's stroppy. She'll need all of us to keep her calm."

" 'Fraid not. Only one support person allowed, as long as all is going well. But if the consultant needs to focus and wants you out, you'll have to leave."

"Well, I'll fill in the forms and Olivia can go in with Cassandra."

The nurse raised her pretty eyebrows. "Sister?" she asked.

"Close friend," I said.

'That's fine. It's good to share the load a bit. Who knows how long her labor will be? Her husband can go in for the birth."

Sebastian rolled his eyes behind her back, and Ben gave me a quick hug. "Come out every now and then and give us a progress report," he said. His voice gave him away. He was excited. Or nervous. Both probably.

"Do you want to go in?" I whispered,

"I get the feeling that would be frowned on. It's OK. You go. You'll be much more useful."

I was scared I would be taken back to my own birth experience, if that was what it could be called. But Cassandra's needs were too insistent to give space for any reflection. "Rub it there, no further down, harder, harder," she moaned as I massaged her back between contractions. A young doctor appeared and inserted an IV line into her arm.

"What's that for?" Cassandra asked.

"Just a precaution in case it's needed at some point."

Janice and the two nurses prodded her from time to time and checked the baby's heartbeat, but seemed more interested in their gossip than their patient. The door pushed open and a gowned man strode in, gleaming wire-framed round glasses caught between his cap and his mask. Without a word he plucked the chart from the end of the bed and read it.

"Right," he said. "Mrs. Brooks? I'm Dr. Adams. I see you planned to have one of those ridiculous home births. Are you the midwife?" He glared at poor Janice who had moved over to stand beside him.

"Yes. Janice MacIntosh."

"Well, at least you've got more sense than most of them. Why you women think you can deliver geriatric mothers is beyond comprehension. Better late than never, I suppose." He looked past her to the nurse. "Nurse, get her into the stirrups."

Cassandra gripped my hand as one of the nurses pulled the stirrups down.

"And you are?" Dr. Adams glowered at me over his glasses.

"She's my sister," said Cassandra.

"Cassandra's friend, " I said. Our words collided in the air between us and him.

"My foster sister," said Cassandra. "Also my best friend."

"Is there a husband?" he barked. "Or is it Miss, not Mrs.?"

Don't say it, Cassandra, please don't say it.

"What's that got to do with anything," she snarled, and then jerked as a contraction began its roll through her.

As soon as Cassandra's body went slack, the nurses forced her legs into the stirrups, telling her to push her bottom down the bed. "Relax your legs, dear," said the nurse. "Let them fall apart."

I squirmed as the glasses appeared between her legs. "Ow," she said. "That hurt." Her grip on my hand almost broke it.

The glasses continued his examination without a word.

"He's just helped your membrane rupture," said the nurse.

After another contraction and more prodding, he stood up and I saw the stain on his gown. "You might need a Caesarian," he said. "The posterior occipital position puts more stress on the fetus."

"I don't want a Caesarian. This is my fifth baby. I've never had any trouble delivering."

"You're a geriatric mother. If you want a healthy baby, you'll take my advice."

"Why can't you turn it?" Cassandra said, the look on her face not one anybody who knew her would ignore.

"If there is a husband, get him in here. He can sign the consent forms in case we need to act quickly. I'm going to change my gown."

"Oh, ow, shit, here it comes again."

"Pant, Cassandra, come on. Huh huh huh huh." I panted along with her, my heart racing. I finally understood why she was so passionate about home births. And why I was thankful for hospitals, even if we were stuck with shits like Dr. Glasses. God in heaven, please let his technical skills be a country mile ahead of his bedside manner.

"Sebastian. Where's Sebastian?" Cassandra screamed.

"He's coming, dear. Your midwife has gone to fetch him."

"I don't want a Caesarian. He'll tell you." Her eyes popped and the bones in my hand ground into each other as the next contraction gripped her. "Shit, I need to turn over. Get me on my hands and knees, that's how I deliver," she screamed.

"Don't be silly, dear. This is a hospital. We can't have Dr. Adams down on the floor, can we now."

"Why the fuck not? I can stay on the bed so he doesn't have to lower himself. It's as hard as a fucking rock anyway."

The nurse's hand reached for the mask on the gas canister. She grabbed the top of Cassandra's head and held the mask over her nose and mouth. "Come on, breathe normally and you'll feel much better."

"She doesn't want gas," I said. "It messes up her ability to pant though the contractions."

"The doctor needs to be able to do his job. This will calm her and she won't need to pant."

The contraction stopped and the nurse took away the gas mask. Cassandra's eyes stared at me. She blinked.

"OK?" I said, smiling at her.

"Where's Sebastian? I want him here."

Ben and I sat in the souless waiting room, unread books in our hands, half empty coffee cups next to the piles of magazines chock full of cute babies and their beautiful mothers, most of whom had some minor claim to celebrity. We'd phoned Aunt Cathie and Uncle William and then Pete and Julie, telling them with our fingers crossed that all was on track for Cassandra to deliver vaginally. We'd reassured Amber who had been joined by Angela, their next-door neighbor. "A nice woman," Sebastian had told us.

"David and Fred are sound asleep," Amber said. "Boys."

I must have fallen into a doze, and woke with a start when Janice appeared. "It's all over," she said, and my heart shot into my mouth. "Cassandra has a daughter. She's beautiful."

"Oh Ben," I whispered.

He put his head against mine and we breathed each other in.

"Cassandra?" he said. "How is she?"

"Sore. It was a hard birth. He used forceps at the end. She'll be torn. These male doctors have no idea how to avoid that." She sniffed. "But she'll be fine. She's feeding the little one now."

"Can we go in and see them?" I asked.

She nodded. "Don't stay too long. She needs her rest. I think it would be better if you went in one at a time, but Sebastian seems to want you both to go in. Don't go saying anything to upset her."

Cassandra seemed almost crouched on the rumpled bed, a white-shrouded baby shape crushed against her chest. Janice went over to the bed and put her hand on the baby's back, as if to protect her from us. The two nurses bustled about, tidying up. Dr. Glasses had vanished, thank goodness. Sebastian rose from the chair by the bed, his smile forced. He leaned over and kissed my cheek. "She's fragile," he said quietly. "A bit confused. Too much gas. It was nothing like her previous births."

"I'm sorry," I said, tears spilling down my face.

"It's not your fault. She'll be fine in a bit." He gazed at her, his hair plastered against his forehead, his expression a mix of exhaustion and worry and love.

"I'll ask her if you can hold the baby," he whispered.

I grabbed his arm. "No, leave her, don't make her just yet."

"I'll be gentle." He moved over to the bed and his fingers stroked her matted hair from her forehead. "Sweetheart, Olivia and Ben would love to see her. Shall I take her for a moment?"

Cassandra's eyes stared at him as she shook her head and clutched the baby tighter. The little sound that came from the bundle became a tiny baby cry. She was hurting her. I leapt forward and stopped short as Ben grabbed me.

"What about me?" Sebastian said. "Can I hold her for a moment; I won't let her go, I promise." He bent over and gently tried to loosen Cassandra's hands from their grip. The bundle somehow transferred to him and he turned towards us. We looked into the small red face, her mouth an O and her eyes squeezed tight. My heart flipped over. I touched her cheek and she turned her face towards my finger, and somehow it slipped into her tiny mouth. I felt the wet softness close around it as she started sucking.

"Get away from her. Give her back to me." Cassandra was off the bed, the nurses rushing to her side, Janice almost falling over as she tried to get to her from the far side of the bed.

"She's my baby. She's Sunny, she looks like Sunny, she's mine. She needs me."

His shoulders stooped, Sebastian stood back as the nurses almost lifted Cassandra onto the bed, caging her with pillows. Pushing past them he leaned over, his shoulders shaking, and settled the baby in Cassandra's arms. Her cries turned to hiccupping sobs as she rocked the mewling baby back and forth.

"It's OK sweetheart," Sebastian murmured. "No rush. You're exhausted. Olivia and Ben can have a cuddle later, when you've had a sleep and feel stronger."

Cassandra peered up at him through her mess of hair. I had a sudden flashback of her holding Sunny's still body.

"They'll only want to see her and have a cuddle," Sebastian said, the starkness in his tone chilling my bones. "They'll give her back straight away. No one is going to take her away until you're ready."

Ben's hand was dragging me towards the door, and not until then did I realize Dr. Glasses had come into the room.

"Out," he said. "Everyone out. You too, Mr. Brooks." His steely eyes narrowed behind his glasses as he turned to Janice. "And you. Perhaps this will teach you a lesson. If you'd delivered this woman at home, the baby might not be so healthy and the mother would have no protection from this nonsense."

Chapter Thirty-Four

"Come on, love. You have to eat something," Ben said.

I shook my head. "Can't. Sorry. What are we going to do?"

"Let's wait until tomorrow and then talk to Sebastian. It was a difficult birth, that's all. Once Cassandra's recovered, then we can all talk about what happens next."

"But she promised. It's your baby too."

"Cassandra knows that." Ben pulled me to him and I closed my eyes and tried to stop my thoughts. "It's premature to worry," he murmured into my hair. "But perhaps we do need to prepare ourselves in case she does change her mind. We've always known she could."

The phone shrieked and we jumped. Ben leaned over and picked up the receiver, one arm still around me. The nausea crawled up into my throat as I heard Sebastian's voice. Ben held the receiver away from his ear a little so I could hear better.

"She's calmed down now. I'm sorry you had to go through that."

"It's not your fault. We're more worried about Cassandra. Is she OK? Physically, I mean?"

"Sore and exhausted. She's asleep now. They gave her a sleeping pill and said she'd probably sleep until midday. I'm about to go home and see the kids. They're worried. Scared. I haven't told them much but they thought this baby would pop out like the others."

"Didn't we all," said Ben. "We should never have agreed to this. Cassandra's too old."

Perfect, youthful, energetic Cassandra too old?

Sebastian's voice echoing down the phone-line interrupted my unkind thoughts. "Well, you have a beautiful baby girl, and there is nothing wrong with her. Eight pounds, four ounces, nursing like she's been born to it."

His upbeat tone didn't fool me. I pulled the phone away from Ben's hand.

"Sebastian, it's me. Is she really OK? Our…the baby? I'm so sorry it's been so terrible for Cassandra. I was frightened that she'd gone back to what she was like after Sunny died."

"I know. Me too. But I think she'll be fine, once she's had a sleep. She even asked me to tell you she's sorry."

"You're just saying that."

"No, she really did say that. She's getting back to normal. Her eyes have lost that strange look, thank heavens. It was probably a reaction to the trauma, and her getting the idea in her head that the baby was Sunny."

"Does she look like her?" My voice was a squeak. "Her little face was all screwed up from being squeezed too hard, so we didn't have a chance to see her properly."

"Crikey, I can't tell one baby from the next when they've just been born. They all look the same to me."

My desperate prayers weren't all answered late that afternoon when we returned to the hospital. But we did see the baby and hold her. She was perfect, and I didn't care that she perhaps looked like Sunny. She already had a fluff of golden hair in tiny curls, and when she made her funny mouth movements, dimples appeared in her chubby cheeks. The small bruise on her cheek from the forceps was already fading.

Cassandra lay back on her pillows looking pale but herself. "I don't know what happened," she said. "It's being in hospital. It's much worse than I even imagined. I'm so bloody sore I have to stand up in the shower to pee."

"I know. It was awful. But you'll be home soon," I said, my eyes not leaving the sleeping baby in my arms.

Cassandra grabbed Sebastian's hand. "Tell them to let me go home."

"Four more days in here. That's what the nurse said."

"I'll die. They can't stop me leaving."

"I can, though. And you're staying put, so get used to it. The kids can come and see you every day."

"They haven't seen the baby yet?" Ben asked, his eyebrows shooting up.

"Tomorrow morning. We wanted you to see her first." Sebastian smiled at me but anxiety was still etched on his face.

"Thank you," I whispered; who to, I'm not sure. Sebastian, Cassandra? Ben held out his arms and I let go our little girl. He looked down at her, his eyes tearing up behind his glasses as she opened sleepy blue eyes.

We left soon after, pushed out by the nurse, a different one from the nurses who'd been at the birth. Sebastian followed us into the corridor. He kissed my cheek. "I can't ask her until she's better and home again. I know it's hard, but it wouldn't be right, or sensible, to raise it now. I'm sure she won't go back on her promise… she just needs some time."

We were all there on Friday when the car pulled up in the drive, Sebastian and Cassandra in front and Amber in the back next to the baby seat. David and Fred were so excited to have them home, and Fred could barely tear himself away from the baby's cradle long enough to sit at the table and eat his lunch. Ben and I left after that, still with no idea what was happening.

"She doesn't even have a name yet," I said, forcing myself to stay dry-eyed.

"Well, Cassandra will have to register the birth soon and she'll need a name for the baby then. She wouldn't want to leave it as Baby Brooks. At least the birth certificate will have only Cassandra's name on it as parent. She can't retract the legal statement that says I'm the sperm donor. It's signed by all of us." He took his glasses off and rubbed his eyes. Then he looked at me, his head on one side. "So don't worry. I'm the biological father, and you and I, my love, are the intended parents."

"But that doesn't hold her to giving us the baby," I said.

"No," said Ben. "It's early days yet, and she seemed perfectly happy for us to cuddle little Miss No-name. Surely she wouldn't want us anywhere near her if she'd discovered she couldn't give her up after all?"

On Saturday evening Sebastian appeared at our door. My heart pounded its familiar crazy beat.

"Cassandra says she is certain she wants to give you bubs as we agreed, but she would love another couple of weeks with her first."

I nodded, my throat too thick with tears and fear to speak.

"Olivia, love, I'm sorry. It'll be a tough time for all of us, but you two especially," sweet Sebastian said, his hand enclosing mine.

"Two weeks. Two weeks in a child's lifetime," Ben said. "In our lifetime. A blip, that's all. Perhaps it was the rough birth.

Cassandra needs to somehow forget that, and being with the baby helps."

"What about her name and the birth certificate?" I croaked.

"She's planning on registering the birth on Monday, and we wondered if you could come over for brunch tomorrow and we'll decide on her name," Sebastian said, his whole face smiling.

My heart leapt out of my mouth and danced around the room.

"Boadicea," shouted Fred. "That's what we should call her."

"Don't be ridiculous," David said. "Boadicea is a warrior, not a cute little baby."

"She fought her way out of Mum. And she won't always be a baby, stupid." He stuck his bottom lip out. "She's like Sunny. She was a warrior princess."

"Come here, sweetie." Cassandra held out her arms to him. "I think Boadicea is definitely one of the names we should all consider."

"Any other contenders?" Sebastian said, in his best lawyer voice. "Olivia, what do you think?"

"I think she looks like a Grace," I said, feeling suddenly shy.

"That's what religious people say before they eat," David said. "We're not religious."

"No. But it also means thank you. Thank you for being." I swallowed and made myself smile.

"Grace," Sebastian said. "That's lovely. I like it."

Ben nodded. "Me too."

We'd discussed names over and over, and he knew I wanted to call her Grace.

A mewling came from the cradle beside Cassandra's chair and she leaned over and set it rocking. "It's perfect," she said. "Let her be Grace."

"Grace Jessie," Ben said. "Grace for thank you and Jessie for Olivia's mum."

I covered my face, my tears choking free. Arms enclosed me, my chest, my waist, my whole body. My hands fell from my face, leaving it grinning like a zombie. I was surrounded by them all, hugging and stroking me; Ben, Sebastian and Cassandra, Amber, David, and 8-year-old Fred. Grace's family.

~

GRACE JESSIE'S BIRTH CERTIFICATE WAS ISSUED, WITH ONLY THE mother named.

It was still terrifying, the waiting. How would Cassandra be able to give her up after breast feeding her for weeks, changing her, bathing her, cuddling her. In the depth of the nights I woke in cold sweats, my dreams black with replays of Cassandra clutching Grace to her heart and screaming words I didn't want to hear. In the sunlight I'd push away my nightmares and tell myself she'd do it for me. This was Cassandra, a woman of her word, this was Cassandra, the almost sister who loved me. This was Cassandra, the friend who couldn't save Lily and wanted to make amends. That was the obsession that haunted me. I wanted baby Grace to be a gift of love, not a price Cassandra believed she must pay.

Four long weeks after her birth we were invited to the Brooks home for a BBQ. I was quivering from my core outwards. Was this it? Was she going to tell us she was sorry, so sorry, she couldn't let her go, but we could spend as much time with her as we liked?

Cassandra and I were in the kitchen, feeding tomato-sauce-stained plates into the dishwasher when sleeping Grace let us know she was hungry, now, right now. Cassandra shut the dishwasher door, stood up, stretched, looked at me and grinned. "Olivia, your daughter's crying. You'd better get her before she screams the house down."

Ben walked into the kitchen while I still had my mouth open, no sound coming out. Cassandra winked at him. "Daddy, there's a bottle of milk in the fridge; I expressed it earlier. Why don't you heat it up? I'm going back outside to have a bloody enormous glass of red wine."

It wasn't all plain sailing. Cassandra was weepy for a while. Sebastian told us this when he explained why they'd decided that they wouldn't see us for a few weeks. "Our counselor thought that would help. Sort of going cold turkey."

It made it easier on us too, but also harder. We had to delay applying for a Relative Adoption until all four of us were ready to fully support it. But oh what heaven it was when I let myself forget that nothing was certain. The scent of her, the touch of her tiny fingers, her kissable toes, her funny little expressions, hanging a row of nappies on the line every day, cuddling her close as she sucked vigorously on her bottle, singing her to sleep in the gorgeous cradle Sebastian had made especially for her, dressing her in the tiniest sundress and cute sunhat, walking hand-in-hand with Ben through the park with Grace in her baby sling, snug against my chest. Watching Ben with her. That was the most precious of all.

When Grace was eight weeks old and we'd been her mummy and daddy for four weeks, the four of us, plus Grace, met with our counseling couple and agreed we wanted to do this. There were tears, and not just from the counselors. But they were good tears and I felt closer to Cassandra than I ever had since we lost Lily and Sunny.

We got all the documentation together. This would be the most faultless Relation Adoption Application the Department of Adoptions had ever received. We attached proof that after Cassandra and Sebastian had decided their family was complete seven years ago, Sebastian had a vasectomy, and included the statement that Ben was the sperm donor, signed by all four of us. Our GP's statement confirmed that she had performed four cycles of intrauterine insemination on Cassandra using donor sperm from Ben, and that it was clear to her throughout that Ben and I were the intended parents of any child or children conceived; further statements from our counselors and our two lawyers confirmed that that was our joint intent. Then there were the statements signed by everyone that we agreed that Grace should be adopted by Ben, her natural father, and me, his wife, and that we owned our own home, had secure and good incomes and could give a child a loving, stable home. We even included a statement from Cathie and William explaining that they had been my foster parents from the age of 13, and had brought me up as Cassandra's sister. Mine and Ben's statement included information about losing our son, my uterus, and then Lily, and our intent to encourage a continued relationship between Grace and Cassandra and the Brooks family as well as with her natural grandparents, Cathie and William.

"It's as watertight as it could possibly be," Sebastian said.

Chapter Thirty-Five

Six weeks later we received a letter informing us that we'd made it through the first stage and could book an assessment to see if we'd pass as suitable adoptive parents. We'd been through this before we'd adopted Lily; the background checks, references and home visits. But it didn't prevent me waking in the early hours rehearsing what I would say in response to the inevitable questions about my relationship with Cassandra. Not so much our relationship, but how I'd feel about her spending time with Grace and remaining a big part of her life.

Every week Grace looked more like Sunny. Even her eyes were changing from dark blue to violet. Why couldn't she look like Ben? Doubts, doubts. They wouldn't leave me alone. What would happen if we decided to leave Brisbane? Ben had put off his sabbatical leave; we'd planned to return to Cambridge for a year. Would we ever be able to do that now? Once we'd adopted Grace, Cassandra would have no legal claim over her, so she wouldn't be able to stop us, but Ben wouldn't go if she didn't agree, I knew that.

Of course, once daylight came, my dark night thoughts faded, and I told myself it would be like old times; all of us happy together, Grace loved by everyone, and no-one ever doubting Ben and I were her true parents.

Aunt Cathie and Uncle William came to stay with Cassandra and divided their time between Grace and her half siblings. "Cathie," Uncle William said, on their first visit to us, "Look at this baby. She's the image of you when you were little. It's like looking at that photo of you with your parents."

I caught Aunt Cathie's concerned look and rushed to reassure her. "It's OK," I said. "I know she looks like Sunny, and Sunny took after you. It's lovely."

"I can see Ben in her as well," Aunt Cathie said. "Some of her funny little expressions…"

"Gee, thanks," said Ben. "Funny little expressions. Poor kid."

"Are you truly alright about it all?" I finally asked.

"We think it's perfect. You have a beautiful baby and we get another granddaughter to spoil," Uncle William said.

"Why is it taking so long to approve us?" I asked Ben, as weeks went by following our final home visit. We'd thought it had gone well.

Ben shrugged. "Government departments I suppose. Always slow. With any luck it'll happen before Grace hits eighteen."

"What does Sebastian think? He knows about these things."

"Actually, I think he's a bit concerned. It's hard on Cassandra too; unfinished somehow I suppose."

"What do you mean? Do you think she's going to change her mind?" My breathing quickened as the panicky feelings that had become part of my being began their rapid ascent.

"Of course not. I don't know, but why should she? Christ, even after we're approved it'll be months before we can adopt her... " His voice tailed off and I turned and busied myself peeling spuds.

Jason Sullivan, our lawyer, phoned at 8am the next morning. He wanted to meet with us as soon as possible. We were at his office by 9.30am, our hands cold with fear as we waited until the client he was seeing had left.

"I'm afraid it's not the best news," Jason said, and my world collapsed. I held onto the sides of the chair. *Please no please no...*

"It's going to be a little more difficult than we hoped," he was saying. "The Family Court Judge asked for a meeting yesterday. He saw Cassandra's lawyer too, before me."

"I thought adoptions were decided by the Adoption Services," Ben said, his voice sounding strange. "What's the Family Court got to do with it?"

"Apparently the social worker interviewed Janice MacIntosh, given that she was your midwife, Olivia, when you were pregnant, and she was also Cassandra's midwife. I suppose it makes sense."

"Shouldn't we have been asked for permission?" Ben asked.

"They have the right to do whatever background checks they think are necessary. Anyway, it's done now. Did you know the midwife had strong opinions about it?"

Ben shook his head as I spoke. "I know she didn't really understand how Cassandra could give her baby away. She never said anything to me but I felt her antagonism. But that's only her; she's old-fashioned."

"Prejudiced," muttered Ben.

"The Judge didn't give me much detail. But apparently Miss MacIntosh told the social worker that Cassandra had been distressed after the birth and had refused to give Grace up. So the two nurses and the obstetrician who were at the birth were also interviewed. That was their recollection as well."

"Cassandra was confused, that's all. It was a difficult birth," said Ben.

"And the obstetrician was horrible. Cassandra hated him." My face was burning as I spat out the words. "She was fine next morning and wanted us to have Grace. She always wanted that. It was her idea from the start, not ours."

"Surely it is all beside the point given Cassandra has applied to have Grace adopted?" Ben said. "It's how she feels now that matters."

"I believe there were some other complications." Jason looked at me, small frown lines appearing between his eyes. "The midwife mentioned that you had some serious psychological issues after you lost your first baby, and again after your daughter died."

"That's ridiculous," Ben said, his voice searingly quiet. "What mother wouldn't grieve after losing her children? That's what Olivia was going through; grief."

"And Cassandra was so psychologically disturbed after Lily and Sunny were drowned that she ended up in a psychiatric hospital and they were going to give her ECT," I said, my voice feeling as if it were coming from someone else. "How does that make her a better mother than me?"

"I don't believe the judge was judging the situation." He grinned and then pulled his face back to serious. "Expressing an opinion. He wasn't expressing an opinion, simply explaining the complexities, as he put it. It was a concern that Cassandra might be giving the child up because she felt guilty about her role in the drowning."

"What are you saying?" Ben said. "Are we being turned down as adoptive parents? I'm her biological father; can they even do that?"

"You're leaping ahead here. Nothing has been decided. If there are concerns, the Department of Adoptions is required to inform the Family Court. So the Judge decided that because of the complex issues, the case should be referred to that Court. That allows everyone to have their say, and permits the lawyers to call multiple witnesses. The Court will appoint a counsel for the child because the primary job of the Court is to decide what's in the best interests of the child. But they'll consider the interests of the other parties as well, especially the birth mother."

It was over. We were going to lose Grace too. I pulled my hand from under Ben's; I needed both hands to cover my face and pretend this wasn't happening, that I wasn't sitting here listening to this. Jason was still talking, talking; taking everything that was left away.

"Take some time to think this through. Talk to Cassandra and Sebastian. It's up to the four of you to decide whether to proceed to the Family Court. If you don't then you'll receive the standard letter denying you registration as potential adoptive parents." His voice stopped and all I could hear was my breathing, my held-back wails.

"So the Judge is giving you a chance. I see that as a positive," Jason said.

CASSANDRA WAS FURIOUS. "WE SHOULD REPORT JANICE TO THE Midwifery Association or whatever they have," she said. "How dare she do this to us. She's meant to be our support and all the time she's collecting any tiny thing she thinks she can use to stop us, just because she's got some religious thing against it. I bet that's why she made me go to the hospital for the birth. Why did you let her?" She shoved Sebastian in the chest and he wobbled before he caught his balance.

"I'm not sure that's entirely fair. She didn't want to take any risks," Sebastian said, his voice flat.

"Ha. And look what happened. We're lucky Grace survived with that shit of a doctor shoving forceps up me. If

I'd had her at home it would all have been perfect, you know that."

"So what are we going to do?" asked Ben. "Cassandra, what do you want to do?"

"What if we just decided we wanted you two to keep Grace and bring her up as yours? There's no law against that, is there? Tell them all to go to hell."

"But she wouldn't be ours," I said, my voice cracking out between my dry lips.

"I think we should take it to the Family Court," Sebastian said. "We'd surely have a good chance. The judge will see that we all want this and no social worker can say that Grace isn't loved and happy. By the time this gets to court she'll have been with Olivia and Ben for at least six months. They won't want to uproot her."

"I agree," Ben said, his voice sounding more like Ben. "I'm the father after all, and no-one can deny that. It seems bizarre that we even have to go through this because of ten minutes observation after a horrific birth when everyone was upset."

"You mean me. It's my fault," Cassandra said.

"You were traumatized. Our lawyer will get an expert witness to testify that what you said then was an understandable reaction, and has no bearing on your true feelings," Sebastian said. "I don't even remember what you said but I'm sure you didn't say that Olivia and Ben couldn't be her parents."

"No, you definitely didn't. I'd remember that. You were so confused, you thought she was Sunny." I reached out for her, my eyes too blurred to see her face. But she was looking at Ben and didn't see me.

"How could they deny Ben his rights if I want him to have Grace?" Cassandra said, her tone sending a shiver through me. "They couldn't. So let's bloody well go to Court and kick their bloody backsides. With luck, Janice traitor MacIntosh will be struck off."

“Along with Dr. Glasses,” I added.

Only Sebastian sat in on the Preliminary Hearing to listen to our lawyers put our case. As expected, given the complexity of the issues and affidavits received from Janice and the medical staff present at the birth, the judge decided it should go to a Final Court Hearing.

One thing worried Sebastian; the lawyer the Court appointed to represent Grace. “He’s in his early sixties, a devout Catholic, and has eight children of his own. He’s got a reputation as being ultra-conservative. I somehow can’t imagine he’s an advocate of surrogacy.”

“Why would the judge appoint someone like that? Does that mean he wants us to lose?” My eyes filled as I watched Grace kicking and chuckling on her blanket on the floor.

“I think it was more because he was the only option. After you take out our two lawyers and me, Barry Braxton is about the only family lawyer left in Brisbane who has experience with complex adoption cases,” Sebastian said. He pulled me towards him in a quick hug. “Chin up. Judge Campbell is known as a fair and astute judge. He won’t be fooled by weak or biased arguments.”

Somehow we got through the next two months while we waited for our court hearing. It was a bizarre situation as our two lawyers each had to call their own witnesses, even though we were on the same side. Grace’s lawyer had a third lot of witnesses. I saw him as our enemy.

“There shouldn’t really be sides in this sort of case,” Sebastian said. "The purpose is not to get a conviction, but to make sure the best thing is done for Grace. If her lawyer decides she is happy with Olivia and Ben, and we all agree, then we'll all be on the same side and the judge will give us his blessing."

The Baby Brooks Case was set down for the 16th of August. Grace would be six and a half months old. It was 1987, over two long years since Cassandra had offered to act as a surrogate for us. I took down the framed photo of Lily and Sunny dressed as bunnies and put it under a pile of sheets in the top of the linen cupboard. I didn't want Grace to grow up feeling she was a replacement for Sunny… or for Lily. Four days before our day in court, Aunt Cathie and Uncle William arrived to hold the fort and look after Fred and Grace, and provide meals for David and Amber. At 15 and 17, they had a problem with being looked after, but food was another matter. Aunt Cathie would as always, be everything to everyone; Priscilla Mather, Cassandra's lawyer, was also going to call her as a witness.

I found myself waking at 4am, night after night, with nothing to do but worry about the court case. Grace was finally sleeping through until 6am and here was I not able to catch up on months of sleep deprivation. The hearing had been allocated three days, which seemed over-the-top. According to Sebastian the time frame was estimated on the number of witnesses—a psychiatrist, a social worker, one of our counselors, Aunt Cathie, a close friend of Cassandra's, and each of us —and that was just on our side. Barry Braxton, Grace's lawyer — how ridiculous that sounds — was calling Janice, Dr. Glasses, his two nurse followers, his own expert psychiatrist, and a specialist child psychologist. Braxton's role, Sebastian explained, was mainly to cross-examine us.

Chapter Thirty-Six

PRISCILLA MATHER, CASSANDRA AND SEBASTIAN'S LAWYER, began. I barely took in her opening statement, I was shaking so much. I knew the substance of what she and our own lawyer would say anyway. That all four of us had planned for this and wanted it, that Ben was the father, and that Grace had been happily living with Ben and me for over five months.

Priscilla called first Cassandra's GP, then Pauline, the female half of our counseling couple, and finally a close friend of Cassandra's. They all testified that Cassandra's intent had been, from before the baby was conceived, to carry a child for Ben and me, and she had never given them any cause to doubt her. The other two lawyers had no questions for them. I relaxed just a fraction.

After lunch it was Cassandra's turn. She was calm and sure, telling the Court about her love of being pregnant and giving birth, that she and Sebastian had decided that their family was complete, and explaining her desire to help Ben and me have a child of our own. She said she felt entirely happy about giving Grace to us to love and adopt, knowing she and her family would remain a part of her life, as our two families would always be close.

I couldn't imagine how anyone could not find her convincing.

How wrong I was. Barry Braxton cross-examined. He started softly, softly, asking Cassandra about her own children, how she felt about them, had she ever considered giving them up? She was already fighting tears when he slid the knife in.

"I note that your first births were home births and your babies were born in the spa bath. Those must have been wonderful experiences."

Cassandra nodded. "They were," she said.

"Your friends Olivia and Ben Appleby lived with you and your family when one of your children was born.." —he looked down at his notes—"David. Olivia was present at that birth and later at Fred's birth. That's true friendship." He smiled at her and I felt a butterfly of hope flutter in my chest.

"I imagine when Olivia became pregnant in 1972, she looked to you for advice," he continued, his voice like warm fat oozing from the spout of a round pink teapot. "She was still Olivia Newman then, and she and Ben Appleby were living with you, is that correct?"

Cassandra nodded. "Yes."

"Can you tell the Court what advice you gave Olivia about birthing options?"

"I can't remember. It was years ago. I suppose I gave her all the usual advice about exercise and eating healthily."

"Did you give her any advice on whether she should have a home birth in the spa bath like you, or a hospital birth?"

"Yes, I thought a home birth would be better. She was very healthy throughout her pregnancy."

"Do you recall Olivia's response?"

"She agreed. She'd seen for herself how much more natural and gentle it was."

"Olivia was a first-time mother and Ben a first-time father. Did they express to you any doubts about a home birth?"

"Yes, at first. Ben thought it would be safer having the

baby in the hospital, but he changed his mind." Cassandra's chin lifted, and she held the lawyer's gaze. I could feel her fury. My palms were sweating as I grasped the sides of my chair.

"Can you describe what happened at the birth?"

Priscilla Mather rose. "Objection Your Honor. This has no relevance to this case."

"What's your point, Mr. Braxton?" Judge Campbell barked.

"I will show this has relevance to Mrs. Brooks' decision to carry a child for her friend, Olivia Appleby, Your Honor."

"Well, don't drag it out. Objection over-ruled."

"Mrs. Brooks, where was Olivia Newman when she went into labor on Christmas Day, 1972?"

"At Killara, where my parents live up near Port Douglas."

"And what happened?"

"The baby was four weeks early. We called in a midwife from Port Douglas and got Olivia into the spa bath but there were complications and Olivia had to be taken to Cairns Hospital." Cassandra glanced over at me, and I could see her eyes were flooding with tears. "She lost the baby and had to have a hysterectomy. It was terrible."

"If you could go back in time, would you advise Olivia differently about a having a home birth for her first baby?"

"Of course I would. I felt sick for her. I loved Olivia, love her. I knew how much having a baby meant to her. It was her chance to have a family of her own."

"Would you say you felt guilty?"

"Yes, I felt guilty. Of course I did. But I was sad more than guilty."

"Do you still feel guilty?"

"She would probably have lost the baby even if she had been in hospital right from the start."

"Just answer the question please. Do you still feel guilty?"

"I suppose so. I suppose I'll always feel guilty."

He looked down as his notes. I could almost see him

grasping the handle of the knife he'd jabbed into Cassandra's heart, getting ready to twist it.

"I understand this is difficult for you, but it's important that the Court understands the complexity of your relationship with Olivia Appleby. Can you describe what happened on January 19th, 1983?"

Cassandra's eyes closed and she grabbed the edge of the witness box, her knuckles so white I could see them glowing from where I was sitting. "Our daughters were drowned at Piha Beach in New Zealand." Her voice was barely above a whisper, but he didn't ask her to speak up.

"I'm sorry for your loss," he said. "Let me help you. One of the children who drowned was Sunny, the eight-year-old-daughter of yourself and Sebastian Brooks, and the other child, Lily, was the eight-year-old adopted daughter of Ben and Olivia Appleby, is that correct?"

"Objection," said Priscilla.

"I hope this is relevant, Mr. Braxton?" said the judge.

"Yes, Your Honor."

"Objection over-ruled."

Braxton pinned his eyes on Cassandra, her hands still gripping the sides of the witness box. "Can you tell the Court who was watching the children in the surf on that occasion?"

"I was. My son David was there too."

"And how old was David?"

"He was ten. He wasn't in the sea right then."

"So you were the only adult watching the children on this occasion?"

"Yes. I tried to save them. They were in shallow water and then suddenly they were caught in a hole. By the time I'd got Sunny to the beach, Lily was too far out to get to and then Ben arrived but he was too late."

Sebastian was up from his seat beside me and I saw Ben's hand on his arm, pulling him down. The police officer standing near the witness box was by Cassandra's side, holding her up.

Priscilla leapt to her feet. "Your Honor, I'd like to request a recess to give my client a chance to gather herself."

"May I ask one further question, Your Honor?" said Braxton.

"If you must, and then the Court will recess for the day," said the judge.

"It was a terrible tragedy, losing your own daughter as well as Olivia and Ben's daughter," Braxton said. "How did you feel when you were unable to save Lily?"

"Of course I felt guilty. Is that what you want me to say?"

"Just the truth. Do you think that feeling of guilt played a significant part in your depression; a depression so severe that you had to be admitted to a psychiatric hospital in the months following that tragedy?"

"I don't know. I had lost my own daughter. I was grieving for her too. My children had lost their sister. Sebastian had lost his little girl." Her voice rose until she was almost screaming. "Of course I was depressed. I was depressed and guilty about not being able to save them, not Sunny, not Lily. That's why I want Olivia to have a baby of her own."

"BASTARD," SEBASTIAN SAID THAT EVENING WHEN WE WERE going over and over it. "He's trying to make out Cassandra's motivations for being a surrogate for your baby are not altruistic but stem from her guilt."

"I'm sorry. I should never have said I felt guilty. I didn't think. I just told him the truth. What else could I say?" Cassandra whispered, her face as white as her shirt.

But it wasn't over yet. Poor Cassandra was back in the witness box next morning, Braxton ready with his knife.

"Your husband, Sebastian Brooks, is a family lawyer, and

two of his specialist areas are in adoption and surrogacy. Is that correct?"

"Yes," Cassandra said, the frown lines between her eyebrows signalling she knew something nasty was coming.

"Does he sometimes discuss his work with you?"

"No, not his cases."

"Of course not, but I meant more generally. For example did he ever discuss surrogacy with you before you decided to be a surrogate yourself?"

"I suppose so. I knew about surrogacy."

"Let me help you. Were you aware he was a member of a surrogacy working group comprised of lawyers as well as surrogate mothers and the couples who had adopted the surrogate child?"

"Yes, of course."

"How long has he been part of that group?"

"I don't know. About three years I think."

"And when did you first decide to offer to act as a surrogate for Olivia and Ben Appleby?"

"About two years ago."

"Who was the first to suggest you consider acting as a surrogate?"

"No-one. It was my idea from the start."

"Can you recall whether your husband was supportive when you first mentioned it?"

"Yes I can. He wasn't sure at first; he thought I should take my time and look into all the aspects very carefully. That's why when we did decide to go ahead he said we must all have counseling and get our own lawyers before making a decision."

"Was it helpful to have his advice, given his experience in the area?"

"Yes, it was. But he never tried to influence me or any of us one way or the other. He wanted to support whatever I decided."

"Did you ever meet any other surrogate parents or parents who adopted a child born of a surrogate mother?"

"Yes."

"Who introduced you to those parents?"

"Sebastian."

"And can you tell us how he knew them?"

"They had some involvement in the working group he was on. When we were all having counseling he asked them if they would talk to us about their experiences." Cassandra's knuckle-white hands gripping the sides of the witness box disappeared. I knew she'd suddenly realized she shouldn't be showing her fear.

"By working group, you mean the surrogacy working group?"

"Yes."

"And did they say anything negative about their experiences in a surrogacy arrangement?"

"No, their experiences had been wonderful."

Braxton smiled sweetly, as if he was happy for Cassandra. He shuffled his papers and I caught the anxious look Cassandra aimed in our direction. My own hands were gripped so tightly they felt as if they'd been wired into claws.

"Prior to the baby's birth, did you discuss with anyone how long you would keep the baby with you following the birth?

Cassandra nodded.

"Can you answer, please?"

"Yes."

"Who did you discuss this with?"

"Our counselors, and Sebastian and Olivia and Ben."

"And were you able to come to a decision you all agreed upon?"

"Yes. But I knew it was my decision like everything to do with my pregnancy and the birth."

"I understand. And what did you decide?"

"To give Olivia and Ben the baby soon after the birth."

"What did you understand by 'soon'?"

"After I had breastfed her straight after she was born so she could have my colostrum."

"And what actually happened after Grace's birth?"

Cassandra looked around as if she were trying to find an escape route.

"Take your time, Mrs. Brooks. Just describe what happened as you remember it."

"It all went wrong. We were going to have a home birth but the midwife made me go to hospital and Olivia and Ben weren't allowed to be present. It was very difficult and I had to have forceps. When she was born, after I fed her, Ben and Olivia came in but I don't think I was thinking straight. Grace looked so like Sunny, our daughter we lost. I was upset. Sebastian took her and I think Ben and Olivia looked at her, but I got out of bed and I can't really remember much, except I was very sore and upset."

Braxton addressed the judge. "Your Honor, can I draw you attention to documents two to five in your folder of evidence."

He turned back to Cassandra and presented her with some papers. "I will be referring to these affidavits in detail later when the witnesses who wrote them are on the stand. They are the affidavits made by Janice MacIntosh, the midwife, and also made independently by the obstetrician and the two nurses present at the birth. They all state that when Mr. Brooks was showing the baby to Mr. and Mrs. Appleby you shouted 'Get away from her. Give her back to me.' Do you remember that?"

Cassandra shook her head. "No, I told you. If I did say anything like that it was because I wasn't thinking straight because I was so upset by the whole birth process and how uncaring the obstetrician and the nurses were. They didn't seem to care about me at all."

"When did you give the baby into Mr. and Mrs. Appleby's care?"

"They made me stay in hospital for five days and they wouldn't have let me give her away while I was there. When I got home I thought it would help if I kept her with me for a bit longer, but Ben and Olivia spent lots of time with us and helped bath and change her and everything. Then I gave her to them to take home. I was so happy…"— her voice wobbled and when she managed to speak again, her words were thick with tears — "… so happy they had their baby at last."

I realized I was wiping tears off my face and looked down, blinking hard.

"So exactly how old was Grace when you gave her away?"

Priscilla was on her feet. "Objection Your Honor. Mr. Braxton is harassing the witness."

"I'm inclined to agree," said the judge. "Mr. Braxton, how much longer are you intending to drag this out?"

"That is my last question, Your Honor. I believe it is in the best interests of my client, the child, to establish an accurate understanding of how difficult it was for Mrs. Brooks to give her child up."

"Objection over-ruled," said the judge. He looked over at Cassandra. "Please answer the question, Mrs. Brooks, and then you will be released from the witness box, and we'll break for thirty minutes."

"Let me clarify the question, Mrs Brooks," Braxton said, his voice sending chills down my spine. "How old, in days, was Grace, when you gave her into the intended parents' care?"

"Twenty-eight days old," Cassandra said, her head high, tears shining on her cheeks and her voice shaking. "She was 28 days old."

Chapter Thirty-Seven

After a late morning recess for desperately-needed coffee, Priscilla called her only expert witness to the box, Dr. Sinclair, the psychiatrist who had assessed Cassandra's state of mind. She had nothing but good things to say, pointing out, without a hint of sarcasm, that it was within the normal range of human emotions to respond by becoming depressed following the death of one's child. "In my opinion," she said, "Mrs. Brooks carefully considered her role as a surrogate for the child of her close friends, and I could find no evidence that she was coerced in any way to make this decision, or that she has any regrets about giving the child up. She is happy with the understanding she has with Mr. and Mrs. Appleby that she and her family will continue to spend quality time with Grace, and she understands that she will have no legal status with respect to the child once she has been adopted."

Then it was Sebastian's turn. He knew what was coming and he knew how to behave in court. He explained how careful we'd all been to respect Cassandra's wishes and feelings, and how we had prepared ourselves with counseling and an in-depth understanding of the legal implications. He agreed he was an advocate for mutually beneficial altruistic surrogacy arrangements and would welcome legislation to ensure that all surrogacies were handled with sensitivity and with the child's interests as paramount. He admitted it had taken him a little while to feel comfortable with the idea of Cassandra acting as a surrogate for a child that he would not father, but that he also wanted to support her desire to carry a child for Ben and me, their dearest friends.

This time I wasn't silly enough to think that Braxton would pat him on the back and let him go. Sebastian responded to his barbs like the sweet man he was, but somehow also managed to remain the lawyer. He confirmed everything Cassandra had said, his calm tone popping Braxton's statements as if they were bubbles stuffed with rancid air. Then came the questions Braxton hadn't been permitted to ask Cassandra.

"After your wife gave the baby to Mr. and Mrs. Appleby, how often did you and Mrs. Brooks, and your three children, Grace's half siblings, see the baby?"

"Not having Grace with us was hard at first for all of us. She'd been with us for four weeks. So I suggested to Cassandra that we stay away from the Applebys for a few weeks to give both us and Ben and Olivia time to settle into our new routines. After about four weeks, when Cassandra felt emotionally ready, we began spending time together again. It worked out perfectly." Sebastian glanced over at us, a smile on his face. Was he really as relaxed as he looked?

Braxton hitched up the back of his trousers. "The four medically qualified staff present during Grace's birth state in their affidavits that shortly after the birth you took the baby out of your wife's arms so Mr. and Mrs. Appleby could hold her, even though Mrs. Brooks was clearly distressed and cried out 'Get away from her. Give her back to me.' Can you tell the Court what you said and did following this?"

"No, I can't. The whole situation was fraught. Cassandra had just undergone a difficult birth in a situation that was far from the home birth she wanted. I would never have insisted she give the baby up if she didn't want to. My memory is that I tried to reassure her that Ben and Olivia only wanted to see her and have a cuddle, and that no-one was going to take her away until… unless Cassandra felt ready. In fact Ben and Olivia didn't hold her or even see her properly until late the next day when Cassandra had had a sleep and was back to her normal self. She wanted them to see Grace. She couldn't even remember what she'd said the day before."

"I put it to you that when your wife was vulnerable after a difficult pregnancy and birth, and clearly expressed her desire to keep her baby, her genetic offspring, a daughter who looked like the daughter she lost, you were horrified and encouraged her to change her mind, using all your experience as a lawyer to do so. I put it to you that Mrs. Brooks did not give up her child willingly."

"Objection, Your Honor. Mr. Brooks has already answered every aspect of Mr. Braxton's colorful accusations," Priscilla interjected, her tone so sharp it made Braxton's knife seem blunt.

"Objection sustained," said the judge. "You will ignore that question, Mr. Brooks. Mr. Braxton, keep your opinions for your summing up."

Brazen Braxton tried a new tactic after that and got stuck into Sebastian about his involvement with the surrogacy working group. Sebastian stayed his calm self, not attempting to underplay his desire to work towards good legislation.

"If your own surrogacy situation failed would this be a blow to your arguments?" Braxton said.

"It would depend on why it failed. If it failed because it didn't comply with the guidelines we are proposing, then that could be viewed as support of those guidelines. If it failed in spite of us following all the guidelines, as indeed we have, then, yes, I suppose it would be a blow, and we would need to consider whether the guidelines required revising."

"Thank you. I have no further questions."

"THE JUDGE IS ON OUR SIDE," I SAID. "HE CAN'T STAND Braxton." We were eating sandwiches in a small room in the courthouse. I'd discovered I was starving. Too much tension. We'd already called Aunt Cathie and Uncle William and given them the good bits, and listened to Grace cooing over the telephone line.

Our lawyer gave his opening statement after lunch, before calling Ben to the witness box. I would follow him, and then Aunt Cathie. Then Jason planned to call two expert witnesses: the social worker who had assessed Ben and my suitability as parents for Grace, and the psychiatrist who had assessed my mental state.

Putting Ben first was a good strategy. He was every bit as composed as Sebastian had been.

I stared at Braxton's back. *Try at your peril to trip him up.*

But he didn't even try. Perhaps Sebastian's calm testimony had convinced him he didn't have a hope? Or perhaps he'd decided Grace would be happy with us? After all, that's what he was meant to be doing; making sure her best interests were met, not trying to turn us into criminals.

Then it was my turn. I took some deep breaths and avoided looking at my quivering hand as I took the oath. But once Jason began his questions I almost relaxed, although my fingers were crossed beneath the witness stand as he thanked me and returned to his seat.

"Miss Mather, Mr. Braxton. Do either of you wish to cross-examine the witness?" Judge Campbell's voice sounded as tired as I felt.

"No, your Honor," said Priscilla.

"Yes, Your Honor," said Braxton.

Shit. Head up. Don't let the bastard get to you.

His questions slid in like slimy worms. He started by forcing me to answer questions about losing our son and my consequent depression, and the 'tragedy' as he put it, of losing my uterus.

"It would be understandable if you'd blamed Cassandra for advising you to have a spa bath birth. It's a long time ago now, but can you recall how long it took you to recover from this experience and forgive Cassandra?"

"I never said I'd blamed her. It was my decision to have a home birth. Cassandra's experiences had been so positive that of course she encouraged me. But I didn't blame her when it went wrong."

"I understand how painful this must be so I won't dwell on it. But when Lily, your daughter, was drowned, how did that change your relationship with Cassandra?"

"We were both trying to deal with our grief."

"Of course. It is a terrible thing to lose a child, and you have lost two children, as well as your ability to have children yourself. It must have made it so much more difficult that your closest friend was the only adult present when the girls got into trouble in the surf. How long was it after your daughter drowned in New Zealand and you returned to Australia that you saw Cassandra again?"

"About a year. A bit longer."

"And since then would you say that you and Cassandra have been as close as you were before your daughters were so tragically drowned?"

"All four of us are friends." I took a deep breath. "Perhaps Cassandra and I took a while to get back to the closeness we used to have, but she and I are sort of like family."

"Do you think Cassandra offered to be a surrogate for a baby which she would then allow you and Mr. Appleby to adopt, because she felt guilty about her part in the deaths of your two children?"

"Objection, Your Honor," said Jason. "My witness cannot be expected to read Mrs. Brooks's mind."

"Objection sustained," said the judge.

"As you are aware, Mrs. Appleby, we are in court to decide what is in the best interests of Grace. Can you tell me why you think that you will be a better mother for this baby than her own birth mother?"

"Ben is her biological father. Isn't that just as important?"

"As sperm donor, yes, but Grace is not a child conceived in love."

"We all love her; she has twice the love."

"Let me return to my question. I'll put it another way. Do you think Cassandra is a good mother to her children?"

"Yes, of course I do. She's a wonderful mother."

"Is it the case that she has chosen never to go out to work so she can dedicate herself to that mothering?"

"Objection Your Honor. The witness can't answer for another person."

"I withdraw that question. Mrs. Appleby, based on your observations of Cassandra's mothering over the past seventeen years, what can you give Grace that in your opinion Cassandra cannot?"

"All my love, I can give her everything Cassandra could give her. I don't have other children so Grace won't have to share our time and love."

"You were an only child. Did you ever wish you had siblings?"

"I can't remember. Sometimes, I suppose. But my situation was entirely different."

"Of course, I understand that. Your mother was unmarried and brought you up without a father —indeed I believe she didn't know who the father was — and she died of an alcohol and drug overdose when you were only thirteen."

"Objection, Your Honor. This line of questioning has nothing to do with the case we are here to discuss," said Jason.

"Objection sustained. Restrict yourself to the case in point," snapped the judge.

"There is a reason for my statement, Your Honor, if you'll bear with me."

"Well get to it and stop wasting our time."

"Mrs Appleby, who took you in after your mother's tragic death?"

"Cathie and William Tulloch, Cassandra's parents."

"How long did you live with them?"

"Until I was eighteen when I went to England to university."

"How would you characterize the relationship you had with the Tulloch children, Cassandra and her twin brother Peter?"

"We were like siblings."

"Ah. So you know what it's like to have siblings. Could you recommend it?"

"Of course, but it's not as important as having loving parents. It's not my fault I can't give Grace siblings. It's not as if I haven't spent my whole life trying." I swallowed my rage and tears and forced myself to stare him down.

Jason sprang to his feet. "Your Honor, I'd like to request a short recess so my client can have a break."

"Yes, I'll grant that. Mr. Braxton, do you have further questions for Mrs. Appleby?"

"I have one more question at this time for the witness."

"We'll take a fifteen-minute recess. Mr. Braxton, I suggest you use the break to consider if further questions for Mrs. Appleby are relevant to the case we are considering and not simply a means to cause upset."

I GULPED DOWN THE STRONG CUP OF COFFEE BEN POURED for me.

"The man's a bully," Jason said. "The judge doesn't like it. Braxton hasn't got a single thing against you. He's grasping for anything that might bolster his own small-minded beliefs about surrogacy."

"What about that photo taken of Olivia in Cambridge? He hasn't entered that yet. What's he intending to do with that?" Ben asked.

Jason shook his head. "I don't know. He might not use it. I'm assuming he thought he might be able to bring up that Olivia was an activist in the abortion rights movement, and argue that somehow that throws doubt on her mothering qualities."

"That's ridiculous. It was 18 years ago. In any case it's a plus. It's a pity not every child has a mother who is willing to stand up for equality and women's rights."

"Exactly. And if this is what Braxton comes out with next, Olivia, you have nothing to worry about. Just give him the briefest possible answers. The less you give him, the harder it will be for him to carry on with his tactics to upset you and show you as someone too emotional to bring up a child. He's trying to convince the judge you wouldn't be as good a mother for Grace as Cassandra, that's all," Jason said.

"Perhaps I wouldn't. She's never put a foot wrong."

"It's not a competition, so that's not the issue. The issue is that Cassandra suggested this surrogacy and fully supports your adopting Grace. The judge will see that."

When Ben released my hand so I could walk my lonely way back to the witness box, the nausea surging up into my throat almost made me turn and run back, out the door, to find a bathroom before I vomited right there in the courtroom. I clamped my lips tight and swallowed the bitter regurgitated coffee. The trial would be over soon and there would be nothing more I could do to keep Grace. I had to show the judge how much I loved her, that I would spend the rest of my life with her at my center.

"I trust the break has given you time to calm yourself," Braxton began, his lips smiling.

I nodded.

"Remember you are still under oath. You will need to speak up when you answer my questions. This won't take long, so try and relax." He nodded at the judge. "Your Honor, I would like to draw your attention to a photograph published in the London Times on April 27th, 1968. I think you'll find it's document seven in your folder of evidence."

My mouth was dry, my heart pounding in my ears. *Keep your answers short.* I repeated Jason's mantra in my head.

Braxton walked over to me and placed the grainy photograph, encased in a plastic sleeve, on the stand. "Do you recognize this photograph, Mrs Appleby?"

I nodded, and he frowned at me. "Yes," I said, my voice almost shouting in my effort to get any words out at all.

"Can you read aloud for the Court the words under the photograph."

"The 1967 Abortion Act which came into effect today, has sparked protest marches across the United Kingdom. The largest march, seen here, included an estimated 1000 Women's Liberation supporters. They marched across central London, waving banners and chanting slogans, and gathered in Parliament Square. A number of protestors who sat in the middle of an intersection next to Parliament Square, blocking traffic, were removed by police officers, who carried them away to vans parked nearby. According to a spokesperson for the protestors, who declined to give her name, they are protesting that the conditions of the 1967 Abortion Act are too restrictive and damaging in the case of a woman requesting an abortion within the first 24 weeks, when abortion is a safe and simple procedure and the embryo too immature to survive outside the womb. In particular, they argue against the requirement that two medical doctors, one of whom would usually be a psychiatrist, must certify that, in a case where the physical health of the mother and the unborn child are not at risk, the woman would suffer mental health consequences if the pregnancy is not terminated. This, according to the spokeswoman, will force women to falsify their mental health status, and thus brand them for life, or even worse, force them to seek an illegal and dangerous backstreet abortion, exactly the situation the Abortion Act was designed to prevent." As I voiced the words I could feel the fury pulsing through me, all over again. The crush of bodies on that mild spring day in London, the police with their shields and batons, the screams of the Pro-Life brigade…I set the photograph back on the stand and looked Braxton in the eye.

"Thank you. Can you point to the woman at the front of the march, next to the woman with the loud hailer?"

I touched the familiar grainy face, her mouth open mid-shout, her hair flying as she moved forward, a banner in one hand.

"Can you read the words on her banner?"

"If it's not your body, it's not your decision."

"Do you believe that?"

"Yes, of course I believe it."

"Do you recognize that woman who appears to be one of the leaders of this protest march?"

"Yes."

"And who is it."

"Me."

Braxton rocked back on his heels. I could almost see a pipe hanging from the corner of his mouth. "Ah. And were you in a relationship with Mr. Appleby at that time?"

"No, we didn't meet until just after that."

"Those were heady times. Free love, bare breasts, drugs, wild music festivals, protest marches. And the irresponsible behaviors that went along with that hippie lifestyle. The contraceptive pill finally available even to unmarried women. But in spite of that, unwanted pregnancies were booming. Isn't that why you were protesting so vehemently? To make it easier for women to enjoy this lifestyle knowing that if they did get pregnant they could get rid of the baby and carry on with no consequences?"

"Objection," said Jason. "Mr. Braxton's diatribe is not only irrelevant but contains no discernible question."

"What's your point, Mr. Braxton?" asked the judge. "If you have a question, ask it."

"Do you agree that my description of those times is accurate?" asked Braxton, his sanctimonious expression making me want to spit in his florid face.

"No. No woman ever had an abortion without consequences."

"Are you speaking from personal experience?"

My stomach churned. *Shit, he knows.* I looked past him at Ben. The disgust that twisted his face as he glared at Braxton's back turned him into someone I didn't know. I swallowed.

"Can you answer the question, please." Braxton's headmaster tone pushed a bolt of poison through me.

"I have friends who have had abortions, yes."

"And you? Have you had an illegal abortion?"

"No."

"Have you had a legal abortion?"

Does he know or is he bluffing?

Jason was on his feet and I closed my eyes for a second and tried to breathe.

"Objection, your Honor. These questions based on a photograph from 1969 are inadmissable on three counts. Mr. Braxton is attempting to harm the good character of my witness, he is bringing up her past which has no relevance to this case, and he is attempting to force Mrs. Appleby to reveal confidential details about her medical history."

"Yes, I'm inclined to agree. If you cannot convince me otherwise, Mr. Braxton, and explain the relevance of your questions related to Mrs. Appleby's medical history, your questions and Mrs. Appleby's responses will be struck from the record." The judge glared at Braxton over his spectacles, and I looked across at Ben, trying to read his expression. What could he be thinking?

"It is my last question, Your Honor. A perfectly straightforward question that requires a yes or no answer about a legal procedure that Mrs. Appleby has clearly stated here and in the public arena that she supports. Its relevance to this present case is to clarify the truth of Mrs. Appleby's statement made before the recess." He looked down at his notes. "I quote from her statement: 'It's not my fault I can't give Grace siblings. It's not as if I haven't spent my whole life trying.' Your Honor, the happiness, health and safety of my client, Grace Brooks, is at stake here. This hearing is to decide whether she would be happier, safer and psychologically more stable with her biological mother, Cassandra Brooks, who has an unblemished record as a dedicated mother to her children, who are, after all, Grace's half siblings, or to be adopted by a woman who has a history of failure as a mother.

"No blame can be attached to Mrs. Appleby or anyone else for the deaths of her two children. However, if she did have an abortion, at the very least this would raise the question of why she stated that she spent her whole life trying to have children. Of more importance, and as she herself read out from the London Times, a condition of having a legal abortion was that in order to have a legal abortion the pregnant woman must be certified by two doctors as being at risk of significant mental health problems if she had the child. My concern is that Mrs. Appleby's mental health may still be at risk if she becomes the primary caregiver for a small baby, especially given the traumatic birth and mothering experiences she has suffered since her return to Australia. I will be later calling an expert witness to give an opinion on mental health issues Mrs. Appleby experienced in relation to these child-related traumas. Her answer to my simple question regarding whether or not she has had a legal abortion could be helpful within that context."

Judge Campbell sighed. "Well, I'll allow it, given that Mrs. Appleby's opinions about abortion have been in the public arena for many years." He turned to me, his expression weary. "You may answer the question, Mrs. Appleby."

It was over. Ben. My baby. I'd lose them both. I could lie. But Ben would get it out of me. I could see it on his face, his whole body. He knew. And what if Braxton had the proof and found a way to use it? That would make everything even worse.

"Mrs. Appleby?"

Braxton's voice felt like a noose tightening around my neck.

"Would you like me to remind you of the question?"

I shook my head. "No. I remember the question. Yes, I had a very early legal termination. I was seven weeks pregnant, that's all."

"And was Mr. Appleby the father?"

"Yes."

"Thank you. I have no further questions."

I was looking at Ben, my eyes swimming. His head was lowered and I could feel his anger as if we were connected by an electric cable deadly enough to power a city.

"Mr. Sullivan, have you any further questions for your witness," Judge Campbell said. *Oh, no more, please.*

"Yes, Your Honor." Jason stood before me, his face tense beneath his calm expression. "Mrs. Appleby, Olivia. I know this is hard, but can you tell the Court why you decided to have a termination?"

"It was a terribly hard decision. But I was only 22, and had just graduated from university and started my first job. I had no money. My relationship with Ben had just begun and we weren't really even a couple. Just casually dating. I didn't think it would be fair to put that on him. He had his whole career ahead of him. He'd only just finished his PhD. If it had happened later, when we were in a committed relationship, it would have been so different. If I had known then that our little boy would die and I'd have to have a hysterectomy, I would never have had an abortion. But I can't go back and change it. It doesn't change how much I want Grace, how much I love her. It has nothing to do with that."

I was sobbing and barely heard Judge Campbell's words. "Thank you Mrs. Appleby. You may stand down. Given the time, the Court will resume at 10am tomorrow."

"Say something," I begged. "Don't close me out. I know how angry and upset you are and you have every right to be. But we have to talk about it."

"It's a bit late for that," Ben said, not moving from the window where he was standing with his back to me, looking out over the dark garden. We were alone. Cassandra had told us that Grace would be staying with them that night, and I knew she was right. I'd told them, she and Sebastian, that I'd never told Ben about the termination. Their shocked expressions couldn't make it any worse. Nothing could make it any worse.

I spoke at his back, my guilt burning into anger. "I was trying to protect you. We hardly knew each other and I didn't think it was your problem."

"Your body, your decision," Ben said, spinning around to face me.

"Yes. You hadn't told me you loved me or that you wanted a long-term relationship. I didn't want you pretending you loved me because I was pregnant."

"Did it occur to you that I would have supported you to

have an abortion if that's what you wanted? That it was my right to support you, as it takes two to make a baby?"

"Yes, but I didn't want to scare you off. I loved you. I loved you so bloody much. You just couldn't see it. I know it was wrong, but it happened and there's nothing I can do about it. Are you going to make me pay for it for the rest of my life?"

"You surely know, Olivia, that it is much more than your having an abortion without asking me or telling me even back then. It is about you lying to me ever since. Not telling me in all these years. You clearly never were going to tell me."

"I wanted to, I meant to, so many times. But it was never the right time. Either we were happy and I didn't want to spoil it, or we were going through hell, and I couldn't take any more pain."

"Have I ever given you cause to think I would blame you, or do something to make your pain worse if you had told me of your own free will?"

I shook my head. "I'm sorry," I whispered.

"I'll sleep in the study tonight," Ben said, his voice so, so tired. "I suppose we'll have to go back to Court tomorrow and pretend we're a happy couple, perfect parents for Grace."

"Don't you think so any more?" My words choked out.

"I don't know, Olivia. I really don't know. Grace will always be my daughter, but right now, I think she'd be better off living with Cassandra and Sebastian and being part of a big loving family."

In desperation I had taken a sleeping pill at 2.30 in the morning, so when Jason phoned at 7.30, I was still caught in a dream so realistic I couldn't for a moment recall if the trial was over or hadn't even yet started.

"Olivia, we need to work out whether Braxton knew about the abortion, or if he really was just fishing. I can't believe he would have taken that risk, so how could he have known?" Jason began, after muttering some vague greeting.

Jason's voice forced me into the real world, more court horrors to come and Ben as far away from me as he'd ever been. I struggled to remember. "Apart from the clinic doctors in Cambridge and my flatmate, who lives goodness knows where now, no-one here knew, I'm sure of that. Could he have got access to my medical records? That's the only thing I can think of."

"That's what I think. But he would have had to subpoena them, and he would have known the judge would almost certainly have ruled the record inadmissible. It's so potentially prejudicial. So instead the slimy bastard tried to discredit you by getting you to admit to having an abortion without him having a shred of evidence. So where could he have got that information unofficially? Who has your records?"

"I suppose they would have been included in my medical records when they were transferred from Cambridge to my Australia doctor when I moved back here."

"So you have a crooked doctor?"

"Oh shit. It was Janice MacIntosh. The midwife. She was my midwife for our son, and she asked me about my previous medical history. I remember being a bit nervous about telling her about the abortion, but I trusted her. I trusted that she would keep it confidential, even from Ben." My voice hitched. "Even from Ben."

Jason was silent for what seemed like minutes. "That's almost certainly who it was. MacIntosh is out to get you, we know that. Well, she's gone too bloody far. I'll discredit her for this. Just you watch. The judge won't believe a word she says after I've cross-examined her. All Braxton's hard work to prove she's a creditable witness will be out the window."

~

On the third day I sat in a daze as Aunt Cathie told the Court how she and Uncle William loved me like a daughter, and were delighted that Cassandra could help us realize the dream we so deserved, a child of our own. Ben sat beside me, his body tensed so there was no possibility that he might accidentally brush against me.

Braxton asked Aunt Cathie only one question: whether she fully understood that if Ben and I adopted Grace she and Uncle William would no longer be her legal grandparents, and the entire Brooks family would lose their status as Grace's relations.

Dear Aunt Cathie. She stood like the rock she has always been and said that of course she understood that, but family was about unconditional love and commitment, and they would continue to love and be there for me and Ben, and for Grace, whatever the legal status of our relationship. Braxton had the sense not to ask her how she would feel if Ben and I refused to let her see Grace.

By the time the social worker and psychiatrist had given their glowing opinions about Ben and my mental stability, financial means, and ability to look after one small girl, leaving Braxton silent, I was feeling almost hopeful. Judge Campbell seemed quite spritely as he left the court having called an early lunch recess, and Cassandra insisted that we go to a café instead of huddling over sandwiches in a back room at the Courthouse. Ben drank a cup of coffee, grabbed a sandwich, and said he needed some fresh air. Sebastian and I both pushed our chairs back, but Ben turned and said, "Alone. I'll see you back in Court."

Chapter Thirty-Eight

Mr. Braxton's opening statement after lunch was brief but not brief enough. He reiterated the arguments he had used in his cross-examination of Cassandra and Sebastian; that Sebastian wielded excessive influence over Cassandra's decision to give up her baby, and that her guilt over her role in the loss of my tiny son and then Lily had influenced her decision. He belabored the point that an adoption should not only be in the child's best interests but also in the best interests of the birth mother. He finished with a flourish: "We have heard evidence that Olivia Appleby has experienced mental health issues in the past, and that these mental health issues are associated with first, her own concerns about her ability to care for a baby when she was 22, forcing her to seek an abortion, and later related to the tragic deaths of her two children. However, those concerns aside, as suitable as Mr. and Mrs. Appleby might currently appear to be as adoptive parents for Grace Brooks, by approving this adoption the Court will be taking away not only baby Grace's birth mother and a loving stepfather in Mr. Brooks, but also three siblings, an uncle, aunt and cousin, and her grandparents, William and Catherine Tulloch. The Court has heard that all of these family members love

Grace dearly. In contrast, Olivia Appleby has not a single family member other than her husband, and Ben Appleby is an only child whose parents live in Scotland. Olivia and Ben Appleby might well now regret that they chose to abort their first child simply because the timing wasn't convenient. If baby Grace becomes the legal daughter of Ben and Olivia Appleby, she will have no siblings, no aunts, uncles or cousins, and her only grandparents will live on the other side of the world."

I winced as I heard the jagged intake of breath from Ben. The chocolate cake that had been all I could stomach at lunch, churned in my gut. I closed my eyes and breathed to the mantra I used to calm myself. *Love grace love grace love grace.* When I opened my eyes Judas Janice was in the witness box, swearing on the bible. I closed my ears but her sanctimonious testimony yanked them open. On and on she went with her dramatic descriptions of the scene after Grace's birth. Thank heavens there wasn't a jury. She'd almost convinced me that Cassandra didn't want to give up her baby and that Sebastian had piled on the pressure.

When Braxton asked Janice about my and Ben's involvement in Cassandra's pregnancy, she made a big issue of how I came to one of her consultations with Cassandra, but Ben never showed any interest. She made it clear that in her opinion Cassandra felt so guilty about the loss of Lily and our son that she was willing to do anything to make amends. Priscilla objected to that, reminding the Court the witness was a midwife, not a psychologist. So Braxton slid into another topic: given her wide experience of visiting families with new babies, what was her opinion of the Brooks family and their home? Janice really got into her stride then – perfect family, wonderful children. Oh, and how Amber, David and Fred adored Grace, such a warm family atmosphere in their warm family home.

Jason cross-examined and got her to admit that she had

very little evidence that Ben took no interest in Cassandra's pregnancy, and that the only time Cassandra had ever expressed reluctance to give up Grace was immediately after the birth when she was confused and distressed.

I struggled to concentrate, my stomach churning. Was he going to confront her about leaking confidential information to Braxton? I didn't know which would be worse, having her caught out, or having it all brought up again, with Ben sitting like a storm cloud beside me.

"You served as Olivia Appleby's midwife when she was pregnant with her son," Jason said. "Is that correct?"

"Yes, but I wasn't at the birth. She went against my advice and traveled to Far North Queensland and had the baby miles from a hospital." She sniffed.

"How often did you see Mrs. Appleby during her pregnancy?"

"I see my mothers regularly. Once a month and more frequently nearer their time."

"So you must get to know them very well. Thinking back, would you say you built a good rapport with Mrs. Appleby?"

"Yes, I get on well with all my mothers."

"As Mrs. Appleby's primary carer at that time, at least in respect to her pregnancy, would you have available to you her medical records?"

"Yes. Most of my mothers had their babies in the hospital but even when a mother had a home birth, it was essential that the hospital was close by."

"Do you rely on the hospital medical records, or do you also gather your own information on a woman's medical history?"

"Yes, I always spend a lot of time assessing my mothers and interviewing them so I can give them the best care. Often the most important information isn't in their medical records." She seemed to puff up as I stared at her. She hadn't cottoned on.

"Can you give some examples of the sorts of information you might gather that perhaps wouldn't be in the official medical records?"

"I need to know about their temperament, that sort of thing. How supportive their husband is and how well they eat, and whether they need support stopping smoking or drinking. All sorts of things."

"What about their past sexual history. Is that important?"

"Sometimes. If they've had any problems. Perhaps if they've had irregular or painful menstruation, that sort of thing."

"What about abortions? Would that be something that would be helpful for you to know about?"

"Yes, of course, Any history of pregnancy, whether it went full term or not. But that would be in their medical records."

"What about an illegal abortion? Would you ask about that?"

"Yes. That would be even more important. Damage could have been done that would affect their current pregnancy."

"Mrs. Appleby told the Court yesterday that she had a legal abortion in 1968 when she lived in England. Did you already know this?"

Braxton stood up. "Objection. Mrs. Appleby's past medical history has no relevance to this hearing."

"Well, you found it admissible when you were cross-examining Mrs. Appleby yesterday," said the judge. "You may answer the question, Miss MacIntosh."

Janice shifted in her seat and seemed to shrink. She knew where Jason was going with this now. "I'm not sure. I don't think so. It was a long time ago."

"Did you review your notes on Mrs. Appleby when you knew you would be called as witness in this trial?"

"Yes, but I don't remember everything. I made a lot of notes."

"You are a witness for Mr. Braxton because you were Mrs.

Brooks' midwife for the surrogacy birth that is at the center of this hearing. Did you tell him you were previously Mrs. Appleby's midwife?"

"Yes, I think so. That was important as I know both women and their husbands well."

"Yes, of course, that would be valuable. Do you recall discussing your notes relating to Mrs. Appleby with Mr. Braxton or one of his team?"

"Only in a general way."

"Do you remember mentioning that she had had an abortion?"

Janice was silent, her eyes skittering away from Jason.

Braxton was up again. "Objection. As a medical practitioner, Miss MacIntosh is bound by rules of patient confidentiality. Mr. Sullivan is out of line."

"The fact of Mrs. Appleby's abortion is already known to the Court. Answer the question please, Miss MacIntosh," said the judge, his expression making me shiver. God knows what it was doing to Janice.

She looked down and nodded.

"Can you speak up please," said Jason. "Did you tell Mr. Braxton that Olivia Appleby had had an abortion?"

"Yes," she said, her voice squeaking.

"Had you received permission from Mrs Appleby that you could share that information?"

"No, but I didn't think it was confidential. It wasn't an illegal abortion. Why should a legal abortion be confidential?"

"I suggest you discuss the matter with your regulatory body," Jason said, making no attempt to disguise the disgust in his tone. He turned to the judge. "Your Honor, I have no more questions for Miss MacIntosh."

"We'll take a recess until 2.30 pm," said Judge Campbell. "Mr. Braxton and Mr. Sullivan, I will see you both in my chambers now."

~

Before we returned to Court, Jason had a few minutes to tell us that Braxton had got a dressing down from Judge Campbell and a warning to clean up his act. But back in court, Braxton continued as if his most important witness had not just shown him up for the weasel he was. He took his time leading the two nurses who were at the birth, and Dr. Glasses with his string of degrees through their testimonies. Memory perfect. According to them, Sebastian asked Ben and me to come in and hold the baby, perhaps even take her away right then, and Cassandra definitely said, almost screamed, 'Get away from her. Give her back to me.'

Then Braxton called his first expert witness, the child psychologist. In her opinion, yes, the Brooks family would be a nurturing place for any child to grow up in, and the children missed baby Grace dreadfully when she was taken away. "My PhD thesis showed that sibling bonds are even more important for an individual than their bonds with their parents," she said. "Siblings will be around much longer than one's parents."

"Lucky for some," Ben muttered.

Braxton's psychiatrist was next on the stand. He'd assessed both Cassandra and I, delving into our clinical states following Lily and Sunny's deaths, and into my depression and even my drinking following our son's death.

"Do you think guilt played a part in Mrs. Brooks' mental condition following the tragic drowning incident?" Braxton asked.

"Definitely. That and unbearable grief," he answered.

"And in your opinion, could guilt be an emotion Mrs. Brooks still feels strongly, even now?"

"Yes. That sort of guilt almost never entirely resolves," he replied.

"What about a situation where Mrs. Brooks is able to give

Olivia and Ben Appleby a child; might that help ameliorate her feelings of guilt?"

"Yes, very likely. Not that a child who dies can ever be replaced by another child, but it was clear to me that Mrs. Brooks loved Olivia Appleby and thought of her as her sister. She expressed to me that she was still saddened by the change in their relationship which she felt had never really returned to the easy and close friendship they'd shared before the tragic drowning. She said she'd do anything to make Olivia happy again."

The hairs on my arms were standing on end as if they were in a sunless grave and not a sweltering court room in the tropics. I rubbed them and swallowed the sickly taste of chocolate that rose into my throat. I knew I'd never eat chocolate again.

THE DAY ENDED WITH ALL THREE LAWYERS SUMMING UP. Nothing new, just an excuse for dramatics. It seemed almost pointless given there was no jury. Judge Campbell had more clues than all of us put together.

Priscilla and Jason stressed the careful process we had gone through and our unanimous decision that this adoption was what we all wanted. Braxton focused on Cassandra's wonderful mothering abilities, her sadness about her best friend's desperate desire for a child, her deep-seated guilt, and her emotionally-charged decision to make amends by offering herself as a surrogate, a decision strongly encouraged by Sebastian because of his passion for surrogacy as a means to provide children for childless couples.

"But is that guilt reason for this mother, Cassandra Brooks, who was never accused of any crime, to feel compelled to give away her own baby to Olivia Appleby, a woman whom she loves as her foster sister?" he said, hitching up his trousers.

"However sad we feel about Mr. and Mrs. Appleby's tragic losses, this does not justify ripping a much-loved baby from her mother's arms. A baby who would indisputably be better off parented by Cassandra and Sebastian Brooks, whose experience in child raising is extraordinary by any measure. With them as her parents Grace would grow up in the home of her sister and brothers, with her grandparents and uncle and aunt around her."

"Thank you," said the judge. He looked over his glasses in our direction, his expression gentle. "This has been a difficult few days for all of you. If any of you would like to speak on your own behalf, you may do so now before I retire to consider my judgment."

I looked at Ben. I hadn't expected this. He raised his eyebrows at me and I shook my head. What more could I say? Then Cassandra stood up. The air between us vibrated, blowing a chill wind up the back of my neck.

"I'd like to say something, Your Honor," Cassandra said, tears in her voice.

"You can speak from there," said the judge. "Take your time. No need to return to the witness box."

"I just wanted to say that I don't want Grace. I love her but I don't want to look after her as my daughter. Sebastian and I decided after Fred was born that our family was complete and that's why Sebastian had a vasectomy. I've been a full-time mother for seventeen years and I've loved every minute, but I've done my bit. I'm over it. I want to do something else now before I'm too old. I want to get a job, that's all. Is that too much to ask? I would never have got pregnant if I thought I'd be forced to be the baby's mother. I only did it because I knew what wonderful parents Olivia and Ben would be and that I would be able to enjoy watching Grace grow up without having to look after a child for another seventeen years."

She was sobbing as she collapsed down, and then I felt

Ben's hand closing around mine. As my own tears choked out of me, I felt them joining me to Cassandra. Cassandra, the girl who had taken me into her heart, and, without hesitation, had shared her family with me ever since that day so long ago when I stepped onto Killara's wide verandah.

"Thank you, Mrs. Brooks," said the judge. "The Court will adjourn until 10am tomorrow when I will deliver my judgment."

Grace came back home with us, and after we'd tucked her up in Sebastian's beautiful cradle, the cradle which would soon be too small, Ben poured us whiskies and we sat out on the back deck—tiny in comparison to Killara's—and I found the courage to talk about my abortion and my unforgivable lie. But I didn't get far before Ben leaned across from his chair and stopped me with his finger across my lips. "It's done. I understand why you had the abortion and didn't tell me. I even see that it was your right, back then, before we were committed to each other. Your body, your decision. But never telling me over all these years… in time I'll get over that too. I know you were just taking the easier way. Why bring it up and risk hurt and upset? I get that. But please never conceal something as important as that from me again."

"No, I won't. I'm so sorry. There's nothing else I haven't told you, I promise."

Ben kissed me, his mouth gentle. He pulled back and smiled, a bit wonkily, the pink light from the setting sun reflecting off his glasses and hiding his eyes. "We have the future to think about now. Cassandra was incredible today. I've never had quite the glowing opinion of her that others seem to have, but after that speech… she's a brave woman. I'm not sure if she meant it all, or if she exaggerated how she felt, to convince the judge that she absolutely wanted us to adopt Grace, but it was powerful."

"I think she exaggerated a lot. She loves kids. They're everything to her. Of course she would love being Grace's mum. She could have a career as well as Grace if she wanted. She did it for me, for us."

Ben nodded. "Well, she'll always be there for Grace. What little girl wouldn't love an Auntie Cassandra? Cathie and William as her grandparents? Killara for her holidays? Amber and David and Fred to spoil her and tease her and love her?"

Hours later my fears were still screaming around in my head. I knew Ben was still half awake too. "Do you think we're being selfish? We can't give her all that. A big, loving, crazy family like the Brooks tribe," I whispered.

"Shush," he whispered back. "Grace can have it all. Boring old us and the Killara clan."

Just before dawn I heard Grace fussing, and tiptoed into her room. "What do *you* want," I murmured, as I cuddled her close. "Will you be as happy with me and your Daddy as you would with Cassandra and Sebastian?"

We straggled into the court in the morning, all of us wanting this to be over. Sebastian was optimistic, or pretended to be. "I think that Cassandra's plea makes it pretty much impossible not to find for you two adopting Grace," he said, pulling a still shaky Cassandra to him.

"Did you really mean that?" I said. I hadn't dared ask last night. "Or did you just say it to make a point?"

Cassandra's eyes flooded again. "I don't know. I truly don't know. Of course if Grace stayed with us she would be loved as much as all our children, but it wouldn't be right, would it? She's Ben's daughter. And I want her to be yours."

Judge Campbell limped into Court like an old man. Did he

have a wife and children and grandchildren? How did he cope, hearing all these heartrending stories? Having to make decisions that would change people's lives, their reasons for living. I glanced over at Sebastian, my heart full. He would be a judge as wise as this man one day.

"This has been a complex and difficult case," began the judge. "While it concerns adoption, this cannot be considered in isolation from the surrogacy arrangements made by the two parties. In 1984 an interim report was released by the Special Committee appointed by the Queensland Government to enquire into the laws relating to fertility issues, including surrogacy, and discussions of these matters are ongoing. I am therefore aware that this case may be viewed as a precedent. However, I have made my judgment today based on the evidence before me." He shifted behind the bench and pulled a startlingly white handkerchief from somewhere in his robes. Taking off his glasses he polished them, held them up to the light, and polished them again. I gripped the edge of my seat. I had no clue what he was thinking. He put his glasses back on, maneuvering the wire hooks over his small ears.

"It is unusual to hear a case in a Family Court where the parties are in complete agreement. Here we have two caring couples who are entirely at one in the course they wish to take; and that course is that the child, Grace Brooks, should be legally adopted by her biological father, Ben Appleby, and his wife, the surrogate mother's close friend and informal foster sister, Olivia Appleby.

"Mr. Braxton, representing Grace Brooks, has performed his duty in examining whether this adoption would be in Grace's best interests, and also whether it would be in the best interests of her birth mother. One of his arguments was that Sebastian Brooks, because of his own strong advocacy for surrogacy and adoption, placed undue pressure on his wife to give up the baby. I did not find the evidence for this compelling. Mr. Brooks has a faultless reputation as a fair and ethical lawyer, and I find that he did not wilfully influence Mrs. Brooks in this matter. Certainly his knowledge informed Mrs. Brooks, and may have influenced her, but I am satisfied she made her own decision. Perhaps Mr. Brooks should have considered the inappropriateness of, in any way, supporting a surrogacy arrangement that involved his own wife, given his professional involvement in the area, but on the other hand, I believe that because of his experience, the surrogacy process was well-considered.

"However, it cannot be said beyond reasonable doubt that Mrs. Brooks wasn't influenced and is still influenced by a combination of factors, including understandable feelings of guilt about her friend Olivia Appleby."

I clutched Ben's hand, cold sweat sliding from my armpits.

Judge Campbell cleared his throat. "My deliberations have encompassed first, what arrangements will be in the best interests of the child. It is clear that both Cassandra and Sebastian Brooks, and Ben and Olivia Appleby, would make exceptional parents and caregivers for Grace. I was not convinced by Mr. Braxton's arguments that Olivia Appleby would not make an excellent mother for Grace. I also found Cassandra Brooks' statement that she wanted Olivia and Ben Appleby to adopt Grace, and that she would continue to play a part in her life, compelling. However, I am also concerned that Grace continues to enjoy every opportunity to form strong bonds with both Cassandra Brooks and Ben Appleby, her biological parents, but also with her half-siblings, the other children of Cassandra Brooks, and with her grandparents, William and Catherine Tulloch.

"My second consideration seeks to guard against later regret on the part of Mrs. Brooks, should she realize that she should not have given up her child for adoption, especially as once the child is adopted by Ben and Olivia Appleby, there would be no legal requirement for them to allow Cassandra

Brooks access to Grace, or to remain located in a city or even a country that made access possible."

Ben's hand squeezed mine so hard I jerked in my seat.

"It is undisputed that Ben Appleby is the biological father of Grace Brooks, and I order that her birth certificate be reissued with her name registered as Grace Appleby, and with Cassandra Brooks as her mother and Ben Appleby as her father, with a notation that Mr. Appleby is the sperm donor. This will remove the necessity of Ben Appleby adopting the child in order to claim his legal parental rights. Given that the Brooks and Appleby families have a long history of close friendship, and indeed that Mrs. Brooks and Mrs. Appleby grew up as foster sisters, there seems no reason for an adoption that will transfer the parental rights of Mrs. Brooks to Mrs. Appleby.

"Therefore to accommodate the needs of all parties, I have decided not to approve the adoption of the child by Ben and Olivia Appleby on the grounds that this would legally sever forever the rights of Mrs. Brooks to the child, as well as the rights of the child's half siblings and biological maternal grandparents."

I watched him, this judge of human happiness, human love, take off his glasses, rub his eyes and put his glasses back on. *He didn't say that, he couldn't, how could he? He's made a mistake, he's speaking again…*

"I further order that a joint custody arrangement be formalized between the biological parents, Ben Appleby and Cassandra Brooks, to the effect that Ben Appleby and his wife, Olivia, will act as the child's primary carers until she is eighteen or leaves home for tertiary study or work, whichever date is earlier. At any time, Cassandra Brooks can take over the primary care of Grace if there is sound reason, and with the agreement of Ben Appleby and of Grace herself, should she be old enough."

He can't, he can't take Grace away from me, how can he? I'm her mummy...

"With the assistance of the counselors who advised them throughout the surrogacy process, both couples will discuss and agree on the details of the access rights of the biological parent who does not have the day-to-day care of the child; that is, Cassandra Brooks. The custody arrangement should be such that the child spends considerable time with her birth mother and Mr. Brooks, her half siblings, grandparents and other Brooks family relatives, and all important decisions about her welfare, religious upbringing, education and health will be made jointly by both biological parents."

I was going to faint. I pushed my chair back and sunk my head on my knees, Ben's hand on my back keeping me from sinking to the floor. *She's not going to be mine, never, never.*

"Olivia, have a drink," I heard, as I forced my body back into an upright position. I took the glass Ben pushed into my hand and gulped the tepid water down, the sound of my swallows echoing around the room. The judge wasn't talking; no-one was.

"Sorry," I croaked.

"Would you like a break before I go on?" said Judge Campbell, and I looked over at him, his face suddenly cruel below his wispy white hair.

I shook my head. "No. Go on."

"Very well," said the judge. "As with all joint custody arrangements, neither parent is permitted to leave Brisbane temporarily or permanently, taking Grace with them, without the other parent's permission. This will remain the case until Grace has attained the age of 18 or has left home for study or work, whichever comes first. This seems the arrangement that is in the best interests of the child and will ensure she has every opportunity to form strong bonds with both her parents, as well as with her step-parents and siblings. By the time she is eight years old the situation must be explained to her, unless circumstances arise that would make this undesirable."

The next minutes, hours, were a blur and then we were back at Cassandra and Sebastian's place and somehow I was sitting in Cassandra's nursing chair with Grace in my arms, her round violet eyes attached to mine, her mouth sucking furiously on her bottle, her hand around my thumb, her cheek wet with my tears.

We were alone. I could hear voices somewhere in the house and a shout from Fred. Why weren't they all here with Grace and me? Did I dream it all? Will I wake up and we will have to go to court and listen to the judge taking my baby away from me? That's what he did. He gave her back to Cassandra because she's a better mother than I am. He didn't let me adopt Grace because I can't be trusted and I might refuse to let Cassandra share in her life.

Chapter Thirty-Nine

Brisbane, February, 1990

Grace's third birthday was staged at Killara. Cassandra had decided that David and Fred could return late to their Brisbane schools after the long summer break because she wanted Grace's party to be on the exact day she was born, the fourth of February.

"We could have the party on Saturday," said Ben. "It won't matter to Grace if it's a few days early. Then the boys can be back for the beginning of the new school year. If they aren't they'll probably get the worst desks, right under the teacher's beady little eyes." He winked at Fred, who winked back.

"No. It's Grace's day. We must all be here to celebrate it with her. Three is a major milestone.

"Since when?" said Sebastian, his eyebrows in his hair. "Sixteen maybe, twenty-one, forty, perhaps. Even five. But three?"

"Trust me. I know three-year-olds. This is when they understand what birthdays are all about."

And I don't of course. Know about three-year-olds. Lily

was only a trial run. No competition for Cassandra's vast experience of three-year-olds, or any other age-year-olds. Not that I'd get a say anyway. The story of my life.

I gritted my teeth, the action reminding me of our teenage years when I would clamp my mouth tight to stop myself telling Cassandra to shut the hell up. Think how Grace will love it, I told myself. Her Poppa telling her his favorite stories, Fred at her beck and call, Amber and David pulling her through the little waves on her blow-up surfboard, Cassandra's over-the-top ballerina birthday cake.

"Mummy, Mummy," the center of attention called out as she bounced through the door covered in sand, her Sunny gold hair a mess of tangled curls. "Mummy, look what Fred found for me. Hold out your hands." She placed a crab with half its legs missing, dead I hope, into my cupped palms and jumped up and down. "It's for you, Mummy," she said. And I forgave Cassandra once again.

Ben had put off his sabbatical leave to Cambridge for three years now. He'd broached the idea with Cassandra when Grace was two, but she'd made it impossible. Not by saying we couldn't go, but by saying we must do whatever was best for us, but if he wanted the truth, she'd rather we waited for another year or two.

So we waited. Then Ben got a chance that fired him up so much he decided to get tough. He was offered a three-year research fellowship on migratory seabirds to be jointly funded by his old Department at Cambridge, and the university here in Brisbane. If he accepted it he would need to spend the first 18 months in Cambridge. After that he could remain based in Brisbane but with regular short trips to the UK.

I couldn't wait. It would give me the motivation I needed

to start writing again. I was over being an editor of other people's novels.

"And it would get you and Grace away from Cassandra," said Ben.

"That's not what I was thinking at all," I said.

"Bullshit," he said.

Cambridge in April was cold and damp, but I didn't care. I felt finally safe. The small 1930s house we were accommodated in as part of Ben's fellowship was not a quaint and crooked cottage, although perfectly pleasant. There were swallows in the eaves, a small patch of grass and an old oak tree at the back, and daffodils and bluebells lit up the woods nearby. I sank with deep joy back into my old world as a writer. Browning and Wordsworth accompanied us as Grace and I trundled along the muddy paths, woollen hats pulled down over tingling ears, and scarves bought from a tourist trap in Trinity Lane wrapped snuggly around our necks. By June the sun had shone enough to pack away the woollens, and on some days even our shorts and T-shirts got an airing. Weekends were set aside for the occasional trip to London, but more frequently our choice was to explore the beautiful countryside and sleepy, timeless villages surrounding Cambridge.

Ben was as happy as a blackbird, back to his old haunts, the fields and woods he had known so well as a student. So many birds, old friends to him, so soothing after the bright loud birds of Australia.

We'd managed to get Grace into a daycare center a five-minute walk from our cottage, so I had free time enough, but it took me a while to settle down to writing again. So much easier to immerse myself in the gloriousness of Cambridge, drinking in the ancient stones and stopped in my daytime aisle-wandering tracks through Kings College Chapel when the massive pipes, without warning, swelled with sound. There from his throne on high sat the organist, so small and so powerful as he rehearsed—I was sure he must see it as a performance — for the next service. Almost every week Ben and I, with a wide-eyed Grace on Ben's knee, sat mesmerized during a Choral Evensong, sometimes in Kings College Chapel, sometimes in one of the many other chapels — St John's College, Trinity College, Christ's College. During the day, without Ben or Grace to distract me, I gave myself over to the literary vibes that permeated every twist and turn of old Cambridge. They set me dreaming and soon enough I found my writing voice again.

I spent two or more hours every fortnight writing to Cassandra, Sebastian and the kids. Ben added half a page at the end and I enclosed Grace's latest art work. I did it out of duty, every stroke of my pen soaked in guilt. Cassandra's letters to me were full of news about mutual friends, the children's doings, and updates on her parents. Fred, bless him, wrote funny letters to Grace, illustrated with drawings she found hilarious.

Sometimes writing to Cassandra brought back memories of my student days in Cambridge and the mad letters Cassandra and I sent each other before I fell in love with Ben and became distracted. It was strange to think how few letters I had written to friends since.

In June we drove to Scotland to see Ben's parents: Don and Bessie to me, Grandad and Nana to Grace. They still lived in the forbidding, beautiful, gray stone house in a pretty valley to the east of the Cairngorm Mountains where Ben had grown up. Don seemed frail and much older than Uncle William, although they were both 78. Bessie was as energetic as ever, and Grace, the only grandchild they would ever have, was indulged with ice-creams and piggy-backs and walks to the park for endless swings. When, after five days, we left, even Don's tired Scots eyes were misty, although we promised we'd try and get back every couple of months.

But Sunday, a month later, the phone shrilled at seven in the morning. Too early for a casual call. I knew from Ben's tense back what it was. His mum had found Don cold and still in his bed when she took him a cup of tea that morning. The doctor when called thought it was likely a massive heart attack; Don had suffered a minor one a year before and had been on medication since. The doctor reassured Bessie that he wouldn't have known a thing, but she was more distressed about not being there for him in the night than by his actual death. She'd been suffering from a bad cold and had been sleeping in the guest room to spare Don her coughing. I felt for her; I'd never believed those 'He died peacefully in his sleep' euphemisms. If there was no-one there how could one know? I suspected heart attacks were excruciatingly painful; surely a heart clenched in an unforgiving cramp would wake even the soon dead from his sleep.

The funeral was exactly as one would expect for a kindly man who had lived in the same Scottish village all his life, as had his parents and grandparents before him. By Christmas, Bessie had moved to the next village to live with her widowed sister, and the house with Ben's childhood laughter in its walls had been sold to a rich young London couple who fancied it as a country retreat.

With only two months before our return to Brisbane, I was ready to send my manuscript to my new literary agent, an American now plying her trade in the UK. My *Daisy's War* agent had given up agenting and Mary-Ann had taken her spot in the same agency. Her aim was to sell books to American as well as to UK publishers, so I fantasized about making it big in America.

Now I had to decide whether I wanted Ben to read it. He had no clue what it was about, only that I'd been on fire once I got into the writing. But if I couldn't let even Ben read it, why had I even bothered to write it? *Courage, Olivia. Real writers write what they must whatever the consequences.* So I told myself, over and over.

Ben took his sweet time. How often I wanted to snatch it from his hands and stuff it in the open fire burning merrily in our small living room. At last he gave his opinion. Grace was tucked safely up in bed, two doors closed between her and us.

"It's fiction," I said, before he had a chance to convert his leaden expression into words.

"Perhaps you can revise it," he said.

"What do you mean? Since when were you an expert on fiction?"

"You must know you can't publish it, certainly not as it is. I don't doubt your agent will love it, but that's beside the point."

"It's the best thing I've ever written. Surely that's what matters. Not what a few friends might think."

"Our closest friends, one of whom is our daughter's mother."

"Cassandra's not that selfish. It's not as if it's about her."

"A story about a surrogate mother who breaks her promise and refuses to give her child to the intended parents? Not about Cassandra?"

"Well if you think like that, it's as much about us."

"Except it's the biological mother who comes across as selfish and grasping."

"That's OK then. Everyone will know she couldn't possibly be modeled on the wonderful Cassandra." Anger burned through me as I snatched the manuscript from his hands and threw it in the fire. It made a weak hiss and the fire went out.

Ben didn't move from his chair. I pulled the bloody thing out and blew on the smoldering corner. Fury flamed my cheeks as I sat back down, as far away from Ben as I could get. "Why should she control what I write? How can't you see what's she's like? She always gets her own way. How is that fair? She's got a husband who thinks the sun shines out of her, three healthy kids, control over our daughter, and parents who support her come hell or high bloody water. What's she ever done that's important? Just stayed at home and everyone thinks she's marvelous."

Ben stood up. "You're right, it's your novel and you can do what you wish with it. You asked me to read it and I assumed you were interested in my opinion. All I ask is that you consider re-writing it. Change it to adoption or something. Turn it around so the adoptive parents are the ones who triumph and the woman who gives up her baby is the one who is destroyed. That would be a more likely scenario, anyway. Set it in 1930s England when that happened all the time. And when you've done that ask Cassandra to read it, and listen to how she feels about it, before you send it to your agent."

"I've put everything into this." My stomach was a burst balloon, angry air screaming out through its limp, torn, jealous skin.

"I know. I'm sorry," Ben said, his tone flat.

"You're not sorry. You care more about Cassandra's feelings than mine."

"Olivia, calm down. I get this has been important to you. Christ, it's been a relief to see you so involved in something other than Grace. It's been therapy for you. So it's not wasted, not a word of it. It's what you needed to do for yourself."

"But not for anyone else. Not to get my career back. Perhaps you think it would be OK to put it in a vault somewhere so it can be discovered and published after we're all dead."

"I've said my piece, and it's up to you now. If you decide to publish it, I'll support you as far as I can. Cassandra will probably cope better than any of us, as long as she doesn't think it will hurt Grace, or even her parents."

"That's unfair. How dare you even think that I would do anything that might upset them." I stepped back as Ben walked towards me, but he passed me by and went into the hall. I heard our bedroom door open and close, but his face stayed in my head, his eyes blurred behind his glasses.

My agent loved it. "Thank goodness you've got your mojo back again," she said. "I'm pretty damn sure I'll be able to sell this. It might outdo *Daisy's War*."

"I was thinking it needed a solid re-write," I said, the lie making me want to throw up.

"Let's send it out first. The lucky editor who gets it can tell you what you need to change."

"I don't know. It's a bit close to home. Ben thinks it'll upset the surrogate mother who had Grace."

"Give me a break," she said. "I thought you were a writer, not some hobbyist."

Chapter Forty

Brisbane, October, 1991

They were there to meet us at the airport, our other family. Not Amber, now twenty-one and at Melbourne University, immersed in her first year of a Masters degree in Psychology. But David showed up having taken the morning off from his university lectures; he had decided to stay in Brisbane for his teaching degree but had escaped to a student apartment, shared with three of his long-time mates. Six-foot-two, yet he still fitted snuggly in a corner of my heart. Even now, remembering, the ghosts of milk ducts deep inside my breasts tightened. My only experience of nursing. It had caused the first serious rift between Cassandra and me but I couldn't regret it, or forget it. Two children I had conceived, three I had mothered, yet not one of them had I been able to nurse.

Of course Grace's idol had skipped school. Now thirteen, Fred had changed so much in 18 months I almost didn't recognize him. No wonder Grace adored him; he was Sebastian all over again, in looks and in spirit. He lifted his little sister off her feet with his hug, and I choked up as he swung her around as if the two of them had found each other after long years parted by war.

Cassandra blocked them out as her long hair wrapped around my head and her long arms around my body. Pulling back, she wiped a stray drop from my cheek. "I've missed you so much," she said. She thought my tears were for her.

Cassandra didn't waste any time reclaiming our daughter. "We've planned a camping trip next weekend to welcome Grace back," she said. "We'll leave Friday afternoon as soon as Fred gets home from school and come back on Sunday. It's a lovely little campsite south of Brisbane by a very safe beach. Grace will adore it."

"But we've only got back," I said. "She's tired. She's only four. Perhaps in a few weeks when she's got to know you all again she can stay over."

"Poof. She's as happy as a kookaburra. Look at her." She pointed out the window to the swing. Up, up, up, she flew, squealing with joy or terror, and down, down, up, to be pushed again by Fred.

"It will be good for her," Ben said. He wiggled his eyebrows at me. "I'll take you out to the movies or a fancy restaurant. No babysitters. We can stay out all night."

This was how it was going to be. Grace's mother being backed up by Grace's father, and me, the one who looked after her ninety percent of the time could go jump.

This was the first time we'd left her longer than a night, and that was more than eighteen months ago, before we went to the UK. Was she pining for us? Part of me wanted her to miss us with a passion, part of me wanted her to have a wonderful time.

"She'll miss us a little, but she'll have a ball," said Ben. "That's what you should wish for."

It was easy for him. He was her father. He didn't have to fret over Grace's golden Sunny looks, every day more vivid. Fear that she'd learn to love Cassandra more than me did not lie in the pit of his brain like a firecracker hiding from a match.

Forty-eight hours finally passed. And there she was, racing towards our car as we drove through their gate. *She's missed us, thank you, thank you.*

"Mummy, Mummy," she shouted, "Daddy, look what Fred made me." Behind her, up in the blue sky, flew a kite. Wings sprang from my heart and she was in my arms, my beautiful girl.

Cassandra wasn't home. "Off to check on her horse," said Fred. "Dad's in his workshop, making a digger."

"A digger?" said Ben, his eyebrows arched above his glasses.

"A wooden toy for the kids' ward at the hospital. It's his latest craze. Diggers and tip-trucks. Better than dolls' houses."

"Ah. He should have been a carpenter or a gardener, not a lawyer."

"Don't let Mum hear you say that. Dad's always threatening to leave the law practice, and Mum never takes it lightly."

"You go check on him," I said, smiling at Ben. "I'll get Grace's things together and we can get home."

"No, no. Not yet, It's only afternoon. Cassandra said you had to stay for dinner. She's got it all ready. She'll be home soon." Grace jumped up and down, her kite leaping with her.

"We'll stay, minx, but as soon as dinner is over it's home time. You have pre-school in the morning," Ben said.

"Thank you Daddy, thank you, thank you," she sang. "Come on Fred, let's fly our kite in the park."

"Crikey, kid. Give a guy a rest." Fred grinned at me. I watched them as they made for the side gate that led into the adjoining public park. Through my mind a five-year-old Fred ran along a wild black-sand surf beach in New Zealand, his kite flying high in the deceptive blue sky, big sister Sunny running behind him. Did he think of that? Was that why he was so devoted to Grace?

Dinner didn't go to plan. Just as we were all working out who should sit where at the big table on the deck, Sebastian dropped a full kettle of boiling water on his bare feet and burnt them quite badly. Cassandra drove him to A & E and we stayed back with Fred to eat Cassandra's gourmet spread of pies and salads, and clean up.

"Dad's always dropping things," Fred said. "He fell over the kitchen step the other day and gave his head a right crack. Mum said he's got arthritis and that's why he's getting so clumsy."

"He's a bit young for that," Ben said. "Has he had it checked out?"

Fred shrugged. "Dunno. I don't think so. Mum's been hassling him to go to the doctor so he probably won't."

"I hope it's not arthritis," I said. "People our age can definitely get it. A woman at work has it and she's only forty. It's horribly painful."

"Poor Dad. He'll be gutted if it stops him making his wooden toys," Fred said, a frown on his so-like-Sebastian face.

Next morning, in the rush to get Grace off to preschool, I almost missed the revelation I didn't want to hear. I was fuming about Grace's excited chatter about the Saturday riding lessons Cassandra had apparently booked her into. Cassandra knew I was uncomfortable around horses. How dare she sign Grace up for riding lessons without talking to us first.

"I've seen Sunny's picture. She looks like me. And now I've seen Lily's as well. Fred showed me in the photo on Cassandra and Sebastian's bedroom wall. Are those Lily's books in my bookcase?"

"What did you say?" I said, and Grace looked at me, her dimples disappearing.

"Did Lily have all my Pooh Bear books?" she said, her voice tiny.

I'd scared her. "Yes, sweetheart," I said, forcing myself to smile. "But she'd be so happy to know that they all belonged to you now."

"Could I have a photo of Lily and Sunny on my wall? Cassandra said they were my sisters."

I pulled her firm little body close, taking three deep breaths before I dared speak. "Yes darling. I have that very same photo somewhere. We'll hang it in your bedroom. Did Cassandra tell you anything else about Lily and Sunny?"

"They died when they were eight. It was a tragic accident. It was a long long time ago, when Fred was five. He remembers it. He told me about the big big surf beach with black sand and it was dangerous sometimes and Sunny got caught in a hole in the sea and so did Lily. He was very sad when he told me and then Cassandra came in and found us and she was sad too."

"We were all very sad," I managed.

"They all go and see Sunny on her birthday and other times as well. Can we visit her, Mummy? Could we go and see Lily on her birthday?"

"Did Fred tell you that? That they go and see Sunny?"

Grace nodded, her eyes enormous. "It's at a place where lots of people go when they die. They get buried and have a stone on top of them. The worms don't eat them because they're inside a box. They aren't scared though because Fred said it's only their bodies in the box, not their thoughts and feelings. That's because they're dead."

"Well, I'll talk about it with Daddy, and we'll see. We'd better get you to pre-school now, or you'll be late."

Grace grabbed her little backpack and wriggled it onto her back. "Ready. Let's go."

"How could she be so slack?" I said. I'd driven straight to the university after I dropped Grace off. Ben was in his office talking to one of his PhD students. My face must have made it clear that his meeting would have to be cut short.

"Calm down, Olivia. I don't suppose it even occurred to her that Fred would tell Grace. Perhaps it's for the best. She had to be told some time. It's likely good that it's out in the open. Little kids take these sorts of things in their stride."

"But it's our place to tell our daughter, not Cassandra's."

"It wasn't Cassandra who told her, it was Fred."

"She shouldn't have had that photo of Sunny and Lily hung on the wall where Grace could see it. I took our copy down when Grace was a baby."

"You're being unfair. We can't expect Cassandra and Sebastian to bury everything that reminds them of Sunny just because that's the only way you can cope. They had it in their bedroom, for heaven's sake, not in the dining room or somewhere where everyone can see it."

"Stop excusing her. You always take her side. She should have discussed it with us at least."

"Christ, Olivia, stop dramatizing. It's done now. Go and talk with Cassandra and tell her how pissed off you are."

"What are we going to do about Grace wanting to visit Lily's grave?"

"Take her to see it, of course. I'll take her in the weekend."

"But I've never seen it. You can't show her when I haven't

seen it." I felt his arms around me and hid my face in his chest.

"Perhaps we could go together," he whispered. "You, Grace and me."

I knew Lily had been buried in a cemetery somewhere in Brisbane, but I'd refused to let Ben tell me which one. I sat in the car next to Ben, Grace in the seat behind us clutching a bouquet of white and blue flowers chosen by her from the florist shop. To my surprise we drove out of Brisbane and into the country. My heart jumped as we passed the turnoff to the house we'd all shared so long ago. Ten minutes later we turned down a no-exit country road. At the end of it was a small wooden church, surrounded with old gravestones. Ben parked the car and led us through a gate, around the back of the church, and through another gate to a grassy park with rows of tombstones punctuated with trees and gardens. Grace gripped my hand. She hadn't said a word since we'd clambered out of the car.

Ben stopped by a row of white stones on a small rise under a wattle tree covered in fragrant yellow blossoms, buzzing with bees. The doll-sized gardens fronting each grave were starred with white flowers. At the base of each stone a vase had been sunk into the concrete, and each one held a pretty bouquet of flowers, still looking reasonably fresh. Someone had been here within the week.

Ben stood back, silent. I read the inscription on the grave on the left. It was Sunny's grave, a simple message of love. The outline of a young girl, her hair short and curly, was engraved on the stone, one hand reaching towards the grave next to it. Lily's stone. Another little girl engraved above the epitaph, this silhouette with long straight hair and arms outstretched, one hand reaching towards Sunny and her other hand to the stone on the other side. The silhouette of a baby. I swallowed my tears and read the words: 'In Loving Memory of Archie Appleby, son of Olivia and Ben. Died at birth, Christmas Day, 1972. *Step softly, a dream lies buried here.'*

I DON'T KNOW HOW MUCH TIME HAD PASSED, BUT THE HEAT had gone from the sun. Grace was dancing up and down the rows of gravestones, her tears quickly shed and forgotten. She'd divided her bouquet of flowers into three, and shared them between the graves of her three siblings. A low ray of sun caught Lily's epitaph. '*Sometimes the smallest things take up the most room in your heart." —Winnie the Pooh.'* Seventeen. She'd be seventeen now. Tall and slim, thick black hair down to her waist.

"Did you put the fresh flowers on the graves?" I asked.

"No, this is the first chance I've had to come here since we arrived back from Cambridge," Ben said. "Cassandra comes pretty often, I think."

"Oh." I screwed up my eyes. Enough tears for one day. "I thought Archie's body had been left in Cairns."

"I couldn't leave him there. I thought you would want a grave for him close by."

"Thank you. I don't deserve you."

"It's a relief to have this over. I had given up on you ever wanting to know where Lily was buried. Perhaps I should thank Fred for precipitating this."

"It's not that I didn't want to know, it's that I didn't think I could handle it, ever. I was scared it would destroy me again."

"Is it OK? Now we have Grace?"

"I think so. I feel, I don't know, washed out, a bit empty. Sad. Happy-sad. The graves are beautiful. And it feels right that Grace knows about Lily."

"I'm not sure how much she understands, but she'll grow

up knowing now. Perhaps we should try and explain about Cassandra being her birth mother soon."

"No, not yet. How could a four-year-old understand that?"

"Four-year-olds don't agonize over details. She'll accept it without a second thought." He looked at me over his glasses, the twinkle back in his dark eyes. "Perhaps Fred will tell her."

Chapter Forty-One

Killara, Christmas, 1991

I survived Christmas and New Year at Killara. Enjoyed it actually. I'd been dreading finding myself alone with Cassandra. The easy friendship we'd shared since we were thirteen had turned into an agony of small talk. But there was so much going on that I soon relaxed, kidding myself that it was just like old times.

Everyone was there, including Pete and Julie. Their boy, Billy, was a year older than Grace, and the two of them spent most of their time together, either giggling or squabbling. It was noted by the adults that Grace was the boss.

Amber was with her fiancé, Matt, and David with his girlfriend, Marinna. She and David had met when he did a teaching internship at an Aboriginal primary school in the small town near Darwin where Marinna had grown up. She'd been the force behind the establishment of a much needed pre-school next to the primary school. David was smitten. She was amazing with Grace and Billy — teaching them bush craft, showing them how to track animals, enchanting them with stories from the Dreamtime.

"You are so lucky," she said to me one evening when it was our turn to wash up after dinner.

"Because I have Grace?" I asked.

"She's a special girl. She has a real feel for the bush and wild things." She grinned. "Are you sure one of her parents isn't a Blackfella?"

"With her hair? I don't think so." I loved this woman. David had better hang on to her.

"That's not what I meant though. You're lucky because you have this family. Cathie and William and all their tribe. This place, this land your family is caring for. This home. Killara. Always there. That's what Killara means."

I nodded, my throat so tight I couldn't speak for a moment. "I am lucky. I have Ben and Grace, and Grace has all this family as well."

"So do you. They're your family. All of them."

I shook my head. "Not quite. Close. We're close. Close enough for me." A roar of laughter came from the living room; they were playing Pictionary. "You're used to having a big family, but I think I'm a small family type. Big families are fun in small doses."

Marinna scrubbed at the rice stuck to the bottom of the big saucepan, her midnight curls bobbing with her efforts. Rinsing it, she set it on the draining board. "Sometimes your family chooses you, and there's nothing you can do about it." She leaned over and kissed me on the cheek, took off her apron, blessed me again with her luminous smile, and sashayed out the door.

Brisbane, 1992

Grace began 'big' school on her fifth birthday, the fourth

of February, which serendipitously fell right at the start of the school year. I had only just got used to waving her goodbye at the school gates each morning, watching her skip off with her friends, when my agent at last got the bite she was seeking from the editor and publisher she thought would do the best job marketing my new novel. When she phoned with the news, instead of jubilance, the iron bar I'd been struggling to ignore clamped down on my chest and pinned me to the ground.

"Olivia, are you still there?' squawked the phone.

"Yes, sorry, I'd sort of given up on it," I said.

"I've been working my ass off to get the right deal," she said.

"I know. Thank you. Can you give me a few days to think about it?"

"What the fuck? This is a great contract. If you're wanting a bigger advance I don't think you'll get it. It's ten years since *Daisy's War* came out and you've published nothing to match it since."

"It's not that. The advance is fine. I'm not sure any more if it's what I want to publish right now. Perhaps I'll take another shot at revising it."

"You're crazy. Mavis is a great editor. Talk to her and she can tell you what she wants you to change. Not much I don't think. She really liked it. I checked out her background before I submitted to her. Two of her kids are adopted. She probably wishes she could have conned some desperate woman into being a surrogate for a kid for her."

I really was on the floor now, sitting with the phone handset held away from my ear, my eyes popping and dry, my breath frozen around my heart.

"I'll set up a time for the two of you to have a chin-wag and you can get the lowdown on any changes she wants. But we should push her. You can't afford to stay off the radar for ever. For fuck's sake don't offer to majorly revise it unless she's really insistent. Which she won't be."

"No."

"Whaddaya mean, no? You want me to go ahead and finalize the contract without you talking to her first? That's good by me if Mavis will go for that."

"No. I mean no, I don't want you to go ahead and I don't want to talk to the editor until I've thought this through. I want to read it again first."

"Christ. Any other writer would be screeching with joy and you're going to read it again? What the fuck do you suggest I tell the editor? She's not going to sit around waiting for you to make up your mind. If I submit a manuscript to her, that means the author actually wants to publish the damn thing."

"I did tell you that I was worried about it because a friend might be upset if she thought it was about her."

"Ha. That's what this is about. Christ. Has this so-called friend told you she doesn't like it, is that it?"

"No, she doesn't even know about it. But my husband isn't happy. He thinks I could make it more about adoption and not about surrogacy. It might even upset our own daughter one day. You know she had a surrogate mother; I told you."

"Well why the fuck did you write it if you're so precious about it?"

My pulse pounded through my chest and throat and head. I needed some air that didn't choke me. "I'll get back to you later," I rasped, and placed the phone carefully back on the receiver. Levering myself off the floor I stumbled to the open door, desperate for the caress of fresh, clean, eucalyptus-fragrant air.

PAGE BY PAGE I STRUGGLED THROUGH IT, STOPPED BY MISERY or rage or bloody-mindedness multiple times a day. The writing was good, the story was focused. I even cried for the characters, in spite of having written the bloody thing and read it numerous times. Then Ben's eyes — sometimes accusing, more often sad — would seem to flicker on the page and I would slam it shut.

I knew he knew how hard this was for me, but for a long time he kept silent. My wakefulness and annoying wriggling at 2am, 3am, 4am every morning finally broke his resolve.

"Olivia, this is crazy," he said, out of the darkness. My eyes were fixed on the window, a plane's spooky lights silently moving through the stars.

"Sorry," I said. "I'll sleep in the study so you can get some rest."

He rolled on his side and put his arm across my rigid body. "Don't be silly. You know I don't like us sleeping apart. Talk to me."

"I don't know what to do. Do you really think I should ditch it and write something else that won't upset anyone? Won't upset Cassandra?"

"Can you change it a bit so that it's not so obvious?"

I shook my head, not daring to speak. Ben gave me a squeeze. "Then talk about it with Cassandra. Ask her if she'd read it and tell you how she feels. I might be wrong; she could be fine with it."

"What if she isn't? Then I'll have to ditch it."

"Or write bits of it differently." He pulled me closer and I turned on my side and looked at his dark eyes in the starlight.

"I hate having to get her permission. This is mine. Not Cassandra's. What does that say about me if I have to get her approval?"

"You might find that it's a relief. She's your friend, not your agent. You love her."

"My agent? I don't even like her."

"You know I'm talking about Cassandra. Whatever else you do, I think you should fire the agent. The softest thing about her are her teeth. Get a new agent who cares about you as well as your writing."

"Agents aren't that easy to get."

"Maybe not, but you won't know until you try. Friends like Cassandra are even harder to get."

I pulled away from him, my head turned again to the stars, the plane long gone. "Why are you on Cassandra's side? Ever since she got pregnant you've liked her more than me. You used to find her a pain in the butt."

"She's still a pain at times, but of course I care about her. You're being childish. She's been a true friend and practically a sister to you since you were a kid. She's Grace's birth mother."

My angst came out in a long sigh. "I'll think about it; asking her if she'll read it. I know you're right about my agent. She's too cut-throat for delicate little me. Perhaps I'll give up writing and stick to editing."

Aunt Cathie has always had second sight. She phoned me the very next morning at the office. Hearing her voice usually made my heart bounce with happiness, but not this time. It felt more like the start of a heart attack. She knew about the novel. Somehow she knew. What else could it be?

"Olivia, love, William and I need to talk to you and Ben. Is there any possibility of your flying up here and having a few days at Killara with us? Just you two. Grace could stay with Cassandra and Sebastian."

"What's wrong? Are you OK? Uncle William?"

"We're both fine. It's our future we want to talk about. Our will. It's not a topic we want to discuss on the phone though. It would help to talk it over with you and Ben."

"You've got years and years yet."

"Of course we have. But it's sensible to have a will."

"Shouldn't you be talking to Cassandra and Pete?"

"We have. Now we want to talk to you."

"Because of Grace."

"Partly. Grace and you."

FOUR WEEKS LATER WE LEFT GRACE AND MY MANUSCRIPT WITH Cassandra and flew to Cairns. In the end I'd simply asked Cassandra to read the bloody thing, telling her that because it was about surrogacy I wanted her opinion before I revised it. "It's totally fictional of course, but you know publishers, they only take novels where the stakes are high and everyone has horrible things happen to them. I might have gone over the top a bit. I don't want to upset you."

"Me? Upset? But of course I'll read it. It'll be like old times. Remember your very first book about the high-country farm in New Zealand and how you were so uptight while I was reading that?"

"God yes. I hope I'm a better writer now than I was then."

"I thought it was great. Why do you always put yourself down?"

I shrugged. "I don't always. But this novel is sort of like *Daisy's War* in that it comes pretty close to home. If you find it upsetting I'll change it."

Cassandra reached out and caught my hands. "You'd do that for me? Oh, Livie, I can't tell you what that means. Of course I'll read it. I'd be honored."

"Don't speak too soon," I said, heat rising in my face. "I want you to be honest. No pretending it's OK if it isn't."

Chapter Forty-Two

Killara, March, 1992

The first night at Killara was like being home again. Just the four of us, Uncle William and I talking about the latest books we'd loved or not, Ben and Aunt Cathie comparing bird lists. Under Ben's influence Aunt Cathie had become a bird fanatic and Far North Queensland was a birder's heaven.

Tomorrow we would get serious. I assumed they wanted to include Grace in their will; perhaps they were grappling with proportions? When it came to inheritance, to Killara, would she get an equal share with Cassandra and Sebastian's three, and with Pete's son, or not quite? I could sort of see how it might be a dilemma.

As I often was in matters of the heart, I was wrong.

"We want Killara to stay in the family. But we don't want to force you three to have to take it on if you really don't want to," Aunt Cathie said.

"We three?"

"You, Cassandra, and Pete. We'd like to leave Killara to the three of you jointly, and leave it up to you to work out how it passes on to your children. Who knows what the distant future will look like? We thought of a family trust but that is so inflexible and difficult to break if our grandchildren or their children aren't as fixated as we are on living here. Some of them will likely not even stay in Australia."

"Me? Why? Surely it should go to Cassandra and Pete? Is it because of Grace and you don't know how to include her?"

"It's not about Grace," Uncle William said. "Of course all our grandchildren, Grace included, will be remembered equally in our wills, but our estate, and especially Killara, will be left to you, Cassandra, and Pete. It is your home."

"That's not fair on Cassandra and Pete. Why should I take what's legally theirs?"

"Legal documents aren't about love and belonging," he said. "We've discussed what we want to do with Pete and Cassandra, and neither of them hesitated, not for a second. They both agreed that Killara must go to all three of you. Our three children."

I think my mouth was open. On the other side of the table I was vaguely aware of Ben's silence. "I'm… I'm… well, I'm moved that you could even think of me like this but you mustn't. I'm not a real daughter, not your real daughter. Leave my portion to Grace. She's your real granddaughter."

Aunt Cathie leaned toward me and I looked down, blinking hard as she covered my hand with hers, the blue veins under her old skin like rivers from her hands to my heart. I didn't move as Uncle William and Ben got up, Uncle William muttering something about making tea. The door closed behind them and I sat there, my eyes fastened on Aunt Cathie's hand as it stroked mine, my throat thick with tears.

"Sometimes, Olivia, when I see you fighting so hard to deny us the joy of being your family, I wish we'd gone against our instincts and legally adopted you. We thought deeply about it when you were 14, although you were so determined to cling to your independence we were almost too scared to even ask you. But in the end, it seemed wrong anyway. We felt that by adopting you we would be usurping Jess from our lives all over again. A legal document wouldn't change how much we loved you, and we didn't want you to feel obliged to love us as parents."

I rotated my wrist and grasped her hand. What had I lost? What had I lost with my stupid ideas about not getting too close, not getting too comfortable living at Killara, never thinking I belonged? I wanted to tell her but my tears were coming too fast and I pulled my hand away and covered my eyes, my face screwing up with the effort to keep control.

"Oh my love, don't cry so," she said. "I'm so sorry. We failed you. You were only a child and we should have found a way to tell you how much we wanted you as our daughter. We hoped you loved us as much as we loved you, of course we did, but we got this idea in our heads that we owed it to Jess… we wanted Jess to always be your mother in your heart."

"Like Cassandra is to Grace you mean?" My voice stuttered out, angry, hurt.

"No, that's very different. Grace has known since birth that she's part of a big loving family. She's completely secure in knowing that you and Ben are her mummy and daddy. To Grace and to all of us, you will always be her mum. Just as Jess will always be your mum. But that doesn't stop Cassandra and Sebastian loving Grace as part of their family too, any more than it stopped William and I from loving you as part of ours."

I blew my nose and jabbed at the tears on my face. "It was my fault you couldn't ask me. I was so prickly, I know I was. I knew it even back then, but somehow I couldn't stop myself. I think I was scared of embarrassing you. Embarrassing myself. You were so kind to me because of Mum, but that's not the same as wanting me in your family forever."

I blew my nose again but nothing seemed able to stop my sobs. I saw Mum in her bed, her chin coated with vomit, the smell making me gag. "I wish you had adopted me. She killed herself, why did she do that? She knew I'd find her body. How could any mother do that to her child? I love Grace so much I could never do that to her, and she's not even mine. And Mum did that to me. I tried to make her happy, to make her proud of me, I tried so hard. I know she had a miserable life, I know all of that. But you were in the same prison camp and look at you. You tell me how strong and heroic she was, so why did she have to kill herself and leave me alone?"

"We don't know if she meant to die. I think she simply took too many pills in her confusion. But even if she did knowingly take her life because she was so depressed she was incapable of seeing her way out of it, if even her love for you couldn't save her, then the blame is not with Jess. It is what happened to her in the camp when the Allies finally came to free us that must be blamed, not Jess."

"What do you mean? What did they do to her?"

"No, no. Our rescuers were wonderful. That's not what I meant." Her shaky breathing sounded loud in the quiet room. I fastened my eyes on her tanned feet in their sensible sandals.

"Darling, I think it's time I told you the last part of Jess's story. I hoped I'd never have to, but perhaps it will help you to forgive her."

I pressed my lips together and looked up. When had Aunt Cathie become so frail? Her golden bouncy waves now pure white and pulled back in a knot, her gentle face still brown but covered with fine lines from her years of sun worship. I forced myself to look into her eyes, still the violet of the deepest tropical sea. But a sea now so desolate I wanted to turn my eyes away.

"I told you that Jess worked for the commandant in the camp, and that she came to respect him. He wasn't a bad man, just a man caught up in that terrible war like so many. It became more than friendship as time when on. I didn't understand it. It seemed wrong to me, but Jess was lonely and he cared for her. Cared for her deeply." She clasped her hands together but couldn't still their shaking. "Olivia, it's hard to understand, I know it is. But in that last year… we'd been in those dreadful camps for so long we had almost no pride left… Jess and Captain Tanaka fell in love. They became lovers."

My body, my head, my heart—everything stopped. I was turned to stone.

"I know it's difficult to take in. I didn't. Not for a long long time," said Aunt Cathie, her voice quivering.

I stared at her as if she were a stranger.

"I'm ashamed that it's taken me until I'm 75 to understand the courage it must have taken for Jess to follow her heart. She was shunned by all the women in the camp near the end because she dared to cross those boundaries, but she loved him. She loved him with all of herself. She believed they would find a way to be together after the war. I pretended to understand, but she saw through me. She must have felt abandoned. After all she had done for me. After all she had done for so many of the women. So many of our children."

Blood throbbed in my temples.

"It was late August in 1945 before we had even a hint that the war was over. Captain Tanaka called us together and told us there was peace and that we'd all be leaving Sumatra. After that we got vegetables and rice, and all of a sudden, boxes of medical supplies arrived. We found out later that the Japanese had been ordered to feed us up before the Allies got to our camp. But we had to wait until half-way through September before we were discovered by the Allies. First two young Dutch soldiers and a Chinese man arrived, and then the British major who'd been searching for all the camps in Sumatra for weeks showed up. A few days later two Australians and another soldier came and told us to get ready to be transported to Singapore in army trucks. We couldn't believe it was really over. But for Jess it was so hard. She couldn't eat, couldn't sleep. Tanaka seemed to be ignoring her. Now that we were no longer prisoners he didn't care about her. All he cared about was going home. That's what she thought."

"Why would she care when you were going home at last? How could her freedom be less important than her feelings for the man who'd controlled her. A Japanese. How?"

"It got worse for her. Unbearable. We were all outside waiting for the first truck to arrive to collect us and the Japanese were in their huts. We heard a gunshot. The Australian soldiers raced into the hut and a few minutes later they dragged out a body, right in front of us. The women crowded around crying and laughing. Hysterical almost. It was Captain Tanaka, shot through the heart. He'd shot himself rather than give himself up. The Japanese way. None of the others shot themselves, only him."

I couldn't speak. My head was a snake pit. What if he'd not killed himself? Would I never have existed? Would my mother have found a way to be with him? I shivered. I was so cold.

"It's hard, I know. It will take time." Aunt Cathie rubbed my arms.

"What happened? What did Mum do?"

"She was distraught. She threw herself over his body. The poor Aussie soldiers didn't know what to make of it. I think they thought she was going to hit him, that she hated him. They hauled her off him and she sort of crumpled up."

"And I suppose all the women jeered." I forced myself to swallow the bile that was burning my throat.

"You know, they didn't. They were silent. We were all silent. I was crying; I think many of us were. Somehow it brought the whole thing home to us all. All those years of loss and deprivation and terror. All the crosses we had put on the graves of our babies and our friends. But for Jess it wasn't over. For her this was the worst day of her life."

I heard the big clock ticking on the wall. I heard an owl's soft call outside the window. My body shivered as the hot tropical air fell on it through the open windows. I saw my mother crouched on the hard dirt of another hot country, her emaciated body covered in sores, her hair hacked short to control the nits, her hands red with the blood of her Japanese lover, her heart shattered. I looked out to the stars and let my tears flow down my face and seep into my shirt.

Aunt Cathie's soft voice seemed to be coming from far away. "By the time we reached Darwin, Jess was very ill with a raging infection. She nearly died."

I hugged myself tightly.

"Jess was pregnant, Olivia."

Did I hear that?

"The doctors had to do a caesarian to remove the six-month fetus. Jess's baby was dead inside her and had been for probably two weeks. I don't know if it was hearing that shot and seeing his body being dragged out like trash, or losing his baby that destroyed the Jess I knew. Perhaps both."

"She had a baby before she had me." My head was shaking; no, no, no. It seemed to be separate from me.

"I knew she was pregnant. I guessed. She changed, became softer. One day I found the courage to ask her. I was shocked, but it meant so much to her that I tried to be happy for her. How she could even get pregnant was a miracle. Most of us had stopped menstruating years before. I've always wondered if the extra meals she got when she was working for Tanaka kept her fertile. Or perhaps it was because she was able to find some sort of happiness with him."

She sighed. "We wanted to take her with us when we left Darwin, but Jess refused. She told us she needed to go home to New Zealand. We should have insisted. She had no family there. That's why we decided it would be wrong to ask you if we could adopt you. It would be like taking away her child all over again."

I was jerked back to now. I was here at Killara. I had Ben and Grace. I didn't need Mum any more. Grace. How I wanted to see her, hold her. "So if we'd been allowed to adopt Grace would that have upset you?" I felt almost curious, as if I were someone else. A reporter perhaps. "You don't think it's right to take a child from her biological mother?"

"That's entirely different. Cassandra wanted to help you and Ben have a baby. We totally supported her in that. We were as upset as you all were when the judge refused it. But he did, and it is not Grace's fault. It is never the child's fault. Jess's unhappiness and depression wasn't your fault. Her death wasn't your fault. The one thing you must hold true is that she loved you. She always loved you. I believe that and you must too."

NEXT MORNING AUNT CATHIE AND I SAT ON THE BEACH BELOW Killara and talked some more. We were both exhausted, but we needed some sort of closure. Poor Ben had held me through the night while I sobbed and shook and raged, and I don't suppose it was much easier for Uncle William.

"It feels as if I never knew her at all," I said. "I can't remember any more how she was when she was happy. I know she was happy sometimes, I know she loved me, but I can't see her like that any more. I can't see her smile."

Aunt Cathie took my hand. "Look in the mirror when you're happy. Then you'll see her."

"I never saw her in me. The same coloring, but that's about all."

"When I first knew Jess in Singapore, she was so very like you were when you were in your twenties. Even as a child I could see her in you. You both had that determination, that independence, that self-sufficiency. For her it came from being brought up in foster homes. Dragged up, as she used to say. For you it came from having to take care of your mum without any family to share the load."

"I'm sorry. I must have been a nightmare for you when I first arrived on your doorstep."

"No. We loved you from the very beginning. You were as feisty as Cassandra, but in your own quiet, contained way."

"Poor Mum. Losing her baby so terribly. I know how that feels. Oh, Aunt Cathie, I know how that feels, and I had Ben and you and Uncle William and Cassandra and Sebastian, and even little Amber and David to love me and help me through it. She had no-one."

"I was so worried about you after you lost little Archie. So afraid. All I could think about was Jess and what it did to her. Losing the only person who truly belonged to her."

"Her Japanese captain?"

"No, I meant losing her baby son. He was her only family. All she had left. All she had ever had. When you became so very depressed I knew you were drinking, and that was Jess's downfall."

"Ben saved me. I didn't believe I had a problem. I needed to dull the pain, that's all."

"Jess didn't have a Ben. When I visited her when you were a toddler, she seemed to have her drinking under control. But I was fooling myself. She tried so hard. I know how much she wanted to be a good mother to you, but she had more than the stress of being a solo parent with no support, no family to help her. She had her demons from the Japanese camps to deal with as well. Today we know so much about the long-term effects of trauma, but back then, it was stiff upper lip."

"You think she suffered from post-traumatic stress disorder?"

"Yes, I'm sure she did. That's why I was so afraid for you when Archie died and then again when Lily died. But I didn't need to worry because you had the strength of a loving family around you."

"Then Grace was born." I smiled through my tears and grasped Aunt Cathie's hand more tightly. "Why couldn't I make up for Mum losing her first baby? I tried to help her, I loved her so much but it was never enough. I didn't know how, what to do."

"You had to grow up far too soon. But it made you who you are, a strong caring woman and the best mother Grace could ever have."

"You're biased. I don't think Cassandra would see me as caring."

"You two have lost your closeness and it makes me sad. But it's never too late to find each other again. Make the effort, Olivia."

"I know. I should make the effort for Grace's sake. Ben's told me that."

"Yes. But that's not the most important reason. Make the effort for you. I think Cassandra is waiting."

Chapter Forty-Three

We flew back to Brisbane on Sunday morning. I was missing Grace terribly. Was she missing us?

I was still hollowed out by my mother's experience, my emotions all over the place. But after talking with Aunt Cathie yesterday, it was grief I felt now, not horror. With grief came glimmers of understanding, flickers of forgiveness. For Mum, for me as a child, for Cassandra.

Cassandra. Had she read my manuscript? I wished I'd never given it to her. The worst timing ever. I could have rewritten it first as Ben suggested and she'd never have known.

We'd find our friendship again. We owed it to Mum and Aunt Cathie. I owed it to Mum and Aunt Cathie. It was me who was the problem. I knew that, I bloody knew it. Why couldn't I relax and stop worrying about losing Grace to Cassandra? I'd change. It was time I stopped being so possessive. The more family who loved Grace the richer she would be.

By the time we got to the Brooks house I was a quivering mess of doubt and determination. It would be all right. If Cassandra had read my novel she'd come round, even if she were a bit upset. She didn't hold grudges. I'd talk to her and tell her how I'd been feeling. Apologize. Tell her about Mum and what she went through. Everything would be OK.

Grace opened the door when we knocked. She was perfectly fine; clearly hadn't missed us for a second. Good. That was good.

Cassandra appeared and I gave her a hug, a real hug. She pulled back and turned to Ben, accepting his kiss on her cheek. Something was wrong. She seemed tired, distracted. Shit, she'd read my manuscript and was upset. Should I ask her?

"Grace, go and get your things," she said.

No invitation to dinner?

"Come on Gracie," said Ben. "Say your goodbyes, and no messing about. I was planning on getting Chinese on the way home and I think they close early on a Sunday."

Liar. He could see something was amiss. My manuscript. Shit.

"Can Fred come and stay next Saturday night?" Grace asked, as soon as we got home.

"If he wants to, of course he can," I said, smiling at her glowing cheeks and messy curls.

"Why on earth would Fred want to spend the night with a five-year-old girlie?" Ben said, grabbing her and tickling her.

"Stop it, Daddy. Stop it," she screeched. "Fred likes me, so there. He says I'm better than most boys. I'll be six next month anyway."

"Fred's a sweetheart," I said. "Of course he wants to come and stay. He probably gets lonely without Amber or David at home any more. No-one to argue with."

"Goodie," said Grace, jumping up and down. "We've got a secret."

"You have? What sort of secret?" I asked.

"We're doing a concert and Fred said we needed a dress rehearsal. We can't do it at his place because it's a secret from Sebastian and Cassandra. It's for Sebastian's birthday. We've been practicing in Fred's bedroom when they're outside in the garden so they can't hear."

"A concert," Ben said, and I could almost see his banjo materializing in his arms. "Who's in it?"

"Me and Fred. It's our surprise for Sebastian. You can watch it and then we can do more practice. But you have to keep it secret."

"So, Miss Gracie, do you think your mum and I'll be invited to the opening performance, or do we only get to see the dress rehearsal?" Ben asked.

"Of course you'll see it, silly. It's soon. Cassandra's having a party for Sebastian."

"Right. I'd completely forgotten it was the old bastard's birthday."

Grace gave him a shove. "He's not old, he'll only be 46," she said. She knew everyone's birthday and exactly how old we all were.

I winked at Grace and poked my finger in Ben's chest. "Same age as you'll be soon."

"Really?" said Ben. "I thought the old bugger was at least fifty."

"Liar, liar, pants on fire," Grace sang, twirling around. She stopped and placed her hands on her hips. "Daddy, you and I can go and watch Fred's rugby game on Saturday afternoon and then he can come back home with us. We can get fish 'n chips for dinner 'cos that's his favorite, and then we'll have the concert. OK?"

"Looks like I don't have a choice. You seem to have it all organized," Ben said. "But perhaps your mum would like to come and watch the rugby too?" He wiggled his eyebrows in my direction, a smirk on his face.

“Watch a scrum of 14-year-old boys knock each other out?” I said. “I don’t think so.”

“Yes, Mummy, you should come. Fred would love you to come. He thinks you’re the best.”

“He’ll have enough people watching. Sebastian always goes, doesn’t he? Cassandra too, I bet.”

Grace shook her curls. “Cassandra’s not coming. She’s riding.” She stuck her head in the air, placed her finger on the tip of her nose and pushed it up.

“Grace, that’s rude.”

“Everyone does that when Cassandra says she’s going riding. ‘Specially when it’s one of her fancy jumping competitions. Fred does it and Sebastian too.”

“Well, it is rude and I hope Cassandra doesn’t see.”

“She does see. She tells them to get knotted.”

"I’m not sure spending all this time with the Brooks family is good for you,” I said, half believing it.

“I’m stuck with them,” said Grace. “They’re family. That’s what Fred says.”

“Fred may be a rugby man but he’s a wise one,” Ben said, winking at Grace. “Perhaps your mum will want to go and watch Cassandra win her jumping competition instead of joining us louts at the rugby.” He turned his traitorous face towards me. “Olivia?” His left eyebrow went up.

Here’s my chance to do something nice for Cassandra. “OK, I’ll come to the rugby,” I said. “It’ll be better than galloping horses.”

I DIDN’T SEE CASSANDRA ALL WEEK. HER STRANGE MOOD THE other day had made me nervous. I thought about going over one morning when the kids were at school and the men at work. Coffee between two friends. *Loved the manuscript, Olivia. Can’t wait ’til it’s published.*

I chickened out. Don't force it. She mightn't have even read the thing yet. I can't begin to explain my feelings about us, apologize for how I'd been behaving; not until we'd got the book out of the way. She's probably too busy organizing Sebastian's birthday bash. Knowing Cassandra, it will be an Event. Once that's over, I'll ask her.

FULL OF FISH 'N CHIPS BEN AND I SETTLED INTO OUR armchairs with a glass of wine and waited for the pretend curtain to rise. We'd been listening to Fred's distinctive laugh and Grace's giggles, muffled by the door, for at least thirty minutes. In front of us a stretch of wooden floor had been cleared of furniture, except for our CD player that glowed expectantly in the corner. The excitement was building.

And then they were there; Fred, already taller than me, in white flares, pink shirt, silver tie, pointy-toed brown leather shoes and a Beatles wig, a guitar slung over one shoulder. The clothes were recognizable from the chest of dress-ups that Cassandra had collected over the years, and the flares and shirt had once been Sebastian's. Grace was in black tights cut off below the knee and a shocking pink midriff-length top exposed her five-year-old tummy. Circling her golden curls and low across her forehead was a purple scarf, and from her small perfect earlobes dangled two enormous circles of silver. Her eyes were surrounded by black eyeliner, slightly smudged, her eyelids glittered with blue eyeshadow, and her lips were painted scarlet. On her feet were her own ballet pumps, thank goodness. I knew how much she loved clomping around in Cassandra's discarded stiletto heels.

Ben clinked his wine glass to mine, his eyes twinkling.

Grace slinked over to the CD player and pushed the button. 'You Should be Dancing' blasted out. Fred put down his guitar, struck a pose, and then went for it, John Travolta no competition for him. We were caught between grinning and mouths open. That boy had always loved dancing but we'd never seen him like this. Grace flounced in and he grabbed her hand and spun her around, and then she was sliding across the floor between his legs and back again, springing up with a carefree style that would have made her ballet teacher weep tears of steel.

After that we were treated to 'You're The One That I Want' with Fred and Grace singing along with John T. and Olivia (the other one). We needed no movie screen to remind us how sensual the original dance moves had been; they were mirrored in our innocent child's every move and facial expression.

As we rose from our armchairs clapping and stamping and shouting 'Bravo,' Fred bowed and Grace jumped up and down before coming to a panting stop.

"Did you like it?" she squealed. "Do you think Sebastian will like it?"

"He'll love it," I said. "It'll blow him to the moon and back."

"We've got one more act," she said, and Fred grinned.

"Don't move, we just have a really quick change," she added, waving gaily as she made for the door, Fred following behind her like the lamb that he is.

"I think this calls for another glass of wine, my dear," said Ben, sweeping a low bow before me. "We'll be able to afford to buy a whole wine-cellar full once those two hit Broadway."

"I had no idea Fred was so talented. How could he dance and sing like that without us knowing, and play rugby as well?"

"God knows. He doesn't take after Sebastian on either count."

"Strange given he looks so like him. Cassandra though; she can sing. And Grace has your musical abilities as well as Cassandra's. The rugby is a mystery. At least Grace can't play that."

"Don't be too sure. If she wants to she'll find a way." He handed me another large glass of red.

They were back, John T. and the other Olivia. Fred had the same clothes on but had removed the tie, unbuttoned the top three buttons of his shirt and taken off his Beatle wig. Grace had on a long silver tube of a dress hitched up at the waist with a gold belt, both items I recognized from the dressing-up chest.

Fred changed the CD and pressed the play button. The two of them stood side by side, holding hands, Grace barely reaching as high as Fred's chest. Hot tears filled my eyes. The music began and my breath caught as the opening chords of James Taylor's 'You've Got a Friend' soared into the room and my heart. Our song.

They sang it beautifully, their voices harmonizing without a single flat note. Two young faces glowing with earnestness and something else. Love. Ben's hand was holding mine, and as they came to the last verse and chorus he stood up, taking me with him. We stood beside them, me holding Fred's hand and Ben on the other side, holding Grace's, and we sang along, the four of us now mirroring our foursome from so long ago.

"Who gave you the idea to sing 'You've Got a Friend,' Ben asked, when we'd all recovered and Ben and I had exchanged our wine for tea.

"It's Mum's favorite CD. She's always playing it," said Fred. "She sings it to Dad. Soppy as."

"Sebastian said you all used to sing it when you lived together when Amber was a baby," Grace chimed in. "He said it was your theme song because you were bestest friends." She climbed onto my knee as she used to when she was smaller. "I wish we all still lived together," she whispered, coiling her sweet young arms around my neck.

~

"I've read your manuscript," Cassandra said, walking into my office at Stoddard and Jones. "I should have phoned first I suppose. Is this a good time to talk about it?"

No, it's not. "Yes of course. Do you want a coffee?"

She shook her head and sat down. "No thanks. I had one at the café next door." She looked at the thick envelope in her hand. "I'm sorry, Olivia. I've been trying to find the courage to talk to you."

"You don't like it." I stuck my clenched hands under the desk.

"It makes me out to be so selfish. All I ever wanted was for you to be happy and for Grace to be happy. How could you think I was using her to control you?" She looked up, her eyes glassy. They narrowed as I stared back.

"It's not you. It's a novel. Deborah — the surrogate mother — she's nothing like you. Why would you even think that?" I was standing now, looming above her for once.

"Shit, Olivia, that's crap. Anyone who knows us will think it is us."

"It will have an author's note at the end that makes it crystal clear that my daughter is from a surrogate birth and that my relationship with the surrogate mother is wonderful and that she is as far from Deborah as it is possible to get. In any case 99.99% of the readers won't know us."

"Re-write it. Ben thinks you could. Revise it so it isn't about surrogacy. If you publish it I'm scared it will destroy whatever is left between us. How could you do it to Grace? What about Mum and Dad?"

"Ben's been talking to you about it? How bloody dare he."

"I talked to him. I didn't know what else to do. I can't sleep for worrying about it."

"What do you think you're doing now if it's not controlling me? You've always tried to control me. This is my career that you're controlling now. I'm a writer, Cassandra. That's what I do. You'd never understand. You've never had a career apart from telling everyone else how to live and riding bloody horses. How would you feel if I told you that you couldn't ride anymore because I didn't like horses? What if I said you had to stop pushing Grace to have riding lessons?"

"Grace loves her lessons. I don't have to push her. If you had your way she'd never be allowed to do anything fun in case she fell and scraped her knee."

"I told you over and over how dangerous the surf was and you promised to watch them and you were so sure it was safe just because it was shallow. Haven't you learnt anything?"

Cassandra shoved her chair back and stood up, throwing the envelope on my desk. It skittered across the surface and fell off the edge. "Publish it then. See how happy that makes you when Grace and Mum and Dad find out what you've done. I wouldn't count on Ben forgiving you either."

The door slammed behind her and I gave the bloody envelope a kick. It hit the rubbish bin and I snatched it up and stuffed it in.

Chapter Forty-Four

Brisbane, October, 1992

"Damn arthritis," Sebastian said. "Soon I'll have to get a bloody walking stick."

"I wish you'd go and see a specialist. They can do things for arthritis now days. I've looked it up," Cassandra said.

"Not this sort they can't. I'll just have to deal with it. I'm thinking of ditching the legal practice and getting out of the city. What do you say to that?"

"You've become as stubborn as a mule. There must be better ways to deal with it other than swallowing aspirin every few hours," Cassandra said, her expression something between exasperation and worry.

I almost felt sorry for her. Months had passed since I'd thrown away my novel, my agent, and my writing career, but I felt we'd come to some sort of understanding. Nothing spoken. We didn't go that far. But we managed a sort of friendship; the civil polite sort. So much for my resolution to apologize and talk honestly about my feelings. What got to me most was how little she needed from me, how little she'd ever needed from me, how little she needed from anyone. It was a one-way street with Cassandra, and she had the right of way.

"There's no way this is arthritis," Ben said, as we sat down with a final very small whisky after Cassandra, Sebastian and Fred had left. It had been an awkward evening. We'd had them over for dinner and Sebastian had spilled more seafood chowder down his chin than went in his mouth. We were all keeping up the pretense that nothing much was wrong, but it clearly was. Once so full of energy, Sebastian now tired easily, and he sometimes struggled to enunciate his words.

Ben poured himself a second final very small whisky. "I think we need to say something."

"Surely they'd tell us if they knew what was wrong?" I said.

"Perhaps they're in denial. But he needs to see a specialist and find out. It might be treatable, whatever it is."

"Do you think it's Multiple Sclerosis?" I screwed my eyes tight shut, as if that could banish the truth.

"I don't know. Perhaps. I think that can affect people in different ways. We need to talk to them. We're their best friends, for heaven's sake. Let's go over there tomorrow and have it out."

"We should have told you sooner," Cassandra said, standing up and sitting down again. "It's so raw I needed to get used to it first."

Sebastian reached out his hand and she grabbed it. We sat there, waiting for someone to speak.

"It's Motor Neuron Disease," said Sebastian. "A bastard of a thing I'm afraid."

"Oh, Sebastian," I said. "I'm so sorry. When did you find out?"

"He's known for ages," Cassandra broke in, her voice shaking. "I finally told him I was coming with him to see the doctor, no arguments. That's when he told me." She glared at him.

"I'm a coward, we all know that." Sebastian grinned, but it didn't quite work. "I wanted to pretend it wasn't going to affect me too badly for as long as I could get away with it."

"Good for you," Ben said. "I'd bloody well do the same."

"What exactly is it?" I asked, not sure I wanted to know.

"Do you want the five-minute lecture or the ten-minute one?"

"Stop it, Sebastian," Cassandra ordered. "If you can't be serious long enough to tell them, I will."

"Sorry. I'll do it. It's a neurodegenerative disease that gradually destroys the motor neurons and as a result my muscles get weaker and weaker and waste away. The neurologist thinks my sort is the common variety, called Amyotrophic lateral sclerosis, or ALS for short in case you can't remember that tag. It's called Lou Gehrig disease as well after a famous American baseball player who had it in the 1930s."

"How long have you known? Are there treatments for it?" I asked, when no-one else spoke.

"I had tests and the like about three months ago and got the diagnosis. But there aren't any treatments so there didn't seem any point in telling Cassandra or you guys. And my sort is not hereditary, thank goodness."

"So, what happens as it progresses?" Ben's knuckles were white as he gripped the arms of his chair.

"I'll end up in a wheelchair and having to have my butt wiped. If it affects the respiratory muscles I'll need a ventilator. Cheerful thought."

"Christ. How long before you get to that point?"

"Depends. Some people go on for years, but mostly it gets you in about five years."

"What do you mean, gets you?" I said, the taste of fear in my mouth.

"Well, unless I want to spend years paralyzed and on a ventilator, I can only hope it will mercifully shove me off this mortal coil sooner rather than later."

Cassandra stood up, hands on hips. "No. We'll find a cure. There are sure to be research studies going on in the US and other countries. We'll get you into them. We CANNOT give up. We will not give in to this."

"Not now, sweetie. Poor Olivia and Ben have just been given the lowdown. Give them time to get their heads around that before you begin the campaign to save me."

"Look at Stephen Hawkins. He's got this horrible disease and he's had it for years and years. And he's the most intelligent man alive."

"He's got a different form of motor neuron disease."

"Are you sure you've got the bad sort?" I asked.

"One of the bad sorts. But even my brand of the disease doesn't usually affect the old noggin. Perhaps I'll even get smarter than I already am." Sebastian pushed a fist towards Ben and missed, grazing his arm. "Whoops. No more boxing for me. But at least I'll still be able to understand your witticisms, even when I can't laugh at them any more."

Five months later we helped Cassandra and Sebastian sell up and move to Killara. He needed a walking stick always now and he had terrible cramps. Cassandra tried to put a positive spin on selling their beautiful home. "It's for big families," she said. "It's time we went home to Killara. Mum and Dad could do with some help. I want to spend more time with them, anyway. I can keep on with my research and campaigning from there just as well as here."

She'd never give up trying to find a cure. Never.

Sebastian seemed to improve overnight once the decision was made. He was full of plans for fixing up Killara; organizing the tradesmen at least. The old house hadn't seen much maintenance of late. Grace was heart-broken until it was decided that Fred would live with us so he could stay at his school.

The day before they were due to leave I saw Cassandra at the bottom of their garden, her stooped back eloquent. I wandered down and stood beside her.

"You'll miss all this. You've put so much work into it."

"Sebastian more than me. He was the gardener."

I took her hand. "He was never really a city lad. Perhaps when he doesn't have the stress of his law practice and living in Brisbane, things will be a little easier for him. Stress does strange things to people."

Cassandra sighed. "I should never have pressured him into all this." She waved her hand at the house. "I pushed him into law, you know. But he did like quite a lot about being a family lawyer."

It almost sounded like a question.

"Yes, he did. And if it hadn't been for Sebastian we would never have been given Lily. Lots of families have him to thank for all sorts of things. So don't start regretting what's happened. Think about how wonderful it's going to be when you're living at Killara. Imagine waking up every day to that view. This view here is incredible. But it isn't Killara."

"But what will I do? I'm only 46."

"You'll make a wonderful vegie garden, ride and swim every day, entertain, look after us when we come and stay, and you'll have grandchildren before you know it."

That got her. She smiled. "Do you think so? Amber and

Matt seem very settled and she's always said she wanted lots of children. I do wish they'd get married though."

"Whatever has happened to the Cassandra I once knew? Since when did you think all that legal knot-tying mattered? Young people have the choice now and if you ask me it's a lot better than it was when we were that age."

"Olivia Appleby, are you saying you wish you hadn't married Ben?" She raised her still perfectly shaped eyebrows above her dark glasses.

"You know I'm not. It's worked for us so marriage is good. But what if it hadn't? What if we'd grown apart and it became a prison? Getting a divorce would have been a nightmare. Much better to not have that to deal with if it doesn't work out."

"I suppose. Although the commitment of a legal marriage surely makes one stop and think before splitting up."

"Perhaps. I sometimes wonder if Ben and I came close to splitting up after Lily died."

"No, you didn't. Don't even think that. You two are our heroes. Whenever we felt shaky we'd cling to you; how you held together."

I looked at her to see if she was kidding. She wasn't. She'd removed her glasses and she had tears in her eyes.

Part Four

KILLARA — STILL THERE

1996

~

"How lucky I am to have something that makes saying goodbye so hard."

— *Winnie the Pooh* by A.A.Milne —

Chapter Forty-Five

Killara, July, 1996

This waiting was driving me spare. I checked my watch. Almost midday. Where was Amber? Perhaps something had happened up at the house; perhaps Sebastian was having such a bad day that he didn't want to see us? We should go right now. Since when did we need an invitation? It was typical of Cassandra, trying to control everything and everybody. Well, she won't stop us from seeing Sebastian, however sick he is. We love him too.

We should have cut short our time in the UK and come back here last Christmas. A year was way too long. I got up from the deck where I'd been fuming in the sun, and started inside. I could hear Ben and Grace banging about in the kitchen. They'd probably decided to rustle up some lunch and give up on Amber.

And then, as if she'd heard my thoughts, she was suddenly there, pushing her way through the bushes that partially hid the entrance to the track that wound up from the Shack to Killara.

"Amber," I said, "Thank goodness, I was beginning to worry."

"Sorry. It's a bit of a mission getting everyone sorted in the morning. Kids and buckets and spades and heaven knows what else. And you know what Mum's like. She's getting worse. Poor Dad has to be cosseted and treated like he's incapable of wiping his own backside. Face shaved, hands washed, planted in his chair on the verandah with Mum next to him to make sure the kids don't jump on his knee or he doesn't leap up and have a bit of a dance around the grass."

"We don't care about that. We could have come up earlier and helped. Is Sebastian really that much worse? He was walking pretty well when we last saw him."

"He can still get around, but he needs a couple of walking sticks inside the house. Lately he's had to submit to using a zimmerframe if he's on uneven ground."

"He must hate that. Is he coping?"

"Most of the time he's fine. You know Dad, he's the world's biggest optimist. Not one for feeling sorry for himself. Mum's the one who's not coping."

"It's harder to watch someone you love suffering than to suffer yourself." Ben's voice came from behind me and I turned as he pulled Amber into a quick hug, and with his other arm drew me close as well. Then Grace was there, more hugs. She'd missed her big sister.

"What about Aunt Cathie and Uncle William? Are they well?" I asked.

"Grandma is pretending she isn't excited about having an 80th birthday party. She and Mum are still horse mad and ride most days. Poppa is exactly the same. Sharp as a tack. A bit more eccentric, repeats himself sometimes—but not as much as most oldies—the old bugger's 84, but he still writes his 40 hours a week.

"What was it Mark Twain wrote?" I said. "'Age is an issue of mind over matter. If you don't mind, it doesn't matter.'"

"Wise, but I wonder how easy it is not to mind when the body can't keep up any longer. Poppa was never one to overdo the exercise, but he keeps fit, probably because he wants to make sure his body stays strong enough to carry his head around. He still swims in the sea every day, rain and shine, unless there's a cyclone stirring things up, or a croc caught inside the net." Amber's grin, so like Cassandra's, lit up her face.

"That hasn't happened again, has it?" said Ben. "I'll never forget Cassandra's face when David came running up the track that day, puffing and spluttering and finally getting out that there was a croc tangled up in the net and would we please get it out so he could have his swim."

"And none of us believed him. He never let us forget it." Amber laughed. "But at least Poppa had to get a new net. That old one couldn't keep a stinging jellyfish out, let alone a croc. It's a wonder we weren't all stung to death every summer."

"How long ago was that?" I asked. "It seems only about ten years but David can't have been more than eight."

"That would be about right. Fifteen years ago. Not that David has changed much. He's still more like a kid than a grown-up at times. It's lovely having them back at Killara. They don't get here often. Too expensive for a teacher. And Marinna always seems to have family stuff to keep her in Darwin."

"Is she back teaching?" Ben asked. "Or has she given up now she has the baby?"

"She's still officially on leave but David says she spends almost as much time at the Aboriginal pre-school she helped set up as she did when she was teaching. Just with no pay. He doesn't mind though; he loves her family as much as he loves us. And most of the kids at the play school are related to Marinna's family." Amber grabbed my hands. "Just wait 'til you see Kirra. She is beyond cute. Looks so like Marinna.

Curly back hair, black sparkling eyes, always chuckling, full of mischief. She had her first birthday last week, right here at Killara. Mum was in heaven, making her a wombat birthday cake—that's her thing, no boring old teddy for Kirra. I think she's Mum's favorite. Not that she'd let on, of course. All her grandchildren are treated meticulously exactly the same."

"I'm glad. About the wombat cake and the birthday, I mean. Cassandra needs that. She's always been the earth mother." I swallowed the ache in my throat.

"Is Fred here?" Grace couldn't keep the excitement out of her voice.

"Tomorrow. Not long to wait. He's hanging out to see you," Amber said.

"Has he got a girlfriend?"

"You'll have to ask him. But he's not bringing anyone."

Grace blushed scarlet as she caught Ben winking at me.

"Billy will be here though," Amber said, smiling at Grace. "He and Pete and Julie are flying up from Melbourne on the same plane as Fred. Your boy Fred has made Grandma's birthday cake."

"Fred should have his own birthday cake. It was his birthday on Monday. He's eighteen," Grace said.

Twice as old as her, I thought. Forever her idol.

"Grief. I'd completely forgotten," Amber said. "Well done you for remembering. We'll definitely celebrate his birthday as well."

"How's his course?" I asked.

"Mum says he loves it. Le Cordon Bleu. Our little bro. He'll be famous one day. That's what Mum and Grandma think, anyway."

"HURRY UP. YOU'RE SO SLOW," GRACE SAID, HAULING ON MY hand as we walked up the track.

"Why don't you run on ahead. Surprise them," Amber said. "I've got something I want to show your parents."

As Grace disappeared up the path to the house, Amber pushed open the door of the shed Sebastian used as his workshop. The high windows hadn't seen a clean in a long time but still let in beams of sunlight, dancing with dust motes as they played over the benches and lathes and other equipment that Sebastian had acquired over the years. The air was scented with old wood and I smiled as Ben closed his eyes and sniffed long and deep, his whole body quivering with the memories.

"He needs a wheelchair?" I'd spotted one to the side of the door.

"It makes it easier for him in here. He has another in the house. Look, the arms of this one fold down so he can get close to his bench and use his tools more easily."

My throat tightened as I looked around the big room, imagining Sebastian wheeling his disobedient body about. I could feel, almost see, the ghost of young Sebastian emerging from the shadows at the back of the room, first a tall silhouette and then as the light fell upon him, a young god with his smooth brown skin and fine features, his burnished hair a mop of silky unbrushed waves. I'd never forgotten that image of him the first time we met. Almost thirty years ago. Where had they gone? Tutankhamun I had thought. Smoky-grey eyes. Kind eyes, generous eyes. Eyes that deepened with love when he looked at Cassandra.

Amber was pulling an old yellowing sheet off something half hidden behind a bench. "This is what he's been working on. He can only do a little bit every day; he gets tired quickly. But he's determined to finish it."

"Oh, it's beautiful." I felt the cursed sting of lurking tears again and blinked them back as Ben sank into a squat, his sensitive fingers stroking the mane of the wooden horse that tossed its head and pranced delicately on its low pedestal. It stood about a meter high, its head and mane glowing with the sheen of oil.

"He's almost done. Now he just has to get it all oiled and polished to perfection."

"It's like the rocking horses we made, but so much more fine and beautiful. He's still a master craftsman," Ben said.

Hearing the catch in Ben's voice I kneeled on the floor beside him, and followed his fingers with my own as we stroked the golden wood.

"Cassandra must be proud of him achieving this," I said.

"You mustn't breathe a word. She doesn't know. Poppa and I are the only ones in on it. I probably shouldn't have shown you but I wanted you to see this and what Dad is still capable of before you saw him. That rocking horse you and Dad made me when I was little is one of my earliest memories from when we all lived together in that big old house near Brisbane." Amber closed her eyes and covered them with her hands. I stood up, feeling the stiffness of middle age, and put my arm around her back. She dropped her hands and smiled at me. "Those were such crazy, happy times. If only we could have them back," she said.

"He's made this for Cassandra?" Ben asked.

"No-one else," Amber said. "His last love letter to his better half."

As we walked the final short distance to Killara, I steeled myself for the changes Amber's words had implied. Will Cassandra have aged, shrunk, as well as Sebastian? We wandered around the front of the big house to the voices we could hear floating above the grass. There they were, as always, sitting in the old wicker chairs on the verandah. Oscar IV, the first Oscar's great-grandson, lay at Sebastian's feet, his doggy eyes following Grace as she performed cartwheels on the lawn. Like every Oscar, nothing would drag him away from Sebastian if he sensed his devotion was needed. Between Cassandra and Sebastian a low table held tall glasses and a glass jug, half full of some pale pink liquid (watermelon and lime juice I'm betting). The condensation on the outside of the jug brought the memories tumbling back and I felt finally home.

Cassandra turned and was up in a second, long slim tanned legs in white shorts, hair still glossy dark, perfectly waving around her shoulders, the gold in her brown eyes still glinting as they caught the light. I was engulfed by her hug and we were both crying and grinning like we always did when we came together after months apart. Perhaps at last we'd bridged the unspoken void between us?

Ben was crouched down beside Sebastian's chair, hugging him, and I heard Sebastian's infectious laugh. The shaking inside me vanished. He was just the same. Ben as always was right; I had been imagining the worst too soon. It was going to be fine. Then Matt was there, Amber's hunky partner, with buckets and spades and their adorable twins, so much bigger than they'd been last July.

"Poppa and Cathie have gone for a walk and a swim with David and Marinna," Matt said, after we'd hugged him and tried to hug the kids, too—at three they were more interested in their buckets and spades —and then they were gone, taking Grace with them, and we were again just four.

Chapter Forty-Six

It wasn't until Sebastian needed to pee that our illusions were shaken. Some subtle sign to Cassandra had her in front of his chair with a wheeled walking frame that we'd somehow not noticed in its hiding place beside the house. She pulled Sebastian up to a standing position and held the frame firm as he maneuvered himself into it. His long loose khaki trousers flapped across his legs and it occurred to me that I had rarely seen Sebastian at Killara in anything other than shorts. His lean muscular brown legs glinting with golden hairs were an integral part of him. No more. His thinness—the fragile covering over his bones that I'd blocked out when I'd hugged him—was startling. He was pushing his walking frame through the French doors, Cassandra following him, her hand hovering near his back. Ben and I looked at each other, the shock in his face reflecting my own stunned realization.

Cassandra returned a few minutes later, her smile bright, and plopped back into her chair. "He'll be a while..." Her mouth wobbled and her smile collapsed as she turned to me.

I was on my knees in front of her, my eyes tearing as her eyes overflowed. "It's OK," I said, "It's OK."

"No, it's not. He's losing his legs. Soon he won't be able to walk, even with the walking frame. I don't know how we'll manage when Matt and David leave. They're the only ones strong enough to lift him up when he falls over. He hates it."

GRADUALLY I GOT USED TO HOW SEBASTIAN LOOKED NOW. IF I closed my eyes and listened to his croaky and sometimes slurred but still Sebastian voice and gentle humor, I could almost forget his gauntness and his shuffling gait. He'd had a 'nap' in the late afternoon and we'd been told we were staying for dinner. For a while it was like old times, although with Amber and Marinna in the kitchen rather than Cassandra and I, and David and Matt outside turning the steaks and sausages on the barbecue.

Aunt Cathie and Grace had disappeared into the library with Amber's twins, their promise of books and stories sure to be a supercalifragilisticexpialidocious treat. The remainder of we older generations sat in the big family room, looking out over the tangled rain forest to the sea, and sipped our drinks of choice. Still gin and tonics for the women and beer for the men. Sebastian drank his from a large mug, holding it with both hands and lifting it clumsily to his mouth.

"I'm refusing to sup my beer with a straw," he said. "When I get to that point I'll give up the booze. It'll be watermelon and lime juice only then."

"You could lace it with whisky," Ben said, his tone mild.

"Bloody right I could. Mate, it's good to have you here, bringing your creative solutions into our lives again."

I loved him so much, darling Sebastian, almost an Australian after all these years. Still with his charming Brit accent, but every so often slipping in some Aussie expressions. I smiled at Cassandra, willing the crease between her tired eyes to relax. "So, Queen Bee, what's the plan for the 80th birthday picnic?" I asked.

"It will be glorious. Everyone home. We'll prepare all the food tomorrow so we can get away by ten the next day. We'll need to get back by mid-afternoon so Sebastian can rest."

"Get the old man to bed before he fades," said Sebastian.

"Enough of your cheek young fella," Poppa said, and the zing of tension fizzed out before it had a chance to flare.

"SEBASTIAN AND I ARE GOING TO SPEND A COUPLE OF HOURS IN his workshop this morning while you lot prepare the feast for the birthday tomorrow," Ben said, as we stood together at the kitchen sink, washing up our breakfast dishes. "I'll push him there in his wheelchair."

"Will he let you?"

"He will. We've already talked about it. He said he'll do anything to get out of the way when Cassandra is doing her thing and bossing everyone around."

"Why don't you take Poppa down there too?" I said.

"That would be nice, but not today. Sebastian wants to talk to me."

"Could you suggest they get a couple to live here at the Shack? A hunky man who can lift Sebastian in and out of the car and do maintenance stuff around the house and garden. Someone with a wife or partner who could help in the house and perhaps even with nursing Sebastian if he needs that in a few years?"

"I think he'll need quite a bit of nursing in a few months, poor bugger."

"It's so unfair. Why Sebastian? Of all the people who don't deserve this…" I didn't even try to blink back my tears.

"That old cry, 'Why me?' Do you think he asks himself that?" Ben said.

"Probably not. He'll be grateful for what he's had, if I

know Sebastian. Grateful that it is his cross to bear and not Cassandra's."

Ben turned towards me and tipped up my chin with his long fingers. "Yes," he said, and kissed me.

We stood awhile, the sun through the kitchen window warming us, Ben's chin resting on the top of my head, his arms enclosing me, my arms enclosing him.

"Do you think Sebastian can still hug Cassandra?" I whispered into Ben's chest.

"I think that when they are lying in bed he'll still be able to hug her. In fact I'm sure of it," my lovely Ben whispered back.

FRED, PETE, JULIE AND BILLY ARRIVED AN HOUR BEFORE BEN pushed Sebastian back up the slope to Killara. We had a late lunch under the giant Jacaranda tree on the lawn. Salads and Marinna's home cooked bread with left over sausages from last night. The delectable smells of the morning's toil wafted out from the kitchen: it had been a baking marathon. Savory and sweet pies, breads, and melt-in-the-mouth goodies, now joined by Fred's rich fruitcake inscribed '*Dear Matriach Cathie—Happy 80th Birthday!*' hidden in the pantry. The baking aromas had Ben sprawled on the grass, hand on stomach, eyes closed, and manly chest rising and falling with every gulping breath. "And all we get are cold sausages?" he moaned.

"What could be more important than a little something to eat?" said Grace, this child of my heart, this lover of Pooh. Nine going on twenty, as quick and bright as the yellow-bellied sunbirds hovering over the nectar-filled eucalypt flowers. "And tomorrow you will eat cake," she added, tickling her father's stomach with a slim brown foot. "But not today."

Sebastian was like his old self, his voice barely slurring as he regaled us with tall tales of our adventures over the years, vying with Pete for the tallest and craziest. Some weren't even much exaggerated.

As Cassandra walked past his chair he reached out and pulled her onto his knee. She began to push herself up, but he pulled her down again.

"Don't be silly Sebastian. I'll squash you," she said, her tone undecided. Nurse? Schoolteacher? Girlfriend?

"Squash away wench," he said and then sang in his almost old voice, "How I love to be squashed by yoo-ou."

Go on Cassandra, relax. Leave the nursemaid behind. Be his girlfriend again. Perhaps she heard my thoughts because she snuggled into him. I reached for Ben's hand and we sat in a little cloud of illusionary happiness as the kids and Oscar, now happy to leave his master in Cassandra's care, frolicked on the lawn. Yet I could feel an unease, a sadness in Ben. Whatever he and Sebastian had talked about this morning had affected them both, but in different ways.

Chapter Forty-Seven

By eight o'clock on the morning of Aunt Cathie's birthday, Ben and I were down at the beach floating in the soft sea. The flashbacks to that Christmas Day twenty-four years ago had finally been banished. Seeing Archie's white stone next to Lily's had been more healing than any therapy.

There was no sign of the family. Grace had stayed the night at Killara, sleeping on the sofa in the library, Billy beside her on a mattress on the floor. She would have preferred Fred, but Billy was a solid runner up.

Wandering back to the Shack we played at eating breakfast, but we weren't hungry. Ben's late-night sharing of at least some of his conversation with Sebastian yesterday had left no safe place for food.

"Sebastian doesn't want to linger on with this disease," Ben had told me. "He thinks he'll be locked in by the end of the year at the rate the disease is progressing."

"Locked in?"

"His mind will be unaffected but his entire body could be paralyzed, including his ability to speak or even to nod his head. Some motor neuron disease victims end up with the ability to blink or move their eyes, and that's about it."

I sat down, fell down almost, on one of our cheerful blue-and-white striped deck chairs. "That fast? Is he certain? How does he know it will affect him that badly?"

"He doesn't, but it's likely. His specialist agrees."

"And then he'll die? How long?"

"If he's put on a ventilator and fed intravenously, he could live for months, years even."

"How could he live like that? He'd have to be in a hospital for the rest of his life. Cassandra couldn't cope with nursing him here."

" That's why he's decided to go on his own terms."

"Go where?"

"Olivia, you know what I'm telling you. He asked me to help him."

"Help him? Help him commit suicide? Is that what you're telling me?"

"No. Sebastian would never lay that on anyone. Not even on me, his best friend. He's booked himself into a hospice in Sydney where he'll be able to refuse all food and artificial ventilation. He's looked into it and talked with the doctors there and it's legal. They can't force him to eat and he'll have a Do Not Resuscitate order on his chart. He's likely to die within two to three weeks. He's already been eating as little as he can get away with."

"But what about Cassandra? What about his children? Do they agree with this?"

"They don't know. Sebastian believes that Cassandra would stop him if she knew. She can't bear to give up trying to save him. Remember Oscar the First? How she wanted to put him through more and more horrible operations just so he'd live a few extra agonizing weeks? That's love, for Cassandra."

"He can't do this now, on Aunt Cathie's 80th birthday."

"There's no good time for something like this, but he's decided this is the best way. He has said his goodbyes to all the family, even if they don't realize it. And Cassandra has all her family here, and you. She'll be distracted at the picnic and Sebastian is going to cry off at the last minute; say he's feeling too tired, insist that they all go on and enjoy themselves. I'll offer to stay with him and keep him company. When you've all safely gone, I'll drive him to Cairns Airport and fly with him to Sydney. He's already booked our flights. I'll see him settled in and fly back next day."

"And Cassandra won't even be allowed to say goodbye? To hold him one last time?" My tears were falling so fast they were soaking the front of my well-worn T-shirt, the one that Ben gave me many Christmases ago, the one that said 'If You Love Me, Let Me Sleep'.

"She can go and visit him when he's settled in. They all can," Ben said, his voice gentle. "It's not about not saying goodbye, it's about fear. Sebastian knows that if he asks Cassandra to come with him, she'll beg him not to go and he won't be able to stand up to her. He never could."

"He did over Oscar."

"Oscar was a dog. Sebastian did it for Oscar. But he couldn't do it for himself."

"What did you tell him," I whispered.

"I told him I would be honored to take him to Sydney. Sad, but honored."

"Oh, Ben, Ben."

"Come here." He pulled me out of the chair and held me up as he hugged me. His warm tears leaked down my neck and I imagined them soaking the back of my T-shirt where it said 'I Love You To The Moon And Back'.

THE BACKS OF THE LANDROVERS WERE BEING STACKED WITH food and cricket bats when we arrived at Killara. Ben had left our rental vehicle at the Shack with his overnight bag already on board. He'd bring the car up later when everyone had left for the picnic.

Cassandra was everywhere, ticking off her lists. There was a brittleness about her that I could see and feel and hear in her voice, but no-one else seemed to notice. Perhaps the brittleness was in me.

Sebastian looked exhausted, and now that I knew what was to come I saw the ticks and jerks and sudden distortions of his face that overtook him every few minutes. Were these new today or had I simply not seen them before? Refused to see them. At one point we found ourselves alone, and he grabbed my arm as I passed with a box of sandwiches.

"Olivia, thank you. I know it's asking too much of you, but thank you."

"It's not me who's helping you," I said, tears again filling my sore eyes.

"Yes, you are. You love Cassandra and that's why I can slip away. I know you'll keep her safe."

"I'm not sure I can. What if she suspects?"

Sebastian pushed his walking frame into the library and I followed, my heart pounding. He turned and shoved the door shut. "She does suspect. Deep down, she knows. We had it out last night. She's pretending it isn't going to happen, that I won't leave, but she knows I must."

"Oh, Sebastian, why now? Couldn't you leave it a little longer?"

"If I did, my courage would fail. And then it might be too late and I wouldn't have the physical capacity to leave without more help than Ben can give me."

"But *I* can't bear to say goodbye. How will Cassandra?"

"She'll have you to help her." His face contorted and his body went stiff, his hands grasping the walking frame knuckle white. "Shit, bloody cramps," he croaked.

"What should I do?" The panic ripped through me.

He shook his head. "Nothing." His whole face screwed up,

the agony stark. Then his body slumped and his face softened back into Sebastian. "I've left something for Cassandra in my workshop. She'll find it one day when she's ready to go in there and tidy up. Ben helped me finish it yesterday."

I sniffed, and hauled a tissue from my pocket and blew my nose. "Do you want me to tell her to look there?"

Sebastian shook his head. "She'll find it when the time is right. But could you help her, encourage her later to find someone she can love? She's only forty-nine and I want her to share her life with someone special. Cassandra wasn't designed to live alone."

"You've always been the only one for her, you know that."

"Yes, I do know that, but she will live forty more years yet…" He grinned. "Fifty even." He let go one arm of his walker and took my hand. "She needs a man to love her. No hurry, but in a year or two, please Olivia, do what you can to help her fly again."

THE FIRST TWO LANDROVERS PACKED WITH DAVID, MARINNA, Fred, Aunt Cathie, the children and the dog had left, and Amber was corralling the rest of us when Cassandra appeared. Her eyes were too bright and her color too high.

"Matt," she said. "Can you give me your car keys. I want you to go on and I'll come later in your car. Sebastian's not feeling up to it. I'm going to put him to bed."

"Oh, poor Dad," Amber said. "Is he having a lot of those ghastly cramps?"

Cassandra nodded. "Yes. I've given him some codeine so perhaps after he's rested a while he'll feel well enough to come."

"That's silly. We can have the picnic right here. We'll whizz after the others and tell them before they start setting up the picnic stuff."

"No, Amber." Cassandra's words were bullets punching through the hot air.

"Mummy, we can't leave Dad here all by himself. And you have to be at Grandma's birthday."

Amber's childish term for her mother squeezed my heart, and my arm found its way around her waist.

"She's right, Cassandra. You must go," Ben said, his tone as firm as her's had been. Not quite as bullet-like, but firm never-the-less. "I'll stay with Sebastian and if he feels up to it later I'll bring him over in our car. The picnic should be at the beach as always, with you at its center. Your mother's been looking forward to this for eighty years. Do it for her. That's what Sebastian would want."

"Matt, keys please," Cassandra said, turning her back on Ben.

Matt scrabbled in his pocket and handed them to her, flashing an apology in Ben's direction.

"Stay until after dark," Cassandra ordered. "Have a bonfire. The children must roast their marshmallows. I'll bring Sebastian over later so we can all enjoy it together."

"Cassandra," I ventured, "Please go with them. I'll stay here with Ben. If Sebastian needs you I can drive over and fetch you. Otherwise we'll bring him over later when he's rested."

"Oh, for heaven's sake. I don't know what all the fuss is about. Olivia, thanks, but I'll stay too." She reached out and took Amber's hand. "Sweetheart, if your dad is still not up to it, I promise Olivia and I will come later, and leave Sebastian here with Ben. You and Poppa go on ahead and make sure Mum enjoys her birthday lunch. Set up the cricket, and swim and have fun like we always do."

Uncle William was walking towards us from the house. I hadn't realized he was missing.

"Poppa," Amber called. "Are you ready? You're coming with us. Mum's staying with Dad until he feels better."

Darling Professor. He looks so old. How hadn't I noticed before?

"Yes, I'm as ready as I'll ever be. Got the books for the kid's stories." He wiggled his eyebrows and waggled the small pile of children's books he held in his hands.

"*The Wind in the Willows*?" I asked. "Coldtonguecoldham-coldbeef..."

He gave me his special smile."Pickledgherkinssalad-frenchrollscress-sandwichespottedmeatgingerbeerlemonadeso-dawater. Yes, I have it." He bent down, still tall in spite of his writer's stoop, and kissed Cassandra on the cheek. "I've just been talking to Sebastian and I think it wise for him to rest awhile. Why don't you and Olivia come with us and leave Ben with him. He can manage perfectly well and can help him into the car later if they decide to come for the cake and marsh-mallows."

"No. We'll come later. Now off you all go," Cassandra ordered. "I need to get back to Sebastian." And she turned and walked, head held high on her long slender neck, into the house.

"COME ON, LET'S GO INSIDE AND SEE IF WE CAN GET Cassandra to loosen her grip. Tell her you want to go, and make her go with you," Ben said.

"Yes sir. Of course, sir. And what if she refuses? Where does that leave Sebastian's plan?"

"It will work out. It has to. Chin up, stiff back, now come."

We could hear their voices as we came inside. They were in their bedroom. The door was open wide and we could see Sebastian lying on the big bed, almost silhouetted because of the bright light bouncing off the sky and rain forest and sea captured in the large picture window in the far wall.

Cassandra was kneeling on the floor beside the bed, her

hands holding his. She was sobbing as though her soul had been torn from her body. "You can't do this. I won't let you. I know what you've planned. You're going to go away and never even say goodbye. After all these years of loving each other and you're going to leave me alone."

"Sweetheart, don't cry so. I want you to listen to me. Hush and listen."

Cassandra's sobs quieted a little. Ben and I stood in the family room, frozen, backs against the wall.

"I don't want to become a burden, a useless body with my mind locked inside my head. Can't you understand that? You who've always been so alive?"

"You'll never be a burden. I love you more than I love anyone. More than all our family put together."

"I'll be a burden to myself. Maybe I'm being selfish, but I can't help that."

"We'll look after you here until you are ready to go, and then you can, I promise."

"No, I don't want to spend my last months here. I love this place and this is not where I want to die in this cruel way. I want to leave here while I'm still able to tell you how much I love you, how much our lives have meant to me, how you've been so much more than my other half; you've been my whole."

"Then I'll let you die here next week. I'll even help you… die. If that's really what you want."

"You know you couldn't. You couldn't stand aside and allow me to starve myself to death. And I couldn't let you. I need to be somewhere where there are professionals who don't love me and who can care for me without losing themselves."

Cassandra was on the bed beside him, her arms around him, her lips on his, on his cheek, on his chest, the sound of her sobs mixing with his as we crept away and outside onto the verandah.

Then we heard her slow footsteps and she came past us,

blind to anything but her loss. I began to go after her but Ben pulled me back. "Let her go. She needs to be alone for a bit. They both do."

So we sat for maybe thirty minutes, not speaking. Aching for them, our dearest friends.

"Ben..."

We heard Sebastian's call and Ben went into him. I followed and stood by the door.

"Has she gone?" Sebastian said.

Ben nodded.

"Will you find her, Olivia, and take her to the picnic. Don't leave her alone. She'll need you. Tonight, when you come back and she finds me gone, tell her I'll phone her in the morning and she can fly down to Sydney and see me. See how well I'm being looked after. The kids too if they want to. But I hope they decide to stay here with Poppa. I'd rather our last contact was here."

I came over to the bed and kissed him. "Goodbye dearest friend. Safe travels. I'll look after Cassandra and you can take care of Ben."

Sebastian grinned, his timeless Tutankhamun eyes swimming. "Attagirl."

Ben started down the track to the Shack to collect our car and I went with him, hoping we'd find Cassandra on the way. But she'd vanished.

"She'll have beetled off to the beach to get herself together," said Ben. "You go and find her and take your time. When you get back to Killara, Sebastian and I will have gone." He kissed me and pushed me away.

I walked the beach, peering into the shady secret places along the edge. No Cassandra. Where the hell had she gone? Wherever it was, she must be in the most dreadful state. Sebastian was her life. She'd do anything for him. Except let him choose his own death. Oh God. Finding out he was leaving, had chosen his best friend to take him, and not her ... what would that have done to her head? What would it have done to mine, if this were Ben?

Maybe she's gone back to the house and I've missed her somehow? What if she's going there now? If she gets there before they leave she'll try and stop them. Poor Sebastian, he couldn't go through all this again.

Back up the track, sides aching, splitting. *Thank god, there's Killara's roof.* Gasping, bent double, clutching my sides, straighten up, walk, keep going. *Hurry, hurry.*

Shit, they're still here: Sebastian leaning on Ben ... Ben easing him into the front passenger seat of the car. Oh hell. I should have waited longer at the beach … I thought they'd be gone... I don't want to see this. Moaning, something's moaning…it's me…they'll hear me. I shouldn't be here…feels like I'm spying. Get back in the shadows of the bush. Cassandra… I have to keep searching … I promised Sebastian I'd look after her.

I can't tear my gaze away. Sebastian's head dropping into his hands ... looking up again as Ben returns with a suitcase and stashes it in the trunk.

Ben's looking behind him at the house …. keep still … he hasn't seen me. He's getting into the driver's side … they're not talking …Sebastian's pale face staring out of the window. What's he thinking? What's he thinking? How can he say goodbye to his home, to everyone that's part of it. How can he bear it?

The engine coughs, catches. They bump along the drive-way, away from me, away from Killara, away, away from Cassandra.

~

I WAS DESPERATE. I'D RUN OUT OF PLACES CASSANDRA COULD be. I should have driven to the picnic hours ago and got help. We needed a proper search party. It would soon be too dark to find her. What had I been thinking? That she'd never harm herself because of her children, her grandchildren, her parents? I'd convinced myself that she'd gone riding somewhere, on one of her trails I didn't know about that wound through this inhospitable, snake-filled tropical tangle of trees and creepers and bushes. She knew it better than any of us, certainly much better than I. Did she even have a torch with her?

I'd discovered hours ago that Midnight, her black stallion, had vanished, his saddle gone too. Her other horse, Maisie, the mare she'd had in Brisbane, now retired, was all alone, and refused to tell me where Midnight and their mistress had gone.

Then I had a lightbulb moment. She'd be in Sebastian's workshop. Hiding there with his lathes and tools and the woody smell that he loved. Running from the stables to the shed I pushed open the door. The light was still shimmering through the dirty windows and my stomach lurched as I saw she wasn't there. I turned to go, but then turned back, pulling away the yellowed sheet that shrouded Sebastian's carved horse. There it was, glowing and complete, the final loving oiling and polishing done only yesterday by Sebastian and Ben. Only yesterday?

There was a thin leather thong tied around its arching neck, a circle of wood attached to it. I took it in my hands. A round, slim box, about seven centimeters in diameter. 'Cassandra' was carved into the lid. It opened smoothly on a tiny hinge, and stuck to the base of the box was a circle of paper, glued there by a wash of clear varnish. When did you write this, Sebastian? Yesterday, or weeks ago when you decided to die your way? The words were written in black ink in a small, fine hand, with a few wobbles.

—For my love—
To everything there is a season…
A time to weep, and a time to laugh
A time to mourn, and a time to dance
Never stop dancing, my Cassandra
—Sebastian—

I whispered the words, closed the beautifully crafted lid, and let the locket swing free. Pulling the shroud back over the horse I went outside into the glare of the three o'clock sun. I knew what I had to do.

At the stable, I took the old cracked saddle from its hook on the wall and saddled Maisie. She stood like a rock, bless her. It was as if the years since I'd last reluctantly saddled a horse when I was fourteen had never been. Staying on her back was not so easy, and I had to swallow my panic with every step. Cassandra was somewhere in this fearful bush, her heart broken, riding her black stallion. Please let me find her safe. Please don't let her be lying somewhere, frightened and lost. I let Maisie have her head, urging her to find Midnight, to find her mistress. She began cautiously but then seemed to sense my urgency and pushed through brambles and up steep red crumbling cliffs, not caring about her rider's terror and scratches and bruises, only about her mission to save her mistress.

I called and called—"CASSANDRA, CASSANDRA." But all I got back was the screech of a gull, the laugh of a kookaburra. Down a steep bank Maisie stumbled, to an almost dry river bed with a shallow stream meandering down it's middle. She began to splash across it, but pitched, nearly falling, as her front legs sank into a deep hole. I swung around, her belly above me, my hands still gripping the reins, my left foot still caught in the stirrup. The water soaked the back of my T-shirt as Maisie floundered and struggled to get her footing. Out the other side, up the bank. She stopped abruptly, her head flinging up as she neighed again and again. I extracted my foot from the stirrup and found my feet. "It's OK girl, whoa, whoa," I hummed, and she quietened and stood still, her flanks quivering, sweat pouring off her.

"Is this too much for you?" I said. "Let's go home. I bet Cassandra's home already, wondering what on earth I thought I was doing, getting on a horse."

I had no idea where we were but figured we'd reach the beach if we followed the river downstream. I just hoped it was our beach. I tightened the girth and got back into the saddle and we picked our way clumsily along the river. Within fifteen minutes I could see the sea, then Killara sand, and with a bit of scrambling we were through the last scratchy bushes, through the fringing palms and onto the beach.

Be there, be there, be there, was all I could think as Maisie trotted the last few meters of track to the house. I fell off her and tied her to a post by the gate. I tried my mobile phone again, Amber's number. But I knew there was no mobile coverage where they were. I'd been trying ever since we'd reached the beach. The house had the same silent feeling but I rushed through each room, praying I'd find Cassandra curled up in their bed, Aunt Cathie's bed, any bed. I went back to the stables but Midnight was still missing. I put Maisie in her stall and gave her a quick rub down and a bucket of water, an armful of hay.

Matt's car was still parked near the house, locked, and no key. Cassandra had the key. So much for driving to the picnic and getting up a search party. Why aren't they home? It was six o'clock and nearly dark. She'll be there with them. She must be. That's what she did, she rode there to join them just as Sebastian asked her. A tidal wave of relief nearly knocked me over. Of course that's what she did. How stupid I'd been. She would never, never do anything silly.

I flicked through the phone directory looking for a number to call. Police? Should I call 000? Is this an emergency?

Then I heard it, a soft neigh through the open window. Could I hear Maisie from here? I turned towards the door and saw a silhouette against the lighter sky on the far horizon, long hair outlined like a halo in the setting sun.

"You're home. Oh Cassandra, you're home."

She walked towards me and fell into my arms. "I'm home, Olivia. I heard you calling my name. I'm home."

Author's Notes

Call My Name begins in the 1960s and much of it takes place in Queensland, Australia, in the 1970s and 80s; a time of immense social upheaval and change in most Western countries. Yet it would be easy to think of *Call My Name* as a story about contemporary women and relationships. Olivia and Cassandra as young women shared the same hopes and dreams as young women of the 1990s and 21st Century, but their choices were both shaped and constrained by the beliefs and laws of the 70s and 80s in the particular location where they lived.

Olivia was a student in England in the new wave of feminism that swept through most Western countries, and like many women of her era (including me!) was passionate about improving women's reproductive rights. Her personal choices were made with care, but no one of us can make personal choices without some risk that some unforeseen situation might arise in the future that perhaps makes us wish we had made a different choice. Our choice of partners, our choice as to what career would be best for us, our choice of when and if we should 'start a family' or focus first on establishing a career and start a family in our late thirties or early forties… these all have the potential to give us cause for regret later on. But choices must be made and we can only hope that in most cases they will serve us well.

In the 1980s, Queensland Australia had only just begun to consider whether surrogacy should have some legal boundaries, and looked to the more forward-thinking state of Victoria for guidance. Adoptions throughout much of the Western world in the 70s and 80s, and certainly in Australia, were 'closed', meaning that once the birth mother signed the documents agreeing to give her child up for adoption (or in many cases being coerced to give her child up), the child was lost to her forever, and the child grew up with little chance of finding out who his or her biological parents were. In most Western countries now, and certainly in Australia, open adoptions where the birth parent or parents are encouraged to have contact with the child, as well as the opportunity to exchange information, are the norm. If the surrogate birth of Grace had been today, it is unlikely that such a court case would have been necessary. The biological father's wishes would have been taken into consideration as well as the surrogate mother's wishes, and as in many surrogacy cases today, the surrogate mother and her family would have been encouraged to have ongoing contact with the child and his or her legal parents.

Societal beliefs and legalities in different countries and states around euthanasia is another area related to personal choice that is undergoing rapid change.

Our current attitudes and laws owe a great deal to the experiences, often traumatic, of everyday people from previous decades who were forced to test the boundaries, and in doing so enabled first society and then the law to change for the better. It is always disturbing and distressing when a country or a state within a country, turns its back on the lessons learned from history. The abortion issue in the US in 2022 could be viewed in this light.

Reading Group Questions and Topics

- 1. What do you see as the main themes of the novel? What is the over-arching theme? How many members in your book club agree about this?
- 2. Do you think the cover and title of the novel work? Why or why not?
- 3. In Chapter 1, it is 1969, England, and we discover that the main character and the narrator of the book, Olivia, had been at the front of a protest march through central London on the day the Abortion Act came into being. The protesters were campaigning against the restrictions on who could have an abortion. Were you aware that abortions in England were illegal before that? When was abortion first legalized in the country or state where you live and what restrictions are currently placed on access?
- 4. When Olivia discovered she was pregnant, she decided to have an abortion and not tell Ben, the father, because their relationship was very new. At that time, how did you feel about that decision of hers?

- 5. When 13-year-old introvert Olivia first met her new foster sister, extrovert Cassandra, Olivia, as narrator, thought (probably in retrospect!) "And there it was, my future set out before me in that single two-second interaction." Do you think the novel went on to fulfill this prediction? If so, what were the characteristics of Olivia and Cassandra's long-term relationship that sometimes bound them together, and sometimes tore them apart? Have you ever had a close non-sexual friendship that has broken up because of a misunderstanding or differing views, or has been ripped apart in a more serious way? If so, were you surprised at how soul destroying this was?
- 6. There are a number of significant friendships in this novel, apart from the main one between Olivia and Cassandra. What other friendships do you recall from your reading of the novel, and what, if anything, do you think they contributed to the main story?
- 7. The two couples at the center of the story decide that Carole King's song "You've Got A Friend" was "their song." The song won Grammies in 1972 for both King (Song of the Year) and James Taylor (Pop Male Vocalist). Do you know the song, and if you don't, are you younger than about 50! Have you and your friends or family ever thought of a song as "yours"? If so, what was it about that song that captured your life at that time? Does it still make you feel the same way when you hear it? Why do you think music can stir us so deeply?
- 8. Motherhood came into the story in many ways, often under tragic circumstances. Given this is fiction, and none of these characters or their stories are real, why do you think such terrible fictional

tragedies can have readers in tears? For you, do these emotional scenes cause you to put the book away (even if only for a short while), or do they make you turn the pages faster?

- 9. Some of the scenes in Cathie's stories about the Japanese POW camps in Sumatra were confronting. Did you know about those camps before you read this novel? How did you feel about the way the women in the camp ostracised Jess, when she did what she felt she needed to do? (The 1981-1985 TV series, *Tenko*, produced by the BBC and the Australian Broadcasting Corporation, will take you much deeper into those camps and the incredible and mostly sustaining friendships formed between the women incarcerated in them.)
- 10. There are many opinions about the ethics of overseas adoptions. Do you think adopting from a third-world or war-torn country is a good or bad thing? Why or why not? If you hold the view that it is preferable to spend money to support orphans living good lives in their birth country, can you see circumstances when it might be better for the child to be adopted by a family of a different culture and taken to a different country to grow up? If so, what do you think might improve the chances of the adoption being a success (ie: resulting in a happy and stable child and family)?
- 11. Surrogacy is quite well understood today, but in Queensland, 1985, it was so new it was yet to have any legal status or safeguards around it. Do you hold strong views about surrogacy? What safeguards do you think are essential in these situations?
- 12. Did the ending of the novel work for you? If you could rewrite the ending, what would it be?

Acknowledgments

The writing of every novel is a journey, and this one was no exception. Thank you to Rebecca Horsfall, Debi Alper and Emma Darwin of Jericho Writers, UK, who assessed various drafts of the manuscript and taught me more than I thought existed about editing and revision (there is *always* more to learn). My many writer and reader friends are always there at the end of a coffee, an e-mail, or a zoom to give feedback on plot, covers and book descriptions, but most importantly, to supply friendship and empathy. As always, thank you.

Thank you to Barbara Probst for her suggestion to include an 'Author's Notes' section, especially as many readers will not be familiar with Australia or the almost historic time period of the 70s and 80s! I am grateful to those generous authors who took time out from writing their next book to read mine, and pen a blurb, and to Naomi Barton, the so-very-talented narrator of the Audiobook.

Thank you to Thala Beach Nature Reserve, the place where (in my imagination) I located Killara. The real Thala is a spectacular eco-resort set on a private headland located between Cairns and Port Douglas and close to the Great Barrier Reef. It has achieved the highest level of Advanced Eco Certification and is a member of National Geographic Unique Lodges of the World. If you ever have the opportunity, go there! Thank you also to the real Killara, our Queenslander home on Great Barrier Island in Aotearoa, New Zealand!

To my family — John, Caroline, Jonathan, Josie and Joachim, and all the grandchildren; well done for bearing with me as I write yet another book, and for not asking me too often why it isn't it finished yet.

Newsletter Sign-Up

Go to 'Jenni's Off-Grid Newsletter' (www.jenniogden.-com) to subscribe to my occasional e-newsletter about living life on an off-grid island, book reviews of books I love, and a little writerly news.

If you enjoyed *Call My Name*, please do review it on Goodreads, and also on your favorite online bookstores (a few sentences—or even just a rating—is all it needs.)

Then sample the first chapters of my award-winning, best-selling debut novel *A Drop in the Ocean*, set on Australia's Great Barrier Reef, and *The Moon is Missing,* set in England, New Orleans during Hurricane Katrina, and on Great Barrier Island, NZ (where I live)!

To receive notifications of my future novels please follow me on BookBub: www.bookbub.com/authors/jenni-ogden

And do follow, like, or friend me on

Goodreads: goodreads.com/JenniOgden

Facebook: facebook.com/JenniOgdenbooks

Twitter: twitter.com/jenni_ogden

A Drop in the Ocean

BY JENNI OGDEN

About the book

Anna Fergusson runs a lab researching Huntington's disease at a prestigious Boston university. When her long-standing grant is pulled unexpectedly, Anna finally faces the truth: she's 49, virtually friendless, single, and worse, her research has been sub-par for years. With no jobs readily available, Anna takes a leap and agrees to spend a year monitoring a remote campsite on Turtle Island on Australia's Great Barrier Reef. What could be better for an introvert with shattered self-esteem than a quiet year in paradise? As she settles in, Anna opens her heart for the first time in decades—to new challenges, to new friendships, even to a new love with Tom, the charming, younger turtle tagger she sometimes assists. But opening one's heart leaves one vulnerable, and Anna comes to realize that love is as fragile as happiness, and that both are a choice.

Read on for the opening chapter…

Chapter 1

On my forty-ninth birthday my shining career came to an inauspicious end. It took with it the jobs of four promising young scientists and catapulted my loyal research technician into premature retirement, an unjust reward for countless years of dedicated scut work.

That April 6th began in precisely the same manner as all my birthdays over the previous fifteen years—Eggs Benedict with salmon, a slice of homemade wholemeal bread spread thickly with marmalade, and not one but two espressos at an Italian café in downtown Boston. On my arrival at eight o'clock sharp, the elderly Italian owner took my long down-filled coat and ushered me, as he had for more years than I care to re- member, to the small table by the window where I could look out on the busy street, today frosted with a late-season snow that had fallen overnight and would soon be gone. He always greeted me with the same words: "Good morning, Dr. Fergusson. A fine day for a birthday. Will you be having the usual?" as if he saw me every morning, or at least every week, and not just once a year.

Perhaps the unusually deep blue cloudless sky, almost suggesting a summer day, should have warned me that something was not quite as it should be. But superstitious behavior is not a strength of mine, and after my indulgent breakfast I walked to my laboratory in one of the outbuildings of the medical school, taking pleasure in the crisp winter air and stopping to collect my mail—in this e-mail era, usually consisting only of advertising pamphlets from academic publishing houses—before entering the lab.

Rachel looked up from her desk with her hesitant smile and gave me a beautifully wrapped parcel—a good novel, as always, the thirtieth she had given me. One for every birthday and one for every Christmas. I have kept them all. "Happy birthday Anna," she murmured, not wanting to advertise my private business to the others in the lab. Two of my four young research assistants were already at work, hunched over their computers. The other two would be out in the field interviewing the families who were the subjects of our research program. Huntington's families, we called them.

The research I had been doing for the past twenty-four years—first for my PhD, then as a research assistant, and finally as the leader of the team—focused on various aspects of Huntington's disease, a terrible, genetically transmitted disorder that targets half the children of every parent who has the illness. Often the children are born before the parents realize they carry the gene and long before they begin to show the strange contorted movements, mood fluctuations, and gradual decline into dementia that are the hallmarks of the disease. Thus our Huntington's families often harbored two or three or even four Huntington's sufferers spanning different generations.

Thankfully I was spared having to deal with them; I have never been good with people, and especially not sick people. I didn't discover this unfortunate fact until my internship year after I graduated from medical school. But as they say, when a door closes, a window opens, and I became a medical researcher instead. Of course it took a bit longer, as I had to complete a PhD, but that was bliss once I realized that my forté was peering down a microscope at brain tissue.

So there I was on my forty-ninth birthday, looking at the envelope I held in my hand and realizing with a quickening of my heart that it was from the medical granting body that had financed my research program for fifteen years. Every three years I had to write another grant application summarizing the previous three years of research and laying out the next three years. Every three years I breathed a sigh of relief when they rolled the grant over and sometimes even added a new salary or stipend for another researcher or PhD student. I had become almost—but not quite—blasé about it. The letter had never arrived on my birthday before; I had not been expecting it until the end of the month. So I opened it with a sort of muted optimism. After all, it was my birthday.

"Dear Dr. Fergusson," I read, already feeling lightheaded as my eyes scanned the next lines, "The Scientific Committee has now considered all the reviewers' comments on the grant applications in the 2008 round, and I regret to inform you that your application has not been successful. We had a particularly strong field this time, and as you will see by the enclosed reviewers' reports, there were a number of problems with your proposed program. Of most significance is the concern that your research is lagging behind other programs in the same area."

I stared glassy-eyed at the words, hoping that I was about to wake up from a bad dream with my Eggs Benedict still to come.

"The Committee is aware of your excellent output over a long period and the substantial discoveries you have made in the Huntington's disease research field, but unfortunately, in these difficult financial times, we must put our resources behind new programs that have moved on from more basic research and are able to take advantage of the latest technologies in neuroscience and particularly genetic engineering."

My head was getting hot at this point; latest technologies and genetic engineering my arse. Easy for them to dismiss years of painstaking "basic research," as they called it, so they could back the new sexy breed of researcher. No way could they accomplish anything useful without boring old basic research in the first place.

"A final report is due on the 31st July, a month after the termination of your present grant. Please include a complete list of the publications that have come out of your program over the past fifteen years. A list of all the equipment you currently have that has been financed by your grant is also required. Our administrator will contact you in due course to discuss the dispersal of this equipment. The University will liaise with you over the closure of your laboratory.

We appreciate your long association with us, and wish you and the researchers in your laboratory well in your future endeavors."

* * *

The other tradition I kept on my birthday was dinner at an elegant restaurant with my friend Francesca. I could safely say she was my only friend, as my long relationship with Rachel was purely work-related, except for the novels twice a year. I was tempted to cancel the dinner and stay in my small apartment and sulk, but something deep inside wanted to connect with a human who cared about me and didn't think of me as a washed-up old spinster with no more to discover. Fran and I had been friends since our first year at medical school, when we found ourselves on the same lab bench in the chemistry lab, simply because both our surnames began with 'Fe.'

Fran Fenton and I were unlikely soul mates. She was American, extroverted, gently rounded, and 'five-foot-two, eyes of blue,' with short, spiky blond hair. I was British, introverted, thin, and five-foot-eight, eyes of slate, with straight dark hair halfway down my back, usually constrained into a single plait, but on this occasion permitted to hang loose. Fran was also, in stark contrast to me, married, with three boisterous teenagers. She worked three days a week as a general practitioner in the health center attached to the university where my lab was, and we did our best to have lunch together at least once a fortnight. I once went to her house for Christmas dinner but it wasn't a success; her husband, an English professor, found me difficult, and her teenagers clearly saw me as a charity case. But the birthday dinner was always a special occasion for Fran as well as me, I think.

When she read the letter she was satisfyingly appalled, and

said "swines" so violently that there was a sudden hush at the tables around us. When the quiet murmur in the room had resumed, she reached over and put her small, pretty hand over mine. I felt the roughness of the skin on her palm and blinked hard as I realized what a special person she was, never seeming rushed in spite of the massive amount of stuff she did — including slaving over a houseful of kids. Her eyes were watering as well as she said softly, "It's so unfair. How could they abandon you like this in the middle of your research? What will happen to all your Huntington's families?" Sweet Fran, always thinking of the plight of others worse off by a country mile than people like us, whereas all I'd been thinking about was myself and how I'd let down my little team.

I blinked hard again and turned my palm up and grasped her hand. I'd been aware how close to tears I'd been all day, but of course I hadn't allowed myself to succumb; not my style at all. In fact my brave little team all remained tearless as I gave them the news at our regular weekly meeting, which just happened to be today. Rachel had disappeared into the bathroom for a long time as soon as the meeting was over, and when she finally reappeared looked distinctly red-nosed. That's when she told me that she would take this opportunity to retire and go and live with her elderly sister in Portland. Dear Rachel, loyal to the end.

Fortunately, the last PhD student we had in the lab had submitted her thesis a couple of months ago. I'd promised my four shell-shocked researchers that I would personally contact every lab that did research similar to ours and put in a good word for them. They had become quite attached to their Huntington's families, which is not a recommended practice for a research scientist, but was a characteristic that I'd learned was essential for effective field workers. Releasing four Huntington's researchers on to the market at once was practically a flood, but they were young and good at what they did and would surely get new positions in due course.

Fran was asking me about other grants, and I wrenched myself away from my gloomy reverie. Taking my hand back, I grabbed my wine glass and emptied it. "Not a chance, I'm afraid," I told her. "The fact is, I'm finished. God knows how I lasted as long as I did."

"Anna, stop it. It's not like you to be so negative about your research. You've done wonderful things. You can't give up because you've lost your funding. Researchers lose grants all the time; they just have to get another one."

"Trouble is, the reviewers' reports were damning. And they're right. I was lucky to have the funding rolled over last time. They were probably giving me one last chance to do something new, but I blew it. I simply carried on in the same old way because that's all I know. I'm a fraud. I've always known it deep down, and now I've been sprung." As all this was spewing out of my mouth I could feel myself getting lighter and lighter. I felt hysterical laughter burbling up through my chest, and I poured myself another glass of wine and took a gulp, all the while watching Fran's face as her expression changed from concern to shock. Then a snort exploded out of me, along with a mouthful of wine, and I put my glass down quickly and grabbed the blue table napkin, mopping the dribbles from my chin and dabbing at the red splotches on the white tablecloth.

Fran's sweet face split into a grin and she giggled. "You're drunk. Wicked woman. It's not funny."

"It's definitely not funny, but I'm bloody well not drunk. This is all I've had to drink today, and half that's on the tablecloth." I wiped my eyes. "Let's finish this bottle and get another one." We grinned at each other and then sobered up.

"So what now?" asked Fran.

I looked at her, my mind blank. My pulse was pounding through my whole body. I forced myself to focus. "I suppose I will have to apply for more grants, but you know how long that takes. I don't think I've got much hope of getting anything substantial."

Fran screwed up her face. I could almost see her neurons flashing as she searched for a miracle.

I tried to ignore the churning in my gut. "I'll be okay for a while. The good old Medical School Dean said I could have a cubbyhole and a computer for the rest of the year so that I could finish all the papers I've still to write." I swirled the wine around in my glass, and watched the ruby liquid as it came dangerously near to the rim. "Given that boring old basic research is no longer considered worthy, I wonder why I should bother, really."

"Is he going to pay you?"

"Huh, no hope of that. Although he did say that I might be able to give a few guest lectures, so I suppose I'll get a few meager dollars for those."

"Why don't you go back to clinical practice? You know so much about Huntington's disease. You'd be a wonderful doctor for them and other neurological patients."

"Fran, what are you thinking? You of all people know that I'm hopeless at the bedside thing and anything that involves actual patient contact. That's why I became a researcher."

"But that was twenty-five years ago. You've grown up and changed since then. You might like it now if you gave yourself a chance."

"I haven't changed, that's the problem. I don't even like socializing with other research staff. You're the only person in the entire universe who I feel comfortable really talking to."

"Well you have to do something. What are you going to live on?"

"That's one of the advantages of being a workaholic with no kids. I've got heaps of money stashed away in the bank. Now at last I'll be able to spend it. Perhaps I'll fly off to some exotic, tropical paradise and become a recluse."

"Very amusing. But you could travel. At least for a few

months. Go to Europe. It would give you time to refresh your ideas, and then you could write a new grant that would blow those small-minded pen-pushers out of the water." Fran sounded excited by all these possibilities opening out in front of me.

I could feel my brain shutting down, and shook my head to wake it up. "Perhaps I could take a trip." I pushed my lips into a grin. "Go and see my mother and her lover in their hide-away. Now there's a nice tropical island."

"Doesn't she live in Shetland? That's a great idea. You should visit her."

Fran didn't always get my sense of humor.

"Fran, it's practically in the Arctic Circle. I do not want to go there. And right now my mother and her gigolo are the last people I want or need to see." I rolled my eyes.

"Don't be unkind. Your mother has a right to happiness, and I think her life sounds very exciting. I thought she was married?"

"She is. And good on her. But she and I are better off living a long way apart." I yawned. "I can't think about all this any more tonight. And it's way past your bedtime; you have to work tomorrow."

Fran frowned. "I wish you didn't have to go through all this. It's horrible. But I know something will come up that's better. It always does."

* * *

But not for the next four months. I closed up—or down—the lab, took the team out for a subdued redundancy dinner, and moved into the cubbyhole, where I put my head down and wrote the final report on fifteen years of work. Then I wrote a grant application and sent it off to an obscure private funding body that gave out small grants from a legacy left by some wealthy old woman who died a lonely death from

Parkinson's disease. I had little hope it would be successful, as all I could come up with as a research project was further analysis of the neurological material we had collected over the past few years—hardly cutting-edge research. At least waiting to hear would give me a few months of pathetic hope, rather like buying a ticket in a lottery.

That done, I dutifully went into the university every day and tried to write a paper on a series of experiments that we had completed and analyzed just before the grant was terminated. But my heart wasn't in it, and I could sit for eight hours with no more than a bad paragraph to show for it.

Boston was hot and I felt stifled. Fran and her family were away on their regular summer break at the Professor's parents' cabin on a lake somewhere, and the medical school was as dead as a dodo. I used to begrudge any time spent talking trivia to the researchers in my lab, but now that I didn't have it, I missed it. Even my once-pleasant apartment had become a prison, clamping me inside its walls the minute I got home in the evenings. I was no stranger to loneliness, but over the past few years I'd polished my strategies to deal with it. I would remind myself that the flip side of loneliness could be worse—a houseful of demanding kids, a husband who expected dinner on the table, a weighty mortgage, irritating in-laws—it became almost a game to see what new horrors I could come up with. You, Anna Fergusson, I'd tell myself sternly, are free of all that. "I'm a liberated woman," I once shouted, before glancing furtively around in case my madwoman behavior had conjured up a sneering audience. If self-talk didn't work, or even when it did, more often than not I'd slump down in front of the TV and watch three episodes straight of Morse, or some other BBC detective series, and one night I stayed awake for the entire 238 minutes of Gone with the Wind.

When Fran finally returned from her lake at the beginning of August, I was on the phone to her before she had time to unpack her bags. Understanding as always, she put her other duties aside and the very next day met me at our usual lunch place. She looked fantastic: brown and healthy and young. I felt like a slug. It wasn't until we were getting up to leave, me to go back to my cubbyhole and Fran to the supermarket, that she remembered.

"Gosh, I almost forgot. Callum was mucking about on the Internet while we were at the lake and came across this advertisement. He made some joke about it being the perfect job for him when he left school, and I remembered how you said after you lost your grant that you should go and live on a tropical island." Fran scrabbled in her bag and hauled out a scrunched up sheet of paper.

"Fran, for heaven's sake, you know that was a joke. What is it?" I took the paper she had unscrunched and read the small advertisement surrounded by ads for adventure tourism in Australia.

For rent to a single or couple who want to escape to a tropical paradise. Basic cabin on tiny coral island on Australia's Great Barrier Reef. AUD$250 a week; must agree to stay one year and look after small private campsite (five tents maximum). Starting date October 2008. For more information e-mail lazylad at yahoo.com.au.

I looked at Fran in amazement. "You printed this out for me? I think the sun must have got to you. Lazylad is looking for some young bimbo. And he wants to be paid to look after his campsite. What cheek."

"That's what I thought at first, but Callum pointed out that thousands of people would give their eyeteeth for an opportunity like this if the cabin were free. But that's the beauty of it; you can afford it. And wasn't your father Australian? You mightn't even need a visa."

"Fran, you're a dear, but can you see me on an island on the other side of the world, singing jolly campfire songs with spaced-out boaties?"

"Have you got a better idea? Or are you just going to continue to fade away in your cubbyhole?"

"No, I'm out of there as soon as I finish this damn paper I'm writing, and then I thought I might try my hand at writing a book." So there, I felt like adding.

Fran's face lit up. "A book? That's fantastic. What sort of a book? A novel?"

I started to laugh. "What happened to you up there at the lake? This is me, Anna. I haven't suddenly morphed into a normal person. I'm still the same old ivory tower nerd, clueless about people. No, I thought I might be able to write some sort of account of my experiences getting research grants and running a lab. All the highs and lows. Perhaps I'll discover where I went wrong." I could hear the gloom in my voice as the words came out of my mouth.

"But that's a great idea. And you'll need somewhere to write it." I could see the mischief in her eyes as she grinned at me.

"I know what you're thinking, and no, I do not want to live on a desert island at the end of the world."

"Oh well, worth a try. It wouldn't hurt to check it out though, would it?"

* * *

Two days later I composed a careful e-mail to Lazylad, not expecting a reply. Surely the cabin had been snapped up by now if it were such a dream opportunity. I got used to holding my breath as I turned my e-mail on each morning, scrolling rapidly through all the usual stuff looking for Lazylad, telling myself I didn't care. But the idea of going to Australia had got stuck in my head.

I had all but given up and stopped daydreaming about writing a book on a deck looking through the palms across an azure blue ocean, when there it was—a reply from Lazylad, who I later found out was actually called Jeff.

Thanks for e-mail. Been away sorry for delay in reply. Cabin still available if you want it. Photos attached. Island called Turtle Island (after the sea turtles here) and is a coral cay just above Tropic of Capricorn about eight hectares in area with a large reef surrounding it. A few eccentric people own houses here and that's about it apart from my small campsite. Only transport is fishing boat or charter. Cabin basic but comfortable, everything included. Solar hot water (roof water) and solar power for lights and computer, gas fridge and stove, no telephone. Satellite broadband from some locals' houses you can use occasionally in return for a few beers. One of the local fishermen brings supplies over about once a fortnight in his boat and locals can hitch a ride for a small fee or more beers. Fantastic snorkeling and diving, birds, turtles, etc. Weather always perfect (almost). If you are interested e-mail me your phone number and I'll call you when next on mainland to chat. Looking after campsite is a doddle. First come, first served (no bookings), take their money, and make sure the old guy on the island does his job of emptying the toilet and the rubbish bins. It would be good to get someone here before I leave for UK on 18th October so I can show you the ropes.

When I scrolled down so I could see the photos my hand was trembling. The first one showed a rectangular wooden building with what appeared to be an open front with a wide deck. A big wooden table and a few white plastic chairs, along with a heap of what looked like diving stuff—a wetsuit and flippers and a tank—sat on the deck. In the dimness of the inside I could make out a bed on one side of a partition and what looked like a kitchen on the other. The cabin was surrounded on three sides by trees with large leaves, and in front of the cabin was a sweep of white sand. The sand had something black on it, and when I zoomed in I could see it was a cluster of three large black birds just sitting there. The second photo showed a narrow strip of white sand, fringed by trees with feathery-looking leaves, and then the truly azure blue sea and sky. The last photo was like something on a travel brochure: a tiny, oval, flat island with green vegetation crowning the center and white sand around the edge, surrounded by blue. In the blue I could see dark patterns, the coral. I grabbed my pendant and brought it to my mouth. The last time I had seen coral sea had been when I was twelve years old, and I had thought then that I never wanted to see it again.

* * *

The Moon Is Missing

BY JENNI OGDEN

About the book

Georgia Grayson has perfected the art of being two people: a neurosurgeon on track to becoming the first female Director of Neurosurgery at a large London hospital, and a wife and mother. Home is her haven where, with husband Adam's support, she copes with her occasional anxiety attacks. That is until her daughter, 15-year-old Lara, demands to know more about Danny, her mysterious biological father from New Orleans who died before she was born. "Who was he? Why did he die? WHO AM I?" Trouble is, Georgia can't tell her. As escalating panic attacks prevent her from operating, and therapy fails to bring back the memories she has repressed, fractures rip through her once happy family. Georgia sees only one way forward; to return to New Orleans where Danny first sang his way into her heart, and then to the rugged island where he fell to his death. Somehow she must uncover the truth Lara deserves, whatever the cost.

Read on for the opening chapter…

Chapter 1

London, March, 2005

"Who am I?" The bubble of Sunday-gardening bliss floating in my chest deflated as I took a step back from my furious daughter. *This is just a teenage thing. Treat it with gentle humor.* I reached out and put my fingers under Lara's chin, turning her head first to the left and then the right. "You look like my daughter, Lara Aroha Grayson. Have I got that wrong?"

Lara pushed my hand away, her mass of dark red curls sparking like the ends of cut wires around her flushed and frowning face. "Stop patronizing me. I'm not one of your awestruck interns." Her eyes, greener than usual, pinned me to the wall, her face even more arresting than when she was in her usual happy mode. "I want to know who I am, where I come from, what bloody genes lurk inside me, make up every tiny cell in my body, make me horrible at math, give me my passion for music."

My pulse took off, ricocheting between my heart and throat. I focused on keeping my expression mildly concerned and forced my damn body to at least act relaxed. Not exactly easy, as my carefully controlled world teetered on the edge of implosion. "Where has all this come from?" I asked, my voice hopefully sounding calmer than I felt.

Lara glared at me, the creases marring her smooth forehead as clear as a red flag to a bull. An image of her in full tantrum, aged about three, flashed in my head, and for a second the corners of my mouth twitched dangerously near a smile. I swallowed it and pulled myself reluctantly back to what was happening right now; the showdown I'd always known must happen one day.

"Have you not noticed? Have you not caught on to the small fact that I have a Social Studies assignment due in one week, and it's worth thirty percent of the entire year's internal assessment mark? What did you think I was doing stuck in my room all bloody weekend while you and Dad and Finbar were frolicking in the garden, basking in the first hint of sun we've had this year, picking fucking daffodils?"

"Mind the language, Lara. And calm down; you look as if you're about to burst into flames."

"Well, at least I've got your attention at last. I cannot, cannot find an entire half of who I am. And it is your fault. You refuse to tell me anything about my father, let alone who his parents and grandparents and great grandparents and brothers and sisters were. Are, I suppose, unless they're all tragically dead too."

"What has this to do with an assignment on—what is the topic exactly?"

"Who am I. Who—am—I? Get it? It's about genealogy. Who do you think you are. All that shit. How my ancestors' characteristics and lifestyle and social circumstances and mad choices and where they came from gave me the blueprint for who I am and how I am different and why that might be and blah blah." Lara's voice rose even higher. "So get this. I don't want to be a neurosurgeon or any sort of doctor or scientist, so that gene of yours didn't make it into me. You can barely sing in tune so I'm making a wild guess that I got my singing voice from my father, like my hair. But what else did I get from him? You've never even shown me a photo of him. How is that even remotely fair?"

"Lara, please lower your voice. You'll disturb the entire neighborhood. This is not a conversation to have when you're upset. We'll sit quietly after dinner and talk about it. I'm not sure what I can tell you that will help though. I haven't any photos of Danny, and I know almost nothing about his family. So apart from his hair and his musical genius… Mind you, my father also has a beautiful voice, so you could have inherited that from him."

"I know Granddad can sing, but what about my other granddad? My father's father? My father's mother for that matter. Could they sing? Were they shit at math? Were they from America, from New Zealand, from England, from Russia, from Timbuktu? Are they even alive? Why don't they want to know me? Why don't they want to know who I am?"

"We'll talk about it later. In the meantime, think about how nurture as well as nature makes you who you are. More so in my opinion. You've incorporated into your being many more qualities and values from Adam than from a man who by a twist of fate was your biological father and died months before you were born." Shit, I sound like a patronizing prune. But I couldn't seem to stop. "Adam's your real dad and he got many of his personality traits and values from his parents and grandparents, and you know all about them and about my background. You can complete your assignment without even mentioning your biological father if you want to; the teacher doesn't even need to know."

"That, mother dear, is not the point, but thank you for the lecture. The point is for me to think about who I am, and I am half blank. I don't want to be half blank. I know lots of good stuff comes from Dad and I've already written about that, but it isn't complete. I'm not complete." Lara sniffed and swiped her arm across her nose, her face now blotched with tears.

"Oh sweetheart, come here." My eyes were threatening to well up as they always did when almost anyone cried, but especially my own two usually uncrying kids. I opened my arms and felt my tears escape as Lara allowed me to fold her in a close hug, her curls wiry and precious against my damp cheek.

* * *

Dinner was tense, Finbar the only one who seemed oblivious to Lara's mood and Adam and my stilted attempts to behave as if the perfectly roasted New Zealand-born Sunday lamb, bought as a special treat to celebrate this glorious and rare London promise-of-spring weekend, was as delicious as

I'd planned. It was the first weekend in a month that I hadn't been on call. Since Peter—the Director of the Neurosurgery Department—had been laid low by old age and cardiac problems, my workload had escalated. This weekend was Jim Mason's turn on call. Over the past month, he and I, as the next two most senior neurosurgeons in the hallowed hierarchy of our large London hospital neurosurgery department, had taken turns practicing for the Directorship role. Near the end of the year, when Peter was officially to retire, we'd both be up for the job, along with who knows how many outside candidates. Just another ever-present stress to add to my mess of anxieties, a state-of-mind I was well attuned to and mostly successful at keeping to myself. Or at least keeping firmly at home, away from Jim bloody Mason's sleazy little eyes.

Adam's hand grazed mine as he reached for some more potatoes. He'd been looking tired lately. Hardly surprising given that he was the one who bore the brunt of my anxiety attacks. For years I'd been suffering only one or two restless nights a fortnight, but lately sleep refused to come, or stay when it did come, night after night. I smiled at Adam, hoping I was beaming my thank you for his valiant efforts to support my crazy work schedule. On top of that, now he'd have to pretend that Lara's sudden desire to find out more about Danny and his genes did not spear him through his heart. He who'd been her father in every way since she was three years old.

I'd managed to catch him alone before dinner to warn him about Lara's mood and the talk I'd promised her once dinner was over. Adam obviously took it for granted he'd be part of any discussion; we'd always believed that sticking together was the best policy. None of this allowing the kids to pit one parent against the other in an unsubtle tactic designed to get the best deal. Not that it always worked.

I snuck a glance at Lara, stabbing at her tender lamb slices as if they were made of leather. Shit, how the hell was I going to convince Adam that Lara wasn't rejecting him; that this was merely another hormonally charged fifteen-year-old's over-reaction? Cross fingers that within a day of handing in her assignment Danny and his mysterious genes would be over-shadowed by the next crisis in Lara's full-on life.

Finbar, bless his sunny socks, was babbling on about the book he was currently engrossed in. At least he was indubitably Adam's son with his thick tawny hair and dark chocolate eyes. Should have been a girly, as his sister was apt to remark of her brother. Perhaps she was right. Our youngest was endowed with a generous nature that was as conciliatory and non-confrontational as his sister's was boisterous and loud. And poised at that lovely age of eleven. Old enough to be funny and interesting and young enough to still want to cuddle his parents.

* * *

Lara was sitting so near the edge of her chair I thought she might slide off any second and land unceremoniously on the floor. That wouldn't add anything positive to the aura of calm Adam and I were trying to project into the tense space between us and our daughter.

"Stop going on about a tragic accident," Lara said, clearly through gritted teeth. "Of course it was tragic. All accidents that kill people are tragic. That tells me nothing. I want details. People don't just casually fall off cliffs. Was he drunk or stoned? Is that what the big secret is?" She bunched the ball of damp tissues clasped in her hands even more tightly.

"No, he wasn't drunk or stoned. That I do know. But I can't tell you much more because I don't know myself. All I can remember is that we were at our holiday house on Great Barrier Island and there was a massive storm. Danny had been away visiting his parents in the South Island and had just come back and we had an argument about something; probably I was mad about him being away so long and not contacting me. It's fuzzy. The next memory I have is …" My voice stopped working and I stared down at my hands gripped knuckle-white in my lap— "The police found him at the bottom of the cliff. It's a sheer drop from the top of the Pa, sixty meters probably, straight onto the rocks and the sea." I shuddered. "Danny was caught on a ledge of rock. Just above…" — I closed my eyes as the sea thundered in my head — "…just above the surf. It was massive that night; pounding, crashing on the boulders."

I forced my eyes open and saw Lara's wide-eyed gaze. Adam's hand was rubbing my back and I fought away the rising panic, staring at the carpet, willing myself to breathe, willing myself not to throw up. I clenched my hands tightly over my mouth, my whole head jittering, my body a swamp of pulsing fear held in by desperation.

"Deep breaths, come on Georgia, slowly now: in, out, in, out."

I clung to Adam's voice, forcing myself to do as he said.

"Don't cry Mum. Please don't cry." Lara's small voice called me back and I closed my eyelids over my tears and thought about relaxing my arms, my fists, my legs, my body. I was floating, absorbing the aroma of Adam's slightly sweaty scent, my face buried in the safety of his chest. I felt a smooth warm hand on my arm and opened my eyes on Lara's red hair. She was kneeling at my feet, stroking my arm, her voice crooning, sobbing. "I'm sorry Mums, I didn't mean to upset you. I'm sorry. Please don't cry. It's all right. I don't need any of that stuff for my stupid assignment. Please don't cry."

* * *

About the Author

Jenni Ogden and her husband live off-grid on spectacular Great Barrier Island, 100 kms off the coast of New Zealand, a perfect place to write and for grandchildren to spend their holidays. Winters are often spent in Far North Tropical Queensland, close to Killara, the fictional home in *Call My Name*, her third novel. Her debut novel published in 2016, *A Drop in the Ocean*, won multiple awards and has sold over 80,000 copies. Her second novel, *The Moon is Missing*, was published in 2020. Jenni, who holds a PhD in Clinical Neuropsychology and was awarded the *Distinguished Career Award* by the International Neuropsychological Society in 2015, is well-known for her books featuring her patients' moving stories: *Fractured Minds: A Case-Study Approach to Clinical Neuropsychology*, and *Trouble In Mind: Stories from a Neuropsychologist's Casebook.*

CPSIA information can be obtained
at www.ICGtesting.com
Printed in the USA
LVHW112327060922
727629LV00003B/11